UNJUST REVENGE

To my cousin Richard

I hope that you enjoy my first novel.

Best wishes from
Isabel
X.

4th July 2014

UNJUST REVENGE

ISABEL BRATT

Copyright © 2013 by Isabel Bratt.

Library of Congress Control Number: 2013913458
ISBN: Hardcover   978-1-4836-7501-5
               Softcover   978-1-4836-7500-8
               Ebook   978-1-4836-7502-2

All rights reserved. No part of this book may be reproduced or transmitted in any form or by any means, electronic or mechanical, including photocopying, recording, or by any information storage and retrieval system, without permission in writing from the copyright owner.

This is a work of fiction. Names, characters, places and incidents either are the product of the author's imagination or are used fictitiously, and any resemblance to any actual persons, living or dead, events, or locales is entirely coincidental.

This book was printed in the United States of America.

Rev. date: 08/19/2013

To order additional copies of this book, contact:
Xlibris LLC
0-800-056-3182
www.xlibrispublishing.co.uk
Orders@xlibrispublishing.co.uk

For my sons, Gregor and Stuart.
With love.

14th July 2013

ACKNOWLEDGEMENTS

Emotional thanks to my family and friends for encouraging me to maintain equilibrium throughout the journey of plotting, researching, writing and publishing *Unjust Revenge*.

It would be remiss of me not to thank the Xlibris team at Penguin Random House Publishing. Throughout each stage *of writing and selling a novel* they were definitive in their delivery and judicious in their endorsements. This put me at ease as there was never any doubt about who was responsible for my manuscript or its stage in the publishing process, at any given time.

After I finished the first draft, four beta readers read the full manuscript and provided me with honest and constructive feedback about structure, style, readability and grammar. To engage them as my *critical eyes* was prudent. To acknowledge their contribution is essential.

Special thanks to my son, Gregor Ridley, for his advice on structure and style; to my son, Stuart Ridley, for his detailed review of characterisation and conversation; to my cousin, Isla Porteous, for her summary of plot strengths and weaknesses; and to my friend, Marion Webster, for her fastidious proofreading.

PROLOGUE

The St Andrews School for Girls in the City of London is undoubtedly for privileged girls. But it is not a school for the super-rich or the super-bitch. Under the direction of Eleanor Marshall, the headmistress, it is a school that parents choose for daughters who they hope will develop into ambitious and talented young adults.

Eleanor Marshall's determination to deliver an educational curriculum that also embraces the needs of the fast-growing teenagers at her all-girls school means that the students flourish from a combination of stimulation, challenge, and reward. Parents and guardians have no complaints with the results.

Beth and Matt Oliver chose this school because they wanted their daughter, Katie, to be well-grounded and they didn't want her to accidentally or deliberately abuse the lifestyle that she had as a result of her parents' successful and high-earning careers.

Beth's demanding job as detective chief inspector (DCI) at the Metropolitan Police (MET) Specialist Crimes Division created a constant challenge for her to juggle her time as an employee, mother, wife, daughter, and friend. This was further complicated by Matt being constantly on-call as one of the consultant paediatricians at the City of London Hospital for Children.

The Olivers were the envy of their friends, but, behind the scenes, the marriage of Beth and Matt had been showing cracks for a few years. Despite that, they continued to work hard together at trying to be the best parents that they could for Katie, their seventeen-year-old daughter, and Jack, their eighteen-year-old son.

Friday, 18 June 2004

Two weeks before end of term, the sixth form students at the St Andrews School for Girls were as excited as they could ever remember being during a school term. For them, the planned final event of their attendance at senior school and the prospect of being two weeks closer to a long summer break had finally arrived.

Eleanor Marshall had surpassed herself this time. The idea of organising a mother-and-daughter fashion show during the last few weeks of term was the perfect incentive for the girls to work hard for the exam results that would make the difference between acceptance and rejection from the university or college of their choice.

The announcements of the fashion show and the scheduled dates for the A-levels were deliberately posted side by side on the notice boards throughout the school on the same day. The fashion show was a carrot, and everyone knew that.

It was no surprise that some of the parents had reservations about the encouragement of frivolous thoughts at such an important time in the school year. They need not have worried. Eleanor Marshall had a plan. Of course, she had a plan. After all, she never shied away from any challenge that could interfere with her resolve that the girls would leave her school with excellent grades, happy memories, and achievable dreams. Her plan *would* have a positive and creative outcome but *would not* detract the impressionable teenagers from the focus needed to study and pass their final exams.

Thoughts of the fashion show hadn't interfered with study time. It soon became clear to students that if they missed scheduled study breaks, they would not be allowed to attend the one-hour Saturday morning meetings organised to share their ideas for the event of the year. No one wanted to miss out on that.

Attendance at the fashion show required the girls to design a dress fit for any event of their choice and their mothers to compliment the design of the dress with an outfit from their existing wardrobes. Mother and daughter would model their outfits together on a catwalk-designed stage after dinner. The girls had every right to be excited.

At just after midday on the day of the fashion show, after everyone agreed that the assembly room had been set up and decorated perfectly for the event, the girls started to pack up their belongings, having earned their promised half day to prepare for the evening ahead.

After the last student had left and after Eleanor Marshall had given the room one last check, she instructed Eddie, the school janitor, to lock the doors and shut the windows to avoid any mishaps before the fashion show.

Katie Oliver and her three closest friends decided to stop off at the local cafe so that they could finalise their plans for a sleepover at Lucy Dawson's house after the fashion show. Their overnight bags, music selection, and snacks had been dropped off at Lucy's the previous evening.

The girls went their separate ways at 3 p.m., their heads full of happy thoughts for the evening ahead.

None of them could have anticipated then how devastatingly bad the evening was going to turn out for one of the pupils.

PART I

Friday, 18 June to Sunday, 20 June 2004

CHAPTER 1

Friday, 18 June 2004
6 p.m.

Katie Oliver, seventeen years of age, approached the top of the staircase at her home and walked down the stairs with the confidence of a beautiful, intelligent, and popular teenager. Her parents, Beth and Matt Oliver, always encouraged Katie and her brother, Jack, to believe that the world was their oyster. This, combined with Katie's enthusiasm and ambition, meant that she often monopolised family meals with one-way dialogue about her aspirations and future plans.

On this particular Friday evening, she couldn't contain her excitement and happiness because she was wearing the dress that she had designed for that evening's end-of-term mother-and-daughter fashion show at her school. With the help of her mother's fashion designer friend, Freya Williams, one month of secret planning and fittings had resulted in the creation that Katie had sketched and visualised so many times.

As instructed by his daughter, her adoring father waited patiently at the bottom of the stairs with his hands over his eyes.

'You can open your eyes now, Dad,' said Katie.

'Wow!' was Matt's immediate reaction at seeing his teenage daughter looking every bit of the adult that she was becoming, too quickly for his liking. 'You look absolutely beautiful, and your dress is fabulous.'

'I know,' Katie giggled with just a hint of girlie shyness. 'I have been waiting for this moment for months now, and I really do feel as though I am dressed for a red carpet event.'

'I had no idea that you were designing such a beautiful dress. It suits you perfectly. I am so proud of you,' said her father.

'Thanks, Dad. My dress looks exactly as I had imagined it would. I don't think I have ever felt so excited.'

Matt beamed from ear to ear as he walked towards his daughter with his arms outstretched to embrace her.

'Hey! Don't crease my dress or mess my hair,' she laughed, teasing him.

'I don't care,' he replied. 'I have no intention of missing this moment to hug my gorgeous daughter.'

The year-end project at the St Andrews School for Girls had very cleverly been chosen by Eleanor Marshall, the headmistress. Emotional blackmail, perhaps, but she didn't feel guilty about that as she knew it would motivate the girls to study hard for their A-levels. That was her intention. Creating the means to an end was part of the school's charter, after all. What better incentive could there have been for a group of teenage girls than to promise them that study time would be replaced by design time after the final examination? What better reward could there have been than to offer planning time for the fashion show if study time was used effectively and homework completed on time?

The strategy worked. Heads were down throughout study time. Heads were definitely up in the clouds during design time. The girls applied themselves diligently to both challenges.

As part of the planning for the mother-and-daughter fashion show, the students had been given a remit to design and make, or have made, a catwalk outfit of their choice. Any design. Any length. Any colour. Eleanor already knew from the gossip that was rife during lunchtimes that there were going to be some eye-openers, no doubt, some good and some bordering distasteful.

The majority of the girls had referred to celebrity fashion images for inspiration from outfits worn by Britney Spears, Madonna, and Kylie Minogue, for example. Some talked of nothing else but designer chic. Others talked of miniskirts, tank tops, skinny jeans, waistcoats, and even Ugg boots, and Doc Martens got a mention from a few of the girls. They were all determined to take full advantage of the opportunity of dressing up for the evening, and they scoured magazines for designer names such as Versace, Dolce and Gabanna, Chanel, and Valentino. The one thing that all the students had in common was their combination of enthusiasm and effort in the preparation for the event, just exactly as planned by their headmistress.

Katie and her group of friends agreed that the designer route was for them, mainly because they didn't want to pass on an opportunity to research celebrity fashion for inspiration.

During her research, Katie hadn't restricted it to current fashion. She had also gone back in time, and it was in the year 2001 that she found the design that she wanted to recreate. Freya was delighted with her choice as it was perfect for her height and frame. It was the Channel dress that Jennifer Lopez had worn to the Seventy-third Academy Awards Oscars Ceremony in 2001. It hadn't been widely publicised by the media, so Katie was sure that no one else would have based their design on it.

In collaboration with Katie, Freya recommended subtle changes to the design to reflect a more youthful look that was more representative of Katie's age. The top was in folds of light silver chiffon drawn tightly across her slim upper body, twisted over one shoulder and caught into the opposite side of the waist of the backless dress. The fabric for the skirt of the dress was in a slightly creased anthracite shiny satin. It fitted tightly at the waist and hips and then hung dramatically in a very full and long skirt. Katie wanted a vivid touch of colour to complete the dress, and she and

Freya debated many options until Freya remembered that she had a large silk red admiral butterfly back at her studio. When Katie saw it, she knew exactly what she wanted to do with it, and so it was stitched where the chiffon met the satin at her lower back.

The only jewellery that Katie wore was a pair of filigree silver drop earrings. Her shoes were originally a white satin strappy sandal, now dyed anthracite to match the skirt of the dress. Her long dark hair was pulled back into a very loose chignon at the nape of her neck. She chose not to carry a clutch bag. Her make-up was limited to red lipstick. The overall effect was absolutely stunning.

Beth hadn't seen the dress and had deliberately not asked about the design. She trusted that the Katie and Freya alliance would produce a perfect result, and she wanted Katie to feel independent and also trusted about her choices. As a vote of confidence, she had allowed Katie to choose what she should wear and was pleased with her choice. Katie couldn't wait to see her mum's first reaction to the result of her efforts.

'What time is your mother collecting you?' asked her father, looking at his watch.

'She isn't. Freya is. Mum is making her way to the school after she closes a meeting at work.'

Matt stopped himself from voicing his disappointment at Beth not spending the afternoon with Katie to help her get ready and then travel to the school together. *It was a mother-and-daughter event after all*, he thought to himself.

Katie appeared to be oblivious to the obvious. She was too excited and disappeared to her bedroom to check how she looked for the umpteenth time.

6.15 p.m.

As if on cue, the doorbell rang.

'Hello! It's only me,' announced Freya as she entered the hallway before Matt had a chance to open the door for her.

'Hi, Freya!' responded Matt, giving her a peck on both cheeks. 'Katie is in her bedroom, no doubt, standing in front of her mirror *again*. She really looks stunning. Thanks for spending so much time with her.'

'She looked great at our dress rehearsal, so I can't wait to see her tonight,' replied Freya.

'She has obviously enjoyed the experience of working with you, and I think she has worn the dress all afternoon. It's a show-stopper. As her father, I think that I would have preferred that she didn't look so grown up, but I guess I can't stop the clock. I just wish that Beth were here to share the moment.'

Sensing an opportunity for Matt to whinge about Beth, Freya quickly diverted the conversation by suggesting that she capture the moment with some photographs. 'Katie, where are you? It's time for photographs to be taken.'

Once again, Katie made a grand entrance, knowing that Freya would be pleased with how she looked. She wasn't disappointed.

'Oh my God! You look absolutely fabulous,' said Freya as she recorded Katie's entrance on camera. 'The dress looks even better tonight. You just *have* to model it at my next fashion show. I *absolutely* insist.'

'Absolutely! And why not? But there is no way that anyone is getting their hands on *this* dress,' replied Katie.

'Nor would I want them to,' said Freya. 'Has your mum confirmed her ETA?'

'Come on, Freya! This is Mum we're talking about. She will, no doubt, arrive during dinner and then dash to the cloakroom to get dressed just before the fashion show begins.'

They both laughed because they knew that had actually been very close to the truth on many an occasion.

'Yes, you are probably right,' said Freya. 'Oh well, let's take some more photographs of that gorgeous dress and then be on our way.'

'Happy to oblige,' said a very happy Katie as she posed for Freya.

'Matt, let's get a father-and-daughter photograph,' to which he agreed without hesitation. Pleased with the result, Freya said, 'One for your study, methinks!'

'Sounds good,' replied Matt. 'Now, let's get a photograph of designer and model.' Seeing the look of disapproval on Katie's face, he rephrased his suggestion. 'Sorry. What I really mean is that we should get a photograph of the *designers*.'

They all laughed and enjoyed that moment before Katie and Freya left.

6.45 p.m.

Katie and Freya arrived at the school and registered at the reception area that had been set up for the event. Katie was given her entry badge-number 14. She asked if she should take her mother's, number 15, but was told that for security reasons, each person had to sign for their own badge.

'Crikey, Mum must have been involved in the registration arrangements,' laughed Katie.

'Now, that wouldn't surprise me,' replied Freya, also laughing.

Katie silently pleaded with her mum to arrive on time and to be seated at their table before the serving of the first course. She then decided to send her a text to ask for confirmation that she was on her way. What Katie didn't realise was that Freya was having exactly the same thought and that she had also sent Beth a text.

7 p.m.

Brodie Carmichael, history teacher and the students' choice for MC for the evening, took to the stage. He knew that the girls had taken the fashion show project very seriously and wanted them to enjoy their evening to the full. He had decided that a black tuxedo suit would befit the occasion and also demonstrate that he, too, was taking the plans for the evening seriously. It worked. He looked very handsome and definitely got the thumbs up from the girls and also from several of their mothers!

'Freya, where is she?' whispered an anxious Katie.

'She'll be here any moment, honey,' reassured Freya. Pleased that she had chosen to wear a formal black trouser suit for the evening, Freya had decided at registration that she would sit beside Katie until Beth's arrival.

Brodie welcomed everyone to the school's first mother-and-daughter fashion show and thanked the students for choosing him as their host for the evening.

'Thank goodness that I have a list of the students and their entry numbers as I don't think that I would be able to recognise any of you from what I can see. Congratulations, girls, on what looks to be an amazing effort. Don't you agree, mums?' This got the applause that he had intended for the girls.

The event had got off to a good start.

He summarised the prizes, thanked the parents who had made generous donations for the prizes, and talked through the programme that had been issued during registration.

Freya was quietly confident that Katie and Beth stood a good chance to walk away with the mother-and-daughter prize because they were both slim and tall, had a good eye for the detail of what suited them, and Kate had chosen their complimentary outfits wisely.

Before leaving the stage, Brodie wished everyone an enjoyable evening and announced that the first course of the dinner was about to be served.

7.10 p.m.

No sign of Beth.

The asparagus and hollandaise sauce starter was served. Katie was starting to feel uncomfortable. She knew that, aside from herself and Freya, the other eight people at her table were already wondering where her mother was.

7.30 p.m.

No sign of Beth.

The peppered rib of beef main course was served, with a vegetarian option. Wine for the adults, non-alcoholic fruit punch for the students, and jugs of water were laid out on the tables. Freya and Katie each noticed the other checking their mobile phones for a text message, unfortunately in vain. Both sent a further text message to Beth.

Freya couldn't help but be sensitive to the occasional comments that were being directed at Katie from the mothers at the table, for example:

'Katie, don't worry. Beth will be here soon. You know that she would have arrived on time if she could.'

Or

'Freya, it is so good of you to stand in for Beth. She is lucky to have you as a friend when she is often torn between work and family commitments.'

Or

And by far the worst came from Sandra, the least popular of the mothers, who said to her daughter, loud enough for everyone to hear, 'Aren't you pleased that I don't work, sweetheart?' And then to Katie, 'Katie, you have every right to be anxious, particularly as you have gone to so much effort with your dress.'

Freya couldn't restrain herself any longer.

'And doesn't she look absolutely beautiful, Sandra? As long as you are happy as a stay-at-home mother and wife, I am pleased for you. But let's not ever forget the significance of Beth's role in our community and how very proud we all are of her each time that she manages to remove a psychologically deranged criminal from our streets.'

Thankfully, one of the other mothers caught the drift of Freya's message. She offered her support by adding, 'And so say all of us, Freya. Beth can't pick and choose her timings as we can. Excusing herself in the middle of interviewing a serial killer because she must leave to attend a personal social event just isn't going to happen, is it? And, frankly, none of us should want to make someone as valuable as Beth feel guilty. Katie, you just relax and enjoy yourself.'

Thankfully, the silence that followed indicated that enough had been said on that particular topic.

Whilst Katie understood and was thankful for the support, she couldn't help but feel upset and angry at her mother. In fact, she was becoming increasingly annoyed and embarrassed.

All the adults at the table agreed about one thing: the food was delicious and the wine was hitting the right spot.

8 p.m.

No sign of Beth.

Just as dessert was being served, Katie excused herself to visit the toilet. She whispered to Freya that she was really going to telephone home to check whether or not her mum had called her dad and left a message. They both knew that this was unlikely to be the case.

Freya couldn't help but notice that all eyes were on Katie as she left the room. Once again, she silently hoped that Beth would arrive soon. From the envious looks that she saw, it was obvious to her who would steal the show.

8.10 p.m.

Katie hadn't returned to the table for dessert. Her summer fruits mousse and strawberry shortcake remained untouched, and Freya's increasing discomfort had started to show.

She wondered if they would consider her as Katie's guardian for the evening so that she could still participate in the fashion show if Beth didn't show.

Freya excused herself from the table as she had decided to approach Brodie Carmichael and Eleanor Marshall to suggest that she stand in for Beth during the fashion show.

But, first, she would check that this suggestion was acceptable to Katie.

She didn't get that chance.

8.20 p.m.

Still no sign of Beth, and, as Freya couldn't find Katie, she updated Eleanor Marshall of the situation, who then sent someone to fetch Brodie Carmichael.

8.25 p.m.

Still no sign of Beth.

And now no sign of Katie.

As Eleanor Marshall and Brodie Carmichael decided what to do, Freya returned to the table to announce that she couldn't find Katie anywhere.

8.30 p.m.

Back on stage, Brodie Carmichael announced that the fashion show was about to begin. He requested everyone to be seated and talked through the specifics of the catwalk and voting procedures. Finally, and uncomfortably, he asked his audience to delete entry numbers 14 and 15 from the voting forms 'as Katie and Beth Oliver will sadly no longer be able to participate in the fashion show.' Freya left the room, angry at Beth and very upset for Katie. With the help of the janitor, she started to search the common areas of the school.

9 p.m.

The initial search of the school and the grounds was in vain as were calls to Katie and Beth. Freya had no option but to call Matt to check if he had heard from either of them. She didn't have answers to his obvious questions and told him that she would join him shortly. She took one final look around her as she drove out of the car park and then followed the bus route from the school to the area where the Olivers stayed in Clerkenwell.

It was dark.
It was raining.
Where on earth would Katie have gone?

CHAPTER 2

Friday, 18 June 2004
9.20 p.m.

As Freya drove to the Olivers, she dreaded the prospect of facing Matt in the absence of Katie or Beth. Had Katie chosen to hide, Freya felt that she and the janitor had done a thorough search of the obvious places that she may have hidden. Rather than interrupt the fashion show proceedings, they had decided to focus their search on the rooms in the registration vicinity and the car park. Before Freya had left, the janitor said that he would update the headmistress and, with her approval, continue with a more detailed search. Freya gave him her mobile phone number and asked him to call or text her with an update, whether or not he found Katie.

Freya was sure that Katie had left in a temper tantrum rather than having to face the probability of withdrawing from the competition in the absence of her mother. She was also furious that Beth hadn't sent a text message to either of them to explain her absence so that they could consider what they were going to say to the event organisers. Surely, Beth could have left the office for a few minutes to have done that. *Poor Katie*. Freya could only imagine how she must have felt when she left the table. She had been looking forward to this evening for weeks. She had looked so beautiful, and it hurt Freya that Beth had not even been there to witness that.

Freya took a deep breath as she approached the Olivers' home as she could see that Matt was pacing up and down the driveway waiting for her to arrive. She wished that she had rehearsed what she was actually going to say to him.

Matt was ready for her.

'Why did you call me earlier to ask if Katie had called? Why have you returned here? Why are you here on your own? Has something gone wrong? Did Beth arrive in sufficient time to avoid any embarrassment to Katie?' And so the questions flowed before Freya had a chance to answer any of them.

Freya made her way into the sitting room, followed by Matt. She suggested that he stop asking questions and just sit down whilst she shared with him the events of the evening so far. She knew that it wasn't going to be easy, and she knew that he would start to blame Beth before she got the first sentence out. She did the best that she could, ignoring Matt's constant interruptions with unhelpful comments and questions.

She had told him everything that had happened and assured him that the search was continuing, internally and externally. She told him that the janitor would call her later with an update. Finally, she talked him through the route that she had taken from the school with her car.

Now very angry, Matt interrupted Freya with a controlled, 'Before I explode, Freya, I want to thank you for being there for Katie and for making an effort to find her. Now, no more storytelling, Freya. No more softly-softly. No more covering up for Beth. Where the fuck is she? And where the fuck is my daughter?'

An uncomfortable silence followed.

Freya understood his anger as she didn't feel too comfortable about the situation herself.

'I don't know, Matt. As well as following the bus route, I have driven up and down the obvious streets between the school and your home. I have even checked out some of the cafes between the school and here. Thank goodness that I took some photographs before we left as I was able to show people a photograph of Katie as she had looked before she left the show.'

'Well, she can't be at any of her friends' homes, can she, as they are all, no doubt, enjoying themselves at the fashion show, and she doesn't have a boyfriend that we know of. In fact, she doesn't tend to hang out with boys at present as she has been studying hard for her final exams and preparing for the fashion show.'

'We need to get hold of Beth, Matt. No matter which meeting she is in, she will want to know what has happened, and she will know what to do.'

'Fuck Beth. If she had arrived at the school on time to support her daughter, we wouldn't be having this conversation, would we?'

'No, we wouldn't, and, if I am honest with you, I also can't understand why Beth didn't contact us before the show was due to begin,' said Freya. 'But, Matt, all of that is for later. For now, none of that helps us find Katie,' continued Freya. 'We need to find Katie. It's wet. It's cold. And she doesn't have a coat with her. She will not be walking the streets in a designer dress, will she?'

9.35 p.m.

Just as Matt was about to shout another derogatory remark about Beth, the front door flew open, and Beth marched into the sitting room. As an aside, she looked gorgeous as somehow she had managed to change into a classic black dress and apply make-up before making her way to the fashion show. At least it backed up her story that she had actually made her way there.

'Where is Katie, Freya?' asked Beth. 'I have been to the school, and Eddie, the janitor, stopped me going into the assembly hall. He told me that Katie had vanished before the start of the fashion show and to tell you that he had searched everywhere for her with nothing positive to report back to you.'

'I'm curious, Beth,' cut in Matt. 'What exactly would you expect her do in the absence of any communication from you? Registration was at 6.45 p.m. It's now three hours later. You weren't there for the dinner and would have made it for the fashion show by the skin of your teeth. Neither Katie nor Freya is a mind-reader.'

Matt continued with a bombardment of angry words towards Beth. 'Katie was probably so humiliated by your no-show that she couldn't face the prospect of withdrawing her entry and watching all her friends and their mothers enjoying themselves,' roared Matt.

'Stop shouting, Matt. Yes, I could see why she would feel embarrassed, but shouting about it doesn't find her. Freya, are you sure that you checked all the obvious routes that she may have taken?'

'Of course I did,' said a frustrated Freya. 'Why didn't you contact us, Beth? Surely, you must have known that Katie would be anxious about whether or not you were going to arrive on time. You would have missed the dinner, but had I known that you were on your way, I could have reassured Katie. That would have stopped her from leaving.'

'Yes, I'm keen to hear your answer to all of that, too,' said Matt as he walked towards Beth and looked at her directly.

'Let's not waste time arguing about this. Why I was late or whether or not I called Freya with an explanation is irrelevant just at present. You both know that I would have a very good reason for letting Katie down so badly. Of course, I knew that she would be furious with me, and I was in such a rush to change and leave the office that I left my mobile phone on my desk. Instead of returning for it, I thought that it would be better to continue to the school and arrange for my phone to be delivered to me at the school later.'

'Oh no, you can't be without your bloody telephone, can you?' yelled Matt.

'Actually, Matt, you know that I can't be without my mobile phone, so let's not even go there,' responded Beth.

'I don't mean to be rude, but arguing isn't going to get us anywhere,' said Freya. 'Why don't I drive around again to see if I have better luck this time?' she offered.

'I'm coming with you, Freya,' said Matt. He turned to Beth and sarcastically suggested that she do something useful by drawing up a list of contact details of Katie's friends.

9.55 p.m.

As Freya and Matt got ready to leave, Beth picked up the house phone to make two calls. The first was to her office to arrange for her mobile phone to be delivered immediately. The second was to Dan Turner.

The second call came as no surprise to Matt or Freya. As Beth's mentor, boss, and close friend, Dan Turner had an excellent track record as detective superintendent at the MET's Specialist Crimes Division. He was held in high regard by his superiors and all staff who had had the privilege of working with him.

Dan accredited his own successful career to Bill Palmer, Beth's father, who had been Dan's boss before he retired, and Dan was promoted to DSI. Dan regularly praised Bill for the quality of his people management skills and his techniques in training, delegation, and encouragement.

'Hi, Dan. It's Beth.'

Beth proceeded to tell him that Katie was missing and outlined what had happened from the summary that Freya had given her. Dan asked to speak with Freya.

'Hi, Freya. I know that it may be awkward to speak in front of Beth and Matt, but I have a couple of simple questions for you that should just require a yes or no response.'

Before Freya had a chance to answer him, his first question was, 'Is this a domestic, Freya? I know how Matt feels about Beth being compromised by duty to her family and responsibility to the Specialist Crimes Division. So please just answer yes or no.'

'Yes *and* no, I think,' said Freya.

'Christ, what do you mean by that, Freya?'

'I have no doubt that Katie probably stomped off in a bad temper, but I don't think that she would just leave me at the school to handle the situation. Where would she go in an evening dress when all her friends were at the school? Where would she go in the dark, in the rain? The janitor saw her outside, but he said that he definitely got the feeling that she was waiting on a taxi.'

'Hmm. I hear what you are saying. Beth says that you checked the routes between the school and home. Any ideas about the routes that you didn't cover?'

'Just one for now,' said Freya.

'Which did you miss out?' asked Dan.

'The park,' Freya whispered into the telephone with her back to the Olivers. Thankfully, Matt was too busy shouting at Beth for either of them to have heard her last answer.

'Do you think that we need to check out that area?' asked Dan.

'Yes,' replied Freya without hesitation.

'Can you pass me back to Beth, please?'

Freya handed the phone back to Beth.

'Freya sounded pretty confident that she had checked the obvious routes, but she didn't check the park. You know that it is too early to register this as a missing person case, particularly as it just sounds like a family tiff at present. It is also well below my level of command. However, I know Katie well enough to suppose that she wouldn't do anything stupid and walking through the park would have been stupid on her own at night and dressed to kill. As it's now time that Katie should be home and as there has been no contact, I am prepared to arrange a low-key check of the park by a couple of our junior officers.'

'Thanks, Dan,' said Beth gratefully.

'In the meantime, can you and Matt start to call around all Katie's friends as soon as you think that they will be home? Check with each of them to find out whether or not there has been any contact with Katie. Also ask each of them if there is likely to be a boyfriend lurking in the background. Someone that you aren't aware of. She is seventeen, after all.'

'I'm sure that there is an explanation. She can't be far. She is probably just trying to make me suffer, eh? And she is succeeding!'

'As a friend, I will call the school and try to talk to someone in authority this evening before they lock up. Hopefully, I can touch base with the headmistress and forewarn her that she and some of her staff may need to work on a Saturday morning if we don't hear anything from Katie then.'

'Hopefully, it won't come to that,' said Beth. 'Hopefully, she will make her way to her friend's house for their post-show sleepover.'

'I'll call you later. In the meantime, just stay calm. It sounds like she really wants to make a point this time.'

Freya suggested that she and Matt change their plan to drive around the area and insisted that she stay at the Olivers to help her friend make the telephone calls.

Matt agreed and said that he would rather walk the streets to look for Katie in any event. Beth agreed that this was what he should do and updated him with Dan's offer to send a couple of officers out to the park. Matt didn't even respond to her as he put on his jacket and slammed the door as he left the house.

'I had better call my parents, I guess,' said Beth. 'I don't want to worry them, but Katie just may have gone there to have a good moan to her grandmother about how bad a parent her mother is.'

'Actually, that's a good idea, Beth. I just bet that is where she went, but wouldn't one of them have called you by now to update you?'

'Yes, but if she has gone there, she won't have been there for very long, will she? If she hasn't, however, Dad would be really cross if I didn't share with him any concerns that I have about his granddaughter's safety.'

'That's the benefit of having a retired chief superintendent as your father,' replied Freya, 'but, yes, you need to make that call.'

'I know,' said Beth 'and I need to make sure that no one calls Jack as there is nothing that Katie's brother can do whilst he is on holiday on a Greek Island. It's going to be a long evening, isn't it? I am still sure that Katie is safe at someone's house and isn't answering her phone as punishment to me for spoiling her evening.'

'I agree with you. It doesn't bear thinking about if that isn't the case,' said Freya. 'By the way, Beth, she looked absolutely stunning,' added Freya.

'I didn't doubt for one moment that she wouldn't. Did you take any photographs?' asked Beth.

'Of course, I did. You know me. Any opportunity for a photo shoot. Seriously though, I wish that you had been there to see her. She was radiant.'

Beth didn't respond, already feeling very guilty at missing out on the opportunity to see Katie before the fashion show started.

Freya showed Beth a selection of Katie's photographs. As Beth looked at the photographs, she understood the extent of what had happened that evening and knew that Matt had every right to be so angry with her. She knew that she was going to have to eat humble pie with Katie and Matt later.

10.10 p.m.

Beth called her parents, and her father confirmed that Katie had not been in touch with them. Beth played down the extent of her worry and tried to make the conversation as casual as she could because she didn't want them worrying needlessly during the night.

Dan called the school and managed to speak to Eleanor Marshall, the headmistress. She agreed to meet with him at the school that evening.

10.40 p.m.

Over the next thirty minutes, Freya and Beth made calls to friends, parents, neighbours, and anyone else whom Katie may have contacted. No one could point them in the right direction of tracing Katie's footsteps after she had left the school. Of particular concern to Beth was that Katie had not contacted the friends that she had planned to stay overnight with after the fashion show.

11.25 p.m.

Matt returned just before Dan arrived at the house. They exchanged polite greetings.

Matt's search was in vain as he couldn't find anyone who had seen or spoken with Katie. She appeared to have vanished from the school gates, which was where the janitor had last seen her. He said that he hadn't searched the park as he knew that the police officers would be doing that and were more practised in a search of that scale.

Dan reported that he had met with Eleanor Marshall and Brodie Carmichael at the school, also in vain. He had arranged to call Eleanor in the morning if Katie still hadn't returned home, and she would then arrange for the teachers on duty that evening to report to the school for interviews.

They all felt helpless but knew that the reality of the situation was that there was nothing else that they could do until Katie had called them or any of her friends. Beth and Matt both started to wonder if Katie did have a boyfriend that she hadn't told them about. They had exhausted their enquiries with her friends.

As suggested by Dan, Beth and Freya made calls to the hospitals in the area, knowing that Katie would easily be identified in her designer dress had she been admitted after an accident. No one of her description had been admitted to the accident and emergency department.

It was a very long night for Beth and Matt, both knowing that there was nothing practical that they could do until the morning. Both silently prayed that Katie was safe at someone's house.

No one managed to sleep, but Beth knew how important it was for her to rest so that she could be on top of her form the next day if Katie didn't show.

Matt stayed in his study, avoiding his wife as he knew that he wouldn't be able to hide the anger that he felt for her and couldn't trust what he might say to her in the presence of Freya.

2 a.m.

Dan called just before 2 a.m. Beth pressed the loudspeaker button and asked Freya to ask Matt to join them. Contrary to what Beth and Matt hoped for, Dan didn't have any positive news for them. Basically, he just wanted to wrap up the evening by telling them that Eleanor Marshall had just called him to report that the duty teachers that evening had volunteered to report to the school early the next morning so that they could offer their assistance quickly if Katie didn't turn up during the course of the night.

Dan closed by telling them that he would visit early the next morning and advised that they all rest in the meantime.

For once, Matt didn't have anything sarcastic to say. Perhaps that was because he respected Dan and was appreciative of his early efforts to support them.

Matt said that he was going to spend the evening in his study and didn't want to be disturbed unless Katie made contact. Beth knew that this was to contain his anger towards her and also to hide his frustration at not knowing where his daughter was.

Freya accepted Beth's offer of the use of the guest room bed. She wasn't particularly tired, but she didn't want to be piggy in the middle of a Beth-and-Matt argument.

Beth couldn't sleep. She was agitated and quietly prayed that her daughter was somewhere safe. She was also angry that she hadn't made more of an effort to contact Freya or Katie earlier in the day when it started to look like she would struggle to get there before or during dinner. Freya was correct in what she had said. Had she explained the reason to Freya, she could then have reassured Katie that Beth would be there in time for the fashion show.

Beth knew that there was no point in trying to console her husband and could understand why he would want to be on his own.

CHAPTER 3

Saturday, 19 June 2004
5.30 a.m.

No one at the Olivers' home had slept the previous night, although they had all managed to get some rest. Naturally, they were all worried about what had happened to Katie and were hoping that the previous night's events would turn out to be something about nothing.

Katie still hadn't been in touch, and there had been no contact from any of her friends or any of the school staff.

This was totally out of character for the person who had decided to take control of the time that her parents and her brother spent at home so that she could ensure that they at least had family breakfasts together as often as possible.

By now, Beth and Matt knew that Katie would not have stayed out all night without at least informing Matt.

Matt had stayed in his study, but he had used the time to look out some recent photographs of Katie from the family albums, had scanned a few, and had printed out batches for the police. 'Oh my God, I can't believe that I am doing this,' he said aloud to himself. He just couldn't get his head around the fact that he may have to face up to the actual disappearance of his daughter at some point that morning.

Feeling very alone, he felt that he needed to speak with his son, Jack. In fact, if Katie was missing, he knew that he would want Jack to be there with him. He had agreed with Beth's suggestion to keep Jack out of the communication loop until they had determined whether or not Katie was actually missing. *Fuck Beth*, he thought to himself. He would decide when he spoke with his son.

He was still very angry with Beth and blamed her entirely for what had happened. There was no way that he was going to let her make all the decisions about today's activities, regardless of her DCI job title.

Matt checked the time difference between UK and Greece and, as the latter was two hours ahead of UK, decided that 5.30 a.m. was a reasonable UK time to call the hotel that Jack was staying at with friends. He felt that the circumstances justified his decision.

Jack was none too happy when he answered the telephone at 7.30 a.m. in Greece, considering that he had only arrived back at the hotel at 3 a.m. Matt sensed his grumpiness, but that changed when he realised that it was his father who had called him. Instinctively, he knew that something was wrong for that to have happened so early in the morning.

'Sorry to interrupt your holiday at such an early hour, Jack, but I just needed to hear your voice,' he choked.

'What the hell's wrong, Dad? Have you been drinking? It's not like you to go all soppy on me.'

Matt interrupted Jack's flow of sarcasm.

'Katie is missing. We don't know where she is, Jack. She left the school before the fashion show and hasn't been seen since. She isn't answering her telephone.'

That brought Jack back to reality with a jolt. 'But last night was the big event. She has been looking forward to the fashion show for months. There is no way that she would have missed it. What happened?'

'Long story, but your mother didn't turn up for the dinner. Freya sat at the table with Katie, but that didn't help to alleviate Katie's embarrassment at her mother not being there with her. Just before dessert, your sister said that she was going to the toilet, but she didn't return. Last night, we all thought that she had decided to leave to avoid the humiliation of being the only daughter in the assembly room whose mother or guardian wasn't there.'

'Oh, no. Poor Katie. Poor Mum,' said Jack.

'Poor Mum! What the hell do you mean by *poor Mum*? She didn't show, Jack. It was a mother-and-daughter fashion show, for Christ's sake. Her mother's attendance was pretty key to the event, wouldn't you say?'

'Yes, Dad. But I don't think that you will need to say any of that to Mum. You know that she will be hurting, and you know that she will know that she is to blame. You also know that she wouldn't show for no good reason.'

'You know what?' said Matt wearily. 'I am so tired of hearing that said about Beth's non-appearances. Do me a favour, and let's not go there, eh?'

Jack sensed the weariness in his dad's voice and, knowing how much he loved Katie, decided to be more sympathetic.

'Katie will probably have stayed out at a friend's house just to punish Mum, don't you think?' As he said that, he knew that Katie actually wouldn't do that as she wouldn't want to worry them. Also, he knew that she was more than equal to the task of returning home and making their mother feel guilty, very guilty.

'We checked with all her friends last night, spoke to their parents, and also called the hospitals. She hasn't made contact with anyone. That is just not like her.'

'I agree. What do you want me to do, Dad?'

'Not much you can do, for now. Dan Turner instructed a couple of his officers to search the neighbourhood last night, with no luck. He will be arriving shortly to listen to what we have to say and to decide whether or not he will officially register Katie as a missing young person. If he does, he will then appoint an investigation team. He has made it clear that he is acting as a friend for now because investigation procedures would not normally kick in until much later, given the sequence of events. I'll call you again after his visit and give you an update.'

'I'm sure that Katie will be fine, Dad. There has to be an explanation.' Like everyone else who knew Katie well, Jack was beginning to think that she must have had an accident and knew that he wouldn't be able to enjoy his holiday until he heard that his sister was safe.

Matt heard the voices in the kitchen and went through to let Beth know that he had contacted Jack.

'Why, Matt?' she asked. 'Do you really think that calling Jack in Greece is going to have any impact on what we do at this end? Besides, was it really fair to worry him so soon?'

'Beth, I wanted to speak to my son. I wanted him to know that his sister was missing. I made the decision to involve him, and so I made that call. Don't worry, he is not going to jump on the next flight, but he is going to stay put at the hotel until I call him again after Dan's visit.'

Sensing that she should tread carefully with Matt, Beth surprised Matt and Freya by saying, 'I understand why you felt the need to do that, Matt. I have already checked Katie's room, and it would appear that she hasn't sneaked back into the house during the night. She appears to be missing, Matt. Let's agree to leave the communication with Jack to you and also any decisions that relate to whether or not he should cut his holiday short, okay?'

'Okay,' replied Matt.

'One thing, Matt. Just please send him my love,' added Beth.

In an effort to make herself useful, Freya had attended to breakfast. She knew that it wouldn't be a sit-down affair, so she raided the fridge and laid out a selection of food and refreshment options.

6.45 a.m.

Dan arrived at the Olivers. He knew by their faces that Katie had not returned home. He expressed his condolences and accepted Freya's offer of coffee and some breakfast. Like the Olivers, he hadn't slept much during the night because he knew that Katie wasn't the type of person to stay out all night to punish one of her parents. He knew that her exit from the school event was prompted by a domestic situation, but his instincts prompted him to start formulating a plan for the next morning.

He confirmed that his officers hadn't been able to find out anything about Katie's whereabouts and had come up with nothing from their search of the school, local cafes, and park on the routes between the school and their home. He added that they hadn't made an attempt to search any of the local woods as they were considered to be too far away from the school at this particular moment of time.

Matt summarised the route that he had followed when he went out to search for Katie.

Dan asked Freya to talk him through the events of the evening one more time to ensure that he hadn't missed anything. He was conscious that, as she did this, Matt's face was going red with anger and emotion and that Beth's face was going chalk-white with worry and guilt.

'Let's use the next few hours at this end to do a sweep-up of second round of telephone calls to all Katie's friends and their parents. Don't speak to one without also speaking to the other.'

'Count me out of that. I would prefer to be out there, looking for my daughter,' said Matt.

'I understand that, Matt, so why don't I assign an officer to you and, together, you can go to the places that Katie would normally frequent, particularly on a Saturday morning? Let's get some photographs of Katie so that you can show them to passers-by, shopkeepers, or cafe owners,' instructed Dan.

Matt informed him that he had already scanned and copied batches of photographs so he was ready to leave the house soon. Dan made a phone call and told Matt that an officer would be with him within ten to fifteen minutes. Dan left the room to get ready.

After Matt returned, Dan started to summarise instructions just as he would have back at the office.

'Beth, start to make the calls to the people on your contact list. Write down everything that is said during each conversation. Matt, you and one of my officers will spend the morning as I have previously described, and remember to issue or show the photographs that you have. Also record the routes taken, preferably highlighted on a local map, and the people that you speak to.

'Freya, I suggest that you get back to your clients and do what you would normally do on a Saturday morning as everything that we will be doing at this end will be routine during the next few hours.'

No one argued with Dan's instructions as they made absolute sense, and everyone knew that they had to be followed whether they felt able to cope with that or not.

Freya, now wearing a tracksuit and trainers given to her by Beth, confirmed that she would attend to some of her own work. She stressed that she was just at the end of a telephone call and would return immediately if needed.

'What are you going to be doing, Dan?' asked Beth.

'I'm going to go back to the school to interview Eleanor Marshall, Brodie Carmichael, Eddie, the janitor, and the group of teachers on duty last night. Eleanor was going to arrange for the

11 a.m.

When they all met again at the Olivers for their scheduled eleven o'clock meeting, they had completed the tasks that Dan had issued, but no one had anything positive to report back. They didn't have one single clue about Katie's whereabouts. Dan reported back that he had seen the CCTV footage and had seen Katie leave the school and walk towards the gates just as the janitor had said. There was nothing of her on the tape after that.

Knowing the Olivers and Beth's parents as he did, Dan had no option but to take on board the fact that by eleven o'clock that morning, Katie had been missing for fourteen hours and no one had any idea about where she could be. He knew what he had to do.

11.15 a.m.

Just after eleven o'clock, in the presence of the family, Dan called his office to report Katie Oliver as a missing person. Bill hugged Beth. Caroline hugged Matt. It was as if they both sensed that Beth and Matt would not be able to hug each other at that moment of time.

Matt withdrew to his study again, saying that he was going to call Jack with an update. This time, he informed him that his sister had been reported as a missing person. Without any hesitation, Jack said that he was going to book a flight home and would call or text his father with his flight details. He forewarned him that he may have to pay for a new ticket if the existing booking couldn't be changed. Needless to say, that wasn't going to be an issue.

For a while after Dan and Matt had returned to the sitting room, there was only silence. No one knew what to say.

Dan had experienced similar moments of silence many times over in his career and respected the need for them. After an appropriate time, he announced that he needed to return to his office to organise the investigation team and asked everyone to stay put until instructed

CCTV tape to be ready for review this morning, so I will have at that also. And, before you ask, Beth, no, you can't come w I have already arranged for some help. Your place is here, those calls and, hopefully, being on hand to take that much call from Katie when she eventually makes it.'

Having spent a lifetime managing kidnappings and wor: both already knew that there would be no such call. Katie the type of teenager who would just disappear in an evening

'Let's all meet back here at eleven o'clock,' said Dan as for the door to drive back to the school. Just as he was a leave the house, Bill and Caroline Palmer, Beth's parents, arri

Bill spoke up before Beth had a chance to say anything, that it is very early in the morning, but I called Dan to fin you had been in touch. Call it sixth sense. He confirmed had and why, so here we are. Saved you a call, Beth.'

Dan and Freya excused themselves.

A police officer arrived to collect Matt.

Beth sat on the sofa between her mother and father an to sob as she explained what had happened the night before.

'I have really messed up this time, Pops,' she addre father.

Bill gave his daughter a cuddle and said, 'There is talking about what you should or shouldn't have done. Le: that negative thinking until later, sweetheart. Let's use ever wisely so that we can quickly find my granddaughter.'

'You know that these are wise words, Beth,' added apparently unaware that there were tears rolling down her

Beth stood up and said, 'I am glad that you are both he calls to make. Do you want to help me with those?'

Beth split the list, giving the hospital contact details to photo of Katie as she was dressed before the fashion show. split the list of contact details of Katie's friends and the between herself and her mother.

otherwise. He asked them to trust him and his team to manage the search for Katie from that point forward.

Beth left the room.

Matt got a call from Jack, saying that he would be arriving at Gatwick Airport at 7.45 p.m. that evening, UK time. Bill offered to meet Jack. Matt couldn't bear to sit around the house, but he knew that he would need to stay at home in case Katie made contact.

Before leaving, Dan asked everyone to sit down whilst he talked them through the basic procedures that he and his team would follow during the course of the next few hours. He offered them some reassurance by telling them that the team that he was going to allocate the search for Katie to was very experienced and knew exactly the level of performance expected by him. As he shook Matt's hand, he told him that his updates would be regular but that Matt should call him at any time even if he just wanted to talk to someone other than a member of the immediate family.

As final arrangements were being made, Matt called his parents, Tom and Susan Oliver, both GPs in Sheffield. It was agreed that there were more than enough people assisting at present and that their role for the time being would be one of support.

Midday

Just as Dan was about to leave, Beth re-entered the room with an overnight bag. Her intention was clear, but Matt couldn't contain his anger. 'Only you would abandon the family at a time like this. Do you actually believe that the investigation team under Dan's supervision is incapable of managing the search for a missing person without you?' he shouted across the room.

'Matt, please don't start an argument,' pleaded Beth. 'You know that we have enough volunteers at home. You must also surely realise that, with my background and contacts, the place that I need to be based is at the MET. That doesn't mean that I am not anxious about Katie's safety. However, I refuse to sit around, waiting for something to happen while my daughter is out there somewhere needing our help. I have the skills to find Katie, and you know that.'

Matt was silent, which demonstrated to them all that he actually agreed with her but didn't want to say so.

Beth's demeanour appeared to be cold, but they all knew that this was a cover-up for how she was actually feeling. They understood that her way of dealing with Katie's disappearance was to move into her DCI role and to get on with the job in hand.

12.10 p.m.

'I am just going to try Katie's phone one more time before I leave,' Beth said, and Dan held back from leaving while she made the call.

To everyone's surprise, Beth shouted in disbelief, 'Katie, it's Mum. Where are you? Are you okay? We have all been so worried about you. Katie, speak to me.'

Silence.

All eyes were on Beth as she switched the phone to speaker, out of habit, and said once more, 'Katie, speak to me, please.'

A man responded by saying, 'Katie can't take your call.'

'I want to speak to my daughter. Who are you?'

'I'm the person who is about to become your worst nightmare, Mrs Oliver, DCI at the MET's Specialist Crimes Division, if I'm not mistaken.' And then he disconnected.

Beth immediately dialled Katie's number over and over again, but no one answered.

'No!' she yelled at her mobile phone. 'This can't be happening. I want to speak to my daughter.'

'Beth, there is no point calling Katie's number again. He isn't going to answer,' said Dan.

As the shock of his daughter being kidnapped penetrated, Matt lashed out at Beth again. 'This has something to do with you, Beth, hasn't it? It was only a matter of time before your job interfered with the safety of our family,' yelled Matt.

'Now, Matt, let's not go there,' said Bill, Beth's father. 'You are naturally very upset, but let's not jump to conclusions.'

'Bill's correct,' said Dan. 'You all need to be there for each other. Arguments will waste time, add pressure, and actually interfere with our investigation.'

Matt sat down with his head in his hands. Caroline joined him, and, with her head on his shoulder, she started to cry. Matt put his arm around Caroline to comfort her.

Bill left the room, unable to control his emotions any longer.

Beth abruptly turned around to Matt and said, 'I am going to my office now. I promise you that I will find the bastard who knows where our daughter is. Please trust me.'

Matt didn't respond.

12.25 p.m.

Beth and Dan left the house and set off in separate cars for the MET offices.

Caroline left the room to look for her husband and found him in Katie's bedroom just staring into space. She started to put away the clothes that Katie had been wearing before she got dressed for the school fashion show. Tears were rolling down her cheeks as she silently prayed for Katie's safe return.

Elsewhere in a basement room of a terraced house in the Kings Cross area of London sat a man holding Katie's mobile phone in one hand and his camera in the other. He smiled as if to congratulate himself at what he had achieved. Actually, he was rooted to the spot, taking in how beautiful the teenager looked. In the corner of the room, Katie was unconscious and spread out on a hospital bed with her ankles and wrists firmly tied to the corner posts. Her kidnapper had also taped her mouth and put a blindfold over her eyes. At that precise moment, he had no intention of doing anything to her other than to record the moment on DVD. He had already taken photographs of her fully clothed when she had arrived, and she was still fully clothed. But he had every intention of taking many more.

CHAPTER 4

Saturday, 19 June 2004
12.30 p.m.

As Dan drove back to his office, thoughts were swirling around his head. *Had Katie been kidnapped? Or had someone found her mobile phone and was having some fun with the family? No, it couldn't be that because the caller made a point of highlighting Beth's name and rank.* Instinct told him that Katie had been kidnapped, but it couldn't be opportunistic if he knew who Beth was. It couldn't have been planned either as Katie was scheduled to be at the school all evening with her mother. If it was opportunistic, then perhaps Katie had verbally threatened him with her mum's job and rank. In any event, he had a strong feeling that this was about to become serious.

He made a call to Grace Fletcher and asked her if she could meet with him at his office as soon as possible that afternoon. After he had briefly explained the events of the previous evening and that morning, she immediately agreed to get there within the hour.

Grace Fletcher is a highly respected psychologist and criminal profiler at the MET, whose advice and guidance had often been called upon by the most senior of ranks in the Specialist Crimes Division. Over the many years of working closely with Dan and Beth, she had become a close friend to both of them.

1 p.m.

Beth and Dan arrived at the MET offices. Beth went straight to her office without saying anything to Dan. He joined her and closed the door behind him.

'I understand the stiff upper lip, and I also understand your need to be here instead of at your home with the rest of your family. But before we go to meet the investigation team, you must let your guard down with me and just be Katie's mother. No one is going to interrupt us, and I am your friend as well as your colleague.'

The tears started to run down Beth's cheeks as she picked up the photograph of Katie that sat on her desk beside the one of her brother, Jack.

'Dan, I should have been there yesterday. I shouldn't even have come in to work. Katie was so excited about this event, and the fact that we were doing it together was a bonus for us both. I could have asked you to manage the negotiation meetings with Galloway and his lawyers. I am not the only person capable of negotiating the trade of vital information for a reduced sentence plea,' wept Beth.

'I know, Beth, but that is history. It's good for you to say those words, but you know as well as I do that within the next few minutes, we have to prime the team and start the detective work.'

Dan continued.

'It should come as no surprise to you that I have made the decision that you will not be heading up this investigation. In fact, in theory, you won't even be part of the investigation team. I have had a chat with the chief, and he has agreed that we can handle it rather than sending it down the line. But, because of your involvement, that is on condition that I lead the investigation, backed up by Colin and his team, I will allow you to sit in on all meetings on condition that you will not interfere with our enquiries. Also, you will not go off at a tangent on any leads that we consider to be worthy of further investigation. You have been around long enough to know that this isn't up for discussion.'

Silence.

'Is that clear, Beth?' asked Dan with his authoritative voice.

'Yes, but I don't want to be protected from any aspect of the truth. The only way that I will be able to formulate my own thoughts, whilst retaining some semblance of sanity, is to know exactly what is being discussed.'

'I understand that, Beth, but I need to hear that you accept the condition of you even being here. That isn't negotiable, and I need you to accept and understand that before we meet the team. Is *that* clear, Beth?' asked Dan.

'Crystal,' replied Beth.

Once that was out of the way, Beth started to weep inconsolably, and Dan moved towards her and took her in his arms. She was grateful for the strong shoulders of her friend and for the opportunity to vent her feelings.

After a while, Beth indicated to Dan that she would be ready to meet the team after she had freshened up. Before she left, he told her that he had invited Grace to join them. She knew that he would and was appreciative of the gesture. She trusted Grace implicitly. As a friend, she and Grace had spent many a shopping spree and lunch together. Sometimes that had extended to include Katie. Out of work, Grace knew them both very well.

'One final point, Beth,' said Dan. 'From now and until we find Katie, you will not work from your own office. Instead, you will work as part of the team either in my conference room or office. Those two rooms are being set up at present as the incident rooms for this enquiry. All telephone calls and meetings will take place in the conference room. You know the tight timescale that we need to work to for a kidnapping, and so it is vital that you don't do anything independently that may interfere with the drive for a early result.'

'As I said earlier, I have reported all of this to the chief superintendent, and I have also updated the commander. Both Simon and James are sympathetic of your situation and want you to know that they will follow our progress closely. You know that they will be there to offer support and guidance if we feel that we need it at any time during our investigation.'

'I know,' said Beth. 'Please thank them on my behalf.'

'Ready to face the team?' asked Dan.

'Yes. I'll join you in five minutes,' replied Beth, making a gesture to him that indicated her need to splash water on her face.

'Okay, but please remember that you are a human being and not a machine. You have worked many years with the team that I have chosen, and they will not expect you to constantly put on a brave face. It is okay to let your guard down from time to time.'

Dan took Beth's arm and directed her towards the door of her office.

1.30 p.m.

Beth wasn't at all surprised at the team facing her in Dan's conference room. They were regarded as their number one investigation team for high-profile kidnappings.

Deliberately positioning himself in front of the team, Dan reiterated to Beth that Colin Thomson would be leading the investigation, reporting directly to Dan on a daily basis. Beth knew that she had no option but to agree, but she had no intention of leaving anything to chance.

'You are all nodding your heads, but you know that is going to be difficult for me to do, particularly as my experience is in leading teams. You know me well enough, Colin, and have worked with me on more cases than I care to count. You have my permission to wrap my knuckles if I step over the line.'

'Yes, ma'am,' he answered respectfully.

The rest of the team needed no introduction. Abe Hunter reported directly to Colin as detective inspector. Rachel Clark reported to Abe as detective sergeant. Pete Lawson and Sophie Andrews were both constables on Dan's fast-track detective training programme. This was as good as guaranteeing them to stay in one of Dan's teams with regular reviews of their levels of responsibility and promotion prospects.

Beth excused herself before the briefing meeting began. She wanted to check if there were any messages on her mobile phone and also wanted to call home to check if there had been any developments. Dan indicated to her that she should use his office as previously agreed.

1.45 p.m.

Grace arrived with two carrier bags full of sandwiches, nibbles, and drinks. Such a gesture from her was typical. She had excellent people skills and was a great advocate of replacing words with actions when deemed appropriate. This was one of those occasions. One of her closest friends needed her.

Also, she was familiar with Dan and Beth's appalling eating habits during an investigation. Aside from a regular flow of coffee, food didn't feature in their schedules except for the occasional snack and drink at the local bar. No introduction of Grace's initiative was necessary.

She knew the team and had worked with them all before.

As she set about laying out the food and drinks, Beth re-entered the room. Grace laid down the plates, hurried over to Beth, and hugged her. She didn't have to say anything. Such was the bond of friendship that these two women shared that her message was clear enough to Beth and the others in the room.

Grace returned to setting out the food as the crime board was being set up by the others. She couldn't help but notice how Dan lingered close to Beth and how the occasional touches of tenderness were only obvious to her. She watched them for a few moments and was saddened that Dan couldn't display his true feelings for Beth because she was married to Matt.

Dan's personal life wasn't as successful as his career. He had been married before but had sadly lost his wife to cancer. He always managed to have an attractive female companion on his arm at MET functions, but, since his wife's death, he had thrown himself wholeheartedly into his career.

A stickler for detail, procedure, and positive results, he left nothing to chance and expected those who worked with him to consistently deliver. Known for strong people management skills, he sets time aside to keep up to date with positive and negative news. He joins them to celebrate positive results, handles personal bad news with sensitivity, but sends out a clear message that poor performance will not be tolerated.

Grace knew that Dan always had a close working relationship with Beth and would never put a foot wrong in demonstrating anything more than a professional admiration of her. He accepted that the closest that he would ever get to Beth was as confidante, mentor, and close friend. As one of the best profilers in the country, none of his emotional feelings for Beth ever escaped Grace's attention.

Dan explained that until further notice, his conference room and private office would be used solely for the investigation and the investigation team would be kept small. The reason for this is because the Oliver family did not want Katie's disappearance to become public knowledge and had requested that the media not be involved. He concluded by saying that all of this would be reviewed as and when required.

Grace took to the floor and insisted that everyone eat something. 'Our priority is, of course, to find Katie as quickly as possible, but a high energy level will increase efficiency,' she said in such an authoritative tone that no one argued.

They all ate, drank, and worked at the same time. In no time at all, the crime boards were displayed and flip charts positioned for ease of use. Beth couldn't help but cringe as the recent photographs of Katie were displayed, particularly the enlarged photograph of her as she was dressed for the fashion show.

Oh God, what have I done? she thought to herself.

Telephones were placed throughout the room, and a conference speaker phone was positioned in the centre of the conference table. A stack of notepads and pens completed the set-up.

The team got down to business.

Dan opened their first meeting as the investigation team director. 'Okay, everyone has been brought up to date. As we all know, speed is of the essence. The first twenty-four hours are vital for leads. Beyond that, the clock is ticking. You all know how I work and the results that I expect. Just do your job and do it well.'

'Beth is very clear that she will not be leading the team. Instead, her role will be one of consultancy. But you know her well. She has requested, and I have agreed that we won't skirt around anything sensitive or relevant in consideration of her feelings.'

Everyone nodded their heads as they directed their gestures of agreement towards Beth.

Dan continued, 'The best that we can all do for Beth and her family is to conduct ourselves as we would for any other kidnapping and to find Katie asap.'

No one would have known that Beth was the mother of the kidnapped teenager in the way that she now responded to Dan.

'Thanks, Dan, and to you all for rescheduling your workloads in order to be able to start immediately. I do not want any special privileges, nor do I want you to hold back on anything that you want to report or suggest. This is a kidnapping investigation of a teenager who has vanished without a trace. We want her back safely.

From this point forward, Dan, Colin, or Grace will direct meetings and delegate responsibilities. You know how it works, so please get on with it without putting a name or face to the victim. To be honest with you all, I am not sure how *I* am going to cope with that.'

Dan caught Grace's attention, and both were amazed at Beth's ability to professionally demonstrate mind over matter even when a member of her family was involved.

2 p.m.

Under Dan's instructions, the team split with Grace setting out a long list of ifs and maybes for stereotypical kidnapping profiles. Sophie assisted her by researching the police database for all kidnappings of teenage girls during the last twelve months.

Colin and Pete marked up the crime board with the timeline so far. Also, at-a-glance information was available for the routes between the Olivers' home and Katie's school, a list of her friends, and details of the school staff who were in the assembly room or in the vicinity of the registration area at the time that Katie left the table to go to the cloakroom. At the insistence of Eleanor Marshall, the headmistress, this list included her name and the offer that she and her staff would be available to assist with enquiries on a twenty-four-seven basis.

Dan, Beth, Rachel, and Abe split the records on another database into sections of Beth's convictions for kidnapping and rape over the last ten years. They formed a plan to record and review those that they wanted to share with Grace at their scheduled evening meeting.

2.35 p.m.

Beth received a call from her father, saying that Jack had contacted his dad to say that he had managed to catch the earlier flight and that he was now arriving at 5.30 p.m. at Gatwick. He asked to speak to Dan.

'Dan, I'm now meeting Jack at 5.30 p.m. at Gatwick as he caught an earlier flight. Would it be okay if we dropped into the office on the way back? Jack will be desperate to see his mother, and I would like to talk to you about offering my services to the investigation team.'

'No harm in any of that, Bill. In fact, you would be a welcome addition to the team. Can I suggest that you call again once you have met Jack to check the lay of the land at that time?'

'Will do, Dan. And thanks for that. It will mean a lot to Jack. How is Beth, by the way?'

'I managed to get her to vent her feelings in the privacy of her office. But she has amazed me since then. She is putting on a very brave face, but I think that is what will get her through this. I think it is probably better for her to be at the office, keeping busy than to sit around at home, listening to Matt's constant reminders about her not turning up in time for the fashion-show dinner.'

'I know what you mean, but, in fairness to Matt, he is coping with this as best as he can. He doesn't know how to manage his feelings and is frustrated because he doesn't know what he can do to help. He is spending most of his time in his study.'

They said their goodbyes, and then Dan announced Bill's offer of help to the team. This didn't come as a surprise particularly as it was his granddaughter that was missing.

2.50 p.m.

Shortly after Dan's call from Bill, his internal telephone rang, and he was told that a small package had been delivered to the front desk for his attention. As part of their internal procedure, the package had been passed through the security check. The caller was able to confirm to Dan that it was a mobile telephone and that it had been cleared for his collection.

Dan decided to collect the package himself and left the room without explanation as there was nothing to suggest that the package related to Katie's disappearance, although he sensed that it did.

Dan returned with an opened jiffy bag in his hand. No one was in any doubt about it being related to Katie's kidnapping and that the kidnapper had made contact.

Beth took a sharp intake of breath as she recognised Katie's mobile phone. This was the first confirmation that the earlier call to Beth had been real and that Katie had actually been kidnapped. The receipt of her phone was marked on the crime board beside a photograph of it.

Abe took the phone from Dan and linked it to a device that was able to project the screensaver to one of the blank crime boards. There was another sharp intake of breath from Beth as she looked at a photograph of her daughter as she was dressed for the fashion show, looking beautiful, untouched and unsmiling.

No message.

Colin instructed Abe to take the jiffy bag and phone to Forensics in the hope that they may find a fingerprint other than Katie's.

'And tell them to get straight on to it', added Dan, 'or to call me if that is likely to be a problem.'

'The kidnapper wants us to know that he hasn't touched Katie. Why?' asked Grace aloud. She added a couple of large question marks beside the note that Sophie had written about the receipt of the phone.

Some considered Grace to be eccentric. Others who had worked with her long enough had become accustomed to her thought process and communication style. She often talked to herself. She often paced up and down the conference room, deep in thought. She often left the conference room without any explanation. She often left the building for several hours without any communication. She always got results, and it was for this that she had earned the title of the most respected profiler at the MET.

As she walked away from the board frowning, she spoke to herself, 'Is this the lull before the storm?' And then to the group, 'Or is his reason for confirming that Katie is in perfect condition simply to forewarn us of a ransom request?'

'I would originally have thought that ransom was the motive, but let's not forget that he specifically used my name and rank during first contact,' commented Beth.

'Yes, that bugs me too,' said Colin. 'We haven't a clue why Katie has ended up with this guy. It could be a planned kidnapping. It could even be that he found her in some sort of trouble, saved her from whatever, and saw an opportunity to seek a reward. I wouldn't think the worst just yet because this could still end up being a regular guy who has found a way to earn some easy cash. He could have got Beth's contact details from Katie, after all.'

'Colin is right, particularly about it being too soon to form an opinion. For now, we must content ourselves with the knowledge that Katie was unharmed at the time that she entered this person's life and this photograph was taken,' added Grace.

Everyone nodded, knowing that they had no clues to suggest that this was a serious crime and hoped for Beth's sake that the evening would end with confirmation that it wasn't.

Dan left the room once again to forewarn the duty reception staff to keep on the lookout for anyone delivering a letter or package for his attention. If that happened, they should try to detain that person and to notify him immediately. He also asked that they start a trace on all phone calls to his office.

Elsewhere, in the basement room at the Kings Cross address, Katie slept in a drugged state, unaware of what had happened to her and oblivious to what was about to happen to her.

CHAPTER 5

Saturday, 19 June 2004
3 p.m.

Dan instructed the teams to spend the next few hours continuing what they had been doing before the package arrived.

As they prepared to do that, he told them that he had considered Bill's offer to help with the investigation and that he had decided to accept his offer. As of the following morning, Bill would work with Grace to help with the profiling of the kidnapper. He reallocated Sophie from Grace's team to join Colin and Pete's team to help with the criminal database search.

Grace was thankful that Bill would be working with her as she hadn't come up with anything so far from her research. She didn't have enough to match the kidnapper's MO so far. All they had was that one telephone call and the comment 'I am about to become your worst nightmare'. In her opinion, that wasn't about to be demonstrated any time soon from what she had seen so far. She would value Bill's thoughts on that.

4.10 p.m.

The duty officer at reception telephoned Dan to inform him that another small package had been delivered for his attention. This time, a smartly dressed gentleman had asked one of the young policemen entering the building to hand the package in to reception as Detective Superintendent Turner was expecting it. He said that he was running very late for an appointment and would appreciate the policeman's assistance.

By the time that the envelope had been passed on, there was no sign of the man, and, as there hadn't been anything suspicious about the delivery, no one had noted his description other than that he had short dark hair and was wearing a dark suit, white shirt, and a striped tie.

Dan was informed that this time the jiffy bag contained a DVD, and, once again, the contents had passed the security check.

Dan sent Sophie down to collect the package and to check whether anyone had any more information on the person who had delivered it. When she returned with the DVD, she had no additional information to pass on to Dan but did say that someone had already checked the CCTV footage and the person who had delivered the package had either accidentally or deliberately avoided being caught on camera. She handed the package to Dan, who had a quick look at it and then passed it on to Abe.

Nothing happened for what seemed like several minutes on the DVD. Then they heard the sound of Katie screaming.

Grace took hold of Beth's hand and squeezed it, as at this point, everyone present started to suspect that this was the start of a series of communications from the kidnapper that would progressively show something more shocking each time.

Katie appeared on the screen still wearing her dress and still looking unharmed except for the wide tape across her mouth. Everyone must have noticed the tears rolling down her cheeks, but no one commented on that. Then they saw someone else in the room—a man wearing a balaclava, disposable gloves, black polo sweater, black slacks, and dark glasses. He was pacing up and down the room, and then the screen went blank.

Katie reappeared on the screen after a minute or so, still dressed and spreadeagled on the bed with her wrists and ankles strapped to the corner posts.

Beth sat down at the table and put her head in her hands. Grace put her arm around her to comfort her.

The video ended.

Grace got up and started her customary pacing in front of the crime boards. No one said anything until she spoke, 'This was meant to shock, and it has, but Katie still hasn't been harmed physically. I don't think that she screamed because of anything that he did or said to her. I think that she screamed when she saw the camera either to draw attention to herself or as a natural reaction.'

More pacing from Grace and more talking aloud to herself. 'This isn't a stereotypical kidnapping. I don't think he has done this before. Neither is it an opportunistic kidnapping. The hospital bed. The camera. The bottles of water. Too organised. I don't think that this guy has done this before. I say *guy* because we have heard his voice and now see that he has the stature of a man.'

'The staging lacks experience or any level of sophistication, don't you think, Dan?'

Grace continued without waiting for an answer, 'I am inclined to think that he is uncertain about what to do next. I am also inclined to think that he may not even want to harm her. Did you notice that he had put a pillow under her head since the first photograph? Prepare yourselves for more deliveries, folks. But also prepare yourselves for a lack of clues about motive, at least for a while anyway.'

'I agree with all of that,' said Dan. 'We will get another video soon as he is staging the kidnapping. He is obviously sufficiently streetwise not to run the risk of us tracing any telephone calls.'

Dan continued, 'I think I'll call Bill and ask him to make his way straight to your house, Beth. I need to update your family on the latest developments, and I would rather do that collectively as I don't have the time to repeat it twice this evening.'

'I would prefer to stay here with the team just in case another DVD arrives,' said Beth. 'I would appreciate if you could explain that to them.'

'I'll stay here too,' said Grace. 'We have hours of work ahead of us, searching the databases, and it is best to use the time that we have to get that out of the way.'

'I agree with that,' said Colin. 'Count me in. The quicker we complete that exercise, the better.'

The others nodded their heads in agreement. They knew how vital the first twenty-four hours were in a kidnapping case. They had planned for a long night, so they carried on working.

5.15 p.m.

Dan eventually got hold of Bill by phone at the terminal waiting on Jack's flight arriving. He shared his thoughts with him. Bill agreed and said that he would see him at the house at some point before seven o'clock.

5.30 p.m.

Dan called Matt and updated him on the receipt of the two packages. He told him about the change of plan and added that he would arrive at the house about seven o'clock.

5.45 p.m.

Dan left the office early as he knew that the traffic across town would be hectic at that particular time.

6.40 p.m.

Dan arrived at the Olivers' home. When Matt opened the door to welcome him, Dan couldn't avoid noticing the look of stress on Matt's face. It didn't bear thinking about what must be going through his mind.

Matt offered Dan a drink.

Dan's first instinct was to refuse an alcoholic drink, but he changed his mind when he heard the note of desperation in Matt's voice. Noticing that Matt was already drinking whisky, he said, 'I'll join you with a whisky, Matt.'

Matt topped up his own glass and poured a fresh glass for Dan. He then sat down opposite Dan, waiting for him to start speaking.

Caroline came into the room to offer coffee but changed her mind when she saw that they already had a drink each. Dan got out of his chair and walked over to give her a hug, and Matt poured her a sherry.

'We may as well wait for Bill and Jack before I start because they will be here soon,' said Dan. He now wished that he had persuaded Beth to join him.

Ignoring what Dan had said, Matt asked, 'Have you brought the phone and DVD with you. What can we expect to see from them?'

'Yes,' replied Dan. 'I will show you the contents of both packages while I am here. The plan for much of the night is for the team to try to finish the database searches. It's a long tedious job, but it has to be done as part of our investigation. Better to get it out of the way whilst we are waiting for the kidnapper to make his next move.'

'How is Beth bearing up?' asked Matt with a genuine look of sadness.

'She is putting on a very brave face, Matt. You must know that if anyone can find Katie, she can. She knows that she could have prevented Katie's disappearance, and the only way that she knows how to deal with that right now is to work around the clock to try and find her. She is living through any parent's nightmare, just as you are.' He was aware too late that he had used the word *nightmare* as used by the kidnapper during that initial phone call.

Matt just nodded his head in agreement but added, 'She should have been there, Dan. She should have been there.'

Dan was thankful that the sound of a car in the driveway indicated the arrival of Bill and Jack and the opportunity for him to avoid a response to Matt's comment.

Bill and Jack were subdued, but Dan could tell that Jack was glad to be back home to support his parents and grandparents.

As Matt and Jack clung to each other, Dan saw the tears running down Matt's cheeks.

At the sight of this, Caroline started to cry, and Bill comforted her.

Dan felt very emotional at witnessing this painful family scene, and, for the second time that evening, he couldn't help but think that Beth should have been there with her family.

Matt poured a whisky for Bill and topped up his own glass. Jack disappeared to the kitchen and returned with a can of coke. All eyes were now on Dan for his update.

He knew that he couldn't hold off any longer, and so he started with the first delivery of the mobile phone. Abe had set up his laptop so that the second video ran on from the first. Whilst they were all shocked to see Katie in the first video, they did express some relief that she appeared to be unharmed.

When the family heard Katie scream, Dan saw the dread in their faces for fear of what would follow on from that. Dan shared with them the comments that Grace had made and highlighted that Katie still appeared to be unharmed.

Dan told them that both jiffy bags had been sent to Forensics to check for fingerprints.

They all had plenty of questions for him. Sadly, he didn't have many answers. He explained about the database searches and the need for a process of elimination first so that Grace could start to profile.

'What are you hoping to find exactly?' asked Caroline.

Dan explained that one database was being searched for similar kidnappings of female teenagers. The other database was being searched for criminals who may have had a grudge against Beth through the trial, conviction, or release processes.

He explained that, so far, they hadn't been able to find any comparable MO matches that they wanted to investigate further but that they still had a long way to go. Knowing that Bill would definitely know what MO stood for, he explained that MO was a modus operandi, meaning the person's method of operation.

'At present we don't have a comparable MO or any DNA, so we have no leads. I know that this isn't what you want to hear, but it is the honest answer. Without leads, the first twenty-four hours is a long slog.

'We are all of the opinion that we will receive more packages, so I must leave now as I want to be there if another arrives this evening. I will obviously be in touch again if we have any breakthroughs.' To Bill, Dan added, 'Bill, your offer of assistance is accepted. I'll see you at the office in the morning.'

'Can I go back to the office with you as I would like to see Mum?' asked Jack.

'That's your choice, Jack, but as Bill is coming in first thing tomorrow morning, why don't you join him? That would give us a chance to continue with our database searches.'

'He's right, Jack,' added Bill. 'There's not much that we can do tonight, but tomorrow it's all hands on deck. You spend time with your dad tonight and let Dan and his team complete the searches without interruption.'

'Okay. I'll stay here tonight and come in with Granddad in the morning,' agreed Jack, 'but I'll give Mum a call now so that she knows that I have arrived and am thinking of her.'

7.45 p.m.

As Dan was leaving, he turned to Matt to forewarn him that he may need to request him to search the hospital database for any incidents that could link Matt to the reason behind the kidnapping.

Dan left him to ponder how he might go about doing that and then made his way back to the office via his apartment to collect a change of clothing.

8 p.m.

Jack called Beth.

'Hi, Mum. I planned to visit you tonight but was talked out of it by Dan and Granddad. Both suggested that I leave you to complete the database searches and then come in with Granddad in the morning.'

'That actually does make sense, Jack.'

'Mum, where can she be? How are you coping? Have you any idea why anyone would want to kidnap Katie?' asked Jack.

'I'm keeping myself focussed on finding Katie, which helps. We have spoken with all her friends and teachers, and no one has spoken with her since she left the school. Dan has put together our best investigation team for kidnappings, and we are all looking for leads. So far, there is absolutely nothing to indicate what happened and where she might be.

'It's good that you are staying at home tonight because your dad needs you, and you can keep an eye on Gran and Granddad for me. Try to get a good night's sleep as tomorrow will be a heavy day.'

'Okay, Mum, but I would have felt better if I had seen you first,' said Jack. 'Just please promise to involve me and ask me to do anything that you think I may be able to assist with. We will find Katie and bring her home safely. Granddad is wanting to speak with

Dan, but I don't suppose that he has returned yet, has he?' asked Jack.

'No, he hasn't,' replied Beth, 'but let me speak with your granddad.'

'Okay. Please take care of yourself. I love you loads.'

'I love you too, Jack. Remember what I said about watching over Gran and Granddad for me. They are very good at putting on brave faces, but don't ever think that they won't be struggling with their emotions just like the rest of us.'

Jack passed the phone to Bill.

'Hello, Dad. How are you all coping at your end?' asked Beth, using all her strength, not to start crying.

'Beth, this is all very hard for us to take in. When something like this is on your own doorstep, all the experience that you have had in the past fails to account for anything. I'm sure that you know what I mean. Anyway, enough of that. How are you coping?'

'I am definitely better here than I would be at home. Here, I know that I must focus on the job that I have been trained to do. I couldn't have done that at home. This doesn't mean that my thoughts aren't with you. I know how you must all feel, especially Matt.'

Beth continued, 'Jack said that you wanted to speak with Dan, but he hasn't returned yet. Assuming that you have, no doubt, called to ask what you can do to help this evening, I am sure that I can guess what he would say to you.'

'Like you said, Beth, I would rather keep myself busy by being of use to you than sitting waiting for a phone call.'

'Well, if Dan were here, he would ask you to sit down with Jack and ask him to think back in time to anything or anybody that Katie may have discussed with him that may be worthy of further investigation. He would also ask you to urge Matt to consider anything in his past or present that may link him to the kidnapping. He will immediately say that there isn't anything but ask him to give thought to any incidents, threats of malpractice, or complaints. And, of course, Dan would also ask you to think back to any incidents that may have resulted in someone having a grudge against you.'

'I hear you, Beth. Dan did suggest earlier that Matt should consider a search of the hospital database, but he didn't seem to take that on board. I'll do as you suggest with Jack and have a chat with Matt. From what Dan said about the lack of leads or DNA, we need all the assistance that we can get.'

Bill continued, 'We won't be able to sleep tonight anyway, so we are as well to spend the time doing some soul searching. I'll see you in the morning about eight o'clock. Goodnight and good luck. Oh, and please remember to take care of yourself. Mum sends you her love, and you know that our thoughts will be with you every minute of the time that it takes to find Katie.'

'Goodnight, Dad, and please pass on my love to Mum. I love you too,' said Beth, now unable to control the tears that were rolling down her cheeks.

Just as Beth finished her telephone conversation with Bill, Dan arrived back at the office. He noticed the tears on Beth's face and guided her through to his office. He gave her a hug and then left her to cry without an audience.

9.15 p.m.

The delivery of package number three was announced. This time, the owner of the public house across the road from the MET offices delivered it. He said that a member of staff found it lying on one of the tables about 8.30 p.m. when she was clearing the glasses away. He had been in the cellar at the time, but as soon as he had returned to the bar, the waitress had passed it on to him. Again, the package was addressed to Dan at the MET offices. The publican had no idea who could have left the package behind. Neither did any of his staff.

It was a DVD again.

'Jesus Christ, this guy's MO is really starting to piss me off,' said Dan. 'It's so amateurish, yet it isn't producing any DNA.'

Abe went through the process of playing the DVD again.

This time, Katie is nude, her mouth is taped, and her eyes are covered. As Abe immediately jumped up to switch off the DVD player, Grace simultaneously jumped out of her chair, put her hands over Beth's eyes, and pleaded with her not to look at the screen.

After a few moments passed, Beth shocked everyone by standing up, walking towards the DVD player, and pressing the play button again. 'I have to see what I have to see. I can't be selective if I am going to find my daughter.'

You could hear a pin drop in the room during the next few seconds as they waited for Katie to reappear on the screen. No one dared to look at Beth, but Grace had a firm grip of her hand.

No one else appeared to be in the room. Just Katie spreadeagled on the bed. Her eyes were still covered and her mouth taped. She appeared to be unconscious.

Each person in the room knew immediately that she had been raped because of the blood stains on the sheet between her legs. Beth, in complete shock, managed to clarify what the others were thinking, 'She was a virgin. She told me that just a few weeks ago. That being the case, the blood stain is either real because he has raped her or it has been added for effect. Either way it has been intended to shock. It has deliberately been intended to shock me. Isn't that right, Grace?'

As Grace squeezed her friend's hand, she said, 'I'm afraid that's exactly what he intended with this video.'

An uncomfortable silence followed.

Grace broke the silence by saying, 'Beth, can we chat about this in Dan's office?' as she led Beth out of the conference room.

'I wish she hadn't seen that,' said Rachel.

'She had to,' replied Dan, 'and *I* now need to show it to Matt, Jack, Bill, and Caroline. I'm going to take Grace with me this time as

I need to speak with her without Beth being there. Can you all make sure that Beth is kept busy? Somewhere in the criminal database, there may be something that triggers a memory of who may have a reason to avenge Beth.'

In Dan's office, Beth sat down and started to cry uncontrollably.

'Grace, I have ruined my daughter's life. I have destroyed her hopes and dreams. She will never forgive me for this.'

Grace didn't even attempt to answer that as she knew from experience that what Beth had just said was probably true. It pained her now to even consider how she would help to repair the damaged mother-and-daughter relationship, assuming that Katie would be returned to Beth alive.

'You must be shattered, Beth. Dan is going to visit your family, so why not use that time to have a rest on Dan's sofa? He won't be back for a couple of hours.'

It should have come as no surprise to Grace when Beth stood up, dusted herself down, and said, 'No. I have a job to do. I have to find Katie.'

Grace didn't argue because she knew that any other mother in Beth's place would have done exactly the same thing.

Beth and Grace returned to the conference room.

Beth, ever the professional but hurting so much inside, shocked everyone by walking over to the crime board and directing the next instruction to Abe.

'Mark up the board, Abe. Update the database searches, Sophie and Pete. We are now looking for the MO of a kidnapper *and* rapist.'

Dan updated Grace and Beth about his decision to take Grace with him to the Olivers' home. 'Don't you think that you should join us, Beth?' he added.

'No. I need to stay here. I need to find the bastard who is hurting my daughter. Please explain that to my family,' she replied.

As Dan prepared to leave the office, he shouted, 'Abe, chase Forensics. I want those reports on my desk when I return, or they will have me to answer to. The rest of you know what to do. Crack on with the database searches and try to find us some bloody leads. If this guy has no previous convictions, we have nothing until he makes a mistake. Let's go,' Dan said quietly to Grace. 'This is not going to be easy.'

Dan left to update the Olivers and the Palmers for the second time that evening. He could have delegated these visits, but that would have interrupted the database searches. Also, out of his respect for Bill Palmer, he wanted to be the person to keep him in the communication loop.

CHAPTER 6

Saturday, 18 June 2004
10.30 p.m.

Dan approached the Olivers' home, knowing only too well that they would already have worked out for themselves that a second visit from him in such a short timeframe could only mean bad news. The expression on Bill's face as he met them at the door confirmed that. This time, Dan was accompanied by Grace, and he was glad of that decision.

'This is bad, Dan, isn't it?' asked Bill.

'I'm afraid so, Bill,' replied Dan. 'But Katie is still alive,' he hastened to add.

Grace obviously knew Bill through work and had met Caroline and Matt at work and private functions. She hadn't met Jack before and was told by Matt that he was in Katie's bedroom upstairs. She set off to find him so that she could form a relationship with him before he watched the video.

'Where's Caroline?' asked Dan.

'She is in the kitchen,' answered Bill. Dan found Beth's mother wearing rubber gloves with enough cleaning products laid out to suggest that she had cleaned every corner of the house.

As Dan gave her a hug, she said, 'I just don't know what to do, Dan. I feel so hopeless. Cleaning keeps me from thinking about what may be happening to my granddaughter and whether or not I will get the chance to see her again. I also wish that I was there for Beth as I know that under that hard exterior, she will be hurting badly inside.'

'I know, Caroline,' was all that Dan could think to say, particularly with the knowledge of what he was about to show her. 'Let's go and join the others.'

Jack already knew who Grace was as his mother had talked about their friendship often. Grace formally introduced herself and sat down beside Jack on Katie's bed. The room was in a mess. School folders, notes, examination papers, and magazines were scattered across the bed, and Jack had obviously been rummaging through wardrobes and drawers.

'Keeping busy?' asked Grace.

'I'm looking for a diary or anything that could give us a clue about where she could be or whether or not she had been seeing someone that her friends didn't know anything about.'

'And have you found anything?' asked Grace.

'No. There isn't a diary, and, anyhow, I already knew that looking for one was a wild card. Katie never favoured keeping a diary. She preferred photographs. She said that they were reality and helped her to keep focussed on the future. She said that diaries were for those who wanted to dwell on the past, as far as she was concerned. Probably just as well, given what has happened to her.'

'Your sister is very wise, Jack,' replied Grace. 'Did you find anything of use in her photo albums?'

'Nothing. All the photographs that she has kept represent happiness and positive relationships with family and friends,' replied Jack, struggling to hold back his tears.

Grace reassured him that she would ensure that she was taking care of his mother.

Matt walked into the room just in time to hear Grace tell Jack that there was no harm in searching for clues and that anything that may be of significance that he found, or already knew, should be shared with his granddad or one of the investigation team.

'We all feel so hopeless hanging about the house. Surely, we should be out and about looking for my sister,' said a distraught Jack.

Matt surprised Grace with his response, 'You need to leave the detective work to Dan and his team, Son. Also, you need to be here for Katie when she returns. She will need her brother. Dan's waiting for us, so why don't we join him and listen to what he has to tell us?'

After they were all seated, Dan came straight to the point, 'Bill has, no doubt, already told you that the second visit to a victim's family within an hour or so is not good news. As far as we know, Katie is still alive, but sadly, she is no longer unharmed. We have received another DVD, and I must forewarn you that the content will upset you.'

Dan gave them a moment to come to terms with what he had just said but was confident that Bill would already have mentally prepared them for what they were about to see. Dan asked if anyone would like to leave the room, looking directly at Caroline and then Jack. Jack moved to his grandmother, put his arm around her, and said, 'We are staying.'

Taking Jack's lead, Matt urged Dan to *get it over with*.

Bill rose from his chair and went over to the sofa to sit next to his wife. He had a strong premonition that they were going to need each other.

Grace sat between Matt and Jack.

For the second time, Dan and Grace watched Katie's ordeal. They had both experienced Beth's reaction and now dreaded watching the hurt that was about to be displayed by her family.

All Dan could do was sit back and watch their reactions as they registered the image of Katie lying naked on the bed with her mouth taped and her eyes covered with a blindfold.

The reaction to the second part of the video was a repeat of what had happened in Dan's conference room just over an hour earlier. Again, you could hear a pin drop in the room during the next few seconds as they waited for Katie to reappear on the screen.

What they saw took no imagination to come to the same conclusions as the investigation team had just over an hour ago.

Bill put his arm around Caroline as she leaned into his chest and cried.

Matt leaned forward with his head in his hands, a position that Dan had witnessed on many occasions over the last couple of days.

Jack looked as though he had gone into shock. Recognising the signs, Grace acted quickly. She hurried to the drinks trolley and poured two brandies. Matt needed no encouragement as the contents of his disappeared in one gulp. Grace persuaded Jack to sip the brandy until it was finished. His natural colour soon returned to his face.

To see Katie's wrists and ankles strapped to the bed posts with the blood stains on the sheet was more than any family member should have to see.

'Oh my God! He has raped her, and that beautiful girl was still a virgin,' said Caroline.

'Yes, she was,' groaned Matt, who confirmed the conversation that Beth and Katie had a couple of weeks ago.

'According to Grace, the blood stain is either real because he really has raped her or it has been added for effect, with the intention to shock,' said Dan.

Jack said nothing. He got up and walked out of the room.

'He shouldn't have had to see that. I had better go to him,' said Grace as she got up to leave the room.

Matt was surprisingly calm. Dan had expected him to either get very angry again or to break down. Instead, he got out of his chair and walked over to the drinks trolley and poured himself a large whisky. He looked at the others and almost whispered, 'Just help yourselves.'

He walked out of the room and headed to his study.

Bill remained with Caroline.

Dan decided to leave Grace with Jack and Bill with Caroline. He joined Matt in his study.

'What happens now, Dan? Each video gets worse. Am I going to lose my daughter forever?' asked a distraught Matt with tears now visibly rolling down his cheeks.

'I can only be honest with you, Matt,' replied Dan. 'We have no leads so far, and his MO doesn't match anything that we have come up with so far. Grace is absolutely sure that he has never done this before. None of us know what he is after. We have ruled out ransom as the demand would have happened before now. As the DVDs have been sent to the MET and the link from Katie to the MET is Beth, we are focussing on her previous cases.'

'However, due to lack of leads, it would be unwise to only focus on that,' continued Dan. 'We have almost finished our database search, so I must urge you to do the same at the hospital or organise our access to your files. You need to look as far back as you can for any child births or paediatric operations that have gone wrong in the eyes of the parents. You need to look for any evidence that could point us to in the direction of anyone who may have a grudge against you. According to Grace, it is possible to carry a grudge around in your head for many years, if not a lifetime.'

'We both know this isn't about me, Dan,' and then with a raised voice, 'This is all about Beth. She enabled the kidnapping in the first place. Now we are all having to cope with her oh-so precious job being the cause. And it would appear that Beth will be the key to us finding Katie.'

Dan didn't comment as he knew that it would have no effect.

Matt continued, 'Have you any idea how it feels for me to have had absolutely no power to have saved my daughter from this maniac and what he has done to her? I am her father. My role is to protect my children. But how can I manage a wife and mother who puts her job at the MET first? I never know whether or not Beth is going to turn up to important events that involve Katie and Jack.'

'Matt, I understand your anger and I understand your hurt. I have been here before so many times with parents in similar situations. It is not unusual to get very angry and to start to blame someone else in the family, usually the spouse. You know that Beth loves her family. You know that the job doesn't come first. Your anger isn't going to bring back Katie.

'We need you to be focussed. We need you to cooperate. If you want to do something constructive to help find your daughter alive, you are going to have to go to the hospital to start the search of your records. If you don't, Matt,' continued Dan, 'I will have no alternative but to issue a search warrant, by which time, it may be too late. I don't like saying that, but I need to get you to cooperate with me on this.

'We have nothing to go on just now, Matt. Think about that. We will never find Katie until we do. The longer that she is out there, the more vulnerable she is. The DVDs are cruel, but they are real. Chances are that you will never be able to forget them. As her father, it is natural to feel that you have not protected her well enough.

'But, Matt, that is for later. For now, we all have to focus on finding Katie alive. That is how you can now help to protect her from further abuse.'

Matt was openly weeping now into his handkerchief. 'I cannot bear the thought of someone that she has never met before forcing himself upon her and destroying a one and only opportunity for her to experience losing her virginity to someone that she cares for, even loves. That is going to tear me apart forever. She will never get a chance to experience that. She will never forget that she was raped. I hear what you say about not blaming Beth, but I tell you now that I don't think that I will ever be able to forgive her. I know that she will be hurting badly, but I have a feeling that I will always blame her and, most likely, so will Katie.'

'Matt, go to the hospital. Take Jack with you. He is desperate to help. Remember that you have a son to think of, too. Make him think that he is needed. Make him feel that there is something constructive that he, and you, can do to try to find his sister. Spend some time with him at the hospital to search for any life-threatening incident, indiscretion, malpractice, or sudden death,' continued Dan.

'We really can't rule out that this may have something to do with you and your position at the hospital. At this juncture, we cannot rule out anything. Do you understand me, Matt?'

'I know that you have to consider all options, but I just can't bear the thought of sitting at a desk, looking at a computer screen when my daughter is out there somewhere with a stranger. I am not there when she most needs me. Can you understand that?' asked an obviously broken-hearted Matt.

'Of course, I do,' said Dan. 'But at least you will be doing something productive. Isn't that more constructive than sitting at home waiting for your daughter's return? There is no point in you continuing to walk the streets as we have already exhausted the search of the routes between the school and home. Until we receive further communication, we don't know where to search beyond that. Go to the hospital, Matt. Help us to do what you can to put together the pieces that will help us to find Katie.'

'Please, Matt,' came a quiet voice from the door to Matt's study. Neither Matt nor Dan knew how long she had been standing there, but Caroline, looking inconsolable with tears running down her cheeks, accomplished that which Dan had been trying to achieve. Matt walked towards her and hugged her.

'Yes, I'll go to the hospital and do what Dan and Bill suggest is the best use of my time.' He turned to Dan. 'But I don't feel comfortable about doing this. As I said before, this is about Beth. This is about her past. Some criminal, some psycho has a grudge against her.'

Matt got up and walked out of his study and headed for the sitting room where his son and father-in-law were huddled on the sofa, grieving for Katie.

'Jack, come on, get your jacket on. You and I are going to the hospital to start searching the records that Dan is so keen for me to review for leads.'

No one said anything, but Jack got up, kissed his gran on her forehead, and hugged his grandfather. 'Take care of each other, please. I'll see you both later,' said their broken-hearted grandson.

'Grace, you and I should head back to the office. I need to be there should another package arrive,' said Dan.

Bill bolted out of his chair. 'I'm coming with you. I don't want to hear any excuses. I want to see my daughter. I need to see my daughter. I have to be able to tell my wife that she is coping as well as can be expected.'

Dan knew that there was no point arguing, but he didn't want to spare any staff to sit with Caroline that evening.

Grace answered for Dan, 'Bill, you can't leave Caroline alone. You know me well, and so you can trust that I am there for Beth when she needs me. She is focussing on finding Katie. That is how she is coping. Stay with Caroline tonight, and you will see Beth in the morning and also start to help me with the profiling of this guy.'

Bill knew when he was beaten and agreed to stay.

'By the way, Bill, we mustn't give up on Katie's friends. Keep yourself busy by calling them again. Keep asking them questions about any strangers that she may have been in contact with recently. Check again if there is a chance of a boyfriend out there, a casual acquaintance, or a recent unusual incident. Check if she is particularly close to any of the male teachers. Anything unusual, we want to hear about it,' said Dan as he started to put his jacket back on.

Matt was already in his car, waiting for Jack.

Jack ran after Grace and said, 'Tell Mum that I love her loads and that I wish that I was there with her. I will definitely come to the office in the morning to see her. Please tell her that.'

11.30 p.m.

Matt and Jack left to travel to the hospital.

After double-checking that Caroline was okay, Dan and Grace left to return to the MET.

Once they had settled in the car, Dan lost no time in asking for Grace's feedback on the family and whether or not she had managed to find out anything new from Jack.

Grace stared out of the passenger window for what seemed like ages to Dan. 'Come on, Grace. We don't have time for you staring into space,' said an impatient Dan.

'Just collecting my thoughts,' she said, but she didn't turn around. Dan knew better than to force her to speak.

Eventually she spoke, 'Okay. Summary is that we aren't any further forward. Jack isn't holding anything back. I thought that when I saw him rummaging in Katie's room that he was looking for something specific, but he wasn't. Bill would have told us if he had anything to add. Other than Jack, if Katie had a secret boyfriend, I think that it would be Caroline that she would take into her confidence. Caroline is desperate to find her granddaughter, so she would have told us about anything untoward. We know that Beth isn't holding back anything from us. As far as they are concerned, there isn't a mystery boyfriend.'

'You haven't mentioned Matt,' said Dan.

'I know. That was deliberate. It *is* Matt who is challenging my thought process. Yes, we understand his grief, but he almost protests too much about Beth and his inability to protect his daughter. Is he hiding something about Katie? Where does he go when he wanders the streets? He knows that we have exhausted our search. He knows that Katie is captive. Is he aware of a mystery boyfriend or acquaintance? Also, he appears desperate to keep busy, so why didn't he jump at the chance to search his hospital records?'

'You don't sound convinced about Matt,' said Dan.

'Hmm! I can't put my finger on it yet, but there is something that is disturbing me about him. I need to be on my own to give more thought to why that is.'

Dan knew that meant that one of Grace's disappearing acts was about to happen when they returned to the office. He knew *her* MO well!

Back at the kidnapper's home, Katie started to come out of her drugged state, and her first thought was that she was restrained and gagged and couldn't see anything. The realisation of that sent her into a panic attack, and, for a ghastly moment, she thought that she had been buried alive. She then realised that it was too airy for that to have happened.

The last thing that she could remember was being outside the school and contemplating whether to make a call to her dad or a taxi firm.

She couldn't remember anything after that.

Her memory of what led up to present time was blank.

Why can't I remember what happened after that?

Where am I?

How did I get here?

Why am I here?

Is this some sort of joke?

These were just some of the thoughts going through her already disturbed mind. Thankfully, she had no recollection of the photographs being taken and had no memory of being raped.

In just forty-eight hours, the world of the confident, respected, loved, and envied Katie Oliver had fallen apart. She didn't know how long she had been tied up. She was scared. She was anxious. She was weepy. She felt sore all over. She wanted her parents. She wanted the safety of her home.

Her head ached, and she felt that her emotions were in a turmoil. Why couldn't she remember anything?

Then she heard footsteps. The mask over her eyes and the tape over her mouth were removed. The person who stood before her was entirely in black—he was masked, wore dark glasses, and was fully dressed in black.

'You are awake,' he said. 'That's good because it is time for some more photographs to be taken. You do want that, don't you? You do want your parents to know that you are alive, don't you?'

'Who are you? What do you want from me? What are you going to do to me?'

'Too many questions, Katie. I haven't decided yet what your fate is going to be, but you should know that I have already raped you and your parents have received a video to confirm that. Whether you live or die is irrelevant to me. The extent of the pain that I cause your parents *is*, however, *very important to me*. What happens to you while you are with me over the next few days will stay in your family's memories forever.'

He approached the intravenous drip fed into her arm and injected the fluid that very quickly make her feel groggy and then unconscious.

'Perfect, Katie. You are doing very well.'

The last thing that Katie remembered was seeing her kidnapper wheel in a trolley and positioning it beside her bed. She didn't remember anything else.

He untied Katie's wrist and ankle bindings, turned her over on to her front, and restrained the wrists and ankles again. He then reached out to the trolley to pick up a scalpel, held it up, and just stared at it for a long time before aiming it at her lower back.

CHAPTER 7

Sunday, 20 June 2004
12.15 a.m.

Dan and Grace arrived back at the office, having already agreed that he would update the team and she would personally update Beth.

Grace found Beth in Dan's office just staring into space. She sat beside her, took both her hands in hers, and then started to update her on her family's reactions to the latest video. She also told her that Matt and Jack were on their way to the hospital to start reviewing Matt's diaries, meeting schedules, and minutes of meetings. In fact, their plan was to check all documentation other than medical records as access to them was protected by doctor-patient confidentiality.

Dan updated the team, and they reported back that they had nothing encouraging to share with him after trawling the databases since Saturday afternoon. They had passed some files over to Beth for consideration but were sure that they weren't a close enough match to the kidnapper's MO.

Dan knew that they would have been thorough and wasn't surprised at the end result. He insisted that they all go home to rest and to return to the office early the following morning as there was nothing meaningful that they could do until then. He added that he would text them if anything of value happened during the night.

He knew that it was pointless to request the same of Beth or Grace. The best that he could do for Beth was to encourage Grace to persuade her to rest on the sofa in his office until the morning.

When Dan went into his office, he found Beth in Grace's arms, obviously upset. He didn't know what to say, so he sat down with his own thoughts about what to do next and to contemplate what the kidnapper's next move might be.

Beth eventually turned away from Grace and walked towards where Dan was sitting. 'We have nothing, Dan. Negative from Forensics. No MO matches. Clutching at straws with criminal records. This guy is either very clever or he is having one hell of a run with beginner's luck.'

Dan picked up from there, 'I know, and, without leads, we have no motive. We are working with guesswork. Thank God that he spoke to you on Saturday morning, or we wouldn't even know if the kidnapper was male or female.'

Grace added, 'I have been searching through the records that the team have passed to me, but, as they predicted, nothing jumps out. I continue to be convinced that the kidnapper is a novice, and we know that this isn't premeditated because Katie wasn't supposed to be out of the school grounds at the time of the kidnapping. I need some thinking time,' said Grace, 'so I'm off unless you need me for anything.'

'It's okay. You do what you do best, and, hopefully, you will have some words of inspiration for us all tomorrow morning,' said Dan. 'Beth, you should go home. Jack and Caroline are both desperate to see you.'

'No. I am staying here until I find Katie. Anyhow, there may be another package delivered tonight,' said Beth.

'And I will be here if it does,' said Dan. 'I have a couple of actions to clear from my desk on another case, and I want them out of the way before tomorrow morning. I have made a few notes from the records that I searched that are at least worthy of further examination. Like Grace, I want some quiet time to go through them in more detail, but I would prefer to do that here just as I would for any other criminal investigation.'

'Okay, so we are all staying here then,' said Grace. 'Dan, if I could work in your office alone and uninterrupted, I am as well being there as at home.'

'A guy doesn't stand a chance with you girls around. It's okay, Grace. I will move to the conference room.' They all managed a smile at this, knowing that Grace's request had nothing to do with disrespect for Dan's position but had everything to do with her own idiosyncrasies during the profiling stages of a criminal investigation.

2.15 a.m.

Shortly after Dan, Grace, and Beth had settled down to their respective actions, Jack ran into the room, waving another envelope followed by Matt and Colin. Matt didn't give anyone a chance to say anything as he agitatedly explained that neither he nor Jack had noticed the envelope taped to the rear windscreen of Matt's car before they left for the hospital. It was only by chance later on that Matt had asked Jack to go to the car boot to collect his briefcase. That was when Jack had noticed the envelope.

'Jesus Christ, how many more packages are we going to receive before we know who this guy is and what he is after?' asked Colin. 'This guy is either having fun, playing with our emotions and patience, or he is extremely juvenile and inexperienced, or he is cleverer than we think and playing for time.'

As Colin took the package from Jack, he explained that he was on his way home when he realised that his wife and daughter were staying over at the in-laws' that night, so he thought that he would be as well back at the office, helping with the investigation. 'We should pass this by security first,' he said to Dan as he walked towards the door. 'Don't worry. I'll be quick.'

'If the envelope had been taped to your rear windscreen at your home, one of us would surely have noticed it. And the guy would need to be mad to even contemplate doing that with so many cars in your driveway. He must have tailed you to the hospital and stuck it on when you and Jack entered the building,' said Dan. 'I'll get Colin to check the hospital CCVT of the car park.'

'I wondered why I hadn't noticed it on the windscreen when I was driving as something unusual on a window jumps out at you, doesn't it?' answered Matt.

Beth left the room and made her way to the cloakroom. There, she took a few sharp intakes of breath and clasped her hands in a praying position. She quietly prayed for the strength to stay focussed until the kidnapper was found. She felt sick and, for a few moments, didn't think that she could go through with watching another video of her daughter's traumatic experiences.

Whilst Beth was out of the room, Dan suggested to Grace that she should join Beth and try to stall her until he had an opportunity to check the content of the DVD. She agreed and left the room.

Colin returned with the scanned packaged, quickly put the DVD into the player, and pressed 'Play'.

Just at that moment, and as predicted, Beth rushed back into the room, followed by Grace. She shouted, 'I don't think so, Dan. I have to see it at some point, so it may as well be now. So let's get it over with.'

Matt felt uncomfortable. He saw that his wife was exhausted and had been crying. He wanted to take her in his arms but just couldn't. He wondered if this was the way that it was going to be in future. Aside from heated debates about their work/life balance, their marriage was solid, and there had never been any hint of either of them being unfaithful. At that moment, however, he genuinely felt that it would be difficult to make love to his wife ever again.

Every person in the room was on tenterhooks, each wondering what could be worse than what they had already seen.

They couldn't have anticipated the horror of what they saw.

The first part of the video showed Katie lying on her stomach and the kidnapper positioning the scalpel on Katie's lower back. He then started to cut into her flesh as he created the letter 'H'. Blood oozed out of the wound and trickled down the left-hand side of her back.

Then there was a long pause.

The second part of the video showed Katie still lying on her stomach. Carved into the flesh of her lower back were the words:

Help

me

Mum

'Is that really blood?' Beth stammered in shock, at which point Matt did walk over to her and put his arm around her. He sensed that she would collapse if he hadn't.

'He has to be one sick bastard to set up a scene like that in front of the camera for our benefit,' said Colin. 'We don't know if Katie was awake throughout that, but I didn't register any movement from her. Did any of you?' Walking over to the screen, he added, 'Look, he has displayed a bloody knife and a lit Bunsen burner on the trolley. What are you making of this, Grace?'

Grace walked up to the crime board, looked at some of the previous photographs, and then walked over to the latest photograph. Silence prevailed as she collected her thoughts.

Matt and Jack sat on either side of Beth. She still looked as though she was about to pass out.

Dan and Colin sat on the other side of the conference table.

Grace had their full attention.

'Okay, bear with me for a few moments. I am just trying to make some sense about what is actually happening here,' started Grace.

They waited as she stared at the crime boards, circled a couple of photographs with her felt pen, underlined some words, fetched a bottle of water, and drank it.

She turned to face them. She was ready.

'Human beings can carry grudges for many years, sometimes for reasons that we would never consider as justification. Some take grudges to their graves. Psychologically imbalanced individuals or people with deep depression allow grudges to manifest in their daily thoughts. The longer that they think about a grudge, the more that they have a need, a desire, to seek revenge. This doesn't mean that their thought process is any quicker, but it does mean that it can be alive in their minds day after day. The longer that they think about it, the more that their recall of the related incident becomes twisted, gruesome, and more malicious. Depression, anxiety, and schizophrenic tendencies develop until the need for revenge becomes justifiable. The actual revenge is generally unjust, but when the person has fulfilled a plan of revenge, he or she does not believe that they are doing anything criminal.

'A person seeking revenge doesn't necessarily look or act like a criminal or a psychologically imbalanced person. The person that we are looking for may be able to separate day-to-day routine activities from his darkest thoughts. Follow me so far?' she asked. Everyone nodded.

Grace continued, 'We already know that Katie wasn't a runaway. I don't think for one moment that she was the target. I do know that she has become the victim. I have yet to make sense of why she was abducted at that particular time as she should have been at the fashion show. We don't know how or why, and we all have unanswered questions.

'Instinct tells me that this has been planned for a very long time. The flow of the DVDs and aspects of the timeline have bothered me. We don't have leads, so let me just brain-dump for a while. It may not make much sense to you, and it may not be in a particular order, but none of what has happened since Friday night follows any MO that I know of. I am having to think out of the box on this one.'

Dan responded for everyone, 'Just you share with us your thoughts in any order that they come to mind. We need all the help that we can get to profile this guy and to find him as soon as we can. I agree with everything that you have said so far, by the way, but, beyond that, I am struggling without leads.'

Beth was quiet, which probably meant that she agreed with what Grace and Dan had said so far. She would have spoken up at that moment if she had anything to add to their current thoughts.

Grace occasionally tapped the crime board with the collapsible pointer that she always kept in her briefcase.

'He is not enjoying harming Katie. Let's examine the evidence. Have you ever known a rapist, kidnapper, or murderer send a photograph of their subject looking their best other than to follow it up with demands? Usually, in that situation, we get some crude suggestion that the family take one last look at what their family member looked like before he or she started to work on them? Why isn't he calling us? Why so many DVDs? Why no demands? Why the staging? What is happening to Katie is absolutely devastating, but let's be honest here. We have witnessed one hell of a lot worse than that. Sorry, Oliver family, but I have to make that point to emphasise my profile of this guy.'

It was Matt who answered for the Oliver family. 'We understand, Grace. Please carry on.'

Grace continued, 'At no point has he given Beth or Matt an opportunity to trade off anything for the safe return of Katie. At no point has he given us the slightest hint of what his motive was for kidnapping her in the first place.

'Why show us a lit Bunsen burner? Did he actually sterilise the scalpel before using it? Why Katie's lower back? She was already on her back, so why not just engrave the message on her tummy?

'This guy set out specifically to rape Katie and to ensure that Beth saw the DVDs. As gruesome and sick as all of this may be to you, this guy is trying to make Katie's ordeal as pain-free as he can. This guy isn't a serial anything. He is showing a level of care that would not normally be evident with old people or with children.' As she tapped the crime board again, she said, 'Aside from the pillow, bottles of water, etc., there's even a box of tissues and a hairbrush in the room. He has to have a grudge against Beth or Matt. I can't say to you that he won't kill Katie, but it is my opinion based on what we have seen so far that he won't go that far. In fact, I think that we may just about have seen all that he has the wherewithal to do to get whatever his message is to you.

'However,' she emphasised, 'whether or not we find Katie is another matter as he wouldn't consider that to be his responsibility. Why turn her over so that he could create the tattoo on her back? He wasn't thinking of Beth and Matt when he did that. He was thinking of Katie. He didn't want her to see the tattoo every time that she looked in a mirror without her clothes on. Why the Bunsen burner? He probably did sterilise the scalpel. Why? Because he is not an expert in cutting flesh and was afraid that this act would result in infection.

'Am I any closer to telling you who he may be, his age range, where he lives, where he works, what his motive may be? No, I am not. Are any of you?

'He is hurting Katie because he wants to hurt either Beth or Matt. What is it that either of you have done to make him want to take revenge? One of you has the answer. I am now sure of that.'

Dan picked up from there, 'I don't disagree with anything that you have said, Grace. In fact, thanks to such a detailed presentation of your thoughts, I have decided to get a search warrant for your hospital records, Matt. I am sure that you and Jack would have done a reasonable job, but we are the experts here. We know what we are looking for, and, based on what Grace has said, we need to move fast.'

Again Matt spoke up, 'Difficult to argue with any of what Grace has said. I can see where you are coming from, and thanks, Grace, for going into so much detail for us. It doesn't make me feel any better, but it does add perspective. It also gives me some hope that she will be returned to us alive.'

Surprisingly, Beth piped up at this point, 'I am also inclined to agree with everything that you have said, Grace, including the part where you don't think that he will kill Katie. I think that this has been premeditated but that the actual acts have been delivered with hesitancy and a combination of anger and hurt. He is being cruel, yet it is as though he has embarked upon an unfamiliar journey of some sort of revenge. If he has, then he is using Katie to get to either me or Matt.'

Beth looked to her husband for support, but it was difficult to read his pained expression.

'I think it's fair to say that we are all on the same page now. Much as I feel duty-bound to update Bill and Caroline, my place is here. If Grace is correct, we must be getting closer to his final communication,' said Dan. 'Matt, are you happy to return home with Jack and update Bill and Caroline?'

'Yes. Let's go, Jack,' he said without hesitation as he stood up and headed towards the door without any words or gestures to the people in the room. Dan knew a broken man when he saw one.

Beth walked over to her son. 'Tell Mum and Dad that we are sure that Katie will not be killed. I have to believe that if I am going to be ready to face her kidnapper because, before this day is over, that is what I am going to do. Tell them that, Jack, and please try to get your dad to understand that I would have given my own life willingly in exchange for what is happening to our daughter.'

Grace responded for Jack, 'He will know that, Beth, but he is in the worst place just now. He is on the outside looking in, and it is his wife who is working at the coalface. He doesn't know what to say. He doesn't know what to do. Jack, we are taking care of your mother. You must take care of your father. Call me any time if you need someone to speak to.'

2.45 a.m.

Jack hugged his mother and Grace before leaving the office to catch up with his father.

Dan walked over to Beth and put his arm around her. 'Beth, you look mentally and physically exhausted. There was no point in me even suggesting that you go home with Matt and Jack because I knew that you wouldn't. But I'll drag you out to my car and drive you home myself if you don't stretch out on the sofa in my office and rest or sleep. Nothing is going to happen until morning other than Colin updating the crime board and Grace and I comparing notes about the recent event.'

'Dan, I know that you are only trying to do what you think is best for me, but if the shoe were on the other foot, you wouldn't be going anywhere either. I will go through to your office for a lie-down, but I have no intention of shutting my eyes until my daughter has been returned to her family,' stated Beth with a look of determination that Dan knew not to question.

He walked her through to his office and took a heavy blanket from one of his cupboards. 'At least allow me to wrap this around your shoulders.'

Beth didn't argue, and, so, with more concern and love for her than she would ever know, he reassured her that the full team would be there to support her in the morning. For now, he just hoped that no more harm was going to come to Katie and that she would be returned to Beth at some point very soon.

As Dan re-entered his conference room, Grace surprised him by saying, 'I know how you feel about Beth. She will also know that you are going to be there for her, no matter what happens.'

'You are going to have to advise me about how we at the MET deal with Beth going forward. She may decide to resign so that she can take care of Katie.'

'I know but one thing at a time, eh? Let's just focus on finding Katie.'

CHAPTER 8

Sunday, 20 June 2004

During the course of the night, Beth and Grace did manage to sleep off and on, but Dan couldn't. Over and over again, he went over in his head the contents of the packages, the rough notes from the database researches, Grace's profiling thoughts, and his own instincts.

Not one single lead. What was he missing?
Was it revenge? If so, was it against Matt or Beth?
What would be the kidnapper's breaking point?

Dan was frustrated at the absence of DNA or leads. Also the type of person that Grace had described could panic and do something stupid as was known to happen when someone was out of their depth. If he was psychologically imbalanced, he could commit suicide, and then they would definitely not have any leads with which to find Katie alive. He could kill Katie first before his suicide. He had enough experience to know that no one could predict the actions of a psychologically imbalanced individual.

His final thought before he dozed off in his chair was that he knew that Beth could have delegated the meeting that evening to Colin or even himself. *What had possessed her not to?*

As Grace was sure that Katie would be returned alive, her waking thoughts were about how much Katie would remember after such a traumatic experience. She knew that she would blame her mother and may never forgive her. Also, she had already read the signs that this may destroy Beth's marriage.

At 6 a.m., Grace had freshened up and left the building for some fresh air and to breakfast alone.

Colin was helping Dan complete the loose ends of another case that he wanted off his desk before the working day started.

Beth went to the female staff cloakroom for a shower and change of clothing.

Just before 7 a.m., Grace returned, accompanied by Bill. 'Look who I found in the car park,' she said. When Beth came into the room, she saw her father and struggled to stop her tears again. They hugged each other.

'Decent coffee!' remarked Abe, seeing Grace with a tray of freshly brewed coffee. 'You are a treasure, Grace.'

'Oh well, we all need to be on top form today, so it's the least that I could do for you.'

Grace approached Beth and Bill and said, 'The two of you need to catch up, so why don't you do that in Dan's office whilst he issues instructions to the team?'

Neither of them argued as they headed for Dan's office.

Dan sat with his team and, as always, encouraged them to table their thoughts or questions. They all had the same thought that the kidnapper wanted to punish someone in the Oliver family for a reason that they still hadn't been able to piece together.

'As Beth is DCI of the MET's largest murder investigation team and as Dr Oliver is a consultant paediatrician at the City of London Hospital for Children, this *has* got to be something linked to one of Beth's previous convictions or a previous child birth complication or death on Matt's watch,' said Pete.

'I agree,' said Rachel, 'and I don't think that Dr Oliver has been as helpful as he should. He has convinced himself that this has something to do with Beth. There are plenty of ex-cons in the database that could be holding a grudge against Beth, but the MO of this just isn't their style. We would be wasting our time to continue with research at this end. I think that we need a search warrant so that we can take a close look at the hospital records.'

'Already done,' said Dan. 'It should be with us before nine o'clock. Matt has a better understanding of why we need to access his files since he heard Grace's profile summary last night. He will cooperate better now.'

Dan summed up his thoughts for the day ahead.

'Okay, we need to get cracking this morning as Grace and I both feel that everything will come to a head today, and we want to be here when it does. Colin will advise Matt by telephone that we have a search warrant for his records and then make his way to the hospital to serve it. Sophie and Pete will join Colin at the hospital so that work can begin immediately.

'Grace wants to share her profile of the kidnapper with Bill and watch the DVDs together again. As to what Beth will be doing, each hour is getting tougher for her, so I'll have a chat with her before deciding what she should focus on.

'If anyone has any ideas, just speak out loud. Matt has asked me to consider media involvement, so I am going to discuss that with Beth and Grace. I have avoided that so far because if our kidnapper is wet behind the ears, as Grace is convinced, going public could tip the balance against us and he may do something stupid.

'Colin, you have mentioned the janitor a few times. How about the male teachers? Katie is a very attractive teenager. How about calling Eleanor Marshall and asking her to arrange for the male teachers and the janitor to be available for interview? I know it's Sunday, but I don't care. Eleanor is cooperative and very efficient. She will probably have them lined up for you before you arrive.

'Abe and Rachel, you handle the interviews and check their reactions to questions about Katie. Check out Brodie Carmichael and the janitor again. Ask them to describe how Katie looked on Friday night. Push them all to speak about Katie and make sure that you get their opinion on how attractive and intelligent she is. Take the photographs with you again. We can't be accused of sexual discrimination as we know that the kidnapper is male.

'Go through the janitor's story again', continued Dan, 'as Colin is convinced that he knows more than what he is saying. If you have any suspicions, run them past me and then pull him in for questioning.'

'You know what, Dan,' said Grace. 'The clock is ticking, and that's a lot of interviewing for two people, particularly if someone like the janitor is hiding something. How about Bill and I go with them? That way, we can kill two birds with one stone. He and I can talk about the profiling on the way there, and then we can interview Eleanor Marshall, Brodie Carmichael, and the janitor whilst Abe and Rachel interview the male teachers. What do you think? Also, I will be on hand if they want me to take a closer look at anyone.'

'Agreed. Beth and I will hold the fort here, which is no bad thing for her,' replied Dan.

Dan left the team to organise themselves and went to his office to update Beth and Bill with his instructions.

'As always, carefully considered and well presented, Dan,' said Bill. 'That all sounds very sensible to me. When do you want to regroup?'

'Let's touch base at noon, and I'll decide whether or not we need to meet at that point,' said Dan.

8 a.m.

Dan called the team together, including Grace, Beth, and Bill.

'We still have an hour to wait for the search warrant, and it will also take that amount of time for Eleanor Marshall to assemble the teachers and janitor for interviews. We have shared everything that we know with Bill, so let's use the time that we have for him to give us his thoughts on this case with the experience that he has but as an outsider looking in.'

'I'm happy to do that,' replied Bill. 'Based on the information that you have already shared with the family, why don't I share with you where *we* think that you are at,' suggested Bill, 'and then Grace and I will discuss her profiling of the kidnapper as we travel to the school?'

Without waiting for an answer, he continued, 'We don't believe that you are keeping anything back from us, and we also understand how frustrating it must be for you to have nothing to show for the hours that you have spent researching. Basically, you are saying to us that you have no DNA, no MO match, no witnesses, no diary with details of stalking, no obvious concerns from friends, neighbours, and schoolteachers, and nothing at present that stands out for either Beth or Matt as a reason why Katie's kidnapper may have a grudge against one or all the Olivers.

'All we have is that the janitor recalls her leaving the school crying and saying that she hates her mother. Sorry, Beth, but that won't come as a surprise to you.

'It can't get much worse than that in a criminal investigation, and I know, more than any of the family, the severe implications of that.' Bill looked at the floor and was silent for a while before picking up from where he left.

'As far as we know, Beth hasn't come up with a name of an ex-con who would use this MO as revenge against her. I trust her judgement on that. Matt has been slow in cooperating, but you will have the search warrant this morning, so, hopefully, you will get something from that.

'We have talked about involving the media, obviously without Beth being there. I have updated Beth this morning, and, like us, we have mixed feelings about going that route. What do you think?'

Dan answered first, 'The reason why we set up small in the first place was to avoid media attention. Based on Grace's description of this guy, and we have no reason to doubt that, I am concerned that media attention could tip an already imbalanced mind. That being the case, he could do some serious harm to either himself or Katie or both.'

'That is exactly why I don't think that we should involve the media at this stage,' said Grace. 'Sorry, Beth, for what I am about to say, but, as you know, the longer that this goes on, the less chance that we have in finding Katie alive. It's at that stage that we should consider media intervention. For now, at least for the next twenty-four hours, I think that we should focus on the instructions that Dan has issued this morning.'

'I agree,' said Bill.

'Okay, let's revisit that thought tomorrow if we still haven't found Katie,' said Beth.

9 a.m.

By 9 a.m., the search warrant had been delivered to the office, and the various teams had set off to their respective destinations. This left only Dan and Beth at the office.

'What shall we do, Dan?' asked Beth.

'We need to manage the office,' replied Dan. 'What I mean by that is that we need to be available for any deliveries from the kidnapper, be on hand to give advice to either of the teams at the school or the hospital, and keep an eye on our emails for any notes that Colin, Abe, or Sophie may send through to us from the hospital records.'

They didn't have long to wait for their first request for assistance.

10 a.m.

Just after ten o'clock, the phone rang. It was Grace.

'We are sending the janitor in for questioning. Abe and I will bring him in and leave Bill with Sophie to continue interviewing the teachers. He was being evasive during the interview, and Bill and I were convinced that he was hiding something. We shared this with Eleanor and asked if we could see his office in the basement. She didn't have a problem with that, and she accompanied us. In his office were a couple of lockers. Eleanor found the key on the key ring beside his phone. When we opened one of the lockers, we were faced with lots of photographs of female and male students plus some of the teachers. No prize for guessing who one of them was.'

'We'll be ready at this end, but make it sooner rather than later and remind Abe to read him his rights.'

Dan updated Beth and booked an interview room.

10.40 a.m.

Abe and Grace interviewed the janitor as Beth and Dan observed from the adjoining room. Abe put the heat on Eddie, the janitor, but wasn't convinced that he was capable of orchestrating a kidnapping, rape, and videos. Eddie lost his parents when he was young and had never married. He had worked at the school for over thirty years and regarded the pupils and the teachers as his family. He had an excellent relationship with them all, and he took photographs at all the events and prize giving ceremonies as his record of his memories at the school. Apparently, some previous pupils still popped in to have a chat with Eddie if they were in the area. Dan and Beth were inclined to believe him, as were Grace and Abe. Abe and Grace returned him to the school where he would later admit to Eleanor Marshall what he had been doing for almost thirty years. Dan took a note to call Eleanor to talk it through with her and then leave the decision-making process about his future employment to her.

'You were right to bring him in,' Dan said to Grace and Abe. 'I would have done the same thing based on what you had seen. He is too involved in the school activities and cares too much to be a kidnapper. Katie's photograph being in his locker was just coincidence.'

'Oh well, back to square one,' said Abe as he left Dan's office.

11.15 a.m.

As Dan returned to his office with Beth, his telephone rang. He raised his eyebrows to Beth as if to say *could this be another delivery?* He wasn't wrong. It was the duty reception officer to tell him that the manager of Greyfriars had just handed in an envelope addressed to Beth Oliver at the MET. The Greyfriars is a favourite haunt for many of the MET staff after work. Known for its excellent coffee choices, it is also used as a break-out meeting place during investigations.

Dan asked if the manager was still there. When he heard that he was, he asked that he be asked to wait, excused himself from Beth, and ran down the stairs to the hallway. At reception, he saw the man he recognised as George Henderson. George had managed Greyfriars very successfully for almost ten years.

'Hi, George. What have you got for me so early this morning?' asked Dan.

'Actually, Dan, I am really angry with one of my staff. You should have had the envelope that I have handed in at the end of our shift last night. Andy, one of our barmen, found the envelope on one of the tables when he was doing the last clear-up. As it wasn't marked urgent and as I wasn't around, he laid it on my office desk.'

The envelope was going through the security check, but Dan knew that it was from the kidnapper. He asked George to immediately contact the staff working the previous night's shift and ask them to report to the MET for a brief interview.

'And by immediately, I don't mean asap or when convenient; I mean immediately, George. Tell them to ask for either Colin Thomson or Abe Hunter. No excuses. We have to try to get a description of whoever left this, and we don't have time on our side,' explained Dan.

'Will do, Dan,' said George, already on his way to the exit door.

'All clear,' said the duty reception officer as he handed the envelope over to Dan. It was just a plain white envelope addressed to *Beth Oliver, c/o MET*. Seeing it, Dan understood why the barman hadn't felt the need to check it out. It didn't have a look of being anything urgent.

Dan decided to take the stairs up to his office rather than the lift as he wanted to read the contents of the envelope before he faced Beth.

A single sheet of white paper had the following message made up of cut-out newsprint letters:

One of the OlivErs iS tOO ArrogAnT tO kNow whY t*H*eir daUgHTer has Had to suFFer. YoU wiLl fiNd heR in GraNGe WooDs.

This wasn't the outcome that he had expected, and he didn't feel quite as confident as he had the previous evening about whether or not Katie would be returned alive.

As Dan entered the conference room, Beth was facing the door, waiting for him.

'We have a letter from the kidnapper,' Dan announced and handed it to her.

As Beth read the letter, Dan called Colin and asked him to round up everyone, including those at the school, and ask them all to get back to the office pronto.

Looking across at Beth, as he had expected, he saw a hint of relief on her face—relief that it wasn't another DVD and relief that there was still hope that Katie may be alive.

'Right, Beth. Start writing the action plan. Everyone will be back shortly, so have it ready and copied for their arrival. I am going to contact Matt and ask him to bring Caroline and Jack here so that you can all be together whilst we search for Katie.'

Before making the phone call, he had already made up his mind that all arrangements and communication would proceed on the understanding that Katie was still alive. In a search party of this nature, it was imperative that all involved covered every square inch of the search area with the determination and intention to find their subject alive. To think otherwise detrimentally affected the quality of the search.

Midday

Everyone had returned to the MET in double-quick time and were seated, waiting on Dan's instructions.

In preparation of their arrival, Dan had already arranged for the letter to be copied for each of them and also enlarged for the crime board.

'Before I issue instructions, there is something that you all need to know. This letter was actually left in the bar at some point last night. The barman who found the envelope at the end of his shift didn't know what to do with it, and, believing that it didn't look very important, he laid it on the desk in the manager's office. The manager didn't find it until eleven o'clock this morning, which means that Katie has been in Grange Woods overnight. Speed is of the essence.' He didn't have the heart to add *if we are to find her alive.*

Instead, he said, 'We must find her as quickly as we possibly can. You all know why.' He knew them all well enough to know that each person in that room knew exactly what he did mean, including Beth.

'Everybody, listen carefully because I don't have time to repeat myself, and none of my instructions are open to question,' he said directly to Beth. 'Is that clear, Beth?'

Beth nodded.

'Colin and Abe, pull together as many on-site officers as you can for an immediate search party. Rachel, organise the number of squad passenger vans that we will need. Pete and Sophie, pull together everything that we are likely to need, including torches, whistles, blankets, waterproof capes, bottles of water, flasks of soup, chocolate bars, and anything else that you can think of. We don't know where to find Katie, so I have no way of estimating how long this may take.

'Grace, give Sophie a list of what she should put together in a separate box for Katie. Also, Grace, can you arrange for the paramedics to be within range of the woods for immediate access to Katie. Also forewarn the appropriate consultant at whichever hospital that you choose of Katie's imminent arrival and the need for a multi-skilled team to be ready to deal with whatever her condition is on arrival, either physical or mental.

'Bill and Beth, I have already called Matt and told him to make his way here with Caroline and Jack. Matt and Jack may want to join the search party, but I will dissuade them from doing that on the assurance that the family will receive regular updates from either me or Grace.'

Beth was about to say something, but Dan cut her short.

'Don't even think of suggesting anything otherwise, Beth. I do not want you with the search party. I am instructing you to stay here and to wait for your family to arrive. You all need to stick together, and you must be at the hospital in advance of Katie arriving.' In other words, what Dan was really saying to Beth was that this was the one occasion when she absolutely had to be the mother, wife, and daughter, and not the DCI.

'Finally, Beth, what you can do whilst we get organised to leave is to ensure that Grace and I are allocated a fully equipped critical incident vehicle van. We need one with the latest equipment in external lighting, mapping, monitors, and two-way communication. You know what's needed for a search of this nature and the expertise that we will need to assist us in that van. We need to be parked beside the paramedics' emergency ambulance so that Grace can accompany Katie to the hospital in order to gauge her physical and mental condition before arrival.'

He would normally have given this instruction to one of the junior staff, but he knew that he had to keep Beth busy in the lead up to the search.

As an afterthought, Dan added, 'Bill, I would like the family to be here before I start my briefing meeting with all those who are going to be involved.'

Everyone jumped into action, and Dan had total trust and confidence in each of them doing exactly what was expected for maximum efficiency in such a detailed exercise.

Dan could tell by the look on Beth's face that she was quietly questioning whether or not there was any hope that Katie would be found alive. She knew that Dan's instructions to his team and the tone of his voice were deliberately issued with much more detail than normal. She knew that the reason for this was to reassure her that he wouldn't leave any stone unturned. Like Dan, she knew that there was no room or time for negativity for a search party such as the one being planned. She just found it hard to believe that it was for her own daughter and that she wasn't in charge.

He walked over to Beth just as she was about to make another telephone call, took the telephone from her, took both of her hands in his, and said, 'I am going to find Katie alive for you, Beth. Don't ever think otherwise.' And for the second time that evening, he gave her a peck on the cheek, but, this time, he took her into his arms at the same time.

Neither said anything. Beth picked up the telephone again.

12.40 p.m.

In just over thirty-five minutes, everything was in order for the search to begin. The equipped vehicles were ready with drivers at the exit. The Oliver family members were in the conference room. The rest of Dan's team and other officers brought in for the search party were also assembled, ready for the briefing meeting.

Dan wasted no time in bringing them all up to speed, issuing clear instructions and stressing the need for regular and precise two-way communication. Looking directly at Beth and Matt, he said that he would personally ensure that they received their instruction to meet Katie at the hospital in time for them to be there ahead of her arrival with Grace.

Dan and Grace led the way from the conference room.

Colin, the rest of Dan's team, and the seconded officers followed, knowing exactly which vehicle they should aim for and which member of Dan's team would be responsible for communication to Dan and Grace.

Bill had managed to convince Matt and Jack to stay with the family. The three of them, together with Beth and Caroline, sat in silence in the conference room, not knowing what to say or what to do.

But to wait.

CHAPTER 9

Sunday, 20 June 2004
1 p.m.

The search for Katie Oliver was just minutes away from starting.

Each of Dan's investigation team had a detailed map of Grange Woods and a search team of six experienced and equipped officers to search for Katie.

The emergency paramedic ambulance was in place, adjacent to the critical incident van occupied by Dan, Grace, and a communication officer.

Regular communication from the field to Dan and Grace had been arranged for fifteen-minute intervals.

Meanwhile, back at the MET in Dan's conference room, the wait had begun for Katie's parents, her brother, and her grandparents. Bill, who had led similar investigations many times during his career and who had interviewed and advised more family members than he could recall, felt like a fish out of water. He couldn't believe that, in this family situation, he didn't know what to say to help them get through this. For a moment, he wished that he had volunteered to join the search party, but he knew that his place was to be with his family. His role was to provide the strength that was going to be needed, and it was on this that he focussed on during the wait.

Beth couldn't settle in one place, so she paced up and down the room. She felt that she was either going to collapse or be sick. During her life so far, she could never recall feeling as anxious as she did at that moment. She knew that she could trust the teams searching for Katie. She knew that she had to be strong for the rest of her family, but she questioned whether she had the ability, or would be given the chance, to put this situation right.

Grace generally wasn't wrong with her profiling, and Beth prayed that she was right about her prediction that Katie would be returned to them alive.

She looked over the table to her mother and father and knew then that she had been so lucky to look back to her teen years and only have very happy memories of them. She walked over to the crime board and looked at the evidence photographs and knew then that her own daughter would never be able to say that, ever. She didn't know what was going to be worse—the waiting for feedback from the search or facing Katie at the hospital.

She looked over to Matt, who had chosen not to speak with her since he had arrived. As he deliberately turned his eyes away from her, they both knew that the loving and trusting relationship that they had once enjoyed would never be the same again. She knew at that moment that this man who had always loved her so tenderly would perhaps never hold her again in his arms.

Finally, she stopped walking about and looked at her son. Poor Jack looked exhausted and traumatised. She had barely spent any time with him since he had returned from Greece. He and his sister had always been very close, and she knew that their relationship going forward would be as strong as before, if not stronger. She noticed that he was wringing his hands and suddenly realised that his mother hadn't been there to comfort him since Katie's kidnapping. She walked over to where he was sitting and sat down next to him. She put her arms around him and drew him into her. It was then that he started to let the tears flow. It was then that she realised that her son was also going to need help after all of this was over, and she made a silent promise that she would be there for him throughout his own torment after Katie had been found. Her first decision was to stay right by his side from that moment and until they had reached the hospital, regardless of the outcome.

They all knew that the only people who would be able to talk about what condition Katie was in when she was found would be Dan and Grace, and a few of them, including Beth, wondered if they would ever be told the true facts.

The previous day, Dan and Grace had both been sure that they would eventually find Katie alive. However, uncertainty had crept in after the setback about the letter from the kidnapper not being delivered at the time he had planned.

They both knew that the overnight delay may have meant the difference between life and death. The paramedics agreed. Grace was also worried that the reason that the kidnapper had decided to dump Katie in the woods was because the wound was starting to show signs of infection. That being the case, Katie's survival would definitely depend upon her condition when she had been moved to the woods. Thankfully in the month of June, the night temperatures didn't plummet as they did during the winter months.

Grace decided that she was going to rely upon her own instincts about the profile of the kidnapper. She was determined to believe that he wouldn't just have dumped her naked body in the woods. Instead, she visualised him carefully sedating her and then wrapping her up in a blanket to keep her warm. If he had done this, and if the wound wasn't infected, she knew that these two actions would give Katie a chance to survive the evening.

In an effort to regain their original optimism, Grace digressed from the previous life-and-death debate that she and Dan had been having. 'I haven't had much to go on with my profiling of this guy, but, if I am even reasonably accurate with my hypothesis, Katie will be alive and her body will have been sufficiently protected just in case it takes several hours to find her.'

Grace continued, 'Assuming that he has kept her hydrated and fed since Friday night, and I am certain that he will have, and assuming that he has kept the tattoo clean, she should also be in a reasonably healthy condition. She is young, she is healthy, and this gives her a fighting chance to survive the trauma and an evening in the woods.

'Also I don't think that she will have been walking around aimlessly in the dark and in fear. I think that he will have sedated her so that she slept until she was found. I just hope that he gave her enough to see her through the night.'

'I can't help but notice that you avoid mentioning the possibility of him having killed her,' said Dan.

'I know. I am determined to remain positive. That possibility obviously exists, and I have never excluded from my thoughts the fact that he may panic or something may go wrong that makes him feel that he has no option but to kill her. We don't know who this man is, so we don't know the details about his mental state before and after the kidnapping.'

'Regardless of how we find her, Grace, the Olivers are going to face a tough time as a family going forward. You will know better than me the sort of mental effect that this will have on Katie. God knows what is going through Beth's mind at present. Thank goodness that she has Bill and Caroline to lean on because she sure as hell won't have Matt's shoulder to cry on at present,' said Dan.

'Thank goodness that Beth has the Palmers as her parents. Their marriage has always been a happy one, and Beth always says that they were extremely supportive parents, even throughout her teens. If anyone within the family has the ability to repair some of this mess, it is Bill and Caroline Palmer,' said Grace.

'I agree. Bill is one of the very few high-ranking officers at the MET who always seemed to balance his work and family life. He never ever slacked at work. Quite the contrary in fact. Yet he was always there for his family. Not many people are fortunate enough to experience the strong bond and happiness that Bill and Caroline have always enjoyed together,' added Dan.

Grace shared some of her post-kidnapping consulting experiences with Dan. Both knew however that she wouldn't be able to reach a specific diagnosis on Katie until she knew the extent of what had happened to her. She would also need to discuss Katie's mental and physical conditions with the consultant allocated to Katie when she arrived at the hospital.

'By the way, I chose the St Rubens Hospital because Miriam Shepherd is on duty today, and she will be the perfect consultant to deal with Katie and her family. She was my first choice, and we are lucky that she is available. Beth and I have both worked with her often. She is also a close friend of mine,' said Grace.

'Good call,' replied Dan. 'I have also worked with Miriam, and she deserves the respect that she gets. I agree that she will be good for Katie and for her family. She is firm yet kind, and her patients always come first. The two of you will make a good team for Beth and Matt to lean on.'

Regularly looking towards the monitors and checking each team's progress, they were disheartened that there was nothing positive to report yet.

2 p.m.

At just under one hour into the search, the fifteen-minute reports from the various search parties were inconclusive. So far, there was no evidence found that confirmed Katie's presence in the woods.

'I just hope that this isn't some cruel ploy to give the family false hope for Katie's safe return to them. If that were to be the case, it would mean that the kidnapper is really starting to twist the knife and I would be less confident about the outcome of this. How about you, Grace? What do you think?'

'Oh, God! Don't say that, Dan. It's bad enough that any of this has happened to Katie and her family, but I am really relying upon my profiling having a reasonable level of accuracy to it. Whilst finding Katie in the woods, with no further action, threats, or explanation, would be bizarre, I am praying for all of their sakes that this is what is going to happen.'

'If we don't find her, I would have to rethink everything that I have said as this would mean that he was starting to act irrationally, and, in that state of mind for someone who is mentally imbalanced, anything can happen.'

'Just what I was thinking,' said Dan. 'In the meantime, let's continue to be optimistic and logical in our thinking. We knew that without specific instructions about where to find Katie, we weren't going to park the vehicles and then find her within ten minutes. It's just been an hour which isn't long in a search of the extent of the area that we have to cover.'

'As always, you are spot on,' said Grace as she took another look at the monitor.

2.15 p.m.

Nothing to report.

2.30 p.m.

Nothing to report.

2.45 p.m.

Nothing to report.

3 p.m.

Nothing to report.

3.10 p.m.

The call that Dan and Grace had anxiously been waiting for was received from Rachel. At 3.10 p.m. on Sunday, 20 June 2004, thirty-eight hours thirty-five minutes after she had disappeared, Katie Oliver had been found.

'Is she alive?' asked Dan.

'To be honest, boss, I don't know. I am walking towards her as we speak, but one of the team with her is looking for a pulse and is shaking his head,' said Rachel.

'Okay, Rachel. We have your location. Hold everyone back, and don't let anyone interfere with the crime scene. I'm handing you over to Grace.'

Dan updated the paramedics.

'Rachel, we are pretty close by, so we will be with you shortly. Is Katie covered?' Grace asked more calmly than she felt.

'Yes. She is wrapped in a thick blanket and definitely unconscious. Oh God, Grace. I think she may be dead.'

'No, she's not. Sit tight, and we'll be with you in a few minutes,' said Grace, not wanting to believe anything other than that Katie was alive.

3.30 p.m.

At 3.30 p.m., Dan and Grace were able to see for themselves that it was Katie who had been found.

Grace ran on in front of Dan and the paramedics. As she took in the scene ahead of her, she truly believed that they were too late. She knelt beside Katie and initially couldn't find a pulse. As she tried again, the paramedics unloaded their gear and took over. There was a huge sigh of relief all around as one of them confirmed that he had found a faint pulse.

Grace stayed with Katie so that she could supervise her transfer by stretcher through the woods and on to the ambulance.

Dan ran back to the surveillance van so that he could get a better signal on his phone before calling Katie's family.

Before Dan had left his office that morning, he had instructed Abe to switch the conference telephone to loudspeaker because he knew that, regardless what he had to say, it needed to be said by him to all of Katie's direct family. He was thankful that he had good news for them.

Bill answered Dan's call after the first ring.

'It's Dan here, Bill. Is your family with you?'

'Yes, we are all here,' said Bill. 'Have you found her?'

'We have found her. Katie is very weak, but she is alive. Grace is with her now, and the paramedics are checking her vital body stats and making her comfortable before leaving for the hospital. If you leave immediately, you will arrive before them. There are two cars and drivers outside the main entrance door waiting for you.'

Dan didn't have to repeat himself as he heard the chairs being moved and imagined them all grabbing their belongings and rushing towards the door.

He was naturally relieved that the call had ended without questions being asked as he didn't want to have to explain to them that they had found Katie naked and unconscious. As Grace had envisaged, she had been wrapped in a large blanket and laid out on a grassy verge beside a large tree deep in the heart of the woods. A bottle of water and a packet of sandwiches had been laid beside her, untouched, which suggested that she had been unconscious through the whole ordeal. The outfit that she had worn on the Friday night to the fashion show was nowhere to be seen.

Rachel told them that she was sure that Katie was dead when she first saw her and that she was afraid to check for her pulse.

Dan felt very emotional as he watched the paramedics gently handle Katie, and Grace didn't attempt to hide the tears that rolled down her own cheeks. From what they saw of Katie, Dan and Grace both knew that her life would never be the same again and her expectations for her remaining teen years would have come to a sudden halt on the evening of Friday, 18 June 2004, when she had been kidnapped, perhaps repeatedly raped, been forcefully scarred, and had lost her virginity in the cruellest possible way.

3.45 p.m.

The paramedics, Katie, and Grace left for the hospital.

From what Grace had witnessed, and how she felt about what had happened, she was even more determined to try her best to make sure that she was appointed as Katie's clinical psychologist. As Katie's need for prolonged counselling was as the result of a crime having been committed, she knew that her relationship with the family and her friendship with Beth would be questioned in court. It would be considered as a conflict of interest.

She made a mental note to contact the commander once Katie was settled at the hospital so that she could request that he support her application. Given his close working relationship with Beth, she expected a positive response.

She knew that the matter could be resolved with the issue of a specifically worded affidavit, outlining the terms of confidentiality deemed to be appropriate and sufficiently protective of Katie. Grace already knew that this would require her to agree to non-disclosure of anything discussed between Katie and herself unless otherwise authorised by Katie. She also knew that there could be a lifetime inclusion clause included.

None of this troubled Grace as she knew that Beth and most likely the rest of the family would trust her judgement and would prefer Grace to be dealing with Katie rather than some unknown consultant psychiatrist.

Grace also resigned herself to the fact that such an agreement would compromise her relationship with Beth from time to time but that she would deal with that on an as required basis. Her friendship with Beth was extremely important to her, but she knew that she would just have to professionally cope with and manage such a complex situation with extreme care. Anyone who knew Grace professionally would know that she was strong enough to be equal to that task.

Dan was relieved that Katie was alive but was resigned to the fact that Beth may resign her position as part of blaming herself for Katie's traumatic experience. He was confident that he could negotiate a long-term absence for her with the commander and made a note to seek advice from Grace about how he should approach that subject with Beth at a later date. For now, he would ensure that he processed an application for an indefinite period of compassionate leave for her.

Dan made his way back to his office out of respect for Beth and her family. Now was not the time for him, in his professional capacity, to be at the hospital. Grace would be there with them and be able to report back to him later about Katie's condition and Beth's reaction to it.

He decided that he would leave his visit to the hospital for later that day.

4.30 p.m.

Dan's team and the search parties reported back to Dan in his conference room. He thanked them for their efforts and reported that Katie had arrived at the hospital and that her family were there to be with her when she regained consciousness.

Dan dismissed the search parties.

He then sat down with his team to go through the post-search formalities. Colin, Abe, Rachel, Pete, and Sophie updated Dan with their respective searches. Rachel summarised the scene where Katie was found and reported that it had already been sectioned off and pegged out as a crime scene. She reported that she hadn't seen anything obvious and didn't give them any hope that SOCO would find anything that would point them in the direction of the kidnapper.

From what they knew about criminal investigations, Dan and his team knew that if this was the case, and if Katie couldn't remember anything about the kidnapper or the location where she was being held captive, there was a chance that her kidnapping and rape could become a cold case. Dan couldn't help but hope that the kidnapper would feel remorseful about the kidnapping and would come forward to admit to the crime.

For now, they would still have to complete their investigation. This would mean following through with the planned interviews with the male schoolteachers, completing the review of the hospital records, reviewing the feedback from SOCO, and considering the feedback from interviews with Katie.

5 p.m.

Dan told his team to pack up for the day and invited them to join him at the Greyfriars for a beer. 'I guess it's time to put George and his staff out of their misery. Apparently, they have been wetting themselves since I instructed George to have them report here for an interview.'

'We'll get those interviews out of the way tomorrow,' said Colin. 'You never know, now that Katie has been found alive, one of the waiters or barmen just may remember something of value about our guy.'

Meanwhile, back at the hospital, the paramedics' report had given sufficient comfort for the duty doctor to confirm that she had a steady pulse. Katie Oliver was alive, and Beth and Matt Oliver were eventually advised that there was no cause for concern about the results from her clinical biochemistry blood tests.

Physically, Katie Oliver was expected to fully recover.

Mentally, Katie Oliver would later be diagnosed as having severe post-traumatic stress. Coming to terms with the extent of what had happened to her and dealing with the associated symptoms of PTSC, particularly the recurring nightmares, was going to be a slow and distressing struggle for her. Her life had changed in just two days.

Elsewhere, at his Kings Cross address, the kidnapper sat at home, reflecting upon what had happened over the last few days. He was satisfied that his actions would ensure that family life for the Olivers would never be the same again and that was, after all, what he had set out to do. But revenge was supposed to give him peace of mind, and yet that wasn't how he felt.

He recalled that the nagging issue for him throughout the kidnapping was that he hadn't expected to feel guilty at terrorising Katie. Originally, the purpose of the DVDs was to record her fear of the kidnapper and her horror during the rapes so that he could share that with her parents. But, because of her look of fear and horror during the second and third rapes, he still hadn't sent those recordings.

The first rape was easy. He had been deprived of sex for over two years and had become naturally aroused when he saw her naked body laid out in front of him. He hadn't expected her to be a virgin, however. And he now felt guilty that this hadn't stopped him from raping her again two more times. He hadn't enjoyed the acts at the time but that hadn't stopped him from ejaculating and feeling satisfied.

As time went on, he realised that he had spoiled the chances of happiness of an innocent teenager. His original plot was to keep her captive for up to a week, but, after a couple of days, he knew that it was wrong to take his hatred out on the daughter.

It was at this point that he had decided to release Katie Oliver and to protect her against any further harm.

PART II

Sunday, 20 June 2004 to Wednesday, 17 October 2012

After being kidnapped, raped, and bodily scarred during the period of Friday, 18 to Sunday, 20 June 2004, Katie Oliver was found in the Grange Woods and lucky to be alive. She was hospitalised on that Sunday evening and later diagnosed with severe post traumatic stress. The dreams and ambitions of this happy and confident teenager had been shattered in just two days.

CHAPTER 10

Sunday, 20 June 2004
Katie in Hospital
1 p.m.

Thanks to Dan's detailed instructions for the transportation of Katie's family to the St Rubens Hospital as soon as Katie had been found, they all arrived there before she did.

Grace's positive working relationship and friendship with Miriam Shepherd meant that Katie would be taken straight to Miriam's ward. Anticipating her condition, Miriam had pre-booked a private room for Katie and had instructed that her family be allocated one of the temporary side waiting rooms on arrival.

After arriving at the hospital, Beth was feeling nauseous, mainly due to the personal emotional stress that she had been ignoring since Katie's disappearance on the Friday evening. She couldn't get the image of Katie as she had been dressed for the fashion show out of her head. It hurt that she had to rely upon the photographs taken by Freya and then the kidnapper to see how her daughter had looked in the dress that she had so much fun designing with Freya.

At the thought of Freya, she sent her a brief text message to let her know that Katie had been found alive and that the family was at the hospital awaiting her arrival.

Beth's thoughts lapsed back to Katie's dress design for the fashion show. She hadn't been involved during the design stages, the fittings, or the dress rehearsal. And now she hadn't even seen her wearing it. At the start of the project, she had said that she would leave the design choice to Freya and Katie, but now she questioned the sanity of that decision.

After what had happened to Katie, she was riddled with guilt and self-loathing. She knew that she was a good mother, but how could she have been so stupid as to jeopardise the evening by not turning up on time?

She didn't have an image of how Katie was going to look when she arrived at the hospital and suddenly realised that she hadn't asked any questions when Dan told her that Katie had been found. But neither had he volunteered any details.

Beth was of no doubt that she had ruined Katie's evening, had been to blame for Katie leaving the event, and was therefore responsible for the tragic outcome. As she waited for her daughter's arrival at the hospital, Beth knew that she would never forgive herself for not arriving on time for the dinner. She also suspected that Katie may never be able to forgive her because had she turned up on time, she would not have been kidnapped and raped.

Beth paced up and down the waiting room, unable to look at any of her family members. She knew that life would never be the same for any of them, and she knew that the rest of the family were probably thinking the same thing.

Matt sensed Beth's anxiety and saw the pain on her face. He knew that she should be in his protective arms as they waited for their daughter to arrive, but he couldn't bring himself to do that.

Instead, he stood at the window, looking over the London skyline and struggled to think about what the future may hold for his daughter.

He wondered if he would ever be able to relieve himself of the helplessness and pain that he now felt for his daughter, the anxiety that he felt when he considered her recovery plan, and the anger that he felt for his wife.

What would he say to his daughter? How would he comfort her? Would she be able to open up to her father? He dealt with heartache and distress at the hospital on a daily basis, and yet, here and now, he was worried about his ability to find the right words to say to his daughter.

Like Beth, he felt nauseous when he gave any thought to the ordeal that his daughter had survived, the extent of which brought tears to his eyes.

He had been trained to cope with family emergencies, traumatic experiences, and even death, and yet he continued to question his ability to do that effectively for his daughter. He struggled to contain his emotions as he dreaded the thought that Katie may not even want to be hugged by him after her experiences with the kidnapper. *Would he ever find out exactly what those experiences were? Would Katie ever be able to discuss them?*

Jack sat in one of the armchairs, not knowing what to do. For the first time in his life, he felt insecure. His parents weren't relaxed in each other's company, and, worse, he had the dreadful thought that he may never see them happy in each other's company again.

The tension between his mother and father was obvious. He loved them both dearly, and it hurt to see them being unable to comfort each other. He sat alone because he didn't know which of his parents he should try to comfort. He wasn't even sure how he should behave in a hospital waiting room that could so easily have been the morgue had Katie not survived.

He sensed that his grandparents didn't know what to do either, other than to hold on to each other, the one action that came so naturally to this couple who had lived together for almost forty-five years.

He wondered if the first visit to his sister would be restricted to his parents. He hoped not. He felt that he should be there to help camouflage the tensions between them as he wouldn't want the friction between them to be the first thing that Katie sensed. But then he realised that Katie may be unconscious. No one had mentioned that possibility.

He was desperate for his sister to arrive, just to see for himself that she was alive and in safe hands. He had seen the videos and had no idea of how the result of the traumatic experiences would affect her in the future.

Jack vowed to remain as close to his sister as before. He decided to take each day as it came. He decided that he would speak with his grandparents or Grace if he needed advice as he had a feeling that his mother and father would be preoccupied for some time to come.

Bill and Caroline sat together on one of the sofas, silent with their own thoughts and yet in sync with what each would be thinking. They had been very fortunate to have enjoyed a happy marriage, and, as a result of that, they had been supportive and caring parents to Beth and wonderful grandparents to Katie and Jack.

Like Jack, they struggled with any thought about the family being torn apart and what would become of that.

They were generally pleased with their daughter's choice of husband and had witnessed many happy family gatherings. Before Friday, they had believed that Beth's marriage would last the distance. Today, however, they were not so sure.

They knew that the couple, like most working parents, had struggled with the juggling of their responsibilities, but their priority had always been to provide a happy, stimulating, and secure family home for their children. Both Bill and Caroline feared that this was about to change for the worse.

For now, they didn't have to say a word to each other. They knew that all they could do was to be there for the family and to respond in whatever way was necessary to help them survive such a terrible tragedy.

The one thing that they were both sure about was that they would always be there for each other and together they would have the strength to help the family whenever they were needed.

1.15 p.m.

Grace came rushing into the sitting room. She pushed both arms out in front of her as if to indicate that they should remain seated. She sat in the chair nearest the door to reinforce that message.

'The nursing staff are settling Katie into a bed. Dr Miriam Shepherd is a wonderful doctor whom I have had the privilege to work with many times. I can assure you all that Katie is in the safest of hands with Miriam. She will be gentle. She will be caring. She will be thorough. And she will be open and honest with you. You just need to be patient for a little longer until she satisfies herself that Katie's vital signs are stable.'

Grace continued, 'Miriam will then allow Beth and Matt to visit Katie for a few minutes, and the rest of you will be able to observe her through the window. I need to forewarn you that her hospital room will be part of the ongoing criminal investigation, which means that there will be the need for tests and interviews that may give you cause for alarm. However, Miriam is formidable when it comes to protecting her patients, so she will definitely control all of that. Also Dan and I will ensure that the situation is managed sensitively.

'In other words, you need to give the medical team the space that they need to follow standard medical procedures after a kidnapping and rape.

'After Katie has regained consciousness and her reflexes have been checked, which may not be today, Miriam will allow one person at a time to spend a few minutes with Katie. If, however, Miriam observes any negative reactions from Katie, she will put a stop to visits. So you need to be prepared for the potential of visit restrictions.

'After you have had a quick look at Katie, you need to think about how you want to organise future visits. It's going to be a slow process, and Katie will perhaps be hospitalised for many weeks. I know that feelings between Beth and Matt are strained at present, but this isn't a time to focus on that. It is a time to do what is best for Katie.

'Beth, I hate to say this, but you may get an adverse reaction from Katie, and Miriam wants to avoid that so soon after the kidnapping. I guess what I am really saying is that you should prepare yourself for that. It's too early to review and make any judgements on Katie's mental state. Do you understand what I am trying to say?'

'Yes,' said Beth very quietly.

The others nodded their heads in agreement, not sure how to respond.

'What I am also trying to say to you is that if Katie demonstrates relaxation with just one person, then that is the best person to spend quality time with Katie in the short term.'

Matt was the first to speak. 'Grace, no matter what is said, I am going nowhere until I hear for myself that my daughter is medically fit. I know that the psychological process may be long, but, again, I will want to see Katie daily, even if it is for a few minutes. I want her to know that I am here for her.'

'I understand that, Matt, and, no doubt, Beth feels the same. I am trying to emphasise that any negative reactions will not be helpful to Katie's recovery.'

'Grace is being tactful. What she is really trying to say', said Beth, 'is that Katie may reject me. Personally, I don't know how I will cope with that, but I will not do anything that may interfere with her progress. Regardless of how she reacts to me, I will spend time at the hospital every day. If I have to, I will observe her progress through her window.'

The silence that followed demonstrated that everyone felt emotional at Beth's words, understood the need for them, and knew that it would break her heart to have to cope with her daughter's rejection.

'Sorry, but that's the way it is. Katie comes first,' said Grace. 'Under normal circumstances, the parents would regularly visit together, but Beth and Matt aren't exactly clinging to each other at present, and we cannot afford for her to sense the tension that is so obviously there between you.'

'Surely you are not suggesting that anyone other than Beth or I should be spending quality time with Katie?' asked Matt.

'No. I am asking you to be sensitive to Katie's reactions and to ensure that the person that she appears to be most comfortable with spends quality time with her.'

As Grace expected, Beth and Matt were demonstrating negative reactions to her advice, but she understood the reasons for that. As Grace expected, none of them were bursting with enthusiasm to take her advice, but she fully understood and expected that reaction.

She left the room to check with Miriam when the parents could see their daughter. To her relief, Miriam agreed that then would be good time before the next set of tests were scheduled.

Grace returned to the waiting room and asked the family to follow her, reminding Jack, Caroline, and Bill that they should use the viewing panel and stay outside the room.

Beth and Matt approached Katie's bed and couldn't believe that someone could look so much thinner, paler, and younger in the space of a couple of days. She looked so vulnerable, and they both felt helpless at seeing their daughter lying there unconscious and hooked up to drips and medical equipment. They stayed for a few minutes, and each held one of Katie's hands and kissed her forehead before leaving the room at Miriam's request.

Sensing Jack's hurt at not getting closer to Katie, Miriam signalled that he should join her in the room. 'Just two minutes, Jack, and then please leave.'

Grace walked them back to their waiting room and then returned to observe Katie. Unless she heard otherwise, she was assuming the position as Katie's psychotherapist.

Dr Shepherd asked to speak with the parents in her office and nodded to Grace that she should join them. When Beth and Matt arrived, she acknowledged Beth, having worked with her before, and offered both of them her commiserations about what had happened.

She told them that she was optimistic that Katie would soon begin to regain consciousness and that the blood, urine, and saliva tests had been completed. She had also managed an internal examination whilst Katie was still unconscious, which pleased her as it was one less thing for Katie to endure. That examination had confirmed that Katie's hymen had been torn and that she was no longer a virgin. She also told them that, in her opinion, she had been raped more than once. She still hadn't ascertained how the kidnapper had drugged Katie but would have the results shortly.

Beth and Matt both knew that Katie had been raped, but hearing the confirmation of that from a doctor made it real and brought back the pain that they had felt when they had watched that particular video.

Grace added, 'She was groggy when she was found. I didn't want her to regain consciousness in an ambulance or at any point until she was settled in her hospital bed and in the safe hands of Miriam, so I authorised the paramedics to sedate her again.'

'I would have done the same,' said Dr Shepherd.

'What about the kidnapper's semen?' asked Beth.

'I am led to believe that none of her clothing was left at the scene where she was found, and I can tell you that she had been thoroughly washed before that. The chance of us helping with a DNA match is very slim, I'm afraid,' replied Miriam. 'In the meantime, I can assure you that there is no way that any detective is getting anywhere near Katie without my say-so, and that includes our highly respected Dan Turner.

'For now, Beth and Matt, your daughter is alive. Think back to how you felt before that news was given to you. My advice to you is that you should all focus on the way forward.'

'Thank you, Dr Shepherd,' said Matt. 'Now that we have seen her alive, you have our assurance that we will cooperate with you.'

'I know Beth well, so please call me Miriam. Let's take one step at a time. Katie will be closely supervised by my staff and, no doubt, Grace. If Katie asks to see any of her family, we will contact you immediately. I understand that you will want to stay here until Katie regains consciousness, but after that, there is really no need for all of the family to stay at the hospital. You may want to arrange a rota so that someone is always here over the next few days, but I will leave that up to you to decide.'

They all shook hands, and then Beth and Matt made their way back to their waiting room to update the others.

'We may as well get as many of the formalities out of the way this evening as we can, so we need to think about how we are going to manage the police investigation. You obviously won't have a problem with the family as the majority of them are familiar with that process,' said Grace.

'I promised Dan that I would give him an update as soon as possible. Be prepared for him turning up this evening as a matter of protocol, but do that in the knowledge that he will be sensitive, particularly given his relationship with the family,' added Grace.

'I know Dan well and respect the way that he works,' said Miriam. 'He will not be a threat to the way that I plan to monitor Katie over the next few days and to chart her progress. To be honest, Grace, I want to hold on to her until we have established her mental state as that could have an effect on her physical condition. Also I want to know whether or not she is pregnant. If she is, we will need to decide what to do for the best for Katie. I have my own thoughts on that, but Katie is over sixteen, so she has a right to be told and to make related decisions.'

2 p.m.

Grace returned to the family and informed them that Katie had regained consciousness and that Beth and Matt could see her briefly as Miriam planned to sedate her again until at least the following morning.

Grace summarised what Miriam had just told her about keeping Katie under her care until she was convinced that Katie's mental state was not going to have any impact on her physical condition. She obviously missed out the part about the pregnancy test.

Whilst she had their undivided attention, Grace also explained that exposure to a psychological trauma such as the one experienced by Katie was often too overwhelming for an individual to cope with. She forewarned them that there may be flashbacks, nightmares, anger, and difficulty in sleeping but couldn't estimate how long they would last for.

She didn't share with them that; from experience, Grace knew that they were in for a difficult and extensive period of time, facing up to and recovering from the almost certain impairment in Katie's social and interpersonal functioning.

Matt took everyone by surprise by actually speaking directly to Beth, 'You have already been warned that Katie may have a negative reaction to seeing you. Rather than both of us going in at the same time, why don't you go in first to see how she reacts to you. If she is pleased to see you, then that is good and I will join you, but if she isn't, I can then follow in to distract her. What do you think?'

'You have no idea how nervous I am at seeing her because she may reject me if she remembers why she left the fashion show. However, this isn't about us, Matt. In the first instance, she needs to see her parents visiting her together. If she reacts badly to me, I will leave the room to reduce any anxiety that she may have.'

'Okay. Let's do that,' replied Matt.

Grace didn't comment, but she was almost certain that Katie would reject Beth unless she had no memory of what had happened to her.

Before walking into Katie's room, Beth stopped Matt and said, 'Matt, let's do this well for Katie. You and I can talk about how you feel later.'

Matt nodded his agreement.

They both walked slowly up to Katie's bed and fought hard to hide the emotions that they felt at seeing her awake. They stood at the same side of her bed. Katie was facing the other way. Beth took her hand and said, 'Welcome back, sweetheart. You have been asleep.'

Katie slowly turned towards them and stared at them for what seemed like a very long time. Beth kissed her forehead, and then Matt did the same.

'Where am I? What's happened to me? I don't remember why I am in hospital,' said Katie.

'You have been unconscious, darling, and are in a hospital close to your home. Jack, Gran, and Granddad are just next door and have asked us to pass on their love to you.'

'I feel so tired,' Katie said, as she had already appeared to be slipping back into a sleep.

'Then you must sleep. Mum and I will sit with you for a while, and then we will visit you again when you are awake,' said Matt, but he doubted that Katie had heard any of his words.

Miriam and Grace joined them, and, before they asked, Miriam said, 'That is a common reaction. The more she sleeps, the better for her. Beth, whilst that was good that she didn't react badly to seeing you, that may change later. I just don't want you to have a false sense of security.'

Beth nodded her head and said, 'Just in case that does happen, I would like to sit with her now for as long as I possibly can.'

Even Matt seemed to understand how she must feel, and so he said that he would update the family and she should stay with Katie.

Matt returned to the family and updated them on how Katie looked and the words that she had spoken. They all sat down again as none of them were ready to leave the hospital just yet.

As Beth sat with Katie, Grace took the opportunity to inform the commander that she wished to be appointed as Katie's psychoanalyst. He listened to her reasons and then assured her that he would do all that he could to make it happen, including the application to the court.

3.45 p.m.

After a few beers with the investigation team, Dan headed back to the MET. He was frustrated at being no further forward than before Katie had been found. He was starting to be of the opinion that they were going to struggle to identify Katie's kidnapper.

His parting shot to the team was, 'I don't want this going cold.'

He hung about the office for a while but then left to make his way to the St Rubens Hospital.

CHAPTER 11

Sunday, 20 June 2004
5.30 p.m.

Dan arrived at the hospital and immediately saw Grace as he entered the ward.

'I didn't expect to see you until this evening. You surely don't expect to speak to anyone about Katie this afternoon?' said Grace.

Silence.

'Jesus, Dan. You did, didn't you? You know the score. Victim arrives. Victim is made comfortable. Body stats checked. Bloods tested. Et cetera. Et cetera. Only one visitor at a time. No one, but no one is allowed to interrogate the patient until the doc gives clearance. Which part of all of that did you miss during the last umpteen years of being DCI and then DSI?' asked an astonished Grace.

'I know. I know,' said Dan. 'I just couldn't sit at the office watching the crap coming back from SOCO. Even when they've nothing to report, they made it sound as though you should be grateful for feedback at all. They haven't found anything at the crime scene so far. Can you believe that, Grace? Either this guy is getting by with ignorance and sheer fluke or he is so much cleverer than we've been giving him credit for.'

Silence.

'Speak to me, Grace.'

'It is ignorance. I'll put my reputation on him not being a serial kidnapper. I have more bad news to tell you. Aside from the fact that none of her clothes were there at the scene, Miriam has confirmed that she was thoroughly washed before being left.'

'Bloody hell! No semen trace?' he asked.

'Nope,' she replied.

'My parting shot to the team before I sent them home was *I don't want this going cold*. Anyway, I've left the SOCO guys to continue working at the scene, and I'm not expecting detailed feedback from them until tomorrow morning. Colin will start rounding up reports during the course of tomorrow.

'I've felt like a spare part during the last couple of hours, so here I am. Of course, I didn't expect to speak to Katie, but I would like to hear what Miriam has to say if she has the time.'

'And, no doubt, you wanted to check on Beth whilst you were here, eh?' asked Grace.

'I guess so,' was all that Dan said.

'How is Katie, Grace?' asked Dan as if to redeem himself for even thinking about Beth.

'She has been allocated to Miriam Shepherd as you know, so that's a good start. You will, no doubt, meet her soon because she will probably sense that you are on her ward.'

'What is she saying about Katie?'

'Too early to say. We don't think there is any physical damage, but, without being able to test Kate's mental condition, Miriam is concerned that anything negative could have an impact on her overall health. She wants to keep her here for a while so that she can keep a close eye on both. Katie regained consciousness not so long ago, and she has had her first visit from Beth and Matt together, but Katie was so tired that she just questioned why she was in hospital and said that she couldn't remember how she got there.'

'Good,' said Dan, knowing that she would need as must rest as possible.

'Katie's recovery is going to be slow, and, like you, I don't have any answers, but I'm hoping to be appointed by the court as her psychoanalyst and counsellor. I have already contacted the commander, so he will, no doubt, be in touch with you about that. Assuming that goes ahead, I will be able to get close to her and monitor her reactions on a regular basis. Whether or not any of that will bring us closer to identifying the kidnapper, I don't know. What I do know is that you are not going to get any answers soon.'

'Well, if it isn't Detective Superintendent Turner. Long time, no see,' said an approaching Dr Miriam Shepherd. 'How are you and what brings you here so soon after the victim has been admitted to my ward?'

'I just wanted to show face and to find out if I knew anyone on the medical team. I'm naturally pleased to find out that you are the consultant. We have never been adversaries in any of my investigations, so that is always a good start.'

'Good to hear it, Dan. Let's go and grab a coffee, and I'll bring you up to speed.'

Dan followed Miriam to her office, where she told him more or less what he had already heard from Grace. She did add that she thought that due to Katie's age, she was going to classify her as vulnerable and request that the psychiatric testing be conducted from her ward. 'It is my opinion that the medical and psychic tests should be reviewed side by side. I think that a transfer to a psychiatric ward would just add more trauma to an already distressed mind. Here, Grace and I can keep an eye on her combined physical and mental health and she'll feel more relaxed in the company of familiar faces.'

'How long are you expecting that to take?' asked Dan.

'It depends on Katie's recollection of events and the effect that her experiences have had on her health and mind. I would estimate best part of a month. She needs to feel safe again, and, from what

I've picked up from speaking to Grace and meeting the family, all is not well between Mum and Dad. That's the last thing Katie needs. She needs to be protected from any further anxiety. Home wouldn't be good for her just at present. Her parents need some time to settle their differences.'

'If she were my daughter, I'd have to agree with all that you said and I would cooperate with your recommendations. It will also give Grace a chance to spend quality one-to-one time with Katie to build up trust and confidence.'

'Good that we are in agreement, Dan. That makes my job so much easier. However, it's going to be a while before I allow any of your team to interview Katie. In fact, I think that I would prefer that any questions that need to be asked are channelled through Grace. How would you feel about that?'

'I don't have a problem with that,' said Dan. 'I know how Grace works, and my team respect her. But, I'll need to assign someone to sit alongside Grace in order to coordinate the Q&A reports. As Rachel found Katie and worked with Grace at the scene, I'm going to assign her to that task.'

'Good. I'd better get back to my patient. Bye, Dan. Much as I enjoy your company, I really don't expect to see you or any of your team lurking around Katie's room any time soon. Is that clear?'

'Crystal,' replied Dan. He knew how it worked.

'But don't you hesitate to contact me or pop in for a coffee from time to time. Hey! I may even persuade you to buy me a drink.' She laughed.

'My pleasure,' replied Dan, also laughing.

The following weeks in hospital

Katie did spend the best part of a month under the combined care of Dr Miriam Shepherd and Dr Grace Fletcher. Grace was eventually appointed by the court as Katie's psychoanalyst and counsellor on condition that a non-disclosure agreement be signed by Grace to ensure that nothing said by Katie was passed on to anyone, including family members, without her personal written authorisation. Visitors were restricted to family at Katie's request.

Katie was diagnosed with post-traumatic stress condition and didn't respond well to any questions about the time that she had spent with her kidnapper. The one-to-one visits continued, and she did eventually spend time with each member of her family. She continued to be very quiet during each of the visits, and, under the advice of Miriam and Grace, none of the family asked her questions about the past.

Her pregnancy test was positive. When she got that news from Grace and Miriam, she started to scream hysterically. She took Miriam's hand and screeched, 'Don't let this happen to me. Please make it go away. Please.'

Over the next twenty-four hours, Miriam and Grace discreetly attended to Katie's request, which also included never to tell anyone about it. It was never discussed again.

Katie demonstrated coldness and anxiety in the first few visits from Beth. She eventually made it clear to Beth and Matt that she didn't want to spend time with her mother but refused to discuss this with Grace or Miriam. Grace had no option but to explain to Beth the dangerous ground that she would be treading if she insisted that she speak with Katie, regardless of how gentle she would be. Beth had no option but to follow advice as Katie became extremely agitated in her presence. Beth resorted to watching Katie endlessly through the viewing window of her hospital room and writing carefully worded notes to her daughter on a daily basis, not knowing if they were ever read.

Matt visited daily but only spent five or ten minutes with Katie. She always appeared to be tired, and he struggled to know what to say to her. To be honest, he was scared that he would say something that could trigger an adverse reaction. As a doctor, he would have known how to cope with that. As a father, he was out of his comfort zone. He could barely look at his wife, and he and Beth fell into a pattern of spending as much time as possible apart.

Katie's two sets of grandparents limited their visits to once weekly for no more than ten minutes and focussed on sending her their love in handwritten notelets. Katie did occasionally ask for Caroline's company, Beth's mother, and, of course, her grandmother was only too happy to oblige.

It was Jack who spent the most time with Katie. Grace was correct in anticipating that it would become obvious who Katie felt most comfortable with. That person was Jack, followed by her grandmother. On hearing that from Grace, Jack virtually put his life on hold as he went back and forth to the hospital on a daily basis. If she was distressed, he would sit with her until she had finally fallen into as deep a sleep as she could. Aside from Miriam and Grace, it was Jack who had witnessed her nightmares. Grace allowed this to happen as she thought the experience would come in useful one day when, hopefully, Katie felt able to talk about the kidnapping and rapes. At present, she was showing no evidence of remembering either. Grace was confident that this was a brother-and-sister relationship that was going to be strong throughout Katie's recovery.

At the end of Katie's month in hospital, Miriam knew that she had done all that she could and that Katie's future depended very much upon Grace's counselling and Katie's ability to accept what had happened to her. Neither Grace nor Miriam was convinced that this was going to happen any time soon, if ever. Katie acted as though her life had been destroyed, and she showed no inclination of trying to get any of her previous life back or to make any plans for her future.

For the first time in her life, Beth felt totally out of control. At one point, she threw herself into the investigation with Dan and his team, but she had to eventually acknowledge that she was too close to the case and, therefore, could not perform effectively. She longed to wake up one morning to find out that it had all been a bad dream. She met regularly with Miriam and Grace and was distraught about this being as close as she could get to her daughter.

Post-hospital
Katie

Katie was discharged from St Rubens Hospital into the care of Bill and Caroline Palmer, Beth's parents and Katie's adoring grandparents. This arrangement had come about at the request of Katie. She continued to meet with Grace regularly. Whilst Grace knew that she had a close bond with Katie, she was no closer to getting her to talk about what had happened. She had no way of telling whether that was deliberate or Katie had genuinely filed the trauma into a part of her brain that couldn't be reached. Katie talked about the fashion show and enquired about who had won the prizes. She asked where her dress was. As the dress had never been returned, Grace suggested to Beth that a replica be made by Freya just in case she ever asked to see it. Beth had no hesitation in agreeing to this as she was just pleased to be doing something that may help Katie in some small way.

This gave Beth an opportunity to meet up with Freya again and to properly thank her for taking care of Katie on the evening that she was kidnapped. The two of them had only exchanged the occasional telephone call since Katie had been found. Beth decided to take Freya out for dinner rather than just call to ask for a replica dress to be made. Freya was pleased to hear from Beth but was shocked at how gaunt she looked.

Grace had asked Katie if she would agree to being hypnotised, but Katie had always refused. She had repeatedly voiced no interest in talking about either her past or her future.

The changes to Katie's life were devastating for all of her family to witness. She asked her father to cancel her place at university and refused to be drawn into conversations about her future. She became reclusive and refused all invitations from her friends to spend time with them, even when her grandmother suggested that she invite a friend over to stay for a few nights. She had her hair cut short, and she dressed daily in a tracksuit and trainers. She read. She learnt to cook with her grandmother. She helped her grandfather in the garden. She never watched television. She did listen to music. She sent a polite note to each of her close friends and asked them to respect her wishes not to socialise. She managed to keep busy, but she seldom managed to smile.

It took her almost one year to announce her plans for continuing her studies, much to the delight of her family. To their surprise, however, it wasn't the fashion design degree that she had originally decided upon. Katie had been accepted to study at Oxford University for an honours degree in psychology, after which she planned to study for a masters in criminology and criminal justice.

Katie had confided in Grace that she had been researching the two subjects for almost six months, that she had met with her previous headmistress for guidance, and that she had applied and been accepted for the courses. Beth and Matt were naturally disappointed that she hadn't discussed such an important matter with them but could understand her need to research it by herself and to discuss her choices with Eleanor Marshall.

This was determined to be the first major breakthrough since Katie's kidnapping the previous year.

Katie obsessively studied for four years and, unsurprisingly, was awarded a first-class honours degree in psychology. A further one year of study gained her an MSc in criminology and criminal justice. She was headhunted and offered an internship from Robson and Mackintosh, one of the city's top criminal law practices.

She dated men from time to time, but any hint of the relationship becoming physical soon brought it to an end.

She occasionally met up with a couple of her old school friends, and she maintained contact with Eleanor Marshall by meeting up a couple of times a year over lunch. At work, she succeeded beyond expectations, to the admiration of the partners and some of her close colleagues.

Despite the inner darkness of her mind, Katie turned out to be a beautiful young woman who once again knew exactly how to coordinate clothes and accessories to make her stand out in a crowd. Those close to Beth and Katie couldn't help but notice the personality similarities between them and were saddened that they had been unable to mend the broken fences between them.

Matt

Beth and Matt's marriage stood no chance after Katie's kidnapping. It started to crumble during Katie's stay in hospital as Matt was unable and also unwilling to forgive Beth for what had happened to Katie. Grace had tried to reason with him many times, but he always told her that he just couldn't bring himself to consider a physical relationship with his wife. He refused counselling with the excuse that he wanted to focus on Katie rather than himself and Beth. He genuinely believed that Katie was in the wrong place at the wrong time and that the kidnapping had been opportunistic.

Beth tried to reason with Matt as she believed that her marriage was worth saving, but she couldn't help but notice the coldness in her husband's eyes as he looked into her eyes. In the end, she ran out of the energy needed to reason with him any further.

Matt eventually moved out of the marital home, and it was him who filed for a divorce due to 'irreconcilable differences'.

He had returned to work after a period of compassionate leave and, after a couple of years, started to date one of the doctors at his hospital. He maintained a close relationship with Katie and Jack and got their blessing when he announced his intention to marry again. After the marriage, his time with Katie and Jack lessened to the occasional lunch or dinner.

Jack

Jack couldn't cope with the breakdown of his family and couldn't come to terms with the way that everything in his life had changed in such a short space of time.

Once Katie had settled in with her grandparents after being discharged from hospital, he decided to take a gap year before going to university. He travelled to Australia, New Zealand, Malaysia, and Thailand. He earned his keep by working in bars from time to time, and he also did some voluntary work in Malaysia. It was in Thailand that he decided to learn to scuba-dive. He took a PADI dive course from beginner to instructor levels and made many friends. At the end of his gap year, he shocked his parents by announcing that he was going to stay in Koh Tao on the east coast of Thailand and that he had accepted employment as an instructor in scuba-diving.

He seldom returned to the UK and, when he did, spent his time between his mother and his sister. He was never comfortable with the way his father had treated his mother during and after the kidnapping and showed little interest in spending time with him and his new wife.

Jack eventually established his own scuba-diving school and enjoyed relationships with many beautiful local young women. He also learnt to play guitar and became reasonably fluent in Thai, French, and Spanish with the assistance of online multimedia learning resources.

Beth

Neither Grace nor Jack was able to persuade Katie to spend even a short time alone with her mother. Beth's only opportunity to apologise for not being there when Katie had most needed her had been restricted to the notes she had written to Katie when she was in hospital. As the first year progressed, Beth would visit her parents' home for afternoon tea on a Sunday, but Katie avoided any one-to-one conversations with her. She would politely answer informal questions in her grandparents' presence about what she had done that day, but that was as far as Beth could reach her. These afternoons became precious to Beth, and these visits continued until Katie started university.

After the separation from Matt, Jack's foreign travels, and Katie's decision to stay with her grandparents, it came as no surprise to anyone when, six months after the kidnapping, Beth had returned to work. She threw herself twenty-four seven into solving crimes and never forgot that Katie's kidnapper was still out there somewhere. She promised herself that somehow she would find him one day.

She never noticed Dan's growing affection for her, but Grace did and promised herself that she would approach the subject with Beth very cautiously during one of their quarterly spa weekends.

Beth did eventually spend more time socialising with Dan, and they fell into a pattern whereby she partnered him to the many formal functions that he was invited to. It wasn't a romantic relationship and was never sexual, but that was because Beth considered him to be one of her closest friends.

Beth never gave up hope that one day she and Katie would reunite and find some way of forming a relationship that could start to grow for them as mother and daughter again. They had no option but to meet and communicate in court from time to time, but this relationship was formal and professional. Even over a cup of coffee in the court's cafeteria, Katie never let down her guard with her mother. Beth was promoted to detective superintendent (DSI) after Dan's next promotion.

Dan

Professionally, Dan's career continued to move from strength to strength. He received a unanimous vote of confidence to be promoted from detective superintendent to chief superintendent when the existing DCS retired. This gave him considerably more operational responsibility and policy decision-making objectives at the MET and also meant that he was in regular demand as guest speaker at police conferences as well as political and MET formal functions.

Personally, he continued to want to get closer to Beth but was afraid that any approach would ruin the special relationship that they already had. He knew that he was a significant person in her life and preferred that to living a life without her company. He did date other women from time to time but purely for a physical relationship. Beth was regularly listed as his partner at social and formal work-related functions. As long as Beth was a single woman, he knew that he would struggle to have a serious relationship with another woman.

Grace

Grace was the pillar of strength for the Olivers during Katie's hospitalisation and the year after discharge. Her professionalism and friendship made it possible for her to embrace their respective ways of dealing with what had happened to Katie. With sensitivity and respect, she guided each through their own personal anguish.

Grace's friendship with Beth was often compromised by the terms of Grace's non-disclosure agreement with Katie and the court. With Katie's approval, Grace developed a communication code that she could use when speaking with Beth, for example, *You will be pleased to hear that my last meeting with Katie was blue.* This meant that it had gone well and that she was detecting signs of improvement in Katie's demeanour. Various colours were used to describe Katie's state of mind, her dress and image, her relationships, and her thoughts about her future. Simple yet effective.

Katie knew that her mother would never stop asking about her welfare, and she acknowledged that it would be cruel for Grace to say nothing at all. It worked, and Beth was grateful that she was at least able to ask basic questions of Grace, and she trusted her to be as open and honest as she possibly could.

Grace entered into a relationship with someone called Freddie Tyler, who owned the Italian restaurant that she, Beth, and Dan frequented. It was an unlikely match, but it worked. She refused to live *over the shop*, and so they agreed to stay at each other's apartments as and when it mattered. This generally meant that Freddie stayed over at Grace's a couple of nights during the week and Grace stayed over at Freddie's over the weekend, a time when he had to be available at his constantly fully booked restaurant.

They enjoyed a relaxing and loving relationship and shared their passions for good food and wine, music, theatre, reading, and coastal walks, not that they had much time to do justice to anything other than wining and dining.

Grace's professional relationship with Katie continued to be pivotal, and, as Katie aged, each acknowledged that the other was a friend that neither wanted to lose.

PART III

Wednesday, 17 October 2012 - Saturday, 20 October 2012

It had been just over eight years since Katie Oliver was kidnapped, raped and scarred. The kidnapper was never identified and had maintained his freedom. The documentation and interview notes relating to the unresolved crime were filed at the MET with the other cold case files. At Katie's request, she was now known by her family, work colleagues, and friends as Kate.

CHAPTER 12

Wednesday, 17 October 2012
8.50 a.m.

Dan Turner now held the most senior operational role of the MET's Serious Crimes Division, reporting to the Association of Chief Police Officers (ACPO). As chief superintendent, he hadn't changed much in looks over the last eight years. He continued to be the tall, dark, and handsome police officer that could take his pick from the unattached women that he met, and many of the attached women were also not averse to having 'if only' thoughts of Dan. His toned body, that obviously didn't happen by chance, helped, of course.

As for Dan, he continued to have eyes for only one woman since the death of his wife, and that was Beth Oliver, his DSI and next in command to him. He had carried a silent torch for her even when she had still been married to Matt.

He had a way of making his presence known as soon as he entered a room, and this Wednesday morning was no different as he walked into the general office occupied by one of his investigation teams.

'Has anyone seen Beth?' he asked.

Everyone either shook their head or said, 'No, chief.'

'Could someone please try to find her and tell her to come to my office pronto as we only have ten minutes to go before our nine o'clock briefing for the 10.30 television broadcast on the Samuel, Godfrey, and Crichton cases?'

No one could find Beth. She wasn't answering her mobile telephone. She wasn't answering her home telephone. She wasn't responding to her page messages, and there were no messages left at reception from her.

Dan had to start the briefing meeting without her.

10.15 a.m.

After the meeting, he called her mobile. No answer. It rang out. He left an abrupt message about not being pleased at having to do the television broadcast by himself.

'Any news on Beth?' he shouted to the group of staff beyond his office, but no one had heard from her. 'Colin, you had better come with me just in case some smart-ass journalist asks a question that I don't have the most up-to-date answer for.'

The two of them left the office.

10.45 a.m.

After the television broadcast, Dan called Beth's mobile telephone again. No answer. It rang out again. He left another short message and asked her to call him immediately.

The morning passed by, and Dan was starting to worry about Beth's unexplained absence. He called Colin and Pete into his office and explained that Beth had still not responded to his messages.

'This is so unlike her. She never misses important meetings,' he said.

'And she always keeps in touch with the office about her whereabouts or changes to her schedule,' added Pete.

'Look, let's not over-dramatise this, but could you both discreetly check whether she has been involved in a car accident or if anyone with her description has been admitted to A&E at the local hospitals?' asked Dan.

'We'll use one of the interview rooms so that the rest of the team don't see us in a side office,' said Colin.

Midday

Colin and Pete had been unable to locate Beth.

12.25 p.m.

A small package was delivered to Dan's office. It had 'security checked' stamped on the front and was dated. It contained an unmarked DVD. Instinctively, Dan pulled down the blinds in his office and inserted the DVD in his laptop. He had a very bad feeling about what he saw next on the screen.

12.45 p.m.

Dan sat down in his chair and dialled the telephone number of Grace Fletcher, psychologist, profiler, and close friend.

'Hi, Grace. I don't have time for pleasantries, I'm afraid. I urgently need to meet up with you. How soon could you be at my office? Or I can meet you somewhere of your choice if that's more convenient for you.'

Grace knew by the tone of Dan's voice that something vital needed her immediate attention. He would never waste her time with something trivial.

'It sounds serious, Dan,' she said.

'It is very serious, Grace. I need you here now, and you should clear your diary for the rest of the day if that's possible,' he replied.

'I don't like the sound of this, Dan. Thankfully, I don't have anything planned for this afternoon that can't be changed for something more important. Give me thirty minutes max. I'll make a couple of phone calls, and then I'll catch a taxi over to your office as that will be quicker than driving over and trying to find a parking space,' replied Grace as she simultaneously buzzed for her secretary on her extension phone.

1.15 p.m.

Just over thirty minutes later, Grace arrived at Dan's office, which had a private entrance from the second floor corridor at the MET.

He embraced Grace and excused himself as he entered the general office to advise his staff that he had an unscheduled meeting and he should not be disturbed for the rest of the afternoon.

Back in his office, he reloaded the DVD as he updated Grace about Beth's non-appearance for that morning's meeting and television broadcast.

'None of us have been able to contact her throughout the course of the morning, and I received an unmarked DVD this afternoon that you need to see.'

What they both saw on the DVD left them cold.

There on a hospital bed was a naked Beth lying on her front with her hands and ankles tied to the corner posts. That was bad enough, but the bloody message inscribed on her lower back brought back a very unpleasant memory from eight years ago.

Help

me

Kate

'Oh my God, Dan,' said Grace. 'The details of Kate's kidnapping were never publicised. This can't be happening again after all these years have gone by.'

Their professional instincts told them both that this was far more serious than Kate's kidnapping eight years earlier, particularly as there had never been a repeat MO since then to the best of their knowledge.

'Why would he wait eight years? Why Beth? Has she always been the target? What could have happened to trigger a repeat of Kate's kidnapping?' said Dan, thinking aloud.

He continued, 'This has been a cold case for eight years. In fact, it was so cold that it was frozen right from the start. We had absolutely no leads. There was no DNA on any of the packages delivered then, and it is a no-brainer to assume that there isn't going to be any DNA on the package that has just been delivered. Kate's clothes were never recovered, and every part of her body was scrubbed clean before she was left in the Grange Woods.'

Before Grace had a chance to say anything, Dan continued his one-way conversation, 'Where do we start? He has skipped the pleasantry of showing us how she looked before he kidnapped her, I see. No point pulling out the cold case files. Nothing of value in them. Besides, we know it off by heart. We will never forget what happened to Kate. You know more than most, Grace, as you have maintained a professional relationship with Kate.'

Grace took over.

'He has involved Kate and Beth again. Is that because he has unfinished business with either of them or both? We always thought that Matt was the one who was hiding something. On the face of it, it appears that we were wrong. And why has he cut to the chase this time? I really don't know who this guy is, Dan. My thoughts about his profile were shared with you at the time, and, as the case became cold, I questioned my own judgement. I started to believe that Kate had been in the wrong place at the wrong time and that he was just some sort of sicko who happened to offer assistance to her or whatever. Obviously, that was not the case.'

'What are you saying, Grace?' asked Dan.

'I must dig out my old notes about his profile and start from there. He seems to want Kate involved. How the hell are we going to achieve that?' she groaned.

'I wondered when you would come to that,' said Dan. 'I have a feeling that the communications this time aren't going to be drawn out as before. If Kate doesn't cooperate, it could be the difference between life and death for Beth. Do you agree?'

'I am inclined to agree with you.'

'Fortunately, the same team as last time are still with us, so there will be no need for preliminaries. I'll call them and ask them to shuffle their workloads so that they can work together. Also, I need to update the commander. He will want to be in on this from the outset, particularly as I am about to suggest that I lead this again.'

'Yes, we need to move quickly to recap as a team. Can I use your office or do you want me to move into your conference room? I want a few minutes to think about my workload and then call my secretary to give her instructions about how to manage my diary and what to delegate to whom. Then I'll be clear to have a think about how best to approach Kate,' said Grace.

'You settle here in my office, and I'll meet with the team in my conference room after I've updated the commander. I'll leave you in peace here while I brief them about what has happened, show them the DVD, and update them on our initial thoughts.'

Dan left the office and asked his secretary to contact Colin Thomson, Abe Hunter, Rachel Clark, Pete Lawson, and Sophie Andrews and request that they drop whatever they are working on at present and report to his conference room immediately.

The team that worked with him on Kate's kidnapping had all been promoted since then and had progressed from strength to strength as a murder investigation team in Special Crimes Division.

Without exception, they had flourished into responsible and highly respected detectives. He knew that they would know exactly what to do whilst he and Grace focussed on Kate.

1.45 p.m.

The commander was in his office when Dan arrived. He had been very supportive of Beth when Kate had been kidnapped and had been very generous with the amount of compassionate leave that he had authorised for her. He had also called in a few favours to ensure that Grace was authorised by the court to be Kate's consultant psychologist. Dan knew that he would support any requests that Dan made as he held both Dan and Beth in high regard. They had never let him down.

Dan briefly updated him, showed him the video, and informed him that he had already sent out requests for the original investigation team to meet with him as soon as possible. He also told him that he had immediately called Grace and that she was already in his office.

'Anything that I can do at this end, Dan?' the commander asked. 'Other than to assume that you want to roll up your sleeves and lead this investigation?'

'You assume correctly. Obviously, Colin will manage the investigation team, but too much is at stake, so I plan to stay close to this over the next few days.'

'Anything else?' asked the commander.

'We need to involve Jack, Kate's brother, as we think he is the only one, other than her grandfather, who may talk her into cooperating with us. Grace is considering the options as we speak, but we will need to plan a conference call with Jack in Thailand and ask him to get himself over here to assist us. That isn't going to be a problem, but we need to get him on the first flight out of Thailand, so it would save time if we book the flight online at this end.'

'I trust you to make the right financial decisions. We can worry about who pays for what later. Our priority is to get Beth back to us safely. I can't believe that eight years have passed and all those bad memories are going to resurface again. Nail the son of a bitch this time, Dan.'

'Grace and I feel the same and will obviously do all that we can to find him. He has missed out the preliminary communication and the rape this time, so we are concerned that he may literally be going for the kill this time.'

'As bad as that, eh? Well, what are you waiting for? Get yourself out of here and find Beth.'

'I'll keep you posted,' said Dan as he headed for the door.

'Dan,' the commander stopped him just as he was about to leave. 'Do you want me to call Bill? If you are struggling for time, I am happy to meet up with him and bring him up to speed.'

The commander had once been Beth's father's boss and they had remained good friends and golf buddies since Bill's retirement.

'Actually, that's a good idea. Grace and I are going to struggle for time to get this moving, and driving out to meet with Bill and Caroline would not be the best use of my time just at present.'

'Consider it done. I'll meet up with him this afternoon at the golf club on the pretence that it would be good to catch up for a beer and to get some golf dates in the diary. I'll send you an email or text to confirm that Bill is aware of what has happened,' concluded the commander as Dan finally made his exit and headed back to his office.

2.15 p.m.

When he returned to his office, Grace stood up and said, 'We have to involve Jack. He is the only one, perhaps with the exception of Kate's grandfather, who has any chance of persuading her to become involved.'

'Those are almost the exact words I have just used with the commander,' said Dan, and he then updated Grace about their conversation.

'Whilst I meet with the team, why don't you discreetly try to find out Jack's contact details?' Dan suggested.

'I've got his telephone number on file, so I'll dig that out. Do you want me to call him or are you thinking a conference call is needed?' asked Grace.

'You get the details and check the time difference, and then we'll have a conference call with him. Not the best way to pass on this type of news but can't be helped, given his location.'

Dan continued, 'I shouldn't be too long as the team have been here before, and Colin will be able to get this off the ground without intervention from me.'

'Okay,' said Grace. 'Can you ask one of them to retrieve my profiling notes from the archives as I would like to read through them this afternoon to refresh my memory.'

The investigation team had already started to arrive when Dan met up with Colin in the conference room.

2.45 p.m.

During the next thirty minutes, Dan had updated them on what had happened, showed them the video, and then handed over to Colin to issue the first set of instructions. He couldn't help but have a feeling of déjà vu as he listened to Colin repeat the instructions that he had issued eight years before.

Colin instructed them to retrieve the files, pull out what may be of any relevance, check the relevant databases over the last eight years using the MO as the search criteria, and start to create a crime board in Dan's conference room, as before. Same MO. Same investigation team. Same procedures to follow. Same need for discretion from other staff in order to avoid the media.

Grace joined them in the conference room and reminded them to retrieve her profiling notes. She also confirmed to Dan that she had Jack's contact details, that Thailand was six hours ahead of the UK, and that Dan's secretary was checking flight times. They agreed that once they had a note of flight times, they would call Jack immediately. Dan and Grace then left Colin to direct the other tasks.

Dan's secretary confirmed that seats were still available that night on the 12.20 a.m. British Airways direct flight from Bangkok with an ETA at London Heathrow at 06.25 a.m. Dan asked her to hold a seat, and he would, hopefully, confirm the booking after his conversation with Jack. He asked her to give him fifteen minutes or so before making the call to Jack and transferring to his conference line.

Dan and Grace took the next fifteen minutes to summarise what Dan was going to say to Jack.

3.30 p.m.

Dan's secretary announced that she had Jack on the line and transferred the call through to Dan.

'Hi, Dan. What's up?' asked Jack.

'Hi, Jack. I'm afraid that this isn't a social call, so I will cut to the chase as we need your assistance.'

'That sounds ominous. Is everyone in the family okay?' asked Jack.

'There is no easy way of saying this, Jack, but I'm afraid that the past has come back to haunt us. It has now been just over eight years since Kate was kidnapped, and I hate having to tell you over a telephone call that it is Beth that has been kidnapped this time. Sorry, Jack.'

'Oh my God! When did this happen and how did you find out about it?' asked Jack.

'Your mother didn't show for an important meeting this morning, and just after lunchtime, a DVD was delivered to my office, showing Beth in the same room and in the same position as Kate was when the *Help me Mum* message was engraved on her lower back. This time, the message is *Help me Kate*. The guy even knows that she has changed her contact name from Katie to Kate,' explained Dan.

'Oh, shit, Dan. I don't know if I can go through this again. But it's Mum that we are talking about, so I have no option. What do you want me to do?' asked Jack.

'I want you to get the next flight out of Thailand to London and to persuade Kate to help us with our enquiries because that is what this message seems to suggest that we need to do. Can you do that?' asked Dan.

'Jeez, throw me in at the deep end, why don't you? Thank goodness that it's a long flight ahead of me as I definitely need one hell of a plan in place before convincing Kate that she should help. Okay, no problem at this end with handing over the responsibility of the scuba-diving school to someone reliable, so I'll check out the flight times and get back to you,' said Jack.

'Thanks, Jack, but there's no need to check out flight times. That's already been done at this end, and we have a seat already in your name waiting for a booking confirmation. You will need to get your skates on because there is a flight from Bangkok Airport at 12.20 a.m., arriving in London early tomorrow morning. You get yourself organised at your end, and we'll book the flight at this end and email the booking reference to you. Just pack your passport and toothbrush as time is against you, and we'll see to everything else at this end. Grace and I will meet you at Heathrow tomorrow morning at 06.25 a.m.,' summarised Dan.

'Organised as ever,' said Jack, followed by a very long sigh. 'I can't believe that we are about to go through all of this again, but I better get off the phone and charge it so that I can talk to you again once I am on my way to the airport. If you're booking flights at your end, I'll need a connecting flight to Bangkok from Koh Samui Airport. There are over a dozen flights a day so that should be manageable. I need to rush if I'm to catch the next ferry over to Koh Samui so I may just have time to grab my passport, after all. Thankfully, I won't have time to think about what has happened to Mum until I am on my flight to London.'

'You do what you have to do, and my secretary will confirm your flight details and booking references. Any problems just call my direct telephone number. By the way, my secretary's name is Penny. Good luck, Jack, and take care.'

Dan gave Jack a note of his direct telephone number and instructed him just to focus on getting to the airport. Dan did suggest that he sleep on the plane as he would need to hit the deck running once he arrived in London and would only have time to freshen up before arranging to meet with Kate.

Dan updated his secretary and asked her to ensure that all arrangements went smoothly to ensure that Jack didn't miss the agreed flights. He also asked her to manage the communication with Jack about times and booking references.

'Okay, Grace. That's one of the important pieces of the jigsaw put in place. How are we going to spend the afternoon?'

'I would like to review my old profiling notes, not that I am expecting to find any fresh clues there. I guess you should contact Matt and then put a plan in place for Jack contacting Kate and having Bill as backup just in case Jack struggles to get Kate to work with us.'

'I'm not inclined to communicate with Matt just now. I'll sort out a fast turnaround for a search warrant for the hospital records, and I'll think about calling him once that is in place.'

CHAPTER 13

Wednesday, 17 October 2012
4.30 p.m.

Grace informed Dan that the team had already managed to get access to the cold case files and had extracted her profiling notes. She flapped two folders at him to suggest that she had her homework ready.

Dan brought her up to speed with his decision about delaying a conversation with Matt, preferring a face-to-face with him.

Colin popped his head around the door just to reassure Dan that the team were now fully employed on Beth's kidnapping and that they would get their recap of the cold case out of the way as quickly as possible. He did ask Dan whether or not they should consider issuing a fresh search warrant that would enable them to conduct a more thorough search of Matt's hospital records. Dan agreed that the original search warrant had limited their search and confirmed that he had already taken it on board to fast track a search warrant.

A tone from Dan's mobile phone indicated that a text message had been received. He updated Colin and Grace. 'The commander has already met and spoken with Bill. He has agreed to return to Bill's house with him so that they can share the news with Caroline. He confirms that Bill is on side to support Jack if needed and Bill has asked that we arrange for Jack to stay at their home rather than a hotel. Excellent! That means that there is no immediate need for us to contact Bill.'

Dan's secretary confirmed that the flights from Koh Samui to Bangkok and from Bangkok to London Heathrow had been booked and that she had sent the relevant details to Jack by email. She gave Dan a note of the Bangkok to London flight and said that she had arranged for a car to collect Dan and Grace at their homes early the next morning. The details were also on the note.

Back in Thailand, Jack was already on the ferry to Koh Samui. He paced up and down as he came to terms with the content of Dan's telephone call. He was a teenager when Kate had been kidnapped and had to grow up fast to cope with all that was going on at that time. He recalled the daily visits to the hospital and dealing with Kate's nightmares and mood swings. Also, he still believed that he carried the scars from experiencing the sudden decline of the family union as he watched his parents' marriage dissolve. He knew that opting to stay in Thailand instead of going to university was an escape at that time for him, and he now dreaded the imminent repeat of the past that was now facing him once again.

Dan had described the video that had been sent to him via DVD, and a flashback to a similar video of Kate made it only too clear to him the position that his mother was in. He didn't want to see photographs of his mother naked, bound and gagged, and God knows what else. In fact, he made up his mind there and then that he would tell Dan that he didn't want to see that or any other video of his mother in a compromising position. The facts, yes, but not the photography.

Jack recalled that Dan had said that the message engraved on his mother's back suggested that the kidnapper wanted Kate to be involved in the search for Beth. He couldn't help but think that if they didn't manage to find the kidnapper first time around, how were they going to change that this time?

It was then that he asked himself whether or not his mother had been the target all along. But, like Dan and Grace, he couldn't begin to think why it had taken the kidnapper just over eight years to shift his attention from the daughter to the mother.

His last thoughts as the ferry boat approached Koh Samui were to consider whether or not his mother's kidnapping may help Kate overcome her nightmares and negative thoughts about her kidnapping and if it may even go some way towards helping mother and daughter rebuild their relationship into something more positive. He refused to think of his mother as being anything other than alive when found.

As he left the ferry boat and headed towards the airport, he wondered if he should call his father. He didn't recall Dan saying anything about being in contact with Matt, so maybe there was a reason for that. He decided to wait until he had met up with Dan and Grace before thinking of how to communicate with his father.

When Jack arrived at Bangkok airport, he had time to pick up some sterling cash and to buy a notepad and pen. He wanted to jot down his thoughts about how he was going to arrange to meet up with Kate and how he was going to persuade her to help Dan and his team find their mother and bring her back to safety. Just as they had for Kate.

Jack boarded the aircraft to London Heathrow on time and immediately started to prepare his strategy for getting Kate to cooperate with Dan and his team. One thing that he was sure of was that he wasn't going to go round and round in circles with her. Time was limited. His mother came first this time.

When he was satisfied with his plan, he allowed himself to sleep to ensure that he was reasonably fresh for the challenges of the day ahead.

Meanwhile, Grace announced to Dan that she was going to take the cold case files home with her as she needed peace and quiet to get through them quickly. She also wanted to pack an overnight bag just in case she didn't have time to go home over the next couple of nights. With that in mind, she suggested to Dan that she stay over at his apartment that evening, which would give them time to update each other on their current thinking and also save time in the morning. Dan agreed. That resolved, Grace left in a taxi to collect her car at her office and then drive to her apartment.

As Grace drove, she started to think about Kate and the negatives and positives about her progress. She had done exceptionally well in her determination to achieve the top grades at university that would earn her a high-quality internship in the city. With the same determination, she was now well on her way to becoming a very successful criminologist and psychologist. Grace had already heard on the grapevine that Kate's career prospects were excellent, and, due to her diligence in court, she was getting the reputation of becoming someone to watch out for in the future.

Only Jack and Grace knew all of this had come at a cost, and they had often discussed negative outcomes that showed no sign of improving. Jack and Grace were the only people that knew the extent of how much Kate continued to blame and hate her mother for what happened to her all those years ago. Grace was privy to the fact that Kate had led a celibate life since the rapes and that her liaisons with men failed miserably at any suggestion of a sexual relationship.

Kate and Grace met up formally once or twice a year to maintain the patient-psychoanalyst relationship. As a result of Grace's absolute discretion during the last eight years and her loyalty to Kate, informally they now enjoyed a warm, friendly, trusting, and mutually valued rapport. The dark cloud was that Grace worried about Kate's inability to care, and she had shared with Kate her belief that she wouldn't be able to experience genuine love in her life until she found a way to start the process of forgiving her mother.

Grace knew the torment that Kate faced daily about her private life. She hadn't had a serious relationship with a man, and she continued to keep her friends at arm's length. She spent too much time on her own and gave the impression that she cherished solitude in preference to socialising.

Grace wondered whether or not the latest news would go some way to changing some of that.

When Grace arrived at her flat, she showered, put on her favourite track suit, and then spread the cold case papers across her dining room table. She was sure that she hadn't missed anything out first time around, but she planned to use the time that she had before driving over to Dan's to review all of it in the hope that something appeared to be more relevant now than it had eight years ago.

By six o'clock, Dan's head was spinning. He was trying so hard to think of something that would point him in the direction of the kidnapper. He couldn't bear the thought of Beth being harmed. No more packages had been received, and he suspected that they wouldn't. If the kidnapper's intention was for them to involve Kate, then he would know that Dan needed time to achieve that. Dan decided to tell the team not to work too late in favour of arriving early in the morning to coincide with the time that he would be collecting Jack.

6.40 p.m.

Dan headed home, changed into casual clothes, and then, like Grace, packed an overnight bag in case he based himself at the office the following evening. He quickly checked that the spare room and bathroom were clean and tidy enough for Grace's overnight stay. He knew that they would be because of the regular service of his loyal housekeeper, who always went beyond the call of duty to ensure that her handsome and generous employer didn't have to include domestic chores in his busy schedule.

Satisfied that Grace would be comfortable, he set about glancing through the contents of the folders that Colin had copied from the cold case files and started a bullet list of the points that he would later discuss with Grace. Normally, he would work in his study, but he needed thinking time. His sitting room had one wall of floor-to-ceiling windows with uninterrupted views of the River Thames and London's city skyline beyond that. This was where he stretched out on the chair and footstool beside the expanse of window, clasped his hands behind his head, and started to focus on how he was going to find Beth.

Beth! Why Beth?
Why the gap of eight years?
Why Kate again?
Speak to Eleanor Marshall about her contact with Kate over the years!
Check which teachers have stayed and left the school.
Is Eddie, the janitor, still there?
Compare MO to last time (review database again).
Matt? Matt's hospital records—search warrant.
Dr Miriam Shepherd's records—anything?

8 p.m.

Dan phoned through a delivery order to his favourite Chinese restaurant and requested that it be delivered at 9 p.m. He opened a bottle of red wine and laid out plates, forks, and serving spoons. Grace liked her food, so, knowing her as well as he did, he fully expected her to want to eat as soon as she arrived. Just in case she had the same thought, he sent her a text, informing her that he had the food covered.

8.50 p.m.

He wasn't wrong. As soon as Grace entered his apartment, her first words were to question when the food was likely to arrive.

As if on cue, the food delivery was announced a few minutes later. Grace set it out on the kitchen breakfast bar, and Dan poured the wine. They ate well and polished off a bottle of wine before moving through to the sitting room to focus on Beth's kidnapping.

Dan started. 'Okay, let's summarise where we are at. During my last call from Colin, he confirmed that there have been no further packages or communications from the kidnapper. The search warrant for the hospital records will be delivered to Colin first thing tomorrow morning. I have arranged meetings with Eleanor Marshall and Miriam Shepherd at 9 a.m. and 10.30 a.m. I want to know which male teachers have left during the last eight years, and I want to pick Miriam's brains to determine if there was anything that Kate may have said during her hospitalisation that could now be regarded as a clue about who the kidnapper is or where he held her captive.'

'That makes sense, but it may be a long shot in both cases. I am sure that the answers that we need to find are either at the school or at the hospital where Matt worked and still works. We both believe that this is about revenge against one or all the Olivers. The school and the hospital are the only links as you have already ruled out Beth's associations with the existing and ex-cons,' added Grace.

'Snap! That's the conclusion that I came to earlier, particularly as Colin has confirmed that they still can't find anything or anyone that we should take a serious interest in. Yes, he and the rest of the team have looked closer at a list of people that came about from a desperate attempt to come up with something. Colin reckons that they are just filling in time with that.'

Dan continued, 'Obviously, one of tomorrow's priorities is for Jack to get Kate on board for whatever reason the kidnapper appears to think that she should be. After we meet Jack, and assuming that he can meet Kate soon after that, can you coordinate the detail of how he handles that and ask him to keep in regular communication with you? We'll also contact Bill in the morning and make sure that he is available to step in if needed.

'That takes care of the Kate-involvement angle. I am going to take Abe to the school with me as he is becoming a very good interviewer. I am going to ask Eleanor to make the personnel files available of the male teachers who were employed at the school eight years ago. I'll leave Abe at the school to review them and to interview anyone who catches his attention. At the hospital, I am going to try to persuade Miriam to release her file notes from the time that Kate was hospitalised. She is never without a notepad and pen and is constantly scribbling notes from conversations, interviews, thoughts, etc. There could be something there that may be relevant to me. I don't think that she would release the notes to anyone else in the team, but she may agree to me scrutinising them in her presence.'

'Actually, Dan, she may be more comfortable with me doing that. Remember that the non-disclosure agreement between Kate and me is still active, so Miriam will know that I can't divulge anything in her notes.'

'I hear where you are coming from, but you need to focus on Jack and Kate. Let's see how I get on with Miriam, and then we can think about how we are going to juggle our time if we need to.'

Dan decided that the plans for the next morning were covered and suggested that they both get some shut-eye before their 5 a.m. collection. Grace didn't argue with that.

'I can't bear the thought of Beth being at the mercy of this kidnapper,' said Dan as they prepared to call it a night. 'He may have become a loose cannon over the last eight years, and he may have more courage now to practise more of the evil thoughts that are going through his warped mind.'

'She must be drugged as she has received extensive one-to-one training in self-defence and can handle herself very well in combat. She is also very fit. I'm wondering how he managed to kidnap her in the first place, strip her, and bind her ankles and wrists to the bed frame,' responded Grace.

'Yes, there is no way that he would achieve that if she hadn't been drugged. Goodnight, Grace.'

Beth's sedative was actually wearing off at the time that Dan and Grace were having this conversation. It didn't take her long to realise that she was bound, gagged, and blindfolded. When she realised that she was lying on her stomach, she had the sudden realisation that this was one of the positions that Kate's kidnapper had photographed and sent to her via Dan.

What are the chances? She thought, as she realised that her lower back was aching.

Oh my God, it couldn't be, could it?

Oh shit, don't tell me that he has used my back as a message board as he did with Kate.

She didn't have time to give that any more thought as the kidnapper entered the room, realised that the sedative was wearing off, and sedated her once again. Beth couldn't do anything or say anything to register her objection to that happening to her.

She couldn't see her kidnapper. If she had, he would have surely reminded her of another image that had stayed with her all of those years. The image of Kate's kidnapper had never left her. The man in black and his voice were as clear to her then as they had been all that time ago.

If she hadn't been blindfolded, she would have seen that her kidnapper was indeed a man in black. She would have seen that her kidnapper was wearing the dark clothing, black balaclava, dark glasses, and disposable gloves that had been worn by Katie's kidnapper eight years ago. She would also register that she was on a hospital bed and in a room that was all too familiar to her.

CHAPTER 14

Thursday, 18 October 2012
5 a.m.

Dan's driver from the MET arrived as scheduled to take Grace and Dan to Heathrow airport to meet Jack. He confirmed to Dan that the flight from Bangkok was on schedule.

06.30 a.m.

Jack's flight had arrived twenty minutes early, and Dan and Grace were there to meet him after he had made his way through customs, travelling light with his hand luggage.

'What's the latest on Mum?' was obviously the first thing that Jack said.

Dan passed on the little update that he had as they walked to the MET car again, and Dan gave the driver instructions to make his way to Bill and Caroline Palmer's address.

'I'm guessing that I am going to be staying with my grandparents, which must mean that they have been updated with my arrival and the reason why,' said Jack.

'Correct on both counts,' replied Dan. 'As soon as Bill heard about your arrival, he insisted that you stay with them rather than book into a hotel. That's probably for the best because it will make communication easier. Talking of communication, I still haven't spoken to Matt, so can you hold back in telling him that you are in the country and also make that clear to Kate when you speak to her later?'

'No problem,' said Jack. 'What's the plan for this morning?'

'Once we get you settled at your grandparents, you should call Kate and, hopefully, be able to meet up with her this morning at some point. I've got meetings arranged with Eleanor Marshall and Miriam Shepherd, so Grace is going to be your contact and mentor for now. You need to make sure that you keep her appraised of your progress or lack of it. Bill is on standby in case he needs to join you or meet up with Kate separately.'

Jack and Grace checked that their respective contact details were up to date, and Grace squeezed one of Jack's hands and said, 'I understand how you feel, and I will be there for you all of the way. Don't hold back on me. Okay?'

'Okay,' replied Jack. 'I am dreading going through all of this again.'

'We know,' said Dan.

7.45 a.m.

They arrived at the Palmers' house. Dan asked the driver to wait for further instruction. The reunion of grandson and grandparents was very emotional. Dan used the time before Jack calling Kate to bring them all up to speed with his plans for the morning and confirmed that there had been no more deliveries of packages from the kidnapper.

8.30 a.m.

Jack called Kate.

'Hi, Sis. You will never guess who this is?' was Jack's opening comment.

'Unless I am very much mistaken and given that you called me Sis, I am guessing that this must be my one and only brother Jack,' replied Kate.

With great difficulty at restraining the emotion that he felt, Jack continued, 'Ah, but can you guess where I am just now?'

'No, Jack, I can't guess where you are,' she responded sarcastically, 'but I'm guessing that you are not in Koh Tao in Thailand, given the cloak and dagger chat so far.'

Grace was the only person in the room with him, but she could see that he was having great difficulty in keeping the casual conversation flowing. She gesticulated in a way that said *Come on, you can do this.*

'Well, I have just arrived at Heathrow airport. A friend of mine told me that he was travelling to London to attend a family wedding and that, combined with Mum reminding me that I hadn't visited her for a while, led to me making a last-minute decision to catch the midnight flight from Bangkok.'

'You are, of course, first on my list of invitations, so how about brunch or lunch today?' asked Jack with his fingers crossed. 'You choose the venue, and I'll pay.'

'How could a girl resist such a passionate plea for her company and at such short notice? Jack, you really do have to learn to have a better play on words if you are going to charm the girls. I am on my way to a breakfast meeting, and then I have two meetings scheduled at my office after that. I can't change the first one, but I could postpone the second, so how about lunch?'

'Terrific,' replied Jack. 'Just send me a text with an address, and I'll meet you there at, say, 12.30 p.m.'

'I can do that. Looking forward to seeing you. Love you,' said Kate.

'Love you back,' said Jack.

Grace patted Jack on the back. 'Well done, Jack. I know how difficult that must have been for you, but mind over matter works wonders in situations like this. You knew that you had to stay strong, and so you were.'

As they made their way back to the sitting room, Jack received a text message from Kate.

> *Really pleased that you are home for a break. Looking forward to our catch-up. I need to be close to my office for an afternoon appointment, so let's meet in the lounge of the Chancery Court Hotel in Holborn at some point between 12 and 1230.*
>
> *Love Kate, xx*

Jack was visibly shaken as he updated Dan and his grandparents. His grandfather walked over to him and said, 'I know that this is going to be a difficult time for you, Jack. It's going to be a difficult time for all of us. But as before, we will be there for each other, and I will personally stay close to help you through this.'

'Okay, there isn't much time as you will, no doubt, want to have some breakfast, perhaps rest, and then freshen up before you leave. Bill, can I trust you to discuss a strategy with Jack and then drive him to somewhere close to the hotel in Holborn? After that, I suggest that you join Grace at the MET so that you can collaborate about his updates or request for support. Jack, remember the laptop because you need to show Kate the video that the kidnapper sent to us. Hopefully, that will be sufficient to shock her into agreeing to our request.'

Jack didn't argue. He had no intention of looking at the video of his mother, but his sister may be able to. Dan continued, 'I will arrange for Rachel to keep Caroline company after you leave for Holborn, and she will stay here until either of you returns.'

'Any questions?' asked Dan.

None were asked.

Not knowing what to do, Caroline said, 'Let's get a decent breakfast inside of you before you do anything else.'

As Caroline left the room, she turned to Dan and asked quietly, 'Will we get our daughter back, Dan?'

It was Bill who answered as he put a comforting arm around her. 'Of course, we will, my dear. Dan and his team will make sure that we do. We got Kate back, didn't we? And we'll get Beth back safely too.' Bill addressed his wife with all the strength that he could muster and with more confidence than he felt.

Everyone knew that these were words of comfort, but they seemed to help Caroline at the time.

9 a.m.

Dan and Grace left just as Dan realised that he was running late for his appointment with Eleanor Marshall at the school.

'How about joining me for my interview with Eleanor?' he asked Grace. 'I am hoping to persuade her to authorise our access to the employee files of the male teachers that were employed at the school at the time of Kate's kidnapping.'

Beth agreed, preferring to keep herself busy with meeting people who may provide her with any clues about the kidnapper than to profile with no leads.

Dan said, 'Sorry, mate,' to the driver, 'but we are going to be all over the place this morning. I had planned to pick up my car, but it hasn't worked out that way.'

'No problem, Chief,' replied the driver. 'I don't have anyone else to drive this morning, so I am at your service at least until lunchtime.'

'Good,' said Dan. 'That will definitely help me to fit in all that I need to this morning. It's going to be a busy one.'

Dan called his office to ask his secretary to phone ahead to forewarn Eleanor that they would be late, say no later than 9.30

a.m. but confirmed that they would still make the appointment with Miriam at 11 a.m.

'They?' queried Grace.

Dan laughed. 'Well, as you agreed so quickly to meet with Eleanor, I assumed that you would not want to miss the chance of listening to me quizzing Miriam.'

'Put it that way, how could I argue?' replied Grace.

Dan called the MET again and asked to be put through to Colin.

He updated Colin and confirmed that he and Grace were on their way to the school and then on to the hospital. Colin confirmed that the search warrant had arrived, that there hadn't been any deliveries, and that he had nothing new to report since they last spoke.

Dan asked to be put on to speaker phone so that he could summarise his instructions to Colin and the rest of the team.

'We now have the search warrant, so it's time to head over to the hospital. Penny is checking whether or not Matt is on duty. I'm not going to meet with him as I have more important things to do this morning. Colin, take Sophie and Pete with you and present the search warrant to the hospital administrator, who will then, no doubt, alert Matt. When you first meet him, take him to one side and tell him that Beth has been kidnapped et cetera. Don't waste much time, listening to any resistance that he has to the search of his files and diaries. You need to get started quickly, you need to work fast, and you need to dig deep.

'Abe, I am hoping that Eleanor Marshall will agree to your examination of the employee files of the male teachers who were employed at the school on the evening of Kate's kidnapping. If she agrees, I will call you, and you can head over there with Rachel. Hopefully, it won't take too long as you will then need to drop Rachel off at the Palmers' so that she can comfort Caroline when Bill drives Jack to meet with Kate.

'Grace is accompanying me this morning, firstly at the school and then with Dr Shepherd at the hospital. Bill will drive Jack to the

Chancery Court Hotel to meet Kate and then meet up with Grace and me at the MET to await progress reports from Jack and perhaps a request for Bill's assistance if Kate isn't cooperating.

'All of this could change by the hour based on Kate's decision, potential leads, or the receipt of another package from the kidnapper. You know how it works, so just do as much as you can as quickly as you can and be flexible.

'Okay. I think that covers everything. Hopefully, everyone understands who is going to be where and what each person is going to be responsible for. Any questions?'

'No, Chief,' was the united response that Dan wanted to hear.

'Okay. Go to it,' said Dan before hanging up.

No sooner had he done that than his secretary called to say that Matt was at the hospital. Dan asked her to relay that message to Colin.

'Why have you decided not to tell Matt personally about Beth?' asked Grace.

'Firstly, we are genuinely up against the clock this morning, and, secondly, he was distinctly uncooperative with us after Kate had been found. And, if I am being pedantic, he really pissed me off in the way he treated Beth and the Palmers during the aftermath of the kidnapping. Are you aware that he hasn't been in touch with the Palmers since he and Beth got divorced and he moved on to pastures new?'

'Yeah, you're quite right. Leave him to Colin, who will be absolutely impartial to his feelings.'

9.30 a.m.

Dan and Grace arrived at the school just in the nick of time to meet Eleanor Marshall at the rescheduled time.

'Thank goodness that we managed to get through all those instructions in the car as it has saved us time, and I know that Colin will manage all of it without the need for further discussion,' said Dan.

'Hello, Dan and Grace,' said Eleanor Marshall as she walked towards them in the corridor outside her office. 'I just wish that it was under different circumstances.'

They exchanged greetings as they walked towards her office and took the seats in front of her desk.

'Now, how can I help you?' she asked as she poured the tea that had been set out for them.

'I'll come straight to the point, Eleanor, as we are up against the clock this morning. I have three requests for you. Firstly, it is no secret that Kate meets with you regularly, and, after we leave this morning, I would like you to go back in time and give careful thought to the conversations that you have had with her. If there is anything that she has said that could be perceived as a clue about her kidnapper's identity or the location of where he kept her captive, I want to know about it. Secondly, I want an updated list of the male teachers who were employed at the school at the time of Kate's kidnapping with a highlight against those who have since left. Thirdly, I want your authorisation to access the employee records of the names on that list and review them under your supervision. And I want to do that this morning. The records will not leave the premises.'

'I will, of course, cooperate in any way that I can. The second request is easy. I feel that I should speak with Kate about the first request before taking that further. And I am struggling with your third request under the terms of the Data Protection Act,' she replied.

'Just as I expected. Of course, you should speak to Kate to let her know that, due to Beth's kidnapping, we have asked you if you are aware of anything new that should come to our attention. Regarding our third request, you know that we can both be covered by a search warrant, but I won't have that until this afternoon, and who knows what could happen to Beth during that time. You have my word that I will arrange for a search warrant dated today to be delivered to you to cover you. In the meantime, all I am asking is that we read the files in your presence and that we will not copy anything until you have received the search warrant.'

'Put it that way, I agree to assist you with your three requests,' said Eleanor. 'I just can't believe that history is repeating itself. What has this family done to deserve this?'

'Thanks, Eleanor. Now if you don't mind, I am going to make a call so that two of the people on my team leave the office immediately to meet with you. It will be Abe Hunter and Rachel Clark. It shouldn't take them much more than an hour. By the way, is Eddie, the janitor, still with you?' asked Dan.

'Yes, he is. I agreed to that on condition that he told the teachers about his photo album, destroyed all the photographs, and got the blessing from the teachers to stay on. He did all of that without question. These days, we allow him to take photographs for our school publications, and obviously we allow him to keep copies of the finished articles. I have explained the difference to him between invasion of privacy and access to materials that are in the public domain,' replied Eleanor.

'Good. His actions certainly didn't come across as being sinister, and he has a genuine care for his job and the pupils for the right reasons,' said Dan.

They said their goodbyes, and Eleanor promised to have the employee list and the employee files ready for Abe's arrival. She also agreed to call Dan direct if she thought of anything that could be helpful to his enquiries after speaking with Kate.

On the way to their car, Dan called the office to confirm the instructions to Abe and asked him to update Colin by telephone.

10.30 a.m.

On the way to meet with Miriam, Dan received a text from Colin to say that the warrant had been presented and that they were now on their way to an office to start their inspection of the files and diaries that related to Matt and his patients.

11 a.m.

Dan and Grace arrived on time for their scheduled meeting with Dr Miriam Shepherd. She was delighted to see them both and enquired after Kate, via Grace. Dan explained the reason for their meeting and, as with Eleanor, asked if she would spare some time to contemplate whether or not Kate had ever said anything to her after the kidnapping that could now be considered as a possible lead to the kidnapper or the location of the kidnapping. She agreed to that but was more reserved at agreeing to Dan's team examining the case notes on Kate's hospital file. Once again, Dan repeated what he had said to Eleanor about the search warrant, discretion, and research with supervision. Eventually, she agreed to review the notes with Grace in the first instance, and Dan accepted that as progress. A time for later that day was pencilled in their respective diaries, but Grace forewarned Miriam that this could change if she had to attend to other leads or if another package was received from the kidnapper.

'Dan or Grace, please keep me updated with your progress. Poor Beth. In fact, poor Beth's family. I hope that she is returned safely and that you get to the bottom of who is doing this and why once and for all.'

'We will, Miriam,' said Grace.

'Oh, and it goes without saying that you should call me on my personal phone as soon as Beth is found, and I will see to it that I am on duty when she is admitted to my ward.'

'Thanks. That's good to know at this stage as it is one less thing to think about,' replied Grace.

Midday

Dan and Grace arrived back at the MET, and, before making their way to Dan's office, he checked to see if any packages had arrived for him during the course of the morning. He didn't know if he was relieved or anxious at the negative response.

On entering the conference room, Dan couldn't help but notice that it was empty, that there was a lack of activity, and that the crime boards were almost empty. Grace read his mind and said, 'Beth is going to be okay, Dan. You will find her, and you will ensure that she is returned to her family safely. I just have a feeling that we are all going to be tested more this time in advance of that happening.'

Shortly after that, Bill arrived at the office and confirmed that he had dropped Jack off in a street close to the hotel.

'He looked dreadful. I know that it's been eight years, but he looked so much older today as he made his way to meet Kate. I couldn't help but think that I should have been with him.'

'We all agreed that seeing you there with Jack may have an adverse reaction on Kate, and we would get off to a bad start if that were the case,' said Grace.

Silence.

'This is definitely the same kidnapper, isn't it?' asked Bill.

'Yes. We are very certain that it is,' replied Dan.

'Why the hell would he wait eight years to make a comeback?' Bill questioned.

'I am trying to figure that one out, but, like the last time, we don't have any leads. We just have to hope that he needs closure as much as we do, whatever that may be for him. Nothing is going to happen whilst we go through the process of getting Kate on our investigation team, which is why we have only received the one package. We have used that time this morning to trigger actions that may give us something new to work with,' replied Dan.

'Have you told Matt yet?' asked Bill.

'Not personally, but Colin spoke with him at the same time as he presented the search warrant to the hospital's administrator,' replied Dan. 'I really don't have a compelling need to speak with Matt, and my time with Grace this morning has been more constructive than that would have been.'

'Just save my daughter for me, Dan,' as an uncharacteristic tear rolled down Bill's cheek. 'I don't think that I would cope with having to watch Caroline's reaction to hearing that she had lost her daughter. I know that you will do all that you can to prevent that from happening.'

'You know me well enough, Bill, that I will do everything in my power to return Beth safely back to her family, friends, and colleagues. None of us want to lose her. I don't have any intention of allowing that to happen. I also don't know how I would cope without her in my life.'

Dan had to hide his own emotional state from Bill and Grace as he realised that he also didn't want to lose the woman that he loved—the woman that he would so dearly wish to spend the rest of his life with.

'I do know one thing, and that is, as much as I love my granddaughter, I am not going to sit back while she procrastinates about whether or not she can, or is prepared, to join the investigation team. I'll give Jack thirty minutes with her before I want an update. If he is struggling to get a positive response from her, then no one is going to stop me from heading for the hotel and making it very clear to that young lady that her grandparents *expect* her to confirm that she *will* help us to find my daughter.'

Dan couldn't argue with that because he felt exactly the same himself.

'And, if that doesn't work, I have a few ideas up my sleeve that should bring her around to our way of thinking,' added a very determined-looking Grace.

'This isn't about Kate this time. It is about Beth,' she added.

'I agree,' said Dan.

'Caroline said the same thing to me,' added Bill.

'And I have absolutely no doubt that either Grace or Caroline would be an adversary that Kate would not want to upset,' replied Dan, feeling more confident that one way or another Kate would be part of the investigation team before the day was over.

CHAPTER 15

Thursday, 18 October 2012
12.15 p.m.

Matt was outraged that Dan had arranged a search warrant and approached the hospital's administrator without discussing it with him first. He was also less than impressed that Dan hadn't told him personally about Beth's kidnapping and decided to call him and tell him so.

Dan took Matt's call, expecting him to express his concern about Beth's kidnapping. He didn't. Instead, he hurled a load of abuse at Dan about the search warrant. After listening to a barrage of abusive language, Dan didn't mince the words in his response. He told Matt that he was less than impressed with his handling of the requests for his cooperation the first time around and that he wasn't prepared to leave anything to chance a second time. He closed by saying that he expected Matt to give Colin and the rest of the team his full cooperation.

No response.

'You do realise that this isn't about getting at you, Matt. It is about finding Beth alive,' said Dan.

Matt had no answer to that either, and their call didn't end on good terms, but Dan made sure that he reiterated to Matt that from that point onwards, he would expect his cooperation throughout the search warrant process. He also added that it was vital that he did not call Jack or Kate at a time that would be in conflict with their handling of a sensitive topic. Thankfully, Matt agreed to that, and they bid their goodbyes.

Dan updated Grace and Bill with the content of his telephone conversation with Matt, much of which they got the gist of from the tone of Dan's one-way part of the conversation.

12.30 p.m.

'Oh well, Jack will be with Kate now,' said Dan. 'Bill, you need to be prepared to make your way to the hotel if Jack calls for your help. I'll organise a taxi for you to avoid the stress of parking if that happens.'

Dan then spoke aloud to himself, but Grace and Bill tuned in anyway.

'Rachel will be with Caroline by now. Abe will still be at the school with Eleanor, and we should hear about how that went soon. Colin, Sophie, and Pete are at the hospital, and I expect that they will be there most of the day, going through a couple of decades' worth of records and diaries. Jack is with Kate. We are sitting here like spare parts just at present, but I can't juggle anyone around until we hear back from Jack. I've already instructed Abe to join Colin and his team as soon as he is finished at the school and to give me a brief update before he leaves.

'Oh, I almost forgot. That leaves the kidnapper. And it's anyone's guess what that bastard is up to at present. Grace, do you think that he will use the same form with Beth as he did with Kate?' asked Dan.

'The obvious difference is that Beth is so much older and stronger than Kate. That could be good or bad. Good because he may be inhibited by her age, strength, and confidence. Bad because he may feel less inhibited at inflicting pain on her. Are you okay at hearing this, Bill?' she replied.

'Yes. I now know how Beth must have felt when she was at this office, trying desperately to hear or see something that could help her find her daughter. I now realise that the determination to succeed in that gives you the inner strength that you need to cope with the personal aspect of it. Carry on,' said Bill.

And they did spend the time going through everything again and second-guessing what may be going on with Beth.

12.30 p.m.

Jack was very nervous because he understood the importance of the challenge facing him with his sister. As soon as he had arrived at the hotel, he had visited the restaurant and booked a corner table that provided the most privacy.

Jack's jaw dropped as he stood up to catch Kate's attention and watch her make her way through the reception area towards him. She looked absolutely stunning, and he couldn't help but notice the turning heads as she walked straight into Jack's arms.

Kate was wearing a perfectly tailored black woollen jacket. Her classically designed black slacks were cut with a straight leg that showed off the long legs of her 5'8" height. As always, her accessories were understated but perfectly matched to complement her outfit, and she carried one of her trademark oversized shoulder bags.

Jack sighed inwardly as he knew that she didn't acknowledge the regular compliments that she received about her beauty or her dress sense. Despite the sadness that she hid, except to her family, she managed to maintain impeccable taste in her choice of clothing and accessories.

They decided to go straight to their table in the restaurant. He had already asked the head waiter to ensure that they weren't disturbed after lunch had been served. When he saw who Jack's guest was, he couldn't help but note that they were a very handsome couple.

Jack and Kate chatted about her work and the ongoing success of his scuba-diving school until Jack couldn't contain himself any longer.

'I need your help, Sis,' he suddenly interrupted the flow of conversation.

'That sounds ominous, Jack,' replied Kate, 'but you know that I'm a sucker for attending to my big brother's needs. Have you got a girlfriend problem? Oh, don't tell me that you want to settle down. Is that it?'

'I wish it were that simple, Kate. I need you to help me help Mum.'

Silence.

'It must be something very serious for you to travel over from Thailand at such short notice.'

'It is,' replied Jack.

'Is she ill?' Kate bounced back, immediately showing signs of agitation.

'No, but her life is in danger.'

'Jack, I have no emotional reaction to that. I have barely spoken to her in eight years and have even successfully managed to avoid coming up against her in court. Even event organisers know better than to sit me next to her at a formal function.'

'Kate, I love you very much, but you also know that I love our mother dearly. Please don't take a back seat in helping us find her kidnapper or potential killer.'

'Us? Kidnapper? Killer? Jack, what's going on? Why don't you start at the beginning and be entirely honest with me. As your sister, that much I am prepared to listen to but only after we have eaten some food. I'm ravenous.'

As Kate ate her lunch and Jack played about with the food on his plate, he summarised the copycat kidnapping and stressed that both Dan and Grace were of the opinion that Beth's life is in danger.

Kate listened. Jack is already concerned that his sister is looking unemotional or at least making an excellent pretence of being so. But then suddenly she started to ask relevant questions, and he thought to himself that perhaps all was not lost.

They had decided just to have one course and a bottle of wine. Jack wasn't in the mood for anything to eat or drink but went along with it as he was encouraged that she was staying relatively calm as she asked more questions.

Kate excused herself to go to the ladies' cloakroom and Jack seized this opportunity to text Dan to advise him that the chat was going better than he originally anticipated.

Jack did not anticipate what happened next.

Kate returned from the cloakroom and took her seat. She leaned over the table and took Jack's right hand before she delivered the blow. Dispassionately she said, 'Sorry but count me out. I really don't want anything to do with this. I have spent the best part of my life trying to rationalise what happened to me eight years ago. I have never tried to forgive Mum because I actually don't want to. Now I think that I should head back to the office and that we should meet up later after Beth has been found.'

Jack tried everything from pleading with her to emotional blackmail, but she wasn't for changing her mind. He also couldn't help but notice that she regularly referred to their mother as Mum one minute and then Beth the next. *Another sign of her confusion*, he thought.

Sensing that she was about to leave again, he knew that he needed to find a way to keep her at the restaurant so that his grandfather could get there in time to make her see sense.

'I don't see you often, Kate, so I don't want you walking out on me. At least finish our bottle of wine and then have some coffee with me. I promise not to mention Mum's kidnapping again,' he almost pleaded.

'Okay, but let's keep the conversation light, eh?' she asked.

'But first it is my turn to pay a visit to the toilet.'

Phew, he thought to himself. He really wanted to get angry with her, but his mother's life was at stake, and he knew that Kate would have left the restaurant if he hadn't changed his tactic.

Jack sent a short text to Bill saying, 'You are needed. Get over here quickly as she is about to leave.'

'That's it,' said Bill to Dan. 'I'm on duty. I need to get there very quickly as, according to Jack, Kate is about to leave.'

'The taxi will be outside by the time that you make your way to the front door. There is always one on standby. Good luck,' said Dan.

'If you need me, call me,' added Grace.

Bill left.

Jack took his time in returning to the table and then held on to the wine bottle for a while before topping up their glasses. He had to stall for time, and so he poured the wine and then said to Kate, 'I have heard about the amazing progress that you are making with your career. It's now time for me to share with you some of my stories from my humble abode.'

'I'd like that,' laughed Kate. 'Your amazing tan certainly makes me feel pale and unhealthy.'

Jack didn't know how he did it, but he managed to keep her at the table with a selection of humorous stories. She was particularly interested in the stories about his voluntary work with the children. In fact, at one point, she said that she would really like to visit him for a few weeks and visit the school with him.

1.25 p.m.

Just when Jack was worried that he was going to run out of stories, he caught sight of his granddad out of the corner of his eye.

As Bill approached their table, he decided that he had no intention of taking *no* as an answer. Remembering how his wife had looked in the early hours of the morning, sitting in her favourite armchair with a handkerchief in one hand and a photograph of their daughter in the other, was incentive enough for him to get the result they both needed.

Kate hadn't noticed her grandfather approaching but realised what Jack had done when she heard his voice. 'Hello, sweetheart. Do you have a few moments to speak with your old granddad?'

For a moment, she forgot why she was there as she jumped out of her seat and hugged Bill. 'I am always available to speak with you, Granddad. How is Gran?' It was then that she realised the reality of the situation and how daft that question was.

'Kate, you know why I am here. Your gran is at home, crying her eyes out and looking completely lost because she doesn't know whether or not she will ever see her daughter alive again. We don't have time for pleasantries.'

Bill continued, 'Jack, can you leave us alone, please? There is a taxi outside, expecting you. You make your way back to the MET and tell Dan that I will catch up with you all later.'

Jack was about to argue that he would prefer to stay, but the look on his granddad's face changed his mind. He knew then that he didn't want Jack to hear what he was going to say to Kate.

Jack pecked his sister's cheek and started to leave the restaurant, feeling very subdued. Bill caught up with him and said, 'I'll have the laptop, please.' Jack gave it to him, knowing then that his grandfather had no intention of leaving without a positive response from Kate.

Bill picked up where he had left.

'Kate, you are intelligent enough to know that this isn't a social call. I am here because Jack hasn't been able to persuade you help us find Beth. What do you have to say to that?'

'Oh, Granddad, you of all people know that what they ask of me is impossible for me to do.'

'Nothing is impossible, Kate. But what is possible is that we could lose Beth to the same man who kidnapped and raped you. We don't know why he has come back to haunt us all, and we still don't know why he picked you in the first place.'

Kate was silent and Bill decided to leave it that way for as long as Kate could stand it.

'I trust you, Gramps.'

'Kate, your gran suffered a great deal of pain when you were kidnapped, and we have continued to suffer because you and your mother have lost the wonderful mother-daughter relationship that you both enjoyed and treasured. I don't have to tell you how we would feel if we lost our daughter.

'I don't like using emotional blackmail, so I am going to appeal to your professionalism. It pains me to ask for your cooperation, but my daughter may be facing death, and I have to do all that I can to save her even if that means putting pressure on you to work with Dan and his team. You are so professional in what you do that I know that you can do this. I know that you can put mind over matter in order to deliver justice. That's what you do, after all. This time, I am asking you to do your job for your brother and for your grandparents.'

Silence from Kate again.

Bill continued undeterred, 'I believe that you know in your heart of hearts that your mother must have been to hell and back when you were kidnapped. What has happened to her now has made me realise that, for your own good, it is time to stop treating you with kid gloves. What happened to you will never go away from our memories, and we have been there for you every step of the way. We understand how you feel, but you have to turn a corner so that you can start to build a future for yourself. I'm sure that Grace will have told you that over and over again. For some reason, our family is being challenged again, and perhaps this is the time for you to start to think about burying the past and considering the future.'

And still Kate had nothing to say.

'Kate, you are a criminologist, and that person cannot walk away from the situation that we are in. You need closure on this as much as we all do. Your relationship with your mother is one thing, but your oath to the Crown is another, isn't it?'

Bill knew that he was stepping over a line that the family had agreed a very long time ago. He also knew that he had no option but to continue saying what must be said.

'We need your sharp-witted and judicious criminal mind to help us find your mother, my daughter.'

'There. I have said what I have come to say to you.'

Bill stopped speaking, and, at that moment, Kate saw the tears in her grandfather's eyes and knew that, regardless of her own feelings, she could not turn her back on the grandparents that she loved with all her heart.

'Gramps, you know that I blame my mother for what happened to me. You know that I will never be able to forgive her. I'm sure that Gran has told you that I haven't had a sexual relationship with a man. I don't see marriage and children as something that I will ever be able to have.'

'Oh, Kate. Don't say those things. You are a young beautiful woman. Please don't rule out marriage and family because that is exactly what you need to aim for so that you can start to feel the feelings that a mother has for her children. You have deprived your mother from the single most important thing in her life, and that was her family. Your dad walked out on her, and you have been unable to forgive her for something that may have been planned to happen anyway. I would like to save this part of our conversation for another day as I think it's time for your old grandparents to spend some quality time with you to help you understand the meaning of life itself.'

Bill continued, 'In the meantime, you are making decisions without giving any thought to the opportunities that you should be considering for your future happiness. There are many choices open to you that you haven't even considered.'

They both took a moment to absorb what the other had said, and it was Kate who spoke first.

'All of that aside, I will help you for two reasons. Firstly, I cannot knowingly do anything that would hurt you or Gran, and, secondly, you are right, I have a duty to try to save Beth.'

Bill noticed that she didn't say *mother* this time, but he didn't care, for now. He knew that he had Kate on his side.

'However, I have a few conditions, and it is up to you to ensure that Dan and Grace understand them fully as they are absolutely not up for negotiation.

'One. I will only work directly with you and Jack, assuming that Jack is staying in the UK until Beth is found.'

'Two. I should be copied into all new communication and should receive a copy of all documentation considered to be relevant from the past. I will only discuss the content of any of this documentation with you.

'Three. I will not attend briefing meetings, but I will comment on related notes by email. I will also be prepared to listen into conference calls and meetings and to email my comments after them.

'Four. I will not be in attendance when Beth is found, be she alive or dead, and I do not want her to know that I have helped to find her if it is the former.

'Five. The family must not think that this is a step in the right direction towards the reconciliation of a broken mother-and-daughter relationship.'

'Kate . . .' Bill started.

'Granddad, take it or leave it.'

Bill knew that he had moved mountains to reach this far, so he quickly decided to quit whilst he was ahead. To himself, however, he made a promise that, should his daughter come out of this alive, he and Caroline would invite Beth and Kate to their home to have an open and honest conversation about feelings.

'Thank you, Kate. You are doing the right thing for your family. I will pass all of this on to Dan, but my priority is to update your grandmother, who is on tenterhooks waiting for my call. You have my word that we will honour your conditions, and I will personally ensure that no one in the investigation team will betray our mutual trust.'

After they exchanged the email and telephone contact details to be used during the investigation and after Bill had called Caroline with the news, they agreed not to discuss the matter any further that day.

Instead, he asked her to promise that she would spend some time with him and Caroline after all of this was over.

'I would love to, Gramps. Please tell Gran that I love her and will do all that I can professionally to return her daughter to her. Gran is a wonderful person, and you are a lucky man.'

Before Bill left, he asked Kate how her career was developing. She told Bill that she had been told by the senior partners that she was going to be considered for junior partner training at her next performance review.

'That comes as no surprise to me. It should be a reminder to you that you can do anything that you put your mind to.' He winked at her teasingly.

Kate hailed a taxi to her office, unsure of what her emotions were at that moment of time.

Bill took a taxi back to the MET.

2.30 p.m.

Bill called Dan with an update and a note of his arrival time.

After that, Dan decided that Bill and Jack should go home to update Caroline and to spend some time together as a family, whilst Dan and his team worked hard to find Beth.

When Bill met up with Dan and Grace, he told them not to spare Kate with any detail about the comparisons that they discussed about the two crimes.

'From this point forward, no one should think of Kate as a victim. She is an astute criminologist. So, in order to get the very best that Kate is capable of giving, she should be treated as any other professional on the team,' he added.

By this time, Colin, Abe, Sophie, and Pete were still at the hospital, and Dan didn't want to pull any of them back from what they were doing. Bill didn't argue with him when he instructed that he and Jack should go home. He then called Rachel to ask her to tell Caroline that Bill and Jack were on their way home and asked her to return to the office to pull together a documentation package to send over to Kate.

3 p.m.

Still no communication from the kidnapper.

'What the hell is going on, Grace? Why no packages this time? When Kate was kidnapped, at one point, we received three packages in as many hours. Should we be nervous about this change in his MO?'

'I am as confused as you are. How will he know that Kate is on board, and why is that relevant to him? Unless we get something back from the team, we are going to have to start from scratch. What on earth could be his motive? He will contact us again, but with what? I just don't see him raping Beth. To be honest, I don't see him getting it up for that to happen. Kate was young and vulnerable. Beth is mature and extremely capable of handling herself. He will know all about that if he ever takes the tape off her mouth.'

'I agree. He will see that for himself, and she will be sedated regularly just as Kate was. But what does he want to do with her? What is he capable of doing? Jesus Christ, Grace, this is the most frustrating case that I have ever had. Have we missed something in Beth's past?'

'I don't think so as the team spent hour after hour last time going through her criminal files and came up with nothing. Our kidnapper is just not a match for the hardened criminals that Beth has been responsible for putting behind bars,' said Grace.

'Yeah, I know. Abe and Rachel didn't come up with anything from their review of the school's employee records so we have to hope that something will come out of the hospital records, or we are left with nothing.'

As Dan and Beth were pondering their options, the kidnapper was also pondering his next move. He smiled inwardly as he thought about their efforts to get Kate to cooperate with the criminal investigation team. He did know that the grandfather had now succeeded in achieving that, but the detectives at the MET would never know how that had been possible, and he wasn't about to tell them.

Instead, he started to prepare Beth for the next step in a journey of unjust revenge. He wondered how the Oliver family would react to what he now had in mind for Beth.

CHAPTER 16

Thursday, 18 October 2012
3 p.m.

It had taken the distance of the ride from the hotel to her office for Kate to recover from the emotional farewell to her grandfather. As she had approached her office, it was then that she remembered that she had a scheduled meeting with one of the partners.

She had the meeting and then told him that she needed some time off work because her mother had been kidnapped. Yes, that's how she put it to him. Even as one of the few partners who were privy to Kate's past, he was shocked at how calm she appeared to be. He played along with her. She wouldn't have wanted it any other way.

As soon as she had mentioned the kidnapping, and knowing who her mother was, he insisted that she take compassionate leave until her mother had been returned safely to the family.

'If she is returned safely to the family,' Kate muttered almost to herself as she left the office to meet with her secretary. They attended to some admin matters, and Kate issued instructions about the changes that needed to be made to her meeting schedules. She then excused herself for the rest of the day.

Kate lived in a two-storey townhouse in Parsons Green, South West London, which her grandparents shared a financial interest in. Kate didn't want to take money from them, but they told her to regard it as an advance of the financial gift that would be left to her in their joint last will and testament. The result was a legal arrangement that was witnessed by Beth as the executor of their will.

Kate loved her house from the moment that she arrived to view it. The location was perfect because of its proximity to the Kings Road for shopping, its walking distance to the parks, and the good selection of small restaurants, bars, and coffee shops. It was also convenient for her to commute to work by tube or bus.

The purchase of her share of her home was her first major investment. The monthly mortgage payments were onerous, but she got personal gratification from the constant monthly reminder that she had been able to achieve this from her own hard work at university and success at work. It also gave her the incentive she needed to continue working hard in order to be promoted to junior partner in the foreseeable future.

Her home is one of the smaller two-storey properties in a tree-terraced street. The ground floor had been redesigned by the previous owner to create a large open-plan sitting room, kitchen, and dining area, all leading on to the original walled patio. Climbing clematis, Virginia creepers, honeysuckle, and trailing rosemary in earthenware pots created a dramatic and colourful outlook from inside the floor-to-ceiling glazed doors. She spent as many summer evenings as she could, sitting outside with a good book and a glass of wine as her only companions. She never felt lonely.

On the first floor, there are two bedrooms, a bathroom, and access to a very large loft space. She hoped one day to be able to convert that into a master bedroom suite and roof terrace at some point in the future.

Kate's home was her haven. There, after a long day at the office, she could relax, read, and listen to a random selection from her huge collection of classical, jazz, and pop music.

Once she got home on this particular afternoon, she took the landline phone off the hook and switched her mobile phone to silent mode. She wanted to consider the personal implications of her agreeing to assist the investigation team in their search for Beth and her kidnapper.

She ran up to her bedroom, kicked off her shoes, and stripped off her clothes. Despite being the afternoon, she decided to wear her favourite pyjamas and thick bed socks. Finally, she took off her make-up, brushed her long hair, and pulled it back into a ponytail.

She went back downstairs and headed for the kitchen. For moments such as this, she always had a couple of bottles of white wine chilling in the fridge. She removed one of the bottles, opened it, and poured herself a large glass. She grabbed a packet of crisps from the cupboard and then carried them over to her sofa. She placed a couple of large cushions behind her back, stretched out her legs, and then took a long drink of the white wine.

Kate took a couple of deep breaths, stared into space for several minutes, and then shouted, 'Shit, shit, shit,' before getting up and walking over to the dresser in her sitting room. There she rummaged through the drawers until she found the packet of menthol cigarettes that she deliberately kept hidden away for the odd occasion when she felt that she needed a cigarette. This didn't happen very often, but today was definitely one of those days for wine, nibbles, and a few cigarettes.

After agreeing with her grandfather's request, she made up her mind in the taxi to her office that she needed a 'PJ' afternoon as she had a lot to think about.

The next few hours slipped away as she tried to get her head into a dispassionate, calm, and unprejudiced state. Normally, all of this was taken as a given with Kate Oliver by her colleagues as she always appeared to be detached from the world around her when she focussed on work. But this wasn't work. This was personal. Very personal.

If she was to perform as the criminologist that her grandparents, brother, and crime team expected her to be, she knew that she first had to sort out the complexities of her mind and the personal issues that had burdened her for eight years. She needed to be in the right mindset for opening up the old wounds that would assuredly happen over the next few days.

'Shit,' she shouted again. She got up, headed for the fridge, and returned with the remains of the bottle of wine that she had opened earlier. The wine had the desired effect of calming her down. She took a deep breath and then started to reflect on her own kidnapping and rapes eight long years ago.

Not a day went by without her having some sort of flashback, even for a few moments. She still felt sick every time that she imagined what had happened to her. She still had to cope with moments of depression at the realisation of how much she had allowed that incident to affect her life. She had tried so hard to move on, but, even with Grace as her mentor and counsellor, she had found it impossible to bury the past and move on with her life.

Grace was more to Kate than her psychoanalyst. She had become a dear friend to her over the years of their regular encounters. Kate once again considered how Grace would feel if she knew that on a couple of occasions, she had met with other consultants so that she could maintain anonymity and be more open with them. She knew that Grace suspected that she was still keeping some facts about the kidnapping and kidnapper back from her. She knew that this was true because she had decided a long time ago that there were some things that she didn't want Grace or anyone else ever to know.

It was bad enough that aside from Dr Miriam Shepherd, Grace was the only person who had had to carry the secret that Kate was pregnant after the rapes. It required the double consent signatures of Doctors Grace Fletcher and Miriam Shepherd to authorise an immediate termination during her early days in hospital after the kidnapping.

The termination was approved on the grounds that it was necessary to prevent permanent injury to Kate's mental health. It was because of this medical judgement that the documentation did not require the signature of either of Kate's parents. Kate knew that, to this day, the termination had neither been revealed nor discussed with anyone in her family, and she intended to keep it that way.

Kate knew that the most difficult professional decision that Grace had ever had to make related to keeping her pregnancy and termination a secret from Beth Oliver, Kate's mother and Grace's closest friend. The combination of the terms of the non-disclosure agreement and Kate being over sixteen provided her with the confidentiality that she had insisted upon. Kate forbade Grace to discuss the matter with her mother or anyone else in the family.

Eight years later, the secret had remained a secret.

And now Beth, her natural mother had been kidnapped in the same way as Kate had and by the same person. Kate instinctively knew that Grace would try once again to get her to agree to hypnotism, and she could understand why she would want to do that. She would have taken exactly the same action. After all, the only way that the case would be able to move forward was if Kate imparted some of the details about the description of the kidnapper.

She wondered if Grace suspected that she had been searching for the kidnapper for over a year. It was mainly due to this that Kate had instructed her grandfather to insist to Dan that she would not attend their meetings and that all communication should be by email or special delivery. Otherwise, she would be taking a chance at the astuteness of both Grace and Dan being able to read her body language when talking about the kidnapper.

She lit her third cigarette of the evening and then *hid* the packet from herself once again. As she sipped her wine, she gave some thought to what her mother might be thinking at that moment. Perhaps she was turning the clock back eight years and trying to form a better picture of the sequence of events of that Friday evening so long ago.

Kate knew that her mother wouldn't be afraid of the kidnapper and that she would be using every minute that she was awake to piece together any detail of him and her location. She, more than most, would push all her senses to the limit and be particularly perceptive to sounds, smells, and voices. Kate knew that the kidnapper wouldn't have stood a chance had he not restrained Beth whilst she was sedated and had kept her that way.

She would already have been working on the assumption that she was in the same room as her daughter had been eight years ago. She would still be able to remember the detail and be able to visualise the layout of the room that had been prepared for her daughter. She would also be able to imagine how that must have felt for her seventeen-year-old daughter.

Kate shuddered as she thought about her own traumatic experience. Not for the first time, she considered the ways that she could try to bury it once and for all so that she could start to live a normal life.

She had enjoyed dates with some really nice men, and, yes, she had started to mellow on a few occasions after an enjoyable evening as a couple. She had become an expert in knowing when to stop, and it was then that she backed off gracefully making some plausible excuse that would not bring embarrassment to herself or her companion.

She thought of Grace and could just hear her saying that it was encouraging that Kate was even thinking about those moments. And then she would try to persuade her to talk about the future. She would ask Kate to talk about the times when she saw herself with a steady partner. Kate recalled a few occasions when Grace had even asked her to lie back, close her eyes, and picture any scene where she was with a partner and to describe how he would look.

She remembered once getting fairly close to normal thoughts when she described a picnic on a deserted beach, with no other sounds than the waves, the trees, and the birds. In her vision, her companion was tall, dark, and very handsome and looked rather gorgeous in his boxer swimming trunks. Grace had got excited because she thought that she was making progress with Kate, but she had laughed. Why? Because how else did Grace expect her to describe her perfect date?

Poor Grace. She genuinely wanted Kate to date more and to enjoy being in the company of males more often. She regularly invited Kate to functions. Each time that Kate took that final look in the mirror before a formal function, she would always recall how wonderful she felt at that special moment on Friday, 18 June 2004, just before six o'clock.

That special moment was when she looked in her full-length mirror for one last look at her design creation for the mother-and-daughter fashion show. Yes, she still remembered the date and time. Yes, she still remembered how wonderful she had felt. She still remembered the big smile on her father's face as she made her way towards him down the staircase. And yes, she still remembered every stitch of that wonderful dress. She didn't think that she would ever forget those precious moments because they were the last time that she had felt genuinely relaxed, excited, and happy.

Perhaps, she thought to herself. *Perhaps one day I may be able to feel like that again.* What she hadn't told Grace was that she actually did think about the prospect of that happening from time to time.

She poured the remains of the wine and started to feel guilty about the hard time that she had given her grandfather. She had no choice. Her terms of agreement had nothing to do with how she felt about her involvement in the investigation team but had everything to do with her keeping well away from any eye-to-eye contact with the other astute members of the team.

6 p.m.

Her declining mood was interrupted by the doorbell ringing. She signed for the special delivery of a large package of documentation. She knew that it would be the documentation extracted from Kate's cold case and Beth's current kidnapping. She decided not to open the parcel until the following morning.

Kate knew that the kidnapper would not make any contact before then.

Just after 6 p.m., Kate felt drowsy, no doubt, due to lack of food and drinking a full bottle of wine. She took her mobile phone off 'silent' and checked her emails and messages. *Nothing that couldn't wait,* she thought and then drifted off to sleep.

6.30 p.m.

Kate didn't get to sleep long as she was awakened by her mobile telephone ringing. *Damn it,* she thought. *Why did I take if off silent?* Drowsily, she looked to see who was calling her. It was Grace, and she noticed that there had already been four missed calls from her. She decided to answer the phone to avoid the prospect of Grace turning up on her doorstep to check that she was okay.

No surprise then when Grace reminded her that this was her fifth call and if Kate hadn't answered, she was going to make her way to her home. She just wanted to check that Kate was okay after the emotional meetings with her brother and grandfather.

'Bless you, Grace. You are so predictable. What would I do without my guardian angel, eh? Anyhow, it hasn't been the best of days, but I am okay, honestly. Gramps got to me, but I guess that you already suspected that before you called me because you will know that he managed to get me to agree to cooperate.'

'You are, of course, correct. Am I that predictable? I'm going to have to rethink my style of communication if that's the case,' Grace joked.

'Have you been told that I have set some conditions?' asked Kate.

'Yes, and I understand why you felt that you had to do that. This is why I would like to meet up with you this evening for a chat. How about I come around to your house? I could be there in just under half an hour. Do you need me to pick up anything on the way?' asked Grace.

'Oh Grace, I am really tired, and I couldn't face anything to eat. Couldn't we do this first thing in the morning?'

During the call, Grace had sensed that Kate had been drinking, probably on an empty stomach, but she couldn't blame her for that.

'I would rather that we got it out of the way this evening. Who knows what may happen before we next get the chance to talk through your emotions. I just want to make sure that you are in a frame of mind that can cope with whatever comes your way. Please, Kate. I promise that I won't stay long.'

Kate knew when she was beaten. 'How can I refuse? But I must forewarn you that I am in my PJ's and I don't plan to change again. This has been a tough day for me, and I need a good night's sleep.'

'I promise that I won't overstay my welcome. Don't worry about the PJ's. You already know that PJ's are my favourite attire when I'm lounging at home. PJ's help me to mentally establish the parameters that my brain can cope with at that particular time . . .'

'Enough, Dr Fletcher!'

They both laughed.

7.15 p.m.

Grace arrived shortly after their telephone conversation.

Grace took in the scene of the room as Kate hadn't bothered to clear away the empty crisp packets, the ashtray with three cigarette stubs in it, or the empty bottle of wine.

'Guilty as charged, Grace,' said Kate as she returned to the sitting room.

'No guilt required. We have all been there, my dear,' replied Grace.

'I'm fine,' said Kate. 'I just don't want to be treated with kid gloves by any of you, and I don't want to be there when they are digging up the past. I will cope with all of that much better in the comfort of my own home.'

Kate didn't give Grace time to answer. 'Now, my dear friend, you know me well enough to know that once I put on my professional hat tomorrow morning, I will be absolutely fine. So let's get down to why you are really here. You see, I suspect that the real reason that you are here is to ask me to agree to being hypnotised. Am I right?'

'Good God, Kate, you don't have to be unemotional all the time.' Grace always made a point of giving Kate back what she gave, and she knew that Kate respected her for that.

'Point taken. How are you this evening, Grace?' she teased.

'I am fine. Thank you,' replied Grace.

'You see, there is no point asking you how you are because you always say that you are *fine*.

'Touché.'

Back at Dan's office, he was stretched out on a sofa. He knew that he should go home and try to get some sleep, but he didn't want to do that. He didn't want to leave the office in case a package was delivered or some other form of communication from the kidnapper.

He couldn't understand why the kidnapper hadn't made any attempt to communicate with them during the course of the day and found it very frustrating that he couldn't figure out what was going through the kidnapper's mind.

His thoughts turned to Beth, and, for more times than he could remember over the last two days, he tried to visualise what was happening to her and found it difficult to cope with any of that.

It didn't help that he felt so helpless just sitting back waiting for contact.

He sent the team home as there was no point in them sitting about waiting for something to happen. They had all agreed that he would call them as and when he needed them.

Abe, Pete, and Rachel estimated that just over another hour was needed to complete their search of the hospital records. Dan had authorised for that to happen early the following morning. So far, they had extracted eight files for Dan and Grace to review.

8 p.m.

Elsewhere, in the same basement room that Kate had been held captive eight years ago, Beth lay helpless. She was awake, but she could only move her head as her ankles and wrists were restrained. She couldn't speak as her mouth was taped. She couldn't see because her eyes were blindfolded.

Beth knew that she had been sedated and that her current state of grogginess meant that she was just coming around, which meant that she would probably be sedated again soon by the man in black.

She wasn't afraid. She was angry. She was very angry. She knew that she had to get inside the kidnapper's head if she was to negotiate or plan any form of escape. She also knew that before that could happen, she had to use the time to profile the kidnapper and try to determine her location.

She had no idea how long she had been captive. Whilst she couldn't see much of the room, she recalled how it had looked eight years ago. It was definitely cold enough to be a basement room. It smelt damp, and she didn't recall seeing any windows on the images that had been sent during Kate's kidnapping.

She couldn't remember anything about her own kidnapping. *How the hell was I not aware of someone kidnapping me?* she repeatedly asked herself. As hard as she tried, she couldn't remember anything. She thought about her body and state of mind. She was thirsty but not thirsty enough not to have been given anything to drink recently. She wondered if he had raped her but then thought that she would surely know if he had.

Before she got too far into refreshing her memory of Kate's kidnapping and trying to second-guess what may happen to her, the door opened and someone walked into the room. *The man in black*, she thought to herself.

He didn't speak, but as he moved towards her, he started fiddling with something beside her. It was then that she realised that she was hooked up to a drip. He didn't speak to her, and, of course, she couldn't speak to him. He then started to make a noise with moving around utensils on a trolley beside her. She could only guess how that looked.

It was at that moment that she thought that he wasn't going to harm her, and she couldn't come up with a plausible explanation as to why that would be.

He left the room without a word.

Just as she was thinking about what she or any other member of her family could have done in the past that was so bad for this man to carry a grudge against them for more than eight years, she started to feel really tired again. She thought about how Kate must have been so scared about what was happening to her.

Beth was barely awake as she heard the door open again and heard the man in black walking back into the room. She wasn't afraid. She knew he wasn't going to do anything to her.

She couldn't have been more wrong as he walked over to her and then smashed his fist into her face.

Beth didn't feel a thing as she immediately became unconscious with the first blow.

She didn't feel anything as he grabbed a wooden post and hit her repeatedly on her sides and stomach.

CHAPTER 17

Thursday, 18 October 2012
8.30 p.m.

'Kate, you know by now that I am always open and honest with you and that I have never divulged anything that you have said to me in confidence,' opened Grace as they were clearing away their plates.

'Grace, I do trust you. Just relax and get on with what you need to get off your chest today. You have my full attention.'

'I still believe that you have kept back some aspects of the kidnapping from me. In other words, I don't think that you have been entirely honest with me. I would wager that it has something to do with your kidnapper's description or perhaps where he lived at the time of the kidnapping. We are now eight years down the line, and I don't understand why you would have wanted to keep secrets to yourself. Now that Beth has been kidnapped, I am hoping that you will want to divulge any facts that remain in your subconscious as one or all of them may help us to find Beth.'

Grace continued, 'I haven't been able to think of anything else since Beth was kidnapped. Her kidnapping has created a situation that will enable you to revisit the past as an adult, and this may actually provide you with the means to help you to move on with your life. Hypnosis will help you to achieve that. I wouldn't suggest it again if I didn't think it would provide positive results. You have refused hypnosis, and I can't help but wonder if that confirms my suspicions of your secrecy.'

'There, I have said it,' added Grace. 'But then you already pre-empted that I was going to suggest hypnotism again.'

'Have you told anyone about your suspicions?' asked Kate.

'No. I have only told Dan that I think that you are holding back on some particular issue, but he thinks it probably has more to do with the rapes than the kidnapping. So your secret, or secrets, are safe with me. I just wish that I could get you to open up about what they actually are. You know that I can't divulge them without your say-so anyway. What are you so afraid of divulging?' asked Grace.

Kate stood up, checked the time on her watch, and faced Grace. 'Of course, I trust you. Go ahead and organise the hypnotism on the proviso that you are the only person involved and that the only person that you discuss the outcome with is me. From there, anything that I authorise to be repeated should only be with Dan. Is that understood?'

'I wouldn't have it any other way. Let's schedule it now before you change your mind.'

'Any time after nine o'clock tomorrow morning,' replied Kate. 'I have already planned to take the rest of the week off, but I want to get a good night's sleep if that's possible. No alarm. You have to think about it and then send me a text later, telling me where and when. Now, you need to leave soon, so why don't we have a cup of coffee whilst you talk me through the procedure. I can't say that I am looking forward to it. You know that I like to be in total control of my life and my thoughts.'

'Gee, I would never have guessed that, Kate. Normally, I would suggest traditional hypnosis, but this only works well with someone who generally accepts what they are told without a lot of questions.'

Kate smiled.

'Hmm! I see that we agree that you don't fall into that category,' said Grace.

She continued, 'Neurolinguistic programming techniques, or NLP, work best with people who question everything rather than accepting facts at face value. It took me many years to master NLP, so you are lucky that I stuck with the study and training.'

'Sounds as though you have already given thought to which technique that you would use with me,' said Kate.

'Yes, often. Basically, I will be directing your unconscious state to find a memory from your past. This would obviously be a memory from the time of the kidnapping. If there is something that you have filed away in your subconscience, we want that to come out into the open. Trapping away facts interferes with the process.'

'Okay, I get the gist. That's enough for tonight. Much as I love your company, I think that you should leave before I change my mind.'

'In that case, I'm off,' laughed Grace as she jumped up and started to put on her jacket.

They walked to the door together, with Grace's arm linked into Kate's. 'You know that I wouldn't suggest this to you, Kate, if I didn't think that it would help you in the long term. I have your best interests at heart because I want to see you relaxed and happy at some point of your life, and I don't think that you will ever achieve that until you have cleared your mind of the past. The memories will always be there, but it is possible to reach a position of acceptance and then be able to focus on the future.

'I want you to trust me on this. I am genuinely optimistic that, regardless of what has yet to come out in the open, it will help you to move on with your life.'

'No, Grace. It is you who must trust me,' she said with a serious tone. 'Just don't you dare have me leaping about your office on all fours thinking that I am a dog,' Kate added with a rather weak attempt at humour.

Grace gave Kate a bear hug and told her not to worry about it but to get herself off to bed and rest.

9.30 p.m.

Grace had mixed feelings. On the one hand, she genuinely believed that she was doing the right thing for Kate's future well-being. On the other hand, she had a hunch that there was something about to come out into the open that she would hope that she didn't have to keep to herself for the rest of her life. She already had enough of those.

As Kate was already in her PJs, she decided to tidy up the kitchen in the morning and made her way to bed. She surprised herself by feeling a mild form of relief at having agreed to the hypnotism. If Grace was as good as Kate suspected she would be, everything would come out into the open. She couldn't help but be apprehensive about the consequences of that happening.

Grace headed for her old and faithful red MX5 and sent an email to her secretary, requesting that she cancel and reschedule all her meetings over the next two days. She phoned Dan and was told that he was in his conference room alone. She decided to join him and perhaps start to review hospital files that had been extracted by the team for their attention. She knew she wouldn't sleep as long as Beth was captive.

'Well, how did it go with Kate?' asked Dan when Grace entered his office.

'She has agreed to be hypnotised but only on condition that we stick to the terms of the NDA. I hadn't planned for anyone to be there with me, so that's fine. After she and I discuss the outcome, she will decide what can and cannot be shared with you, but only you, I should add.'

'That's really good news, Grace. Well done. Let's just hope that deep down, there is a small part of her that does want to save her mother.'

'I agree. I think that meeting up with Jack and Bill yesterday was very emotional for her, and her resolve was down when I met up with her. I got the feeling that she went straight home soon after meeting Bill and that her only companions for the early part of the evening were a bottle of wine and a couple of cigarettes from the reserve pack that she keeps hidden away.'

'What time have you scheduled for the hypnotism?' asked Dan 'And can I inform the team?'

Grace nodded her head as authorisation for Dan to tell the team about the hypnotism and suggested that he also update Jack, Bill, and Caroline. She told him that she had given some thought to when and where she should hypnotise Kate and had decided to arrange it for nine o'clock in the morning at Kate's house and arrive at eight o'clock to give her time to set the scene. She then proceeded to send Kate a text message, confirming the detail.

10 p.m.

As she updated Dan with her thoughts, Colin and the rest of the team came into the office. During catch-up telephone calls with each other, it became apparent that none of them could concentrate at home, preferring to be at the office beside Dan and Grace, helping to find Beth.

Dan was again reminded of his team's dedication to the job, and their actions reinforced his trust and confidence in their work ethic.

They talked about Colin and Abe's continued suspicions about the janitor. 'Perhaps we are clutching at straws, but it's just too coincidental that he was the only person on the premises who spoke with Kate, didn't ask her where she was going, didn't offer to fetch Freya, didn't offer to hail a taxi, and didn't even wander out of the school grounds to watch which direction she headed,' said Abe. 'And then there are those photographs in his locker. I was never convinced that they were as innocent as he made everybody believe. Maybe it is because we have nothing else, but I keep coming back to him.'

'You have done a background check and come up with no previous on him. Eleanor Marshall rechecked his references and spoke to the people who gave them. All clean. There are only so many times that you can interview the man,' said Dan. 'You need some evidence before you can bring him in again, so no more talk of the janitor and your suspicions until you actually have a lead.'

Dan asked Colin to join Grace and him to help review the files that Abe and the rest of the team had chosen to download for him.

He then instructed the rest of the team to put their heads together and think about any specific questions that they would like Grace to consider before she hypnotised Kate the following morning.

As Colin spread the hospital files over the conference table, Dan sent a brief email to Kate, thanking her for agreeing to the hypnotism.

When Kate received Grace's email, she was relieved at her choice of venue as she couldn't get to sleep because she was so nervous about the potential of a formal procedure. She had responded to Grace with '*Grace, you are a treasure. I haven't been able to sleep so far because I was nervous about being in your office. Being at home will be much better, and I will be more relaxed. I just may sleep now! x*'

Grace replied, 'My *aim is to relieve your subconscience of the burden that has been carried around for too many years. I will be honest with you when I share with you what you said during the hypnosis. Whether or not I record it is your call, but you can think about that before we meet. Sleep well. Love Grace. x*'

Grace knew that this was a major step forward for Kate, and she was very proud of her. She wished she could have told Beth, which led her to think of her closest friend being tied up and who knew what else. Beth would know that they would all be working hard to find her. Grace didn't call Bill, Caroline, and Jack as Kate had told her that she would prefer to do that, adding, 'I owe them that.'

Grace returned to the conference room and updated Dan and Colin.

Dan, Grace, and Colin then agreed upon a process of elimination when reviewing the hospital records that the team had extracted from Matt's hospital records from the time that he had been promoted to consultant.

10.30 p.m.

Dan, Grace, and Colin worked quietly together. Grace checked the time and estimated that she had approximately three hours before she would head home to get a few hours' sleep before she left for Kate's house in the morning.

'Holy shit!' Colin interrupted her thought process. He waved a file in the air and continued, apparently to himself. 'Please, please, please make this out to be what I think it is.'

'Holy shit!' he repeated with emphasis on the words for effect. That caught everyone's attention.

'Collect your thoughts, Colin, before sharing with us what appears to be an epiphany.'

Colin scribbled down a few notes, flicked through several pages of the file, and added some more notes.

'You look like the cat that has licked the cream,' joked Dan. 'I know a lead when I see one. Are you ready to share it with us any time soon?'

No answer. Grace shrugged her shoulders at Dan as she held up both her hands with fingers crossed. Colin rose slowly and walked over to the crime board. He stood there for a few moments and turned around to face Dan and Grace with a huge grin on his face. The rest of the team had already gathered around the table in anticipation of what they were about to hear.

'I have a feeling that his smile is going to lighten up our day,' said Grace to Dan. 'Come on, Colin. Don't keep us in suspense any longer.'

'Honestly, guys, I really do believe that I have just come across our first lead. Hold on to your hats,' said Colin as he positioned himself in front of the conference table to ensure that he had everyone's attention.

'Okay, we need to go through this in detail later, but I'll summarise the reasons why I consider this to be a real lead for us.'

'Alison and Murray Thomson embarked upon an IVF programme in August 1996 after Alison had experienced four early-stage miscarriages, two before they married and two during the first year after they married in 1992. Their gynaecologist doctor during the nineties was a registrar called Matt Oliver. One of the consultants who recommended them to join the IVF programme in 1998 was none other than our Consultant Paediatrician Dr Matt Oliver.'

Colin now had the attention of the full team, and each of them had a feeling that he was definitely on to something. They couldn't wait to hear more.

Colin continued, 'After several failed attempts, Alison Thomson became pregnant in April 1998 and gave birth to a premature baby girl in November 1998. There were complications during the pregnancy and again at the birth. Mother and baby were transferred to City of London Hospital for Children. Unfortunately, Baby Thomson was too weak and died. The parents were inconsolable and apparently blamed Dr Oliver for the death of their child due to the inefficiency of his team as they didn't think that they acted quickly enough to save their baby.'

Colin spread out a bundle of handwritten and typed letters on the table.

'These are all letters from Murray Thomson, making repeated accusations and threats to the hospital and Matt. In one letter, he asks how Matt and Beth Oliver "would feel if their daughter had died after she had just been born or how would they feel if anything happened to her now". Quote and unquote. Don't you see? He knew the Oliver's first names at that time, and he also knew that they had a daughter.'

'Well done, Colin,' said Dan. 'You are on to something here. Anything else jumping off the pages that we need to hear about now?'

'Mr Thomson regularly threatened to make the death of his daughter public. Matt and his team referred the matter to the board of governors, and there is an extract from a report here that exonerated them from malpractice and stated "after due process, the death of Baby Thomson was deemed to have been an act of God and that the board was satisfied that medical protocol had been followed".'

'Well done,' said Dan. 'In fact, holy shit, you are definitely on to something here. Don't you agree, Grace?'

'Absolutely. Well done, team, for bringing it along in the first place. It fits the profile of the person that we are looking for. And, from what you have said, Murray Thomson definitely felt that he had just cause to have a grudge against the Olivers. Actually, that isn't correct. He had a grudge against Matt Oliver,' said Grace.

'That arrogant bastard has never entertained the notion that Kate's kidnapping could have had anything to do with him. How the hell could he forget those threatening letters? The Thomsons wouldn't stand a chance against the hospital's board of governors and their legal team. If I'm not mistaken, there will be a copy interdict in that file somewhere that outlines the legal process that would have been followed if the hospital had received any more further threats from the Thomsons.'

Grace looked at her watch. It was 11.45 p.m.

'Much as I would love to help you some more, I must leave now. I know that the hypnotism isn't scheduled until nine tomorrow, but, in light of this new information, I need some quiet time to think about how I need to reconsider my technique and planned questions. She won't know anything about the specifics between the Thomsons and Matt, but the death of the daughter may have been mentioned.'

They had all agreed that the hypnosis should still proceed as Grace may be able to find out something else to help find Beth.

The mood lifted in the room as Grace prepared to leave, and she felt hopeful of Beth being found after what she had heard.

'Right, Colin, forget the janitor for now. Rachel and Pete, think about questions for Grace and email or text her as soon as you can even if it's just to confirm that you haven't come up with anything other than those that you have assumed that she will ask.

'Colin, Abe, and Sophie, work on the Thomson lead. I want to know all there is to know about the Thomsons, especially Murray Thomson. Where he worked then? Where he works now? Where do they live? Hell, I want to know their blood groups. You know what we need. Follow every related link that you can find,' instructed Dan.

'It's a pity that we have found this close to midnight. There is only so much information that you will get during the night, but do what you can and then get back on to it first thing in the morning. Remember to take cat naps as we're going to be busy tomorrow, and, hopefully, we're going to find Beth tomorrow. Grace, how long will you be with Kate tomorrow morning?'

'I don't know. Depends on what is said and her emotional state during and after the hypnosis. If she is agitated or upset, I need to stay with her. If she is exhausted, I will prescribe a strong sleeping pill so that she can get a peaceful sleep. Assuming the latter, I will revisit her at some point later to ensure that I am there for her when she awakens,' replied Grace.

'Okay. I suppose that it goes without saying that anything crucial to the enquiry has to find its way to the forefront of our investigation as the clock is ticking, and we haven't a clue what this guy's plan is for Beth.'

'You know that I can't guarantee that, Dan, but I'll do my best to get Kate to agree to vital facts being shared with you, at least.'

'Good. I'm going to spend some time in my office as I also want some quiet time to think through the possibility of that happening, together with where this lead could take us and how we will manage it.'

Dan stopped in his tracks, turned to Grace and Colin, and said, 'One thing is for sure. If the facts that you have unearthed, Colin, have something to do with Kate's kidnapping, it means that our Dr Oliver could be accused of perverting the course of justice eight years ago, and I will take great pleasure in bringing that to his attention during a taped interview. This is serious. Let's move quickly, Colin.'

'Good as done, Chief,' replied Colin, without having the need to say anything. Colin and his team were extremely loyal to Dan and knew exactly how they needed to perform to stay in the team that reported directly to Chief Superintendent Daniel S. Turner.

Grace headed for her MX5 for the third trip that day.

Colin gathered the team around him, desperate to get started.

Dan made for his office after he had poured himself a large mug of strong coffee. He then collected a fresh ruled pad and pen. To those who knew him well, that action was no surprise as he always started a new notepad when he wanted to clear his mind or when he wanted to issue a fresh set of instructions. His final thought that he shared with the team on leaving the room was, 'And still the kidnapper hasn't communicated with us. What's different this time? Damn it, I meant to ask Grace that before she left.'

Dan's first note on his new pad was to call Grace in her car to ask that very question. He then picked up his phone to call the commander with an update.

At the kidnapper's basement in his home, Beth was unconscious from the earlier beating to her face and body from the kidnapper. The kidnapper had no intention of raping her. He had already ensured that he had inflicted irreversible damage to the Olivers first time around. For that to have worked so well, Kate Oliver had to be the victim.

CHAPTER 18

Friday, 19 October 2012

During the small hours of Friday morning, Rachel and Pete thought through everything that they wanted to know about the kidnapper and the location that Kate had been kept captive in 2004. They knew that Grace would already have identified the obvious questions that they had jotted down but decided to include them in their email anyhow.

Colin, Abe, and Sophie split their Thomson family investigation into three parts. Colin reviewed the two-way correspondence from Murray Thomson and the legal counsel representing the hospital's board of governors. He recorded all of that and every written side note in chronological order. Abe worked his way through the medical entries and tried to learn as much as he could about the relationship between the Murrays and Matt Oliver. He prepared a bullet list of his findings. Sophie worked at the computer to access the databases that she was authorised to access. She focussed on the years leading up to 2004 and then planned to fill the gaps between then and 2012. Like Colin, she was preparing a log of her findings in chronological order and left gaps for the information that would need to wait until the following morning.

When Rachel and Pete had finished their work for Grace, Rachel helped Colin wade through the medical notes, and Pete helped Sophie paint the much-needed picture of Murray Thomson.

They all took turns at resting but didn't manage to sleep due to the adrenaline rush that they had experienced at finding a lead that could point them in a direction that could find Beth, their DSI.

Dan remained in his office, piecing together a chart of where they were at and where they needed to get to if they were to find Beth alive. There were too many gaps for his liking, but he remained hopeful that the answers would be found from the hospital files and the databases that he and his team were authorised to access. His instinct that Matt was somehow the key to identifying the kidnapper had been with him at the time of Kate's kidnapping and again at Beth's. He took a note to find out why his team had been unable to access the legal correspondence at the time of the first search warrant in 2004. This was the lead that they needed then, after all. This was the lead that would have prevented Beth's kidnapping.

7.50 a.m.

Grace arrived at Kate's apartment and let herself in quietly as she didn't want to disturb Kate. As far as she knew, she was the only person who had a spare key to Kate's home.

As she was drawn into the comfort of Kate's sitting room, she was convinced that Kate would respond better in the comfort of her own home, a place where she felt safe. So far, so good.

Grace tiptoed upstairs to Kate's bedroom and saw that she was still asleep. This was a good sign as it meant that she must have been reasonably relaxed during the night. Kate's current behaviour and cooperation was the best sign so far in the long journey to get Kate to bury the past and to move on with her life in a positive way.

Grace tidied up the dishes from the previous evening as she decided the best way to set the scene for as positive an outcome that she could achieve. She knew that this was most likely the one and only chance that she would get to hypnotise Kate. Grace believed that a successful hypnotism relied very much upon knowing the person well and setting a scene that reflected their needs before, during, and after hypnotism.

Firstly, she checked the fridge. Yes, Kate's favourite Sauvignon Blanc wine was there, and there were also a selection of nibbles. She didn't expect to need either during the morning but acknowledged that they may come in handy later on in the day. She knew that Kate would be nervous about the feedback after the hypnotism, and a glass of wine was what she would normally have after having faced a personal situation that she was anxious about.

Secondly, she prepared the coffee machine to be ready for switching on when she heard that Kate was up and about. She set up a tray with coffee cups and Kate's favourite almond croissants that Grace had bought en route. She knew that this would help to relax Kate.

Thirdly, she tiptoed again upstairs and entered the bathroom. There, she checked that the ingredients for a relaxing bubble bath were available. This included bath oil, bubble bath, and scented candles. Completing the scene was a soft towelling robe and slippers. At some point after the hypnotism, she would encourage Kate to have a long soak and listen to a selection of classical music as she came to terms with the hypnotism and its results.

Grace knew that she wouldn't go to these efforts for the majority of her clients, but Kate was special. She was the daughter of her closest friend. She had become a dear friend to Kate. And she had been the young victim of a traumatic kidnapping and rape through no fault of her own.

Back downstairs, she lit the wood-burning stove and puffed up the abundance of cushions that Kate had on the sofa and armchairs in the sitting room.

As she checked her work, she couldn't help but laugh inwardly. 'Crikey, you would think that I was setting the scene for an evening of passionate sex instead of planning hypnotism,' she said aloud.

Happy that the ambience was as she wanted it, she took off her jacket, kicked off her shoes, sat at the kitchen table, and opened up her briefcase. She began to read the summary of the notes that she had scribbled after leaving Dan's office almost six hours earlier.

She had already definitely decided not to share the latest Thomson development with Kate before the hypnotism as stress had to be avoided for the moment. Dan would, no doubt, update Kate during the briefing in the scheduled daily conference call.

Reflecting on Colin's earlier find, she considered it to be a very positive lead. The timeline fitted, and there was also a motive. As she and Dan had suspected all along, Matt held the key to finding the kidnapper. During research, Colin and the rest of the team had come across other deaths during an operation, or still birth, or a post-birth complication. None had fitted the profile of someone with the degree of grudge as demonstrated by Murray Thomson after the death of his daughter.

She trusted that Dan had sufficient information to eventually get the result that they needed. For the moment, she was content to put all thoughts of Murray Thomson to one side.

For the next ten minutes, Grace highlighted her written questions in a tried and tested colour code sequence.

Satisfied that she was ready, Grace decided to waken Kate. She didn't have to. As if on cue, she heard Kate walking about upstairs.

Grace switched on the coffee machine.

Kate made her entrance, obviously having showered. *Even presented in a pair of jogging trousers, a sloppy sweatshirt, and wet hair, she managed to look amazing,* thought Grace.

'Good morning,' said Grace. 'I must have been lost in thought as I didn't hear the shower.'

'I have actually had a good night's sleep. So what do you think of the outfit? Suitably relaxed for hypnotism, do you think?' asked Kate.

'Perfect,' replied Grace. 'The coffee machine is on, so just you relax whilst I do the honours.'

'No argument there,' said Kate as she made for the sofa and stretched out.

As Grace walked through with the tray of coffee and croissants, she said, 'I don't know how you manage it, Kate. Even in your running gear, you manage to look a million dollars.'

'Is that your chat-up line for your clients before hypnosis?' teased Kate.

Grace ignored Kate's effort to lighten her mood, knowing that she never took praise seriously anyhow.

They chatted during breakfast, and Grace was pleased to see that Kate was as relaxed as she could have hoped for. The previous evening's wine and a good night's sleep had obviously helped.

After breakfast, Grace suggested that Kate select relaxing background music and then settle in a lying position on the sofa.

'Loving it so far, Grace,' Kate shouted through to the kitchen. 'Coffee, croissants, relaxing music, and chilling out on the sofa first thing in the morning. I guess there's a first time for everything.'

'I just want to try to relax you as best as I can before the hypnotism,' said Grace.

'Then may I suggest that you start off by being relaxed yourself. You look tense, and, as your patient, that is having a negative effect on my mood,' again teased Kate.

'Touché. You are, of course, correct. There is so much at stake here, and I am so close to you and your mother. Don't worry, professionalism will kick in the minute that you dose off.'

Satisfied that she and Kate were seated comfortably, she began, 'Talking of dozing off, I'll summarise the process again for you. You don't actually go to sleep as most people think. Hypnosis is actually a deep form of relaxation and is completely safe. Think about it as a form of meditation. You will be aware and in control throughout. It is impossible for you to get stuck in a state of hypnosis and you definitely can't be made to do something that is against your will. NLP also works on the subconscious. Your subconscious mind holds all your past memories. Because your negative thoughts are being controlled by your subconscious mind, I will be integrating hypnosis and NLP to work directly on the subconscious.'

'In other words, we know what the problem is and why it started, so I want to help you release the emotions that are connected to the problem.'

'That actually sounds interesting, and I would like to explore it further with you after the hypnosis. For now, let's get the show on the road so that I can put it behind me.'

Just as Grace expected, Kate was putting on a brave face and wanted the hypnosis out of the way.

'Before we start, I want you to know that you are the most caring person that I know. You have just made me feel very special by going to a lot of effort to do this as well as you possibly can for me. Thank you, Grace.'

Grace jumped out of her chair and hugged Kate. She was thrilled by Kate's words to her and quietly thought, *So far so good*.

'The actual hypnosis should last about an hour or less if I think that you are becoming anxious. You will remember everything that happens. Would you like to sit or lie down, although I think I know the answer to that?'

As Kate pumped up the cushions on the sofa and stretched out, she answered, 'The sofa wins every time.'

'Okay, did you switch off your cell phone as I asked?'

'Yes.'

Grace took the landline phone off the hook and then put a note on the outside door stating *No callers today please*.

'I am shortly going to ask you to close your eyes and imagine being in a happy place. We have talked about this before, so that should now be easier for you to imagine. Then I will want you to feel your entire body relaxing, working from the feet all the way up to your neck and head. Concluding the hypnotism is easier than inducing it. All I have to do is to ask you to stop imagining, and I will start counting from one to five until you feel wide awake and refreshed. Finally, we will talk about the two-way conversation that we had. Any questions?'

'Sounds straightforward,' replied a fairly relaxed Kate.

Grace began the hypnosis induction process.

Kate remained reasonably relaxed during the hypnosis mainly because Grace avoided any discussion that they had already had over and over again about the kidnapping and rapes.

Her main agenda was to find out anything that could point the investigation team towards who the kidnapper may be and where he may be keeping Beth against her will. Kate visibly became anxious at any mention of the kidnapper, and so Grace treaded carefully.

When the kidnapper didn't have a name, all that she could get from Kate was that he was always dressed in black, always wore a balaclava, and always wore dark glasses. However, when Grace asked Kate if the name Murray Thomson meant anything to her, she replied, 'That name sounds familiar.'

At the point where Grace felt that she should end the hypnosis, Kate was not demonstrating a level of anxiety that concerned her, so she decided to ask the two remaining questions that were highlighted in red on her notebook, meaning *proceed with caution*.

Firstly, she asked whether or not Kate thought that she would be able to identify the kidnapper. Grace was shocked when she replied, 'Perhaps I could.'

Deciding not to pursue that response, she asked her final question. 'Kate, do you have any idea where the kidnapper lives?'

'Maybe,' was Kate's final answer in a hypnotic state.

Oh my God, thought Grace. She now had loads more questions that she would like to ask, but her professional code of practice prevented her from doing that. Instead, she concluded the hypnosis session. She could only hope that Kate would open up more when they discussed the highlights. Better still, she would prefer if Kate agreed to her sharing those two particular highlights with Dan so that he could question her formally.

Kate was wide awake in no time at all and felt sufficiently refreshed to start the feedback session.

'Well done, Kate,' said Grace. 'That went really well. I am optimistic that you can begin to make changes to your life, some of which you haven't even realised could happen.'

'Good,' replied Kate. 'But, Grace, this particular session was not arranged to help me focus on my life ahead. It was arranged so that you could, hopefully, get some answers that could help Dan to find Beth.'

Never one to flannel Kate, Grace replied, 'As always, you are as shrewd as ever and direct with your thoughts. You are correct, of course, but I don't take back what I have just said to you. The hypnosis was a success, but we will talk about the personal aspects of that another day.'

Grace summarised that Kate had repeated that the kidnapper had accused her of living a privileged life and had asked how she would feel if she were ever pregnant and lost her child through no fault of her own. Kate initially confirmed that the kidnapper had never threatened her, but, later on in reply to another question, she said that he once said that if she didn't cooperate with him, he would just have to make sure that she could never have any children of her own. The rest of the responses confirmed that Kate must have been unconscious during the rapes. Grace knew of the multiple rapes because of Dr Shepherd's feedback after internal examination.

Not for the first time in the last eight years, Grace felt nauseous just at the thought that she and Dr Miriam Shepherd were the only people that knew that Kate was pregnant after the kidnapping and that they had arranged the safe termination under the terms of their non-disclosure agreement.

She had never been able to share this with Beth but had never given up hope that one day she would be able to do so with Kate's blessing. For now, she had not mentioned it during the hypnotism, preferring to remain thankful that the experiences had not resulted in any physical damage and that Kate could still become pregnant and have a natural childbirth.

They talked about the general feedback and the responses to the last two questions. Eventually, Grace couldn't believe her luck when Kate agreed that Grace could share most of it with Dan and the team, including those responses.

But then came Kate's punch line. 'After all, these are vague responses, and neither actually gives you specific detail about him or where he lives.'

'Very clever, Kate,' replied Grace, 'but I think that I will leave that to Dan to work with.'

A moment or two lapsed before Grace continued, 'But I think that you can, Kate. I think you could describe your kidnapper, in which case you could also describe where he lives. If that is the case, I suspect that you could lead us to him. And, Kate, if that is the case, you have the ability to save your mother and my dearest friend.'

Silence.

Kate's mood visibly started to change.

It was at that point that Grace decided to tell Kate about the information that the investigation team now had about Murray Thomson and the link between him and her father recorded in hospital files dating back to 2004.

'Dan is getting closer, Kate, and if you can clarify any information or supposition that he and his team have, then you must do the right thing. Now is the time to put your demons to bed. Now is the time to do the right thing for your mother.'

'Grace, I'm tired. I want to take that bath now. I then want to go to bed for an hour or so. I need to think. I think that it is time for you to leave.'

'Is that it, Kate?'

'For now, yes,' said Kate. 'Now please leave.'

Grace knew that professionally Kate's reaction was perfectly natural and that she should honour her request. Regularly, Grace was compromised between the professional and personal relationship that she had with Kate and her family. This was one of those occasions. However, she was there in a professional capacity, and it was in a professional capacity that she would leave.

10.40 a.m.

Knowing that there was no more to be said that morning, Grace put on her shoes and jacket and made to leave Kate's apartment.

'I will leave you alone now, and, yes, you should have the bath and a short rest. From what I saw, you shouldn't experience any anxiety about the hypnosis process,' said Grace.

Grace continued gently, 'But, Kate, we will need to speak again soon. We will need to talk about why you think that *perhaps* you could identify the kidnapper and why *maybe* you could point us in the right direction to save Beth.'

As Grace reached the door, she turned to Kate and said firmly, 'I am not a priest, Kate. Please don't expect me to behave like one after a confessional. That would be cruel and that would be expecting too much from me, don't you think? Rest well, and I will call you in a couple of hours. If you haven't already, can I suggest that you clear your diary for the rest of the day and perhaps tomorrow also.'

Grace walked to her car and then sent a text message to Dan to say that she would be back at the office within thirty minutes. She also forewarned him that they had some serious talking to do.

She would share with Dan information that could help the investigation, as authorised by Kate. But then she was going to check her legal position about where she stood with her belief that Kate could identify the kidnapper and direct them to his home. She spent the rest of the time driving to the MET, thinking about how she could get the truth across to Dan, only Dan, without actually breaching Kate's trust and violating the terms of the non-disclosure agreement that she had signed eight years ago. This was another question that she would put to her lawyers. She would also ask Dan if they should discuss this with the commander.

All of a sudden, Grace felt tired and decided then that after Beth was found, she was going to make enquiries about legally making the non-disclosure agreement null and void for anything that was discussed from that point forward.

11.15 a.m.

Back at the office, Grace had a brief private meeting with Dan. She shared with him her belief that Kate could identify the kidnapper and his home but that she needed to discuss the conflict of interest with him.

'Is that likely to lead us to Beth right now?' he asked. 'If not, I suggest that we listen to Colin's update first.'

'That makes sense. Let's do that,' replied Grace.

Colin summarised what he and his team had found out about Murray Thomson during the course of the night and between nine and ten that morning.

'Murray Thomson has no criminal record, and so we have no DNA. However, his wife, Alison Thomson, committed suicide with an overdose of pills prescribed for depression in March of 1999. As to where he works or lives now, feedback is vague at present, but I have gone to the top of the tree to demand that the details that we require are sent over to us within the hour.

'We are getting closer. Murray Thomson is our guy, of that I am sure. But we still need to cross the t's and dot the i's,' Colin concluded.

'Well done, team,' replied Dan. 'You know what you have to do. Kick ass if you have to. Keep on top of everything until you can come back to me with something concrete. In other words, find Murray Thomson. Go! Go! Go! And if you are not getting the cooperation that you need, transfer the call through to me and use my title. I want Beth found safely this afternoon. I also want the kidnapper behind bars this afternoon. Use the next hour wisely.'

Midday

To Grace, he said wearily, 'Okay, let's have that chat in my office.' Dan was obviously not expecting the feedback that Grace had for him.

As Dan walked towards his office, he mentally reminded himself to talk to Grace about the lack of communication from the kidnapper and whether or not she was regarding that as a good or back omen.

As Grace walked towards Dan's office, she battled with her conscience about how much information she should share with Dan and how far she would be prepared to go to save her friend.

CHAPTER 19

Friday, 19 October 2012
Midday

Dan and Grace settled into their chairs in Dan's office.

'Grace, before we talk about Kate and before I forget again, can you explain to me why you think that the kidnapper hasn't been communicating with us at regular intervals this time?' asked Dan.

'It could be because he is struggling to know what to say to us. It could be because he simply wants to be found this time. Remember that I have always said that Kate's kidnapping was a first for him. I never said that it was random, but he always acted as someone who was out of his comfort zone. He is definitely someone with no previous experience of what he has been doing.

'*Or* perhaps he isn't comfortable at photographing Beth or creating any evidence about her time as a victim. If that's the case, he will be in awe of Beth and the position that she holds at the MET. Let's be honest, it was a brave move to kidnap the detective superintendent. He won't have raped her. He will already have experienced Beth's wrath, and we know that she can be a formidable force to be reckoned with when she chooses.

'Personally, I think that he wants to lead us to either him or Beth. He is waiting for us to contact him, which is why he directed us to

Kate. Why that was we don't know, but I now have my suspicions. Now *he* hasn't left us any clues that would enable us to find him, but that is what I want to talk to you about, so we'll come back to that.'

Grace continued, 'Remember how he just dropped Kate off in the woods without any demands. We don't know how he managed to get Beth to be submissive, but now that she is tied up, presumably at his home, he probably doesn't have a clue about how he is going to get rid of her.'

'That should be a worry to us', said Dan, 'because we don't know where she is. She can't escape as her arms and ankles are restrained, and she will be giving him a hard time when she is conscious. If this becomes too much for him, he may panic and kill her. He could overdose her with whatever drug he is using to sedate her. Let's face it. He doesn't have the experience to follow through with a premeditated murder.'

'Why wait eight years to kidnap the mother of the daughter that he kidnapped and raped back then? What has happened recently to make him revisit what has become a journey of revenge?' asked Grace.

Dan interrupted, 'I'm sensing here that you think that someone else is involved? If not, what else could have happened to reopen the old wounds that he obviously has had? None of the Olivers have been in the news recently, and, as best as I can recollect, there haven't been any photographs of them in the media either.'

'Dan, something has triggered the kidnapping of Beth, and, after eight years, it certainly isn't for a walk down memory lane. Something specific has happened to open this cold case.'

'Okay, let's hold those thoughts. Now, tell me about your time with Kate.'

Grace summarised the hypnosis as best as she was able to do within the terms of the NDA. She paused before asking for confidentiality about the grey area that she was about to share with him.

'That sounds ominous. Grace, if you have something that could lead us to the kidnapper, I would seriously struggle with not being able to use that,' replied Dan.

'I know, which is why I am going to tell you this in a way that doesn't compromise either of us. I just need to know that you understand my position and that you will work with me to get out of it what you need, but in a way that doesn't suggest that there has been a breach to the non-disclosure agreement.'

'I understand. Just tell it as it is, and then, if necessary, we will involve the commander and one of our preferred legal advisors.'

They mutually agreed with an informal handshake. Grace then proceeded to share with Dan the detail of her questions and the verbatim responses from Kate.

'Before you comment, you need to know that Kate authorised me to tell you that. However, when I later questioned her about these responses, she appeared to be unperturbed. Then she defended her position by saying that they were vague answers that didn't in any way suggest that she actually remembered any detail. In other words, she hinted that the way in which the questions were asked and answered would not stand up in court.'

'Okay, I can see that this is troubling you, so spill all. This isn't about the NDA as we can get around that. What's your gut feeling on this, Grace? Just get it off your chest, and then we will talk about implications, conflicts of interest, or anything else that could stop us using the information to question Kate.'

Grace inhaled a couple of times before she began.

'I got the impression that Kate definitely *can* identify the kidnapper and lead us to him. The why and the how can be discussed later as our top priority is to find Beth. But, Dan, I think that Kate is involved in Beth's kidnapping. I asked her this question when she was fully awake, and she refused to comment. I have told her that I will revisit this with her during the course of the afternoon, and I still fully intend to do that. My concern is that if she does open up to me, she will know that I can't use any of that unless she authorises me to do so.'

'I don't like the sound of this, Grace,' said Dan. 'If you are right and she does know who he is, has that been in her memory bank for eight years? Surely, you or Miriam would have picked up on that. She was only seventeen, so she wouldn't have been clever enough then to hide something as major as that.'

'Yes, but she is now a very sharp criminologist, and if she has managed to get this information, she will know that she has to share it with us. Kate is a strong-willed person, and, even under hypnosis, I suspect that she wouldn't let anything slip that she wanted to keep secret,' said Grace.

'It sounds to me that she has somehow been able to find out who her kidnapper was. Christ, Grace, do you know what that may mean?'

'I am only too well aware of what that may mean, Dan,' replied Grace.

'Quickly tell me what your lawyer's advice was because surely you have already been in contact with him,' said Dan.

'Correct,' said Grace. 'The answers given by Kate about the kidnapper and where he lives were vague. Her words, remember. Also they aren't about Kate's actual kidnapping or rape as she has always emphatically denied knowing anything about who he is and where he lives.

'The reason that I gave for wanting to hypnotise her now was to determine if there was anything that she hadn't already told me that could be used to find Beth. As Beth's kidnapping is a current crime, then the answers relate to finding Beth's kidnapper. In short, he feels that bringing Kate in for questioning would not be a problem, provided that you bring in Matt to question him about the information that you have retrieved from your new search of the hospital records under the terms of the search warrant.'

'Precisely what I was thinking,' said Dan. 'Grace, we need to bring her in for questioning. We need to bring her in now. Kate will know that she must cooperate, so this won't come as a surprise to her.

'We have a crime to solve, perhaps two. It is time for all of us to forget our relationships with Beth, Kate, and Bill. These two crimes are linked to the Oliver family, and I intend to find out why, after I have found Beth.'

'I think that's wise, Dan,' responded Grace. 'We are all emotionally involved, but there are some facts coming up to the surface that you must consider as leads and then manage them just as you would with any other case. I don't think that I am going to change my opinion about the kidnapper, so it is really down to your detective work now. My imagination has gone into overdrive about some of Kate's responses, but I'll curb that for now until I have had time to talk to her some more.'

Dan told Grace that he had previously invited Bill and Jack to come into his office so that he could update them with the latest developments. 'I don't want either of them to go off at a tangent with Kate, so I will hold on to your information until we have discussed it further. Hopefully, the guys will find contact details for Murray Thomson and interview him today.

'Grace, you have been a tremendous help, as usual. I'll leave you to focus on Kate and look forward to your feedback later today. If we find out where Murray Thomson is, that will become our priority before updating the family. I'll keep you posted.'

'I am going to go over to Kate's now to check on her. I expect that she will be rested as she wasn't showing any signs of anxiety when I left. I don't intend to spend long with her. If you don't mind, I would like to base myself here until we find Beth. I can assist Colin and his team with sorting out their leads from the hospital records, and I will also be able to access psychological records much quicker than you can, given my contacts,' offered Grace.

'That's a good idea, Grace. If we find Murray Thomson, I would like you to observe his interview from the viewing room. I want to focus on the questions and not be sidetracked by his emotions or body language.'

'That's not a problem. I would like to see this through to the end,' said Grace.

Dan continued, 'Until we come up with Murray Thomson's whereabouts, I have decided to call in Kate, Matt, Jack, and Bill for recorded interviews. If we find Thomson, then their interviews will either be cut short or postponed.

'I may upset one or all the Olivers during questioning. With Matt, I need to get to the bottom of the Thomson baby death, mother's suicide, and threatening letters. With Kate, I need to ask her outright whether or not she has anything to share with us about the description of the kidnapper and where he lives. I also intend to ask her if she was involved in her mother's kidnapping. With Jack and Bill, I need to ask them individually if they have picked up any clues from Kate over the years about the kidnapper's identity—after all, they have both maintained an extremely close relationship with her.

'I'm not expecting Bill to have held back anything, and I need to keep him on the sideline just in case he can help me talk some sense in to any one of them. If Kate has any leads for us, then I need to hear them today, and, for that to happen, I fully intend to use whatever interview technique is needed to achieve that. Frankly, I don't care if she suffers a setback as I'm sure that you will get her back on track after I have finished with her.'

Grace thought about what Dan had said for a few moments and then replied, 'Kate wasn't anxious when she answered my questions about her kidnapper's identity and his home. I don't think that they were vague responses. The more that I think about what she said, the more I believe she does know something that could help you find Beth. I need to determine with her whether or not she thought that those answers would come out during the hypnosis and if that was the reason that she agreed to it in the first place. You see, Dan, she may want us to find Beth, but she cannot bring herself to come forward and openly tell us that and then help us with our enquiries.'

Dan called in Colin to join them so that he could update him and also instruct him as to how the interviews should be managed. Abe, Rachel, Pete, and Sophie were all on telephones, trying to locate Murray Thomson.

Colin was the first to speak.

'I have already summoned Matt Oliver for an interview. He is getting ready to join us as we speak so he should be ready for interviewing within the hour. Who do you want to interview him?'

'Oh, that one is definitely mine,' replied Dan. 'I am looking forward to wiping the arrogance off his face. I plan to throw the book at him. I look forward to watching him squirm as I suggest that he may be charged with perverting the course of justice in the matter of our cold case that involved the kidnapping and raping of his own daughter.'

To Colin, Dan instructed, 'I then want to interview Jack, Bill, and then Kate in that order so can you take the necessary action to organise all of that. Coordinate Kate's interview with Grace as she is leaving shortly to speak with her again. Colin, you will sit in on all the interviews.

'However, if we find Murray Thomson before any of the interviews, he becomes our priority, and we postpone the other interviews.

'Grace, I think that you should sit in on Kate's interview. I don't want to be accused of abusing medical ethics with her if she becomes agitated during questioning. In other words, I would like you to keep us on the right track.'

'I don't have a problem with any of that,' said Grace as she got up to leave his office.

1 p.m.

Dan, Colin, and Grace walked into the conference room just in time to witness a group hug. They smiled to each other, knowing that this could only mean one thing. One of them had found information that would lead them to Murray Thomson.

They were quite correct.

'Go on then, Sophie. Tell them. It's your moment of glory,' said Abe.

'Murray Thomson is alive as we already suspected,' she said, pumping both arms into the air above her head. 'And we now know where he works.'

'Well done, but don't keep us in suspense. Who is this guy and where can we find him?' asked Dan.

'I sneakily used the warrant that we had for the search of the hospital records to urge a friend of a friend to pull out all stops at HMRC to access the employment details of Murray Thomson and to report back out with our original enquiry. Sorry, Chief, but I told them that I was calling on behalf of Special Crimes Division Chief Superintendent Dan Turner.'

'Okay, ten out of ten for initiative, Sophie, but, come on, tell us what we all need to know,' urged Colin.

'You are just not going to believe this,' said Sophie, red faced with excitement.

'It's not the bloody janitor, is it?' asked Dan. 'Because I will have to eat my hat if it is. I haven't had him down as the kidnapper right from the outset, but I know that you lot have all had a thing for him. Go on. Put me out of my misery.'

'No, the janitor is in the clear, and he doesn't have a pseudonym,' replied Sophie.

Silence.

'It's only the bloody bursar at the school,' shouted Sophie, jumping up and down. 'He has worked there since the late nineties and still works there.'

'Bloody hell! Good job, Sophie. Now we know why the kidnapper knew the details about the Oliver family. He would've had access to all student records as part of his job. And he would have the details of where the parents worked as required by the application process. How the hell has he managed to stay off the radar until now?' asked Dan.

'We don't have those answers, Chief,' said Abe, '*yet!*'

'Never mind that for now. All we need is his home address. Come on, Sophie, tell us that you have managed to get that too, or do we need to call Eleanor Marshall, the headmistress?' asked Dan.

Sophie waved her arms above her head for the second time, this time with a piece of paper in the right hand. 'Yes. It is 29 Lovatt Road in the Kings Cross area.'

'And is Mr Thomson at school today?' asked Dan.

As he asked this question, Rachel waved the phone in the air. 'On the case, Chief.' They all watched her as she spoke and then listened to the response. 'Surprisingly, our Mr Thomson has been off sick for a few days and may not be back this week.'

'Good work,' said Dan. 'Well, what are we waiting for?'

1.20 p.m.

'Right, never mind any interviews for now. Someone cancel Bill and Jack, but leave Matt to make his way here. He can stew for a while. Let's proceed with determination to find the kidnapper and with optimism that we will find Beth alive.'

Dan continued, 'Colin, you and Pete head for Thomson's home address and take him by surprise. Sophie, as you found his address, you have earned yourself a place on the team of the arresting officers on condition that you write up your notes on how you managed to get his personal details immediately you return. We need to be covered on this every step of the way. Abe and Rachel, can you stay here for now and make the arrangements for an emergency paramedics' ambulance and a SOCO team to be at the scene after our arrival? Grace, can you prepare a hospital and a competent medic team for the strong possibility of Beth's arrival?'

Turning back to Grace, Dan said, 'Grace, you come with me so that you are there for Beth, assuming that she is at that address and regardless of her condition.'

'I have already decided to call Miriam Shepherd directly,' replied Grace. 'She is still at St Rubens Hospital and she has already offered to be on call for Beth at any time. She knows the background, so, together with me, we will know exactly how to treat Beth.'

As he prepared to leave, Dan added, 'Not one word to anyone. I don't want any of the family to know that we have a name and address, and there are no exceptions on this. Is that understood?'

'Yes, Chief,' they said in unison.

'Assuming that this is our guy, Colin and I will bring him in. Pete will call you, Abe, to arrange backup so that you can sweep his home for clues before SOCO arrive. Rachel, don't be too anxious to get SOCO there promptly as I want a quick look around before they invade the space. Grace will accompany Beth to the hospital. And, on the way back, I will have to think about how we are going to manage the interviews going forward. Murray Thomson will be our priority until I say otherwise. Oh well, let's see what happens at 29 Lovatt Road first.

'That's it for now, guys, and well done again, Sophie. Let's take it one step at a time. This may be a false lead, so don't get too excited just yet,' said Dan as he was heading for the exit door, followed by Colin, Pete, Sophie, and Grace.

Dan and Grace pretty much drove to number 29 Lovatt Road in silence, each with their own thoughts. Whilst both were willing Beth to be safe, each was confused about the amateur nature of both kidnappings, the involvement of the Oliver family, and Kate's responses about the kidnapper during her hypnosis.

Grace broke the silence by taking a return call from Dr Miriam Shepherd. She basically told Grace to concentrate on finding Beth alive and leave everything else to her. Grace knew that she could trust her entirely.

After Grace's call, Dan broke another silence by speaking his thoughts aloud, 'This is weird, Grace. We move from having a cold case to a copycat kidnapping of a member of the same family eight years later. It looks very likely that the kidnapper is Murray Thomson who can be linked to Matt Oliver at the hospital and to Beth and Matt Oliver on the school register of parents and guardians. Did we miss something eight years ago? Why were there no leads then? What changed? Why Beth? Why now? If Murray Thomson is the kidnapper and if we find Beth today, we move from a cold case to potentially solving both crimes in one afternoon.'

'The exact same thoughts have been going through my head. This definitely is a surreal situation. I almost expect to find Beth unconscious and naked in the woods, covered with a blanket and a bottle of water and packet of sandwiches laid beside her. It's the concept of lapsed time that I can't get my head around,' added Grace.

'One thing at a time, eh? Let's just hope that we find Beth unharmed and have her settled safely in the hospital before the day is out. And, if Murray Thomson is the criminal that we have been searching for, he will be in a holding cell here. Then, we will have plenty of time to consider the whys and wherefores, particularly as Beth will, no doubt, be able to assist us with filling in some of the gaps.'

2.15 p.m.

When they arrived at Thomson's home address, they saw that Colin and Pete were standing outside the front door.

'Why haven't they gone in as we agreed?' asked Dan. As they approached the house, he noticed that Colin was reading from a piece of paper.

'You are not going to believe this, Chief,' Colin said as he handed the note over to Dan. 'An envelope was pinned to the door.'

Dan took one look at it and passed it to Grace with no comment. Grace saw immediately that the note was in the same style as the one delivered at the time of Kate's kidnapping. Before she read it, she had a premonition of what it was going to say.

**YoU won'T fiNd hER here. SHe is in the GrANge WoODs
I will BE easy TO find so SHe is yOUr priORity.
ReVEnGe haS Not beEN swEEt.**

'This is truly bizarre. Grace, you spoke too soon in the car. Can you issue an instruction for the ambulance to be where it needs to be in the Grange Woods? Colin, I don't think that we are going to need a search party. Just in case that we do, can you call the office and ask Abe and Rachel to make the same arrangements as last time but to keep everyone on standby until we have checked the area where Kate was found in 2004?

'But, before we head for the woods, let's do a very quick tour of the house as I suspect that we will find Mr Thomson in one of the rooms.

'Remember that I don't want anyone discussing any of this until I issue further instructions. Hopefully, Beth will be where he says she is, and, hopefully, she will be alive. This being the case, the first time that any of the family will hear about that is when Colin and I meet with them individually. Is that clear to everyone?'

'Yes, Chief.'

'Colin, make sure that this is also clear to Abe and Rachel.'

The entrance door to 29 Lovatt Road was not locked.

CHAPTER 20

Friday, 19 October 2012
2.30 p.m.

Dan, Grace, Colin, Pete, and Sophie made their way into the Thomson's home, not knowing what to expect.

The full townhouse on three levels clearly belonged to the Thomsons as there were no internal divisions.

A staircase led to four bedrooms and a bathroom. Colin, Pete, and Sophie ran up the stairs to quickly check the rooms.

The sitting room, dining room, kitchen, cloakroom, and various cupboards were on the ground floor. Dan and Grace checked those rooms but didn't go beyond the two doors that led to the garage and basement rooms.

Based on the note that Murray Thomson had pinned to the door, Dan was working on the assumption that Beth would be found in the same location as where Kate was found all those years ago. He planned no more than a quick glance of the basement rooms before setting off to the woods as he knew what they would find, and, that afternoon, it would be sectioned off as the crime scene.

It didn't take Colin long to come across key evidence in one of the bedrooms. 'Chief, you had better get up here,' he called downstairs.

In what was obviously Thomson's bedroom, they found Murray Thomson lying on his bed, on his back, fully clothed, staring into space—and dead.

On the floor lay the 'man in black's' clothes, shoes, and accessories.

On the bedside cabinet was an empty bottle of pills, an empty glass, and an almost full bottle of water. Propped against the glass was a hand-written note.

To Beth and Kate Oliver

I am not getting any personal peace from this journey of revenge, and so it must end now.

All my wife and I ever wanted was an apology from Dr Oliver and a demonstration of his staff's sympathy and understanding of the devastation that we felt when we lost our baby girl and my wife lost her last chance to ever give birth.

Perhaps he will now comprehend the level of helplessness that I felt when I was unable to do anything that would save either my baby daughter or my adorable wife.

Murray Thomson

'Okay, nothing that we can do for Mr Murray now,' said Dan. 'Pete and Sophie, can you do a sweep of his room and the bathroom? Grace, you can join them if you want to get a closer look of our kidnapper. Colin, let's take a quick look at the basement rooms just to confirm that one of them is also a scene of crime for the SOCO guys. Two minutes, guys, and then let's get the hell out of here and find Beth.'

Colin and Dan entered the basement from the door in the kitchen as they had quickly established that the door from the hall led to the garage. In a large basement room that could be accessed from either the kitchen or the garage, they were not surprised at the layout as they had seen it before on the DVDs sent to the MET. What they were surprised to find was Beth lying on the bed with her ankles and wrist bound to the bedposts.

'Oh no! It can't be!' shouted Dan. The sight of a very still Beth with an unrecognisably bruised face and body led him to believe that she was dead. It was Colin who walked over to her and checked for a pulse.

'She has a pulse, Dan,' was all that Colin could say.

Dan ran out of the room and yelled upstairs, 'Grace, get yourself down here now. It's Beth.'

Dan returned to the room and checked her pulse himself. 'You're right, Colin. There is a pulse. Thank God for that.'

Grace ran into the room. 'Oh shit. What the hell has he done to her?' she said as she too checked immediately for a pulse.

There was no need for any instructions to be given. Grace took over.

'The ambulance should be parked outside by now. Someone tell the paramedics that we have a body that can wait until later but that Beth and I must be on our way to St Rubens Hospital immediately. I'll supervise Beth en route.'

She then called Miriam Shepherd's cell phone and told her that Beth was in bad shape and that they would be on their way to the hospital within the next few minutes. Grace didn't wait for Miriam to say that she would be there. She just knew that she would.

'Grace, I'm coming with you,' said Dan.

'No, you're not,' replied Grace. 'You do what you do best and leave me to do what I do best. Beth is strong. Beth will survive this.'

The paramedics arrived at the scene, and Grace and Dan both watched in horror as they prepared Beth for the ambulance ride to the hospital. Grace watched their every move, and Dan knew that she would be there for Beth every step of the way, as would Miriam when she arrived at the hospital.

They had found the kidnapper and Beth, but Dan knew that there were gaps that needed to be filled. For a moment there, he had thought that Beth was dead. When they had found her in the basement after reading the note directing them to the woods, his first thought was that she had died before being moved and that Thomson had panicked and then committed suicide.

The ambulance left for the hospital with an unconscious and badly beaten Beth. Grace wondered why Thomson had made no attempt to wash her, as he had with Kate before she was found. Based on the evidence before her, it was obvious that Beth had a broken nose and some broken ribs. Beyond that, she wasn't prepared to hazard a guess.

Without asking, Colin called Abe and asked him to call off the search party and anything else that he had arranged. He told him that they had found Beth, but that, per Dan's earlier instruction, no one should be told that until Dan issued a fresh instruction. He asked him to report Thomson's death by suicide to the medical examiner's office and to inform SOCO that they would only be needed at 29 Lovatt Road.

Dan instructed Colin to stay with him in the basement and then asked Pete and Sophie to work together and check the rooms out for anything that they should know before SOCO arrived.

In the basement room, Colin recorded the hospital bed, restraints, bedding, pillows, a saline drip, a Bunsen burner, a shelf full of small bottles of water, a packet of straws, a box of tissues, a camera and tripod, and a trolley full of medical utensils.

As Colin did that, Dan wandered through the house and concluded that it must look the same today as it had been eight years ago and long before that.

The only sign of life was in three rooms. In the upstairs' bathroom, some male toiletries, toothbrush, and toothpaste were laid beside the sink. In the bedroom, the bed and bedroom furniture were ancient, as was the bedding. In the kitchen, the fridge had an unopened bottle of milk, a couple of eggs, a few slices of bread, a piece of cheese, butter, and a couple of cans of beer.

This was a home without any soul for a man who had lived a lonely and depressing existence since the death of his baby daughter and his wife. In fact, the decor and overall feel of the house suggested that it had always been an unhappy home. Dan couldn't see anything that suggested that this was a home of a happy marriage and happy childhood. He was sure that Murray Thomson was an only child.

Dan wondered how Murray Thomson had slipped through the medical system. Clearly, he had been very depressed and perhaps even suicidal since the deaths of the people that he had loved most. Not for the first time in his career at the MET, he was shocked by the godforsaken world that he was living in. Regularly, he came across the lack of care and attention for the people who actually needed it most. And Murray Thomson had definitely been one of those people.

Colin informed Dan that SOCO were on their way and shouted to Pete and Sophie to be quick as the crime scene would shortly be taped off.

'Nothing else we can do here for now. Colin, you and Pete stay here until SOCO arrive. Sophie, you and I will head back to the MET.' When they reached Dan's car, he asked Sophie to drive as he wanted to make some calls.

Firstly, he called the commander and updated him briefly, saying that he would meet up with him later at the MET.

Dan then sent a text to Grace, confirming that he was on his way back to the MET, that he had updated the commander, and that he would personally share the news with Bill and Jack together, Matt, and then Kate, in that order.

He phoned Rachel and asked if she could buy in some decent coffee and pastries for the team as, no doubt, like him, they hadn't eaten all day.

His last thought as he approached the MET was that he had enough on Matt and Kate to hold them overnight, and, the way that he was feeling, he was tempted to do just that.

A call came in from Grace as he entered his office. She told him that Beth's blood pressure and pulse were normal and that she was about to get full external and internal examinations. She was able to confirm that there were no head injuries but that her nose was broken. Dr Miriam Shepherd was trying to complete as many tests as possible whilst Beth was still unconscious, even if that meant additional sedation.

He briefly updated Abe and Rachel and then headed to his office. He suddenly realised that he was tired and hungry and that he needed five or ten minutes to himself to compose himself before starting any of the interviews that Abe had arranged for his arrival.

'In light of what has happened, I've decided to change the order of the interviews, Abe. I am going to see Bill and Jack together before I see anyone else. It will be an emotional time for both of them, so can you ask one of the girls to make them as comfortable as possible? No one needs to sit in on that as there is no need for it to be formal.'

After making the call to Bill and Jack, Abe requested that the interview room be set up for three people and that he be called when Bill and Jack arrive.

5.45 p.m.

Dan greeted Bill and Jack and apologised for the short notice in changing their earlier appointments with him. He explained that he had been called out about an important development regarding Beth's kidnapping.

Seeing the anxious looks on their faces, he didn't waste any time in sharing the good news with them.

'We have found Beth alive. Grace escorted her to the hospital, and she is being closely monitored by Miriam, just as Kate was. He passed on the update that Grace had given him. We didn't get a chance to forewarn you about any of this because we didn't know that we were going to find Beth. We had a very strong lead about who the kidnapper was, and we followed that through to his house.'

Dan explained about the mix-up of the notes and about how they had come to find Beth. 'There is some bad news, and that is that Beth had been badly beaten before we found her. Superficially, she has a broken nose and several broken ribs. I can say no more than that because Miriam has barely started to carry out internal and external examinations, and these will be followed by various tests.

'And before either of you ask, the answer is no. Miriam has stipulated that no visitors will be allowed this evening because Beth is likely to be unconscious throughout the night and may be kept unconscious, depending upon what Miriam finds from her examinations and tests. However, so far her vitals are normal.'

Bill and Jack hug, and Dan gave them a moment to pull themselves together. The sheer relief that Dan saw on their faces was reward enough for him.

'Can I phone Caroline?' asked Bill in a quiet voice.

'Of course, you can, Bill,' answered Dan, 'but don't you think that it would be better for you to go home and tell her personally?'

They both agreed and got up to leave.

'Please tell Caroline that I will sit down with the three of you soon to tell you about our leads and how they led to us finding Beth. For now, all that matters to you is that Beth is in safe hands and you will be able to visit her tomorrow morning.'

'Have you told Kate and Matt?' asked Bill.

'No, and I ask you both not to go there. In confidence, I tell you both that I am about to interview Matt and then Kate. Don't ask any questions because I won't answer them. I now know the *who* and the *where*, but I don't know the precise detail of the *why*. I believe that between the two of them, I will get the answers that I need. I must ask you to keep all this to yourself and to resist making any telephone calls to either of them tonight. I can say no more than that, but I hope that you both trust me enough to go along with my request.'

Bill took Dan's offered hand in both of his hands and looked Dan straight in his eyes. 'I always knew that if anyone could find Beth, it would be you. I never lost confidence in your ability to find her for us. Thank you, Dan.'

'I'll second that,' was all that Jack could say because he became emotional again, just listening to his grandfather's words.

Dan returned to his office, by which time Colin and Rachel had returned. He asked Colin to join him in his office in five minutes. Then he spent a few minutes to reflect on the turn of events and to take a moment's pleasure at the emotional time that he had just had with Bill and Jack.

Colin and Dan sat in disbelief as they recalled what had happened during the last few hours. Whilst they were happy with the results, the detective in both of them wanted answers to the questions that remained unanswered.

'We have an element of closure today, Colin. Beth is safe and we identified the kidnapper. Sadly, he is dead. I say we call it a day after we have briefly interviewed Matt and Kate. I will recall them for more detailed interviews tomorrow.'

6.50 p.m.

By the time that Dan and Colin joined Matt Oliver in his interview room, he was very grim-faced.

'Well, Dr Oliver, how are you this evening?' asked Dan.

'Pissed off at having to come here at all and then having to hang about for hours without explanation. What is it with you and your determination to implicate me in Kate's and now Beth's kidnappings?' snapped Matt.

'And here was me thinking that you would be keen to hear if there was any news about your ex-wife, the mother of your son and daughter,' responded Dan sarcastically.

'Naturally, I am anxious about Beth's kidnapping, and I hope that she is unharmed and found safe soon. Have you got any leads? Sorry for being so grumpy, by the way, Dan. It's just that this whole kidnapping has brought back bad memories of Kate's kidnapping. To this day, I just can't bear to think about it,' said Matt.

'I know, Matt,' said Dan sympathetically but certainly not feeling it. 'Anyhow, enough of that for now. I do want to formally interview you about the kidnappings of Kate and Beth, and I also need to warn you that you are on very shaky ground about your lack of cooperation with our enquiries for both.'

Matt started to defend his position, but Dan stopped him.

'Not now, Matt. I have some important news for you,' said Dan. 'We have found Beth. She was unconscious when we found her and has been badly beaten. She is at St Rubens in the capable hands of Miriam and Grace. I can tell you no more than that at present.'

'Thank God that you have found her alive,' said Matt. 'What happened all those years ago between Beth and me is water under the bridge. I have never truly forgiven her for not being there for Kate that evening, but I do know that she didn't do it on purpose. If it hadn't been that evening, it may have been another place and time. I loved her very much, you know, but I never coped well with the compromises that we all had to make for her job. I would never want her harmed. You have to believe that.'

'I find that difficult to believe, Matt. You see, I consider that failing to cooperate with police enquiries is harmful. In the case of your daughter's kidnapping, it was very harmful indeed. I am going to leave you for now as I need to speak with Kate about Beth's safe return. But I want to leave you with this thought, Matt.'

A very serious Dan leaned over the table and looked Matt straight in the eyes and said, 'We now have evidence that proves that it is you who is responsible for the kidnapper's grudge against your family. That evidence could have, and should have, been found eight years ago. But we didn't have the good doctor's cooperation then, did we? Whilst I am away, I want you to think very carefully about how the information that we have extracted from the hospital's records could have helped us to find your daughter sooner and perhaps prevented rape and would certainly have avoided Beth's kidnapping. We had to resort to a search warrant to access your files. I also want you to consider whether or not you think that we may have a strong-enough case against you to charge you with perverting the course of justice.'

Dan's parting shot to Matt as he turned on his heels to exit the interview room was, 'A lot to think about, Matt, eh?' and, to Colin, he said, 'Ask someone to bring Dr Oliver a cup of coffee.' And to Matt, he said, 'Don't go anywhere. I'll be back.'

Outside the interview room, Colin turned to Dan and said, 'Well, you certainly gave him something to think about.'

'That was sweetness and light compared to how I intend to conduct my formal interview with him.'

Dan decided to return to his office to call Grace for a progress report on Beth before meeting Kate.

7 p.m.

When he arrived at his office and saw that his team were still working, he decided to send them home. Beth was safe and the kidnapper's days of revenge were over, which was all that mattered for the moment.

None of his team argued when he told them to pack up for the evening and to reconvene at ten o'clock the following morning. He told them that he would be with the Palmers for the early part of the morning and asked that they focus on writing their reports and tidying up any loose ends.

7.15 p.m.

Grace reported that Beth had gained consciousness briefly but that Miriam had instructed that she be sedated again. Her priority was that Beth rested throughout the night and had a peaceful night's sleep. Grace said that she was going to stay with Beth until she was asleep for the evening.

Grace asked Dan if he wanted her to return to the MET. At that point, he decided that he was only going to update Kate about the safe return of her mother and to delay her formal interview until the next morning. Also, he wanted Grace to be there when he interviewed Kate, so he told Grace not to bother returning to the office.

He made his way back to the interview rooms and told Colin that he would update Kate and then arrange separate formal interviews with her and Matt before discharging them for the evening.

To be honest, he was keen to visit the hospital on the way home to see for himself that Beth was okay. He knew that she would be asleep, but he also knew that he would have a better chance of catching up on his own sleep after seeing her settled in her hospital bed.

He updated Colin, who, like the rest of the team, was also thankful for an earlier-than-planned finish. The two of them set off to meet with Kate and to leave Matt stewing for a while longer.

7.25 p.m.

Dan embraced Kate, and, sensing her agitation, he was glad that he had decided that tonight was definitely not the night to give her the hard time that she must be expecting. That could wait until tomorrow.

'Sorry for keeping you so long, but we have had a rather busy few hours. We have found your mother alive. She is at the hospital with Grace. She has been badly beaten, but feedback from the various tests so far is positive.'

Kate didn't say anything, and Dan couldn't read her reaction, so he continued, 'We followed a lead and found the kidnapper. We have good reason to believe that he was the same person who kidnapped you. He is in custody.'

He used the *custody* word deliberately to see how she would react. She didn't flinch about any of the news that he had passed on to her. He didn't want to say much more at that point. He knew that she would speak to Grace if she had anything that she wanted to say or find out.

'Kate, you should know that I have already met with your father, brother, and grandfather. I had no particular reason for keeping you to last. I just saw people as they arrived. Based on information that we have received, a family reunion would not have been appropriate.'

'Dan, you don't need to explain, but I appreciate you taking the time to do so and to update me about Beth being found,' said Kate.

Dan quietly wished that Kate had used the word *Mum* rather than *Beth*.

'I need to meet with your father again this evening before I leave, but my plan is to spend some time with your grandparents first thing tomorrow morning to talk them through the events that led to us finding Beth and then drive them to the hospital to visit her. They are emotionally drained at present, so, hopefully, after seeing her, they will start to relax,' said Dan.

He continued without interruption, 'I would then like to schedule some time with you to talk through the Grace's feedback from your hypnotism. What time would suit you tomorrow?'

'I have taken some time off work, so I can be free to meet with you at your convenience. How about lunch?'

'Actually, Kate, our meeting isn't social. I would like to interview you here. How about 1 p.m.? Best to eat something before you arrive.'

'I understand,' said Kate, 'and, yes, one o'clock is fine. Can I leave now?'

'Yes, you can. I'll walk with you to your car.'

Dan winked to Colin, confirming that it wouldn't be long now before they could set off home.

On reaching Kate's car, on impulse, Dan turned her around and looked her in the eyes. 'I know that this must be difficult for you, Kate. Take care of yourself. It's good to know that you have Grace there for you as a close friend and mentor.'

'Thanks, Dan. I appreciate that. You take care too. I know how you feel about Mum. Might be a good time to let down your guard a bit on that score, don't you think?' Kate gave Dan a peck on his cheek and jumped into her car.

Dan pondered what she had said and was sure that she had just said *Mum* for the first time in his company.

'Right, Colin. Quick chat with Matt, and then you and I are out of here. I would love to keep him in overnight, but it's probably enough to ensure that he won't have a good night's sleep.'

Colin nodded in agreement, and they made their way to the interview room that Matt had now spent almost three hours in.

8.15 p.m.

'Okay, Matt, all the family are now aware of Beth's safe return. They have each gone their respective ways, and all I need to do now is to ensure that I have told you the same as I have told them.'

He continued without giving Matt a chance to interrupt, telling him where Beth was, the current prognosis about her recovery, and the fact that the kidnapper was in custody.

'Where is Kate?' asked Matt. 'I need to speak with her. I need to see for myself that she is okay.'

'That's not possible. She has gone home. I suspect that she will catch up with Grace at some point, but I doubt if that will be at the hospital. She didn't give any indication that she would visit her mother. Kate was calm, almost too calm.'

'It's good to hear that, at least. I'll give her a call just to let her know that I am thinking about her and offer to meet up if she wants to,' said Matt. 'I'm not surprised that she didn't suggest visiting Beth. So much time has passed by that I wonder if their relationship has gone past the point of any return.'

'It's never too late to repair a relationship. We are all hoping that Beth's kidnapping will go some way to lay some sort of foundation that Grace can use to bring them together amicably in the future.'

'That would be healthy,' said Matt.

'I agree,' said Dan. 'Now, I am going to let you go home, but I will have to interview you formally tomorrow at some point. How about 11.30 a.m.? Would that suit you?'

'Not really, but I'll be here. Do I need a lawyer?' he asked rather sheepishly.

'You aren't under caution, so I wouldn't have thought so, but it is your prerogative to have legal representation if you would feel more comfortable.'

'No. I don't think I will bother. Can I go home now? My wife will be worried.'

'Yes. That's us for this evening. Colin, can you please escort Matt to the exit?' asked Dan.

Colin and Matt left the interview room.

Dan made his way back to his office to clear his desk but was pleased to find that the team had done that for him before leaving. He called Grace to find that she was still at the hospital and had decided to stay overnight. 'Talk about déjà vu,' she said, as she had done exactly the same on the evening that Kate had been found and admitted to the same hospital.

'Jack and Bill popped in to see Beth. They just stayed for a few minutes as she was still unconscious at that time. They were just relieved to see her tucked up safely in bed but were naturally disturbed at how she looked.'

'Yes, I am meeting with them around about nine o'clock tomorrow morning.'

Silence.

'I am assuming by that pause that you, too, would like to come to the hospital to see for yourself that Beth is in safe hands.'

'I thought you would never ask,' replied Dan.

'I didn't,' said Grace, 'but I did expect to see you at some point. I'll be here. Bring a fresh coffee with you, please.'

'No problem,' said Dan.

Colin arrived just as Dan was packing his briefcase.

9.10 p.m.

Colin and Dan left the office together.

Colin set off home, thankful that he would be able to spend some time with his wife in his arms before another day at the office.

Dan stopped off for a couple of coffees. He drove to the hospital, parked, took the lift to the fifth floor, introduced himself to the staff nurse, and was directed to Beth's room.

CHAPTER 21

Friday, 19 October 2012
9.55 p.m.

Dan was shocked at how Beth looked. Her face was badly swollen, her nose was bandaged, and already the yellow and black bruising was spreading across her face.

Grace was sitting beside Beth, holding her hand. On seeing this sight, Dan wished that he could openly do the same. He did lean over Beth and gave her a peck on the forehead. He did the same to Grace.

Dan and Grace didn't want to leave Beth's room, so they decided to check with the duty staff nurse if it was okay to sit beside her bed whilst they discussed the kidnapping investigation. The response was negative simply because Dr Shepherd's instructions very clearly stated that she should get as much rest as possible overnight.

Contrary to their wishes, they had no option but to sit outside the room for their catch-up.

Grace told Dan that all tests were clear and there would be no long-term physical damage. 'The staff are clearing the drugs from her body slowly as Miriam doesn't know which cocktail Beth has had during the last couple of days. That way, she expects Beth to be fully compos mentis when she awakens. As far as her mental state is concerned, I think that Beth is strong enough to have tolerated whatever happened at Thomson's, even if he had raped her. There is no sign of that having happened, by the way.'

Thank God for small mercies, thought Dan.

Grace continued, 'As you can guess from the bandaging on her face, her nose was broken. Also, several ribs were broken, and she is badly bruised around the middle, so she is heavily bandaged in those areas. God only knows what he hit her with to break the ribs, but she won't be running any marathons for a while.

'Beth's job has trained her to cope with horrific crimes, and she tends to shrug off anything that happens to herself. I don't think that she will dwell upon what happened to her. She'll be more interested in crossing the t's and dotting the i's when she finds out that Thomson is dead. If anything, she will torture herself even more about Kate's kidnapping now that she has experienced the how, where, and who for herself.'

'Thank God that she is back with us,' said Dan, 'and thank God that we found the bastard who did this to her and Kate. At least, we will eventually be able to draw a line under the two crimes and not live in fear of them being repeated.'

'I agree,' said Grace. 'I also hope that it will go some way to open a door for Beth and Kate to start talking to each other. Kate must surely realise that she and her mother have now been a victim of revenge against Matt and the hospital.'

'Good luck with that. At least, you now have an opportunity to move it all forward, and I'm sure that you will have the blessing and cooperation of Bill, Caroline, and Jack to do that.'

Dan updated Grace on his meetings with Bill and Jack, Matt, and Kate.

'Now that the kidnapper has been found, albeit dead, I have decided that there isn't the need to formally interview Bill or Jack. For the same reason, I didn't feel the need to prolong my interviews with Matt and Kate earlier, but I have arranged formal interviews for tomorrow at 11.30 with Matt and at 1 p.m. with Kate.'

Dan continued, 'Kate didn't seem to have any negative side effects after her hypnosis. In fact, she didn't show any signs of anything at all, but that's Kate. She asked if I wanted to meet up over lunch tomorrow, but I explained to her that our discussion was going to be formal. She didn't bat an eyelid.

'When I meet with Bill, Caroline, and Jack tomorrow morning, I'll talk them through the sequence of events leading up to finding Beth, and then I'll bring them here to visit Beth. I'll call you first to check if Miriam is happy for Beth to receive her family.'

'That sounds fine. You're going to have a busy day. How can I help?'

'I'm looking forward to sharing positive news with the family, and Matt's interview will be straightforward. The less time that I spend with him, the better. There is no display of remorse, and he still isn't acknowledging that his full cooperation during Kate's kidnapping would have avoided a cold case and then Beth's kidnapping. The commander and I are going to discuss this in detail and decide how to approach the hospital. Despite having a search warrant, we did not get full access to their records, in this case, the legals.

'I plan to make Matt sweat, but I won't be pressing charges about him perverting the course of justice. Let's be honest. By the time that goes to court and members of the hospital board talk about conflict of interest and privacy codes of practice, any jury will rule that he has probably suffered enough over the last eight years. I will, however, send a strongly worded letter to the hospital's board of governors as there is no way that I am going to let him walk away with a clear conscience. The result will undoubtedly be a politely worded letter as the governing members will probably not think that he actually did anything wrong.

'I need to talk to you about what Kate actually authorised you to share with me after the hypnosis. Last time we spoke, you appeared to be keen to give me a hint about that which she didn't authorise. Am I correct?'

'Dan, I have battled with my conscience ever since the hypnosis. For eight years, I have held back information about Kate from Beth and you. That burden has just grown again. I have sought the advice of the court's lawyer. As I started to tell you yesterday, he feels that if I am careful about how I word what I would like to say to you, I will avoid being in breach of the non-disclosure agreement.'

'Good. You are making the right decision. We have to put all this to bed this time, and, if that means that Kate is implicated in Beth's kidnapping, then I have to put that on to the table. So you have a choice. We either have that conversation now or we meet up early tomorrow morning before I make my way to Bill's.'

'Let's do a bit of both,' offered Grace. 'I'll give you something to think about tonight, and then we can have a breakfast meeting tomorrow morning. I'm assuming that you don't need me for Matt's interview, so, from there, I'll accompany you to Bill's and then drive them to the hospital. I will then meet up with you at your office with enough time to answer any questions that you have before interviewing Kate. That is if you still want me to sit in on Kate's interview.'

'Sounds good to me,' said Dan. 'My brain is already in overdrive, so what difference are a few more meaty details going to make? As far as the family know, Murray Thomson is in *custody*.' Witnessing Beth's frown, he added, 'Well, he certainly isn't going anywhere, is he? So, technically, he is in custody, albeit at the morgue.'

'I guess that I can't argue with that,' she said as she stood up. 'I need to stretch my legs so I will get another couple of coffees. Won't be as good as those that you brought in, but they will be hot and wet.'

As Grace went for the coffees, Dan walked back into Beth's room and then leaned over her bed to take a closer look at her. This time, he did take her hand. 'Thank God that you are unharmed. I don't know how I would have coped without you in my life,' he whispered to her.

Grace witnessed this through the viewing window and decided to give him a few moments alone with Beth. She knew how he felt about Beth and took a mental note to have that conversation with each of them at a later date.

When Dan returned to the corridor, he was surprised to see Grace carrying a tray with two mugs and a plate of biscuits and cake. She read his mind.

'Staff nurse took pity on me as I have had so many coffees from the machine today. She made the fresh coffees for us and raided the staff room for the biscuits and fruit cake.

'Staff nurse also took the initiative to call Miriam regarding our question about whether or not we should sit with Beth as we talked. Apparently, Miriam said that it would do no harm if it was contained to you and me. Yes, Beth needs rest, but Miriam also wants to gauge her reaction to reality.'

'Does this mean that we should continue with our discussion in Beth's room?' asked Dan.

'It certainly does, Chief Superintendent,' replied Grace, 'but let's be careful about what we say about Kate.'

They took their seats at either side of Beth and talked about the peculiar events of the day, and then Grace talked about the hypnosis in more detail.

'To be honest, Dan, the majority of the hypnosis was about what I had already heard before. Just as I was about to give up the idea about finding out anything new, I decided to ask a couple of random questions about the kidnapper and the location where she had been held captive.'

'I asked her if she remembered what height the kidnapper was. Kate replied that he was the similar height to Jack. I asked if she ever saw the colour of his hair. Surprisingly, she said that she had and that it was dark brown.'

'Up to now Kate has always given us the impression that the kidnapper always wore a black balaclava in her presence,' said Dan.

'That's true,' replied Grace, 'which urged me to carry on. I asked her if he wore glasses, and she replied that he didn't except when he wore his balaclava. I asked how old she thought he was, and she said that he was in his thirties. "What makes you think that?" I asked, and she said that he had a young voice.'

'Grace, do you think that Kate at seventeen years of age would have been able to put an age to the voice?'

'We are on the same wavelength. You will now begin to understand the suspicions that I want to share with you, but let's not go there for now,' she whispered, nodding to Beth and reminding him that they needed to be discreet in her presence.

'That's when I threw in what I thought would result in a negative response. "Kate, now that you have had more time to think about the kidnapper, do you think that you would be able to identify him from photographs or an identity parade?" Kate said that perhaps she could. I asked if she had any idea of where she was held captive. She floored me with saying that maybe she did.'

Dan remained silent.

'I decided to end the hypnosis then. She showed no signs of being anxious, but I knew that I was in danger of turning the hypnosis into an interview and that this would have a negative effect on her subconscious. After the rest period, I did eventually tell her what she had said. That's when she shrugged and said that they were vague responses that didn't demonstrate that she actually remembered any detail. But I have already told you that.

'I asked her if I could share those particular questions and responses with you, and, to my surprise, she said that I could.'

Dan remained silent.

'Say something, Dan,' said Grace.

Dan stood up and indicated that they should speak outside. Grace nodded in agreement as she followed him outside the room.

'Mentally, is Kate able to cope with directness about her personal life and aspects of the kidnapping?' asked Dan once they were seated in the corridor.

'Her family and very close friends treat her with kid gloves. They avoid conversations about relationships, sex, or a future that includes marriage and motherhood. They never talk about the kidnapping and rape. To be honest, I don't necessarily agree with that, and I don't think that she will ever move on until that has changed. At work, she is immune to personal feelings. I think that she is so good at what she does because of that. There is no conflict of interest because she avoids close encounters.'

'What makes you think that Kate is in some way involved with Beth's kidnapping, and how would you suggest that I proceed with my questioning of her?'

'When I was asking the questions that have been asked many times before, it was almost as though she were answering them as the teenager that she then was. When I paused for a few moments and then asked the questions about the kidnapper, it was as though she was answering them as the adult that she now is. I couldn't help but register that change, and later it made me think over and over again that it was the adult who thought that she could recognise him and not the teenager of eight years ago.'

'I understand your dilemma,' said Dan, 'but if I am being honest with you, I have been starting to have those thoughts myself. None of the second kidnapping stacks up for me, Grace. The eight-year gap, the change in the MO, and Kate's casual reaction to the lack of communication all bothered me. The commander and Bill were troubled by that too.'

'I knew that I was right, but I guess that I just didn't want to hear the words spoken aloud,' said Grace.

'Is Kate capable of such vengeance after all this time?' asked Dan.

'I wouldn't have ever believed that she was, but a person who has suffered post-traumatic stress syndrome and has allowed herself to be tormented by the memories for eight years could. Kate is a very special person, and it is devastating to consider her involvement. But she is a human being who is at the mercy of her brain function and subconscious mind just as we all are.'

'Put that way, we can't ignore our suspicions,' replied Dan.

'No, we can't,' replied Grace.

A moment of silence followed as they each considered the implications of what they had just said.

'I have no option but to present my questions as I see fit,' said Dan.

'Go for it, Dan,' agreed Grace. 'But in order to protect me from the NDA, you must present your questions just as you would in the line of duty with any other suspect. You have already had your suspicions about Kate, so that shouldn't be any problem for you.'

'I have no problem with that. In fact, it makes the line of questioning more credible,' said Dan. 'Now let me give you some advice. There is no point in finding the kidnapper, solving the mystery of the motive, closing the cold case, and solving the current case if you don't try to achieve some closure for Kate and for Beth. As you just said to me, go for it.'

'A word of caution about Kate. She could have thought so much about the kidnapper over the years that she actually started to form a description of him. This does happen, and the reason will surprise you. She may have formed a description of the rapist for no other reason than to convince herself that he was not a scruffy little man but a respectably clean and decent-looking guy. You have no idea how many victims of rape need to believe that. In some ways, it makes the rape feel less nauseous or unclean. Can you understand that?'

'Yes. Actually I think that I can,' replied Dan, 'but this does mean that I have to tread carefully with her.'

'On the other hand, if she did set out to find him, she may have felt compelled to do so and she may have emotionally blackmailed him to kidnap and harm Beth. We know that she hasn't been able to move on from the past, so she may have considered that one way to do that was to find him and face him.'

'I can understand that too and now have the clarity that I need for this afternoon's interview with Kate,' replied Dan.

They decided to return to Beth's bed to continue with the next part of their conversation.

Dan continued, 'I have had a strictly off-the-record and confidential conversation with Eleanor Marshall, and she has given me some background information about Murray Thomson. She was absolutely shocked to hear about his death and the circumstances leading up to it. She said that he was a reliable employee and that he got on well with the teachers and any parents that he met. He didn't have the need to have contact with the students and very seldom met with parents as the payment of fees was computerised and communication with parents was by email. I wouldn't be surprised if neither Matt nor Beth has met with him before. There is a photograph of each student on the registration forms, so he would have no problem in identifying Kate at that time.

'He was an only child and lived at the current address during his teens. His father died when he was nineteen. He returned to the house after studying accountancy at university. He left when he got married but then returned again when his mother became ill and later died. The title of the house was transferred to him after his mother's death.

'We now have a record of his career history up to his employment at the St Andrews School for Girls. We know that wasn't coincidental with Kate's kidnapping because he joined there almost two years before the kidnapping.'

Dan referred to his notes and continued, 'We know that, as bursar, he had access to the family's contact details. The motive for kidnapping Kate was revenge. Why? Because his child died just after birth under the medical management of Kate's father. His wife was unable to cope with the loss of her baby daughter, particularly as it was her last chance to give birth to her own child. She committed suicide a few months later. We know that his wife had many miscarriages before being accepted for IVF treatment, as recommended by Dr Matt Oliver.'

Grace added her analysis.

'We can only assume that Murray Thomson became very depressed and didn't get the medical attention that he undoubtedly needed. Morbid depression turned into a journey of blame and revenge. With the correct care and medication, he could have come to terms with his misfortune and got on with his life. He was allowed to slip through the psychiatric assessment process, and he didn't even receive any prescriptive drugs for his depression. He should have been referred to his GP, who would have recognised the signs and referred him for psych tests.'

Dan picked up the story.

'During his legal battle with the hospital and the conclusion that there had been no malpractice, he became more embittered. He checked out Dr Matt Oliver in more detail and found out that his wife was DCI Beth Oliver and, together, they had two children, Kate and Jack. Rachel checked local press articles before Kate's kidnapping and found a couple of articles about the Olivers and the privileged life that they led. It would have been easy for him to find out that Kate attended the private girls' school where he was working as bursar.

'We can only assume that it was Murray Thomson who gave Kate a lift on that unfortunate night. He probably couldn't believe his luck when he saw her outside the school, looking lost and upset. The hospital bed and the other add-ons in the basement room just didn't arrive overnight. According to Eleanor, his father was a general practitioner who provided private consultations from his home. That had to be in place as part of his plan to capture Kate or one of the Olivers at the first chance that he got. He wanted to ruin their lives, just as he believed that Matt Oliver had ruined his.'

Grace agreed with all that Dan had said. 'He was, no doubt, able to carry out the rapes due to years of sexual frustration. Let's be honest. Which man wouldn't get sexually aroused when facing the prospect of having sex with a beautiful teenager? Yes, he raped Kate, but, in his mind, he was doing that for his wife and daughter, so he didn't consider that he was doing anything wrong. No doubt when he found out that Kate was a virgin, reality was a different story. By Eleanor Marshall's account, he was a decent person at school, but he was obviously a very tormented guy at home. Nevertheless, he was someone who knew the difference between right and wrong.'

11.35 p.m.

'Which is why he came after me,' said a very weak Beth from the bed.

'Bloody hell, Beth. You gave me the fright of my life,' said Grace as she leaned forward and kissed her on her forehead.

Dan stared at Beth for what seemed like minutes, and then he, too, leaned forward, took her hand, and kissed her on her right cheek. 'Welcome back, Beth. We have missed you.'

Grace dashed out of the room to fetch a doctor. Dan sat beside Beth, not letting go of the hand that he still held. He felt really emotional, and it took all the strength that he could muster to hide that.

Thankfully, the duty doctor entered the room at that point and instructed Grace and Dan to leave to enable him to examine Beth.

The two of them returned to the corridor chairs again.

Grace sent a text message to Dr Miriam Shepherd, Beth's consultant. 'She's awake,' was all that she felt that she had to say to Miriam.

'I'm on my way,' was the prompt and succinct response.

'I wonder how much she actually heard,' said Dan.

'It wouldn't surprise me one bit if she hasn't been listening to pretty much all of it,' said Grace. 'Thank goodness that we had the majority of the Kate chat in the corridor.'

'We didn't say anything in the room that I wouldn't have shared with her at some point anyway,' said Dan.

'What do you mean? At some point?' said Grace. 'If I know Beth as well as I think I do, she will be out of that bed, dressed and demanding a progress report before she even considers what day it is. Miriam won't allow that to happen obviously, but you catch my drift. Beth will need closure too, remember.

'Miriam is a match for her but wouldn't you just love to be a fly on the wall to hear the debate that they will have about what Beth can and cannot do?'

'I think we both know how that will go,' answered Dan. They both laughed out of relief to have Beth back.

'It's good to have her back,' said Grace.

She spoke too soon.

Almost at that precise moment, the doctor came, rushing out of Beth's room and shouted out for the crash team.

Midnight

Grace and Dan could only watch on in horror as doctors, nurses, and a crash trolley approached Beth's room. At the rear, they saw Miriam running behind them.

Beth's door was closed, curtains were drawn around her bed, and the blinds at the viewing window were closed. Grace and Dan were left out in the corridor in ignorance of what could have happened.

Next, the door was opened, and Beth's hospital bed was rushed down the corridor surrounded by doctors and nurses.

'We're taking her into theatre now,' was all that Miriam said as she hurried past them. She spoke to one of the nurses, and she ran back to Dan and Grace and told them that it would be a couple of hours before they could get an update and that Dr Shepherd had suggested that they call in her close family.

Grace left Dan saying that she was going to try to find out more before calling the family. Shortly after that, a grim-faced Grace returned and told Dan that Beth had gone into cardiac arrest. She had been unable to find out anything else other than that.

Dan called Bill and explained that Beth was in theatre due to a complication found during the doctor's examination. He didn't want to alarm them too much with the exact detail on the telephone, and he knew that Bill, Caroline, and Jack would all make their way to the hospital immediately after his call.

'We're on our way,' said Bill, confirming Dan's assumption.

'There's nothing that we can do but wait for Bill and the others to arrive. We aren't family, so we won't be able to find out any more than I already have,' said Grace.

Grace grabbed a couple of coffees out of habit, and then they both just sat in shock outside Beth's room, waiting for the family to arrive.

They didn't have to wait long. As predicted by Dan, Bill, Caroline, and Jack arrived at the same time.

Before they had arrived, Grace had spoken to the staff nurse, explained the situation, and asked if they could use a side waiting room until Dr Shepherd came out of theatre. This was arranged before the family arrived.

Dan explained his reason for not saying too much on the telephone to Bill, and then Grace told them that Beth had gone into cardiac arrest just after becoming conscious and saying a few words to them.

Bill was the obvious choice to represent the family at that moment as he and Grace made their way to reception to introduce him and to request an update about what was happening in theatre.

Almost ten minutes later, one of the young doctors who had been observing in theatre was instructed to explain to the family that Beth had gone into cardiac arrest and that they had found internal bleeding. A punctured artery was currently being cauterised by Dr Shepherd. The doctor had been authorised to report that the operation was going well at present.

With a feeling of déjà vu, the family waited again in a waiting room at St Rubens Hospital for a health-status feedback about one of their loved ones.

As before, silence prevailed.

1 a.m.

Almost an hour after Beth had been taken into theatre, a nurse knocked at the door and told Grace that there was someone at reception who wanted to speak with her.

Grace left and returned fifteen minutes later to announce to the family that it was Kate who had requested to speak with her. She admitted that she had called Kate to inform her of her mother's setback. Jack jumped out of his seat and headed for the door.

'No need, Jack,' said Grace. 'Kate has left again. We should all be relieved that she did what she had to do as we know that took courage. She wants to be alone, and I have promised to give her regular updates. She sends her love to all of you and wants you to know that she will be thinking of you.'

'I'm going to find her,' said Jack as he left the room. 'She shouldn't be on her own at a time like this. Call me immediately that you hear anything.'

No one stopped him as they knew that it was the right thing to do.

1.50 a.m.

Miriam entered the waiting room and immediately told them that the operation had been a success and that Beth was in recovery.

'Just a minute. We need to contact Jack,' said Bill.

'I'm already on the case,' said Dan as he sent a text message, telling Jack that Miriam was ready to give an update and that his mother was in recovery.

Jack arrived without Kate and indicated to Miriam that she should proceed. 'If you don't mind, I will be videoing your feedback as I want to send it on to my sister.'

'I have no problem with that,' said Miriam. 'You will already have been told that Beth went into cardiac arrest. The crash team resuscitated her in her room, and then we took her into theatre. She was bleeding internally from a punctured artery. It is my opinion that the blunt trauma during her beating caused a small tear on the artery and that the extent of pressure from the internal bruising caused it to expand and erupt. I have cauterised the artery successfully, and she is expected to make a full recovery.'

The family was obviously relieved, yet very emotional, at that news.

'She is in the recovery room just now, but I'll let you know when she is going to be returned to her room. As before, you won't be able to visit her, but you will be able to observe her.

'After that, you should all go home, get some rest, and then return in the morning when you may be able to visit her after my rounds,' added Miriam.

'Gran and Granddad, you go home. I'm going to stay here to be close to Mum, and I'll call you early in the morning with an update,' said Jack.

'No need to call us, Son, as we'll be back here at the crack of dawn,' was all that Bill said as he helped Caroline out of her chair.

The two of them looked shattered but indicated that they understood the sentiment behind Jack's gesture.

'Where is Kate?' asked Grace.

'She is downstairs in the cafe,' said Jack. 'She was waiting on me sending an update after Mum came out of theatre. That's why I wanted to video what Dr Shepherd was saying.'

'Send her a text to tell her to wait there for me,' said Grace, which he did.

'Okay, here is what's going to happen,' continued Grace in her authoritative voice. 'As Miriam has already said, you aren't going to be able to see her before morning. So Bill and Caroline should go home as Jack suggested. I am going to go home with Kate as she shouldn't be on her own tonight. Jack is going to spend the night in the waiting room, which leaves Dan. What are you going to do?'

'I'm going to keep Jack company as *he* shouldn't be on his own tonight either,' replied Dan.

'Perfect. We have a plan,' said Grace. Noticing how stressed and tired they all looked, she added, 'Beth is strong and healthy. I never doubted for a moment that she wouldn't pull through. She's already on the road to a full recovery, so you can look forward to hearing that for yourself tomorrow morning.'

2.30 a.m.

Everyone was weary but took some comfort from what Grace had said. As they prepared to leave the hospital, or settle in the waiting room, each was probably praying for the moment when their eight-year nightmare would be finally over.

No one got much sleep that night. They were confident that Beth would survive her ordeal, but they couldn't help but reflect on all that had happened to their family during that time.

During the night

Dan was glad that he had chosen to stay with Jack as it was obvious that Jack needed someone to talk to about all that had happened. Lots of coffee kept them awake, and so they were able to be told when Beth had been returned to her room and to see for themselves that she was settled. Once that had happened, they managed to get some sleep for an hour or so.

Grace and Kate sat up all night, and Grace told Kate that she was proud of her decision to visit the hospital and meet with Jack. She was also pleased to witness Kate being emotional; not much, but a hint that the potential was there.

5.30 a.m.

Dan woke Jack.

'Miriam is with Beth, and it looks as though she is speaking to her. Perhaps it's time for you to make your presence known.'

Jack was out of his chair in a flash and heading for his mother's room. He returned approximately fifteen minutes later.

'She's awake, Dan, and I was allowed to sit by her bed for a few minutes. She is tired, but she knew that I was beside her.'

'That's good news, Jack. Why don't you message that out to the others? I'm sure that they will already be awake anyway,' said Dan.

As Jack attended to that, Miriam joined them.

'Phew! That was a close call, Dan,' she said. 'But she is going to be okay. I can't let you visit her as she needs all the rest that she can get today. You can go back to being chief superintendent now.'

'I've got interviews lined up with Matt and Kate. I'll wait until someone arrives to keep Jack company, and then I'm off home to freshen up and then make my way to the MET.'

6 a.m.

Grace was first to arrive, closely followed by Bill and Caroline.

'Good sign, guys,' said Miriam as she left Beth's room. 'Her first question this morning was to ask when she would be likely to go home.'

'I told her that there would be no going home for a while and that, if necessary, I would strap her to the bed if there was any talk of discharging herself any time soon. She hasn't lost her sense of humour because she said, and I quote, "There is going to be no more strapping of me to a bed, so I'll bow to your professional opinion".'

They all laughed, very much relieved that Beth was safe again.

'I don't have to tell you that she needs plenty of rest and that you should only visit her one at a time and spread the visits out well. I'm going to disappear for a few hours, but I'll be back late morning to check on her again.'

'Well, there's no need for us to visit Bill and Caroline this morning,' said Grace to Dan, and to the rest of them, 'Beth is in good hands, so you can relax and enjoy being part of her recovery today. I need to sit in on Dan's interviews today, and so, like him, I am going to go home and freshen up.'

'How does ten o'clock sound to you?' asked Dan.

'Perfect,' replied Grace.

Smiling, Dan and Grace made their way towards the elevator.

CHAPTER 22

Saturday, 20 October 2012
7 a.m.

After Dan had arrived home, he stripped off his clothes and stood under a cool shower for fifteen minutes. He then sent an email to the team to update them on the evening's events and confirmed that it was business as usual that morning. After that, he sat by his sitting room window with a mug of coffee. He was hungry but decided to grab something to eat on the way to the office.

What a night, he thought to himself.

8 a.m.

Dan's door bell brought him out of a semi-deep sleep. It was Grace.

'I couldn't sleep after I woke up after a few hours' sleep, so I decided to meet you here and accompany you to the office. And I knew that you wouldn't have eaten, so I am the bearer of fresh croissants.'

'Excellent,' said Dan as he led the way to his kitchen to pour Grace some coffee and a top-up for himself.

They talked briefly about Kate's kidnapping eight years ago, and both agreed that, based on the information that they now had, it was clear that Murray Thomson was responsible for that. His motive was seeking revenge for the death of his baby daughter due to a complication after birth, closely followed by his wife's suicide. The kidnapping hadn't been planned for the night of the fashion show as Dan had since found out that he hadn't planned to be at the office that night, nor could he have anticipated Beth's non-arrival. As it was so close to end of term, he was working later than normal to make sure that all fees had been paid and that the books balanced. Basically, Kate had been in the wrong place at the wrong time.

'This explains the janitor's ambivalence when we questioned him. He never gave a second thought at seeing the bursar leave the building at the same time. If he had followed them out of the gates, he would have seen that Kate accepted a lift from the bursar. She had no reason not to. Knowing that the hospital bed and restraints were ready for action at his home and that it was already dark and raining, he couldn't resist the opportunity of striking whilst the iron was hot.'

Dan continued, 'And as for drugging her, we have now found a selection of sedatives and chloroform in the glove compartment of his car when we searched it. There is also a selection of cocktails at his home. He had obviously researched their availability, found some in the science labs at the school, and then built up a stash in his car just in case he ever did get such an opportunity as had been presented to him that evening.

'Because it was raining heavily, there was no attention drawn to the fact that, instead of parking on the street as he normally did, he parked in his basement garage. With entrance doors from the garage to the kitchen and also to the basement storage room, he was able to carry Kate into the latter and set her up for the photographs that he sent us. He then stripped her, no doubt, again when she was under the influence of sedatives, laid her out on the bed, and then strapped her ankles and wrists so that she couldn't move. The rest we know. Case closed,' said Dan with finality.

'What I'm struggling with is that if Kate accepted a lift from the bursar, as we believe she did, why is it that she didn't recognise him later?'

Grace interrupted Dan, 'Medically and psychologically, we know that Kate went into deep shock after the kidnapping and rapes, and she has suffered from post-traumatic stress throughout the last eight years. When that happens, victims often file facts away in their brain that they don't want to acknowledge or think about. That's their way of protecting themselves. It's common.

'She was already very upset and angry with her mother, so she accepted the lift from the bursar without giving him another thought, and there was probably no conversation in the car. He may have sedated her immediately, so there wouldn't be much of him to remember in any event. Her first recall of the kidnapping would be at seeing a tall masked man forcing her to be photographed and, no doubt, doing so under threats that she couldn't handle. For anyone, rape is hugely traumatic, but also remember that Kate was a virgin. It is definitely not out of the question that Kate never recalled the detail of the last person that she saw on that evening. All of that can be proven from hundreds of case studies.'

'Okay, I accept that. But surely, if that's the case, it is equally not impossible for her to have a sudden recall of that detail.'

'I'm afraid that is also possible. If Kate decided that she wanted to find the kidnapper herself, she could have subconsciously enabled that detail to come to the surface. If that is what happened, then I have no doubt whatsoever that Kate would have embarked upon a journey to find the kidnapper.'

Silence. Both were deep in thought, coming to terms with something that they would rather not have to consider.

'Let's continue this conversation in the car,' said Dan.

'Okay, but let's take mine as it is parked on the road,' said Grace.

Once they were settled in Grace's car, Dan resumed the conversation.

'If Kate can recall detail that has been locked away for many years, then we are both implying that Kate could have had something to do with Beth's kidnapping.'

'I hope that isn't the case, but I can't rule that out as being a possibility.'

'Holy shit, Grace. This interview is going to be a barrel of laughs.'

'Just forget everyone else involved and trust your own instincts. That is why you hold the most senior operational position in the Serious Crimes Division.'

They agreed that Dan should do all the talking and that Grace should only step in if she believed that Kate wasn't coping well mentally with the opening up of old wounds. However, Grace knew that if she was ever going to get Kate to face up to what had happened in her past, decide to live with it, and to move on so that she could enjoy a healthy life, now was the time. Also, she had to admit to herself and Dan that she was curious to see how Kate would react to coping with such pressure under Dan's microscope.

10 a.m.

They arrived at the MET.

Dan called Jack for an update on Beth and was given positive feedback. Bill and Caroline were still at the hospital, and the three of them planned to stay there until lunchtime.

Grace called Kate to check whether or not she had managed to sleep. She admitted that she actually felt better at having visited the hospital and had managed to have a few hours of quality sleep. She said that she and Jack had kept in touch and that she was meeting him and her grandparents for lunch.

10.30 a.m.

Colin was waiting for Dan. The rest of the team were pulling together the facts relating to both cases and had started to set out the first draft of their reports. The blanks would, hopefully, be filled in after Dan's interviews with Matt and Kate and the summary of Abe's interviews with Kate's ex-headmistress and the janitor. They had a quick briefing meeting, and Dan talked Colin through his plans for the interviews with Matt and Kate.

Colin answered an incoming call and advised Dan that Matt had arrived, that he was being taken to interview room one, and that he was alone. Before they left the office, Dan drew Colin to one side and forewarned him of the sensitivity to Kate's interview. Colin was naturally surprised at the turn of events, but, like Dan, he had not been convinced about how the second kidnapping had unfolded. He and Dan made their way to conduct the first interview of the day.

11.30 a.m.

'How is Beth?' asked Matt as he shook hands with Dan and Colin.

'She took a heavy beating, and she had a broken nose and several broken ribs when she was admitted. Last night, she suffered a cardiac arrest, and it was touch-and-go for a while. Dr Shepherd repaired a punctured artery, and she is now back on the ward. She is strong and is expected to fully recover,' replied Dan.

'Bill, Caroline, and Jack are with her now at the hospital. Caroline is hoping to persuade her to recuperate at their home when she is eventually discharged, and Jack is staying in the country until then so that he can spend some quality time with her.'

'I had no idea,' was all that Matt had to say.

'It all happened in the early hours of this morning, so there hasn't been time for Jack or Kate to speak with you. Jack stayed at the hospital throughout the night, so he'll be shattered. You'll be able to speak with either of them after the interview has finished. My understanding is that they are having lunch with their grandparents.'

'Thanks. I'll call them when I leave here.'

Dan had no intention of prolonging the interview with Matt, and so he dispensed with any further informal conversation, set the scene for the interview, and nodded to Colin to switch on the recording machine.

'We will be closing the case of Kate's kidnapping and rapes this morning, but we have a lot of unanswered questions about Beth's kidnapping which, by the way, would have changed to manslaughter had Beth not survived the cardiac arrest,' was Dan's opener for the interview.

'So, Matt, can you explain to us why you think that we managed to find the lead that we needed from your records this time when we found nothing of value last time?' asked Dan.

This took Matt off guard, and it was a while before he spoke. 'That's an unfair question. I am a busy man. The burden of responsibility that I have is significant. I am not aware that I ever knowingly stopped you from accessing my records.'

'Good response. However, I didn't make any reference to you stopping access. I am referring in particular to the legal files, which were definitely not included in the first search. I am curious as to why you, the administration team or the board of governors, didn't include the legal files in our examination.'

No response.

'Did you know that the legal files had been omitted from the files presented to us after receiving the search warrant?' asked Dan.

'I didn't check. I just assumed that everything that you needed would have been given to you,' replied Matt.

'Are you suggesting that the powers that be deliberately withheld those files?' asked Dan.

'I am not suggesting anything of the sort. It must have been an oversight. It wouldn't have been deliberate,' said Matt.

'Well, Matt, from where I am sitting, I don't see it that way. The search warrant specifically requested that we get sight of all hospital files that related to medical, administrative, and legal documents. You never gave it the attention that it needed. Your son spent more time looking through files than you did. My staff all agree that they didn't get the cooperation that they needed,' added Dan.

Matt started to speak, but Dan cut him short. 'You never even appeared to spend any time thinking about what could have happened in the past that was worthy of examination. What you did do was to spend every minute of every waking day to blame your wife and make cruel accusations to her in the company of her son and her parents. That's arrogance, sir.

'Had you cooperated with us, and I repeat the word *cooperated* just in case you are having difficulty in understanding which page I am on, I believe that you could have come up with the name Murray Thomson. It isn't every day, after all, that someone in your position becomes the focus of attention of the board of governors because of an accusation of malpractice of one of the hospital's most senior paediatric consultants.

'Now, I don't work at the hospital, but I am capable of comparing that situation to what would happen at the MET under similar circumstances. I think that you will agree that it is a fair comparison. If it had been me, I would have been in front of the commander on several occasions for questioning. I would have needed legal representation, and I would most certainly not have forgotten such an embarrassing and stressful experience, even if I had been exonerated.

'Now, I want you to tell me whether or not you ever considered the situation with the Thomsons as being worthy of being brought to our attention. I am assuming, of course, that you actually did take some time out of your very busy days to reflect upon the Thomson threats of malpractice. You see, as of late yesterday, the record shows that baby Thomson, mother Thomson, and father Thomson are all dead. All dead because of your handling of baby Thomson's death.'

Matt started to speak, but Dan interrupted him once again.

'We have a letter from the kidnapper on file that was written just before he took his own life. Allow me to read it to you,' and Dan slowly read through the suicide note that Murray Thomson had left at his bedside.

'Now, Dr Oliver, how would you like to respond to all that I have said? I will be happy to remind you of any of the content if you require.'

Matt was silent. He just stared into space.

'I'm waiting for some answers, Matt,' said Dan.

More silence.

'Dr Oliver, why did we not receive the legal files to research during Kate's kidnapping? Can you explain to me how you miraculously seemed to forget a lengthy accusation of malpractice? And, finally, can you tell me how you feel at hearing that baby Thomson, mother Thomson, and father Thomson are all dead because you and your staff didn't manage to find the time to tell them how sorry you were at their loss. Start speaking, Matt. This interview has been very one-sided up to now.'

Matt looked as though he was going to pass out and was perspiring profusely.

'You seem to be struggling to find the right words, Matt. Whilst you consider what you are going to say, because you aren't going to leave here until you do answer my questions, let me tell you how we feel.

'We all believe that had you shown one jot of respect to our investigation, diverted your misplaced accusations to your wife towards actually helping to find your daughter's kidnapper, and had supported all the people who were working around the clock to find your daughter, you may have helped us to find Kate before she was raped, and you would most certainly have prevented Beth from being kidnapped, scarred for life, and beaten within an inch of her life.

'And why? Your daughter was kidnapped, raped, and scarred, as was your wife, by a medically depressed man who wasn't coping with the loss of his own daughter.

'You are still very quiet, Matt. I do hope that I am making myself clear. You see we need to know that you have understood everything that I have said because it describes interference with the administration of justice, otherwise known as perverting the course of justice. This is a criminal offence, and I am going to do all that I can to make sure that you fully understand the implications of what you did or didn't do to assist us. You could be facing up to two years' imprisonment, Dr Oliver. Did you know that?

'Now speak and don't miss anything out,' Dan concluded. 'There's no hurry. We aren't going anywhere.'

Knowing that he was in trouble, Matt did start at the beginning. He told them about Alison Thomson and how she had been referred to him after her fourth miscarriage. Each time, she had carried the baby outside the womb. As the hospital was running IVF trials at that time, he considered her for that because he could see how desperate she was to give birth to her own child. She was accepted and eventually became pregnant. Under close supervision, the pregnancy went well, and she was expected to have a normal child birth.

He explained how complications were noticed during her seventh month of pregnancy. The father couldn't cope. He was always agitated and very angry. The mother got very depressed. He accepted that, with hindsight, more time should have been allocated to the mental imbalance that the Thomsons were demonstrating. He accepted that they both should have been referred to the hospital's psychiatric ward and that they both should have received counselling during the pregnancy, birth, and post-natal depression.

'Was either of them counselled?' asked Dan.

Sheepishly Matt said that neither was.

'Let me get this straight,' said Dan. 'You and your staff went about your business of delivering healthy babies and totally ignored the pleas for help from the parents who had so tragically lost their last chance to have a child of their own. Now just to be clear for the record here, you skimmed over how she became pregnant, enjoyed a healthy pregnancy, and should have experienced a normal birth. What you didn't say was that this pregnancy came about as a result of using the last of the saved eggs. You failed to mention that this was the Thomsons' last chance to have a child of their own.

'You must have felt like God himself when they sang your praises during the pregnancy. Yet, one slip, questions seeking the truth, one accusation, and they are dropped. How many times each day did one of your staff say "I'm sorry, but Dr Oliver is unavailable"? How many, Matt, because we will check?'

Matt hung his head in shame.

'They are all dead. The Thomson family no longer exist. That is on your conscience, Dr Oliver. If you displayed to them a fraction of the ambivalence that you displayed to my investigation team when they were searching for reasons for your daughter's kidnapping and rape, then you don't deserve to be a doctor.

'Next question. Why were the legal files not included for our research first time around?' asked Dan.

'I genuinely don't know. I didn't check the files presented to you, so I guess that I just assumed that everything you needed would be there,' replied Matt.

'Did you ever take time to think about the questions we were asking you? Did you ever consider that the Thomsons may be holding a grudge against you?' asked Dan.

'I was too angry at Beth and so sure that the kidnapping was a result of her job. I couldn't bear to think of my daughter being anywhere other than safely in her own bed. I couldn't even bring myself to consider the potential of rape. I could only vent my anger at Beth, and she wasn't even there to help us. According to her, the investigation couldn't run without her. So if that is arrogance in your book, so be it.'

'But the kidnapping had nothing to do with Beth. The kidnapping had everything to do with you, and you didn't for one moment consider that possibility. You can't even display remorse at hearing that. Now, why didn't you come forward when Beth was kidnapped? I had to get a second search warrant for my team to find out that, which you have known about for all those years.

'Who in the Oliver family was responsible for setting up the payments for Kate's school fees? And I should forewarn you that I already know the answer to that question?'

'I was,' said Matt.

'Familiar as you were with the name Murray Thomson and knowing that he was the school bursar, why did you never ask us to check him out, if not post Kate's kidnapping, during Beth's?'

'I just didn't give it any thought during Kate's kidnapping because I was sure that only a criminal or serial rapist would do what happened to Kate. I didn't bring him to your attention when Beth was kidnapped because Kate had already checked him out.'

'What?' shouted Dan and Colin at the same time.

'Did you just imply that Kate had already spoken to you about Murray Thomson or did you find out by some other means that Kate had been to the hospital to check out the database? Which?'

'Kate met with me almost three years ago and asked if I recalled a patient called Murray Thomson. The name was familiar, and I told her that. She suggested that I check out his file from the database and that she would like to do that with me. I couldn't refuse because I thought that in some way, this may be part of her coming to terms with the kidnapping at long last. We accessed the file from the database, and we both agreed that he wouldn't have been able to do something as awful as that.'

'Are you qualified to make that judgement?'

'He was too a nice guy to have kidnapped and raped Kate.'

'This just gets better and better. Colin, have you ever charged a nice guy with murder, kidnapping, or rape?' asked Dan.

'All too often, it is the nice guy who has committed the crime, and statistics can prove that,' replied Colin.

'Exactly,' said Dan. 'You are in serious trouble, Dr Oliver, as is your daughter now.'

'Now there is still one question that you haven't answered. The Thomson family are all dead. Alison Thomson committed suicide because she couldn't face living without her daughter or the prospect of not being able to have a child of her own. Murray Thomson committed suicide because he couldn't face living without his daughter and his wife. How do you *feel* about all of that?'

Matt lifted his head and looked Dan straight in the eyes and said, 'You win, Dan. I feel ashamed, tormented, and embarrassed at all that you have told me this morning. But I didn't pervert the course of justice. I just didn't give enough thought to the assistance that you were seeking. I couldn't get beyond missing my daughter, worrying about my daughter, being angry with my wife, and feeling sorry for myself. There, you have it! Satisfied?' replied a very subdued Matt.

'No, I am not satisfied, Matt, but I do feel sorry for you because you are going to have to live with this for the rest of your life. In that respect, Murray Thomson did get revenge for the deaths of his daughter and wife because you now have to live with the consequences of your lack of action. And, for what it's worth, I don't think that you deliberately tried to pervert the course of justice, but I still think that you were arrogant in your approach to responding to our repeated requests for your assistance.

'Interview over at 12.20 p.m.,' said Dan to Colin, who switched the recording machine off.

'Colin, can you please escort Dr Oliver to his car?' asked Dan as he stood up and left the room.

CHAPTER 23

Saturday, 20 October 2012
12.35 p.m.

Dan joined Grace in the interview viewing room, and they both made their way to Dan's office to exchange notes about the interview and to prepare for Kate's interview.

Dan called Jack and reported back to Grace that Miriam was happy with Beth's progress and that they could visit her later that day.

Grace had called Bill to enquire about how he and Caroline were coping with the latest ordeal. She reported back to Dan that Bill sounded tired but that he and Caroline were looking forward to having a reasonably relaxed lunch with their two grandchildren.

'Let's hope that goes well because it is just the tonic that Bill and Caroline need just now,' said Dan.

'I agree. Beth will, no doubt, sleep much of the afternoon, so they will be able to relax in each other's company without worrying about her. I told Bill as much, and he said that his aim was to do just that,' replied Grace.

Dan called in Colin to join them, and the three of them focussed on the bombshell that Matt had landed on them towards the end of the interview.

'I really want to charge him with perverting the course of justice because technically that is what he has done. The reality is that I don't think it was done with intention or in any way to protect himself. As I have said before, he won't be charged because a good lawyer will present the patient confidentiality policy. I can also hear him reminding the jury that Dr Oliver is an acclaimed doctor and not a criminal lawyer. Let's keep the heat on, but, at some point, I should tell him that we are not pressing charges. I'll send a letter to the hospital's board of governors, and I'll copy that to the medical council.'

They all agreed.

'Colin, push the team to complete their reports on the Katie Oliver case and pass them on to me for signing, and I'll endorse the recommendation to close the case,' concluded Dan.

'So let's now focus on Kate Oliver as a suspect in a kidnapping and GBH crime. What are our thoughts on that?' asked Dan.

Grace started, 'I think that you have no alternative but to treat her as a suspect based on the feedback from the hypnotism about his description and where he lived.'

'Let's not forget Matt's faux pas about her examination of Murray Thomson's hospital records,' added Colin.

'You almost need to forget about Kate's past and focus on the present in relation to Beth's kidnapping and grievous bodily harm. Let's remember that Beth could have been dead after her cardiac arrest,' said Grace.

'It's not looking good for our Miss Oliver, is it?' asked Dan.

'You mustn't worry about applying pressure to her. I'll be keeping a close eye on her and will prompt you if I think that you need to relax the style of questioning,' said Grace. 'As far as Beth's kidnapping is concerned, I have my suspicions that she was involved, but I am reserving my opinion about whether or not she actually has it in her to have done something as awful as that. But if I am being honest, and knowing what we now know about Murray Thomson, I don't if he has it in him either.'

'If she has, how the hell do we deal with that professionally? Even worse, how do we share that with Beth?' asked Colin.

'Exactly my thoughts since I left Matt. He is easy to deal with by comparison to what we are about to face during and after our interview with Kate. What a bloody mess!'

'Colin, what has she done that's illegal?' asked Dan.

'She has perverted the course of justice by not sharing with you her suspicions about Murray Thomson being her kidnapper, for starters,' replied Colin.

'Correct. And yet she will bounce back with saying that she didn't report that because she didn't think that he was that person after her investigation. There is no law against her making enquiries,' said Dan. 'Accessing the hospital records is more about Matt's indiscretion than Kate's. But had she shared her suspicion with us, we would have acted upon it and would have come up with the same conclusion as we did yesterday.'

'One step at a time, Dan,' suggested Grace. 'Let's see what Kate has to say about it all. You ask the questions, and I'll pay very close attention to her responses and body language during each question.'

'Grace is right, Dan. After the ball-breaker interview that you have just had with Matt, you are more than capable of achieving perspective at this interview,' said Colin.

1 p.m.

It was announced that Kate had arrived and been shown into interview room two.

Dan and Colin arrived together, and Grace deliberately arrived a few minutes later to gauge Kate's reaction to her involvement. Grace suspected that she would be put out at an apparent solidarity.

Kate didn't ask, but Grace updated her on her mother's progress and her plans to stay with her parents for a few days after she had been discharged.

'Last night was a shock to everyone. I am relieved to hear that she is okay as I wouldn't wish her any harm,' Kate said calmly.

Colin went through the formalities of recording the names of those present at the interview and the timing of it.

'Kate, we have asked you here today because we now know that the person who kidnapped you is the same person who kidnapped your mother. That person is known to you and your family as Murray Thomson, the bursar at your senior school. Your father dealt with him directly in setting up the direct debit mandate for your fees. Mr Thomson is now dead. He committed suicide just after he informed us where to find Beth,' he added without even checking for her reaction to that comment. 'Except she wasn't where he said she would be. We found her in the same basement that he had previously held you captive.'

Again he didn't check for reaction as he knew that Grace would be watching her like a hawk and recording her findings.

'You agreed to help us with our enquiries, but you didn't get a chance to do that, did you? That was because we found Beth before directly involving you. You did, however, agree to be hypnotised, despite having refused to do so for many years before that. Grace has passed on to me the questions and answers that you authorised her to share with me.

'I have interviewed your father this morning, by the way. Did you know that?' sidetracked Dan.

'No, I didn't,' replied Kate.

Disregarding her response, Dan continued, 'I want to focus on the answer that you gave Grace when she asked you if you thought that you could identify your kidnapper. I'm assuming that's because you have been conducting your own investigation and came up with a name that you since reviewed on the hospital database.'

Dan knew that his knowledge of that would come as a surprise to Kate, and so he created a lengthy silence before the next question so that Grace could determine whether or not his knowledge of that had unsettled her.

'Given your line of work, Kate, I'm curious why you never reported your own investigation or discussed your suspicions with us, at the very least after your mother was kidnapped.'

Jesus, Grace was thinking to herself. *I don't know why I even considered that Dan may be uncomfortable at the new direction that his questioning of Kate should take.* He never failed to amaze her with his level of professionalism.

Again Dan paid no attention to her reaction to what he had said.

'I have a dilemma, Kate. You see your name keeps cropping up since Beth's kidnapping. Then I hear that you may be able to recognise the kidnapper. Then I hear that you actually researched Murray Thomson. Can you understand the predicament that I have? No need to answer that.'

'So, Kate, do you or do you not think that you could have identified your kidnapper before he kidnapped Beth?' asked Dan with a 'don't mess with me' look on his face.

Kate, correctly sensing the need for formality during the interview, answered in a way that demonstrated to Dan and Grace that she had given thought to the questions that she would be asked and had rehearsed her answers.

'I didn't give much thought to the kidnapper during the early years after the kidnapping. I couldn't bear to. I had nightmares about all sorts of men keeping me captive and raping me. I threw myself into my studies. The more I understood criminal justice, the better I became in solving crimes and putting guilty people behind bars, the more I started to try to recall the memories that I had about my own kidnapping.

'I still have nightmares about the rapes, the actual kidnapping less so. Initially, I could only remember a man with dark clothing, dark glasses, and a balaclava. As time went on, I started to believe that there was something about the man that I recognised. Through a process of elimination, I knew that the only thing that could be was his voice because his face had always been covered up.

'The memories won't stop, you see. I haven't been able to stop them. I decided that I had to try to find him in an effort to make them stop. Can you understand that?' she asked.

No one answered, so she continued.

'Grace has always said that I won't be able to face the future until I have found a way to bury the past, or words to that effect. For many years now, I have always felt that I must go back and face what happened to me. I must go back and face my kidnapper. I must ask him why he did what he did.

'As you are, no doubt, aware, I have kept in touch with Eleanor Marshall over the years, and I join her for tea in her office or lunch from time to time. I wouldn't have thought any more about the voice of my kidnapper had Murray Thomson not been in her office during one of the days that I was visiting. I chilled when I heard him speak to her, and I couldn't explain why. I couldn't forget that feeling over the next few days.

'This was the start of me feeling stronger at the prospect of facing up to the past and even coming face-to-face with my kidnapper. Several weeks later, I met with Eleanor again, and I asked her if she could find an excuse to invite Thomson into her office.'

Excellent response, thought Dan, but he didn't say so.

'Okay, I am sure that Grace will have a plausible explanation for that. However, can you explain why you approached your father almost three years ago, asking if you could access the hospital's database with him? You only wanted to look at one record, didn't you? You only wanted to examine the file notes on the Thomson family's loss and the resulting stream of letters and threats of malpractice accusations that followed that.'

'Yes, I did approach Dad for information about the Thomsons. I knew that he had lost his child and wife because Eleanor Marshall had told me so. Dad told me the sad story of his wife's miscarriages and death of their baby daughter. I suggested to Dad that he and I examine the file notes just so that I could eliminate the nagging and recurring thought that it may have been my kidnapper's voice that I had heard in Eleanor's office that day.'

She has thought all of this through, thought Dan but again didn't react.

'So you examined the Thomson family case notes, illegally I might add, and what did you determine from that?'

'I was of the opinion that at the heart of all that, Mr Thomson had said in his letters and his threats of malpractice, he was just a very sad man who had lost his wife and child and hadn't found a way to cope with that. In fact, in many ways, I could compare him to how I was feeling.'

God, you are good at this, thought Dan after another premeditated response.

'So how did you come to that conclusion?'

'I met with Eleanor, and I actually told her about what I had done and asked her what she thought about Mr Thomson. She had no hesitation in saying that he was a trusted employee, a good person, and just someone in life who had had to deal with more tragedy than he actually deserved. That was good enough for me, so I eliminated him from my enquiries and convinced myself that many men could have sounded the same as Murray Thomson.'

He couldn't have written the script better himself, thought Dan.

'Do you think that you may be able to identify your kidnapper?' said Dan, knowing the answer before he asked the question.

'No, I don't. Try as I have, my memory is blank,' she responded, looking him straight in the eye.

Her courtroom experiences were definitely helping her with Dan's line of questioning, thought Grace. *She is bloody good at this, but Dan is better.*

'How did you feel about your mother's kidnapping?' asked Dan.

'I was worried that she would have to experience that which I had,' responded Kate.

'And yet we had to persuade you to assist us with our enquiries. You obviously weren't worried enough,' said Dan.

'How do you feel about us finding her badly beaten with a broken nose, several broken ribs, and a badly bruised body? So badly bruised that she ended up with a punctured artery and went into cardiac arrest. How would you feel today if kidnapping had changed to manslaughter? Would you still be as blasé in your responses if your mother was dead?'

Ouch, thought Grace.

When Kate didn't answer, Dan said, 'Please answer the questions, Kate. How did you feel about hearing that we had found her alive and then hearing that it was touch-and-go as to whether or not she would live?'

'I was initially relieved that she hadn't come to any harm, but then I was obviously concerned when I found out that she had been assaulted. I wouldn't wish that on anyone,' was her response.

'And your mother?' asked Dan, again looking directly into her eyes. 'Would you wish that on your mother?'

Kate held the look and said, 'I wouldn't wish that on any mother.'

'For the record, Miss Oliver has no response about how she would have felt if her mother had died last night as a result of cardiac arrest.

'Were you continuing with your search for your kidnapper at the time that your mother was kidnapped?' asked Dan.

'No, I wasn't, but I hadn't ruled out trying again at some point,' answered Kate.

'You must be relieved that you no longer need to do that as your kidnapper has been found. He is dead.'

1.45 p.m.

Dan deliberately allowed a lengthy time of silence and then abruptly said, 'I think we are done here.' He said with a look that was as good as he felt that she deserved at that moment.

As Dan got up to leave the room, he turned to Kate and said, 'When you researched Murray Thomson's hospital files, you must have taken a mental or written note of his address. What is his address, Kate?'

'It is 29 Lovatt Road,' she replied.

'Good memory after discovering it three years ago. Tell me, have you ever visited that address?'

'Except for being held their captive, no,' she replied.

'Colin, could you show Kate to the exit?' He deliberately didn't suggest Grace because he didn't want her and Kate to a conversation at this juncture.

Deciding to keep the interview formal, he left the room without any pleasantries.

Colin escorted Kate to the exit door without a word.

2.00 p.m.

Grace followed Dan to his office in silence. Each had a lot to think about. When Colin returned, Dan pulled together the team and summarised the outcome of his interviews.

He told them his reasons for not charging Matt with perverting the course of justice but that he would hold off formalising that decision for a few days. He told them of his intention to write to the board of governors at the hospital and the medical council.

He didn't go into too much detail about Kate's interview because he wanted more time to think about it. In the meantime, he instructed the following actions:

He asked Colin and Rachel to visit the hospital with the same warrant as before and to check how many times any of the Thomson records had been withdrawn for examination, and by whom, during the last three years.

He asked Abe and Sophie to visit Eleanor Marshall at the school and to ask her how many times she had had a conversation with Kate about Murray Thomson or any member of his family. They should also note the content of the conversation.

He asked Pete to request phone records for Matt, Kate, and Murray Thomson and to note telephone calls between Kate and Matt and also Kate and Murray Thomson during the last three years and up to the time just before Beth's kidnapping.

He and Grace withdrew to his office to talk about what they had just witnessed in the interview room.

'Matt had obviously forewarned her about the conversation that I had with him about accessing the hospital records on the Thomsons. She will, no doubt, have already had a discussion with Eleanor Marshall. And I wouldn't put it past her for already having a conversation about all of this with one of her senior partners. She is clever. But is she honest? What do you think, Grace?'

'That was some interview, by the way. Well done,' said Grace. 'Anyhow, I agree with what you say. She knows about your reputation as a formidable and judicious interviewer, so she will have well and truly covered her back before meeting with you. I don't think that the hospital's board would be particularly impressed by her looking at hospital records, but unless she orchestrated Beth's kidnapping, she hasn't committed a crime, and she knows that.'

'I agree. But who do you think did orchestrate Beth's kidnapping? Matt? Kate? Murray Thomson? Correct me if I am wrong, but, given what we now know, I can't think of anyone else, can you?' asked Dan.

Dan didn't wait for her to answer. 'I can't close this case with that detail hanging over me.'

Dan continued with his thoughts, 'Matt may be subject to an internal enquiry and get his knuckles wrapped from the board, but you can be sure that he will be protected by confidentiality clauses in his contract. He did pervert the course of justice, but, given that it was eight years ago, given that the kidnapper is dead, given that Kate is alive, given that he will hide behind confidentiality, code of practice, etc., etc., it will go nowhere in court. He will definitely not be charged as guilty, and so I am not prepared to waste the tax payers' money in what would end up being a sham.

'Beth was released and is now in the safe hands of the hospital. Aside from a beating and a tattoo from a dead man, that's going nowhere in court either, as her kidnapper has committed suicide.

'The team has done a good job, but we aren't going to get any convictions here unless we get Kate to admit that she organised Beth's kidnapping. Perhaps you could get her to agree to another hypnotism session. And I don't believe for one second that she would agree to that, do you?'

'Actually, I don't think that she would agree. Dan, I now believe that Kate did organise her mother's kidnapping as part of her own revenge. I think that she had persuaded herself into believing that she wouldn't be able to move forward herself unless her mother had been punished for what she did. And what better way to achieve that than to make her mother experience a kidnapping by the same man? She must have figured out that Murray Thomson was her own kidnapper, and she, no doubt, faced him at Lovatt Road and blackmailed him into repeating the crime.'

'And she agreed to the hypnosis with an appearance of cooperating with us when she was just stalling for time as she knew what we would find in the hospital records,' said Dan.

'So, Dan, how do you prove any of that?'

'That's why I asked for the telephone records because, now that Murray Thomson is dead, they are all that we would have to prove a connection between Kate and him. Don't hold your breath because after witnessing her confident performance during the interview, I already know that we will find nothing. She is one clever lady. We could question Matt again, but she will have prepared him for what he should say if questioned on that topic.'

'Oh my God, Dan. Are you saying that you don't think that you could get enough to charge her?' asked Grace.

'Without an admission of guilt from Kate or evidence of her relationship with the kidnapper, we have nothing, and she knows that. You haven't spoken about her mental state or body language, but I already know that, given the nature of the questions, you were surprised at how calm and confident she was.'

'Spot on,' replied Grace.

'We may get lucky, but I am not holding my breath. Worst case scenario is that I will meet with Kate down the line at some point, and I will tell her exactly what I believe happened. I suspect that I will inform her that she must live with the knowledge that we know and also that her firm will never do business with the Special Crimes Division as long as I am chief superintendent if I ever find out that she set out to harm Beth or worse.'

'You must follow your conscience on this,' said Grace, 'but there is something that you haven't mentioned.'

'Beth,' was all that Dan said.

'Yes, Beth,' repeated Grace. 'If you don't share with her what you know, she will find out by herself as the first thing that she will do after she returns from work will be to read the case notes, and there is no way that they won't include a verbatim transcription of today's interviews.'

'I know,' was all that Dan said.

'And what are you going to say to Bill, Caroline, and Jack?' asked Grace.

'Nothing that need worry them. That is up to Beth or Kate to decide whether or not to come clean with them. That is not our responsibility,' replied Dan.

'Have you given any thought as to how you are going to deal with this, Grace?' asked Dan.

'I need some quiet time to do that, but my relationship with Kate is now obviously compromised. This is a real mess, Dan. We don't even know how Beth is going to handle this. The only chance we have of maintaining the close relationships that we have with Beth and Kate is for everything to come out into the open.'

'Okay, later this afternoon, I am going to talk all of this through with the commander just to keep him in the loop. Then I am going to repeat all of that to the team and congratulate them on their good work. Reports will be written, the cold case with a positive result, and we will all get on with finding dangerous criminals.'

'I think that's wise,' said Grace.

What each didn't reveal to the other were the thoughts that were going through their heads at that time.

Grace had no intention of letting this go. She was going to have a very frank conversation with Kate to get the truth from her about Beth's kidnapping.

Dan did intend to close the cold case but not Beth's kidnapping and GBH. His team would return to their specialised crime cases, but he had no intention of letting Kate off the hook. He was going to have a long and confidential talk with her at some point soon, and he was going to get to the bottom of what actually went down during the last couple of days.

He was morally bound to make a judgement call regarding Kate because if she had organised Beth's kidnapping, that would make her an accessory to the crime.

'Dan, in all of this, we must always remember that Kate was the victim. She was the injured party right from the outset.'

Dan nodded his head in agreement. Instinctively he knew that if Kate was accused of being an accessory to Beth's kidnapping, it was most likely her own kidnapping that would sway any jury's decision in favour of the defence.

3.20 p.m.

'Come on, let's get a cab to the hospital and find out what Beth has been up to today,' said Grace. Not waiting for an answer, she added, 'What shall we take her?'

'I'll happily leave that up to you,' said Dan.

CHAPTER 24

Saturday, 20 October 2012
4 p.m.

The combination of the kidnapping, the beating to her face and body, the cardiac arrest, and then the operation to cauterise the punctured artery had all taken their toll on Beth during the last twenty-four hours. Walking towards her hospital bed, Dan and Grace couldn't help but notice how weak she looked and the magnitude of the bruising on her face. Neither of them dared lean forward to give her a kiss on the forehead, nor could they hold either of her hands as they were both hooked up to drips.

Sensing their discomfort, Beth said, 'I know. I must look a mess.'

'You look just wonderful to us,' replied Grace. 'The fact that you are alive and recovering is what matters right now.'

'Welcome back,' said Dan. 'You gave us all quite a fright last night.'

'Nothing that rest won't cure,' said Beth, sounding braver than she felt. 'But I don't have the energy to sit up just yet.'

'Don't worry about that. We are under strict instructions to limit this visit to ten minutes, so you can doze off again after that,' said Grace.

'Miriam won't tell me anything, but I would really like to know how you found me,' said Beth.

'We can't have that conversation until Miriam gives us the all clear,' said Dan. 'All you need to know for now is that a positive lead pointed us in the direction of the kidnapper's home, where we were able to take him into custody and send you off to hospital with Grace.'

'And there is no point trying to get information from Bill or Jack, as they are also under strict instructions not to go there,' added Grace. Changing the subject, Grace asked if Beth needed anything brought in for her.

'I haven't a clue,' replied Beth. 'Mum brought me in the usual toiletries and the customary nightdress, slippers, and housecoat that are all suitable for a stay in hospital. They'll be in one of the cupboards, so could you check them for me?'

'I need to make a couple of phone calls, so I'll leave the two of you to chat about that,' said Dan as he made his way to the door.

What he really planned to do was to check if Miriam was around and to ask her advice about when he should tell Beth about Murray Thomson and his death. Miriam caught sight of him from the far end of the ward and signalled to him to join her in her office.

Her response to his question was not what he expected.

'Normally I would be telling visitors not to cause any level of anxiety for my patients, but Beth is different. To be honest, she is probably going to get more anxious about not knowing the facts as she will be after hearing the truth about how she was found and the demise of Mr Thomson.'

'I didn't expect that response,' said Dan.

'I'm full of surprises. The best that I can do right now for Beth, as my patient, is to release the pent-up emotion that will be troubling her in and out of sleep. It's just after 4 p.m., so why don't you disappear to allow her to rest and return at sevenish with the promise that you will answer her questions then.'

'Will do, but I think that I'll steer clear of the suspicions that we have about Kate. Can you share what we have arranged with the family?'

'They will, no doubt, be back shortly, so, yes, I'll see them then. Also, I'll be around when you return, so I'll be on call for you then unless I have to cope with an emergency.'

'Thanks, Miriam. It's good to have you around.'

Dan made his way back to Beth's room as Grace was sorting out the contents of the overnight bag that Caroline had delivered earlier.

'There are a couple of items that I need to buy, so I'll do that now and return later,' she said.

'Actually, it's time for us both to leave, according to Miriam. I've just asked her advice about when we can talk shop, and she reckons that avoiding that will cause more agitation than not. So here's the deal, Beth. We are leaving now. You are going to rest. Grace and I will return at 7 p.m. for the maximum of a fifteen-minute interrogation from you. Then we'll follow on from there the next morning. Okay?'

'Okay. I get it,' said Beth, looking as though she would be asleep again before they had left the hospital.

4.45 p.m.

Grace left to buy the toiletries that Beth had requested.

Dan went home to give some more thought to his next move with Kate and also to telephone the commander with an update.

They agreed to meet up again at 6.45 p.m. in the hospital cafe so that Dan could share with Grace the extent of what he planned to divulge to Beth about the Thomson family, Murray Thomson's demise, and how they came about the leads.

As they went their separate ways, the two things that they had in common were their relief that Beth would fully recover and apprehension about how Kate's involvement would unfold.

Just as Dan arrived at his apartment, he received a call from Grace.

'How do you fancy dinner with me tonight?' she asked. 'It's actually Freddie's suggestion. He has just had a cancellation for a table for four this evening, and he has asked if we would be interested in taking it over as his guest. That's provided that Beth doesn't present us with any more surprises when we visit her later.'

'Now that's an offer that I can't refuse. Please thank Freddie and tell him that I would be delighted to accept his invitation. Will he be able to join us?'

'It's Saturday, and he's fully booked, but he'll probably be able to join us once his other diners have settled down with their main courses,' said Grace.

'I'll look forward to that,' replied Dan.

Dan pulled out the notes that he had written after Kate's interview and considered each point in detail. Everything pointed to Kate having orchestrated Beth's kidnapping, but unless she confessed to that, he was on thin ice in terms of evidence.

She had been very clever throughout her own investigation. Neither she nor Eleanor Marshall had done anything illegal during their conversations about Murray Thomson. Kate hadn't done anything illegal in looking at Murray Thomson's hospital file, although the opposite could be said about her father's involvement in that. He couldn't prove that Kate had ever been to Thomson's house. What she said under hypnosis could not be used as evidence. Without evidence to any of that, he struggled to think how he could charge her with perverting the course of justice on the basis that she hadn't shared her private investigation with his team.

He called the commander, updated him on Beth's progress, and then had a discussion with him about Kate and his suspicions about her involvement. At the end of the call, they both agreed that Kate would never admit to organising the kidnapping, and, without that, there wasn't sufficient evidence to justify spending tax payers' money on a lengthy legal battle.

'I still intend to write the letters to the hospital's board of governors and the medical council about Matt, and I still intend to have a private and very serious conversation with Kate. Everything will be above board in terms of report writing, and the case will be closed based on our discussion this evening. The problem is that Beth will undoubtedly read the full file when she returns to work, but I guess that will then become a matter for her conscience and not mine.'

'That's just it, Dan. Your priority is to ensure that the accurate reports are written, signed, and filed and that the team are made aware of your final decisions. They will respect your judgement. What happens after that with Grace can be covered in three-way conversation in my office when she eventually wants to discuss it in more detail. And that goes for whether or not she brings that up as a private matter.'

'We're in agreement on all of that, but I think that I'll let Kate sweat for a few days before arranging a private meeting with her.'

'Good. Now please give my kindest regards to Beth and tell her that she isn't expected back at work until she gets the sign-off from Dr Shepherd. Also tell her that she has an open invitation to join you and me for lunch after she has been discharged. Enjoy your evening, Dan,' closed the commander.

With the exception of updating the team and reviewing the related reports on Beth's kidnapping and GBH, Dan was satisfied that he had done all that he could in relation to closure of the case.

He showered and dressed smartly for the evening ahead at the hospital and then on to dinner with Grace and Freddie.

6.45 p.m.

Dan and Grace met at the hospital cafe, and Dan updated Grace about the decision that he and the commander had agreed about the way forward with Kate. They both knew that it wouldn't end there as they had yet to address their social conscience and how that would affect their future relationships with Beth and Kate.

7 p.m.

Dan and Grace found Beth sitting up in bed chatting to Miriam. She still had a drip to her left hand, but the other drip and the medical equipment had all gone. She didn't look any better, but they both knew that the disappearance of the monitors was positive.

'She insisted on being freshened and sitting up for your arrival,' said Miriam.

'So how is the patient this evening?' asked Dan as Grace dispensed with the toiletries that she had brought.

'I am really pleased with her recovery so far. By tomorrow, the final drip will be withdrawn, and we will probably try to get her out of bed for a short walk around the room. Her willpower is strong, and so the exercise will continue over the next week, when we should start to see a reduction in the bruising. Next week at this time, she will be feeling and looking a lot better. But that doesn't mean that she will be discharged. I have managed to get her to agree to a one-day-at-a-time recovery programme,' summarised Miriam.

'That sounds positive,' said Grace.

'Don't mind me, folks,' said Beth. 'I haven't forgotten why you are here, Dan, so it's time for you to answer some of my questions. Miriam has agreed to fifteen minutes, so let's get on with it.'

'No comment,' was all that Miriam said in response to that.

Before Dan started to pass on information to Beth, he asked her to summarise for him what she remembered about meeting Murray Thomson and the time that she spent with him.

'Well, what you probably don't know is that I got a call from a man saying that important information about Kate's kidnapping had come to his attention by chance and he wondered if I would be interested in hearing about it. Obviously, I said yes, and we arranged to meet at his home in Lovatt Road. When I suggested a public location, he said that the reason that he had suggested his home was because he was pretty much a full-time carer of his aging father, who was a doctor. He asked me to arrive alone as he didn't want any involvement in a police enquiry after passing on the information to me that he had.'

'I didn't know any of that, but I did wonder how he had managed to overcome and sedate you. I guess that he served you a cup of tea after you arrived?'

'Yes, I did fall for that old trick,' replied Beth. 'He drugged me, stripped me when I was unconscious, strapped me to a bloody uncomfortable bed, and then carved a message to you guys on my lower back. After that, he made threats about all sorts of unpleasant things that he would do to me if I didn't cooperate with him. When I was awake at one point, I remember making it very clear to him what I would do to him if he even considered any of them. Which is, no doubt, why he decided to make me look like this when I was unconscious. So over to you now.'

Dan spent the next fifteen minutes summarising the lead from the hospital records, the ID of Murray Thomson, their visit to the Lovatt Road address, the two letters from Thomson, his suicide, and finding Beth. He elaborated on his interview with Matt.

'That sounds too straight forward and, no doubt, begged the question as to why we didn't manage to get that level of detail during Kate's kidnapping. Naturally, I am seriously annoyed at having to have gone through all of this when it could and should have been avoided. But the most important thing is that we all now have closure on the last eight years. Grace, this surely means that Kate can start to move on with her life.'

'Yes, she can,' was all that Grace said.

Dan told her how he planned to deal with Matt.

'So what is it that you aren't telling me?' asked Beth.

'What do you mean by that?' asked Dan.

'Yes, I can see how you can have closure on the cold case, but you haven't mentioned why I was kidnapped and why Thomson waited eight years to orchestrate that. Also, he wouldn't have become suicidal just because I was a difficult victim. Why did I take a beating from him? Why didn't he send you videos of that happening? And there are a lot more questions from where that came from. Spill the beans, Dan.'

Dan didn't want to discuss anything else with her that evening, but he knew that he would have to come clean at some point because she would read the reports on file.

Thankfully, Miriam appeared then, pointing at her watch.

'Time up, guys,' she said. 'It's time for more beauty sleep, Beth.'

'Thank God for that,' said Dan. 'She was starting to give me a hard time.'

'Give us a couple of more minutes, and then I promise that I will settle down for the night,' said Beth.

When Miriam left the room, Beth turned to Dan and Grace and said, 'I would appreciate if you could both do something for me. Dan, could I see you alone tomorrow morning at, say, 10 a.m.? Grace, could you do everything in your power to get Kate to join Jack and my parents' visit at 10.30 a.m.?'

'That's a lot of people to see at the one time, Beth. I don't think that Miriam would approve of that,' said Grace.

'I have discussed it with her, and she has approved on condition that the visits are brief and that I rest between them. The visits will only last between ten and fifteen minutes each.'

'All sounds very ominous,' said Dan.

'It isn't. I just have a few things that I would like to share with my family, so, Grace, please don't take no for an answer from Kate.'

'Okay, but we must leave now,' said Dan. 'You take good care of yourself, and I'll see you tomorrow morning.'

Grace lingered and asked, 'Are you going to tell me what this is about?'

'No, Grace,' said Beth.

7.30 p.m.

Miriam returned to the room.

'Time to examine that rather elaborate tattoo on your back,' said Miriam, and then to Grace, 'and what's this I hear about a dinner reservation this evening?'

'As you know, my partner Freddie owns a restaurant that serves the best Italian food in London. Dan and I have hardly eaten during the last few days, so Freddie has invited us both to be his guests for dinner this evening.'

'Any room for one more?' asked Miriam and then added, 'Only joking.'

'Hey, that's a great idea,' said Grace. 'It's Saturday night, so Freddie always has an Italian surprise on the menu that I promise you would love.'

Miriam looked at her watch and said, 'You know what? It's a good time for me to make an exit, and hubby is at a conference this weekend, so I would be delighted to join you.'

'That's agreed then. Dan and I will be making our way there now, but we'll wait for you before ordering. I'll text you the address.'

'Don't mind me,' was all that Beth said, but she was smiling as she did so.

'Another time, my dear,' said Miriam sarcastically.

'Another time, I promise,' added Grace.

CHAPTER 25

Sunday, 20 October 2012
10 a.m.

Dan arrived outside Beth's room but didn't enter as the blinds were closed. He was just about to make his way to the reception area when Miriam opened the door, and a nurse opened the blinds.

'She's all yours now,' said Miriam.

'The arrangements for this morning sound pretty heavy so soon after all that she has been through,' said Dan. 'Are you okay with this?'

'As I said before, she is more anxious about what's on her mind than about getting it off her mind. I'm not happy with it, but I know that she will only start to focus on her own recovery after she has met with each of you. She has promised to keep the visits brief and has assured me that they will be free from any stress.'

'Oh well, here goes,' said Dan as he entered the room.

They exchanged greetings, and then Beth said to him, 'How long have we worked together?'

'You've worked in my team for just under fifteen years now.'

'During which time I have had two promotions to my current title of detective superintendent, the position that you held until a few years ago.'

'Yes, but where is all this going?' asked Dan, knowing her well enough to know exactly where it was headed.

'I think you know where it is going. I am obviously a good detective given my current job title, and so I want you to tell me what's on your mind. You see, I have been in the company of Murray Thomson now, and Grace's profiling was very accurate. Despite what he did to me, he wasn't a bad man, and he was definitely inexperienced at the kidnapping, rape, and GBH malarkey.

'Now if I was the SIO on the second kidnapping, eight years after the first kidnapping, I would have the bit between my teeth about the *why* as I am absolutely sure that you would have done.

'So, Dan, am I correct in thinking that you haven't a mind to close the second case because you have niggling doubts about the *why?*'

'Beth, I would have preferred not to go there with you so soon after what you have been through, but I know that you will, no doubt, start your own enquiries if I don't come clean. You are quite correct in what you say. We know the *who*. That's Murray Thomson, but we can't question him because he is dead. We know the *where* because we have been there. But, yes, like you, I am troubled about the *why*. And, yes, I have a couple of leads that I am pursuing.'

'I have had nothing else to think about when I was awake during or after the kidnapping, so I have been doing my own detective work, and there is only one answer to my question, isn't there, Dan?'

'Yes, but let's talk about that later.'

'No. I have to hear myself say it out loud so that we can move on to the next part of what I want to talk to you about. Dan, between us, we have significant detective experience. Murray Thomson had no reason to kidnap me and put me through what Kate went through all those years ago. You know it, and so do I.'

Silence.

'Clearly you are not going to say it, so I am. The only person who could have wanted me to experience what Kate did eight years ago was Kate. It is Kate who organised my kidnapping, wasn't it, Dan?'

'I wish my answer could be different, but, yes, I believe that she did.'

'That's all I wanted to hear, and I would have been disappointed if you hadn't been following any leads that you have. But I haven't asked you here today to talk about Kate. We will have that conversation once I am out of here.'

Beth continued, 'Today, I want you to drop any further investigation into my kidnapping.'

'Why?' asked Dan.

'I have watched my family suffer for eight years now, and there's not a day goes by when I don't mourn the rift between Kate and me. There's nothing that I could have done about the dissolution of my marriage. But as a mother and a daughter, I am going to make it my mission to ensure that our family ordeals end now. I feel so strongly about this that I am prepared to put my career on hold whilst I do that. That isn't some sort of threat, by the way. Being told that I almost died just made me rethink my priorities. I have lost so much time with Kate and Jack. I don't want to lose any more time. You have sufficient answers to close both cases. All I am saying is that anything more than you already have is irrelevant.'

Dan was watching the clock and knew that there wasn't time to reflect on what she had asked. After all, it was very clear.

'I would like you to discuss my request with the commander as it is important to me that I don't jeopardise the open and honest communication that we all have. Can you do that?'

'I already have,' was his response.

'And what did the two of you decide?'

'We decided to take appropriate action but not to make any charges.'

'Is there anything that I need to know about that before I meet with my family?' asked Beth.

'No. Clearly you and I have a lot to talk about after that,' replied Dan.

'I don't have a problem with that. In the meantime, what am I authorised to say to them today?' asked Beth.

'The official line will be that we have sufficient information to close both cases and that Murray Thomson's journey of revenge ended with his suicide.'

'Thanks, Dan. Now I must have fifteen minutes' rest before the family arrive. Whether or not that will include Kate, I don't know.'

'Grace has confirmed that Kate will join Jack and your parents at 10.30.'

Dan left the hospital and called Grace and then the commander from his phone. To Grace, knowing that she would be with Kate, he simply said, 'She knows,' and hung up. To the commander, he summarised Beth's request, which both of them had already agreed during their earlier conversation.

10.30 a.m.

Grace and Kate arrived first at Beth's room, as previously arranged by Grace. She knew that Jack, Bill, and Caroline were already in the corridor, and she also knew that they wouldn't have any gifts for Beth with them. They all knew that the next fifteen minutes were going to be awkward for everyone, and so the visit was planned, following Grace's lead.

Also prompted by Grace, the five temporary visitors' chairs were positioned two at one side of the bed and three at the other. There was no time for Kate to have to say anything as Grace led the conversation until she saw the others enter the room.

Grace noticed that Kate relaxed slightly after the others had arrived.

'Thanks for joining us, Kate. I have something that I want to say to you all.'

No one said anything.

'This morning I met with Dan so that I could tell him what I remembered about my kidnapping. He then told me about how he had determined who the kidnapper was and where he lived. I also know about Murray Thomson's demise. You probably think that there is now enough information to close both cases. Well, there is, and there isn't. In theory, he does have enough information to close both cases, but there are a couple of loose ends that he is still investigating that will explain why the two kidnappings were eight years apart.'

She took a sip of water and then continued.

'My family has suffered a great deal over the last eight years, not least of which is you, Kate. Not a day goes by when I don't reflect upon what happened to you. Not a day goes by when I don't think about you. I don't know if I could have prevented what happened because Mr Thomson had already planned his revenge against Matt. Perhaps what happened to me was punishment for my part in when it happened that Friday evening so long ago.'

Beth continued, 'I want the suffering to stop. I want us to be family who comes together regularly to enjoy each other's company. For that reason, I have requested that the investigation be closed. Murray Thomson is dead, and surely that must be an end to it. I have told Dan that I don't want to hear any more about either kidnappings or loose ends. He has discussed this with the commander, and they have both agreed to close both cases. I am authorised to share the official line that will be shared with the team today. It is that we have sufficient information to close both cases and that Murray Thomson's journey of revenge ended with his suicide.

'Our past has been cruelly interfered with, but we all still have a future ahead of us. When you leave here today, I would like Kate to accept Grace's help to stop the nightmares. I would like all of you to find a way for us all to be a complete family again. I will go along with whatever you decide, but my suggestion is that we all visit Jack in Thailand after Miriam considers that I am fit to travel that distance. No need to respond now, but please think about it.'

Jack spoke up, 'Personally, I think that's a wonderful idea, so it definitely gets my vote.'

Bill picked up from there. 'As head of the family, I had planned to arrange a similar gathering, and so I endorse everything that Beth has just said. Let's move on. It won't happen overnight, but together we can work this out. It would be unfair to put Kate on the spot today, but I want her to leave here today, knowing that she has a full family who love her very much.'

'Thanks, Dad,' said Beth. 'Now, time is up, so you must leave before Miriam asks you to.'

Jack got out of his seat, walked over to Beth, gently cuddled her, and promised that he would spend some quality time with her during the next few days.

Kate decided that she wanted to be alone after meeting her mother but promised Jack and her grandparents that she would visit them the following day and stay overnight.

In recent times, she had accepted that she couldn't change the past and what had happened during the last few days had been the start of making her feel emotionally stronger.

She pondered the thoughts that had passed through her mind that day.

Perhaps the hypnosis had helped her, after all.
Perhaps her decision to conduct a private investigation into her own kidnapping had helped her to face her demons.
So why had she always made her mother suffer?
Why had she been unable to forgive her mother?

Why had she decided not to make her father suffer after finding out that he had held the key to finding the kidnapper all the time?
Could she do what the rest of the family asked of her?
How did she actually feel about her mother after she almost died?

In honesty, she didn't know!

EPILOGUE

Three months later . . .

The alarm ringing at Beth's bedside at 6.30 a.m. reminded her that the day had arrived for her and Kate's skin graft operations to remove the ridiculous tattoo that they each had at the base of their back as a result of Murray Thomson's handiwork during their respective kidnappings.

This was the first thing that Grace had insisted upon when Beth had been discharged from hospital as she firmly believed that neither of them could focus on the future whilst such a blatant reminder of the past existed. Grace had taken care of everything, from the first appointments with the plastic surgeon right through to arranging cars to collect them that morning and drive them individually to the hospital.

Beth smiled as she realised that she had another two hours before the car would arrive for her. She lay back in her bed and reflected upon all that had happened since she had been discharged from hospital.

Matt had been suspended from St Rubens Hospital, but everyone knew that this was a gesture made by the board of governors in response to the formal complaint written by Chief Superintendent Dan Turner and copied to the medical council. Everyone knew, including Matt, that it was just a matter of time before he returned to his position. During his suspension, he had invited Beth out to lunch and apologised to her for the unnecessary pressure that he had put her through after Kate had been kidnapped. She held her head high and said that it was water under the bridge, and, for the sake of Kate and Jack, they both agreed to keep in touch and to be civilised with each other at family gatherings.

Jack had returned to Koh Tao, in Thailand, from where Beth knew that he schemed with Grace and Bill to get Kate to agree to a family holiday in Thailand. She hoped that would happen soon because she missed him, and she believed that a family holiday would be the best tonic for all of them. She wondered when she would see him next. What she didn't know was that Jack had arranged a surprise visit after the skin graft operations. This would coincide with interviews at a couple of universities to start his investigation into which teaching degree would best suit someone like him who spoke fluently in Thai and eloquently in French and Spanish, played the guitar, and had a history of working voluntarily with under-privileged children in Thailand.

Grace had managed to get Kate to agree to a block of six hypnosis/NLP sessions and was making good progress in getting Kate to talk more openly about her feelings. Beth was delighted that Kate had relieved Grace of the non-disclosure agreement that had been signed after the kidnapping, and, according to Grace, their conversations increasingly were more about the future than the past.

With Grace's encouragement, the three of them had met for lunch on several occasions, each more relaxed than the previous one. Beth was also pleased to hear that Kate's work/life balance was improving and that she was spending less time on her own at home with nothing other than a bottle of wine and her music collection as company. She had started to visit the local spa with friends and was making a real attempt to accept invitations to social gatherings.

All the family hoped that this would help Kate to form meaningful relationships with both sexes.

And what about Dan, she thought to herself. He had surprised Beth by inviting her out for dinner soon after she had been discharged from hospital. It had been an enjoyable and relaxed evening, and, since then, they had regularly had dinner together, agreeing that it was good to spend time together out of the office. That morning, she particularly recalled the previous evening when Dan had taken her out for dinner to keep her mind off the skin graft operation. After their taxi ride home, he had escorted her to her door, taken her in his arms, and then pecked her on either cheek. She had surprised herself by responding with a brief kiss on his lips. Now, she couldn't get the thought out of her head that she would have been happy to have had a proper kiss with him. That thought remained with her as she prepared to get ready to be driven to the hospital.

As she dried her hair, she concluded that the last few months had taken a turn for the better and she had optimistic thoughts about the future. Like the rest of the family, she hoped that a holiday to visit Jack in Thailand would be a positive turning point.

She wasn't surprised to see Grace in the waiting car. Since her own kidnapping, she had come to realise just how good a friend she was. Both were in good spirits and chatted on the way to the hospital. Kate had already confirmed by text that she was also en route.

At the hospital reception area, Grace and Beth waited for Kate to arrive, and the three of them made their way up to the consultant's reception. He came out to welcome them and talked them through the procedure and the timings once again. They were pleased when he confirmed that as it was a mother-and-daughter operation, he had booked the largest of the theatres and that they had been set so that operations could be performed at the same time by himself and his colleague plastic surgeon.

Grace could see that they were both nervous, Kate more than Beth because each time she thought about the tattoos, it brought back nightmares about the past. Beth, on the other hand, just wanted to be rid of it.

After Beth and Kate were taken through to their private rooms, Grace called Dan, Jack, and Beth's parents to let them know that both had turned up and were on their way to theatre. She knew that it was just a matter of time before Dan would turn up to sit with her as they waited for them to come out of theatre.

As Beth and Kate lay side by side on their beds just outside the operating theatre, they shared their enthusiasm about having the tattoos removed. Beth said for the umpteenth time that she hoped that this could be a fresh start for them, just as she had taken every opportunity to tell Kate how much she had missed her being a close part of her life.

'Mum, we have already agreed to take one day at a time, so you don't have to repeat that every time you see me,' said Kate.

'I know,' said Beth with tears in her eyes. 'But before the anaesthetist arrives, I just want to make sure that you know that I would never have done anything to harm you. You have turned out to be a beautiful young woman, and I am extremely proud of your success at work.'

There was always so much that Beth wanted to say to Kate, but she knew that much of it must wait for another time.

She turned to Kate and was surprised to see that she also had tears in her eyes. Just then the anaesthetist arrived, but Beth asked her if she could give them another few minutes.

Seeing that they were both upset, the anaesthetist agreed but said that she couldn't give them any longer than that as the consultants were ready to begin.

Beth reached out her hand to Kate, and Kate took it.

'This is it, Kate,' said Beth. 'In a couple of hours, our outrageous yet unique tattoos will cease to exist. You have a good future ahead of you, and you are highly respected at work. In no time, you will be a junior partner. It just makes me sad that you achieved all of that on your own without me there to listen to your plans.'

'Stop,' said Kate. 'You just don't understand anything, do you? You don't really know what is going on in my head and the type of person that I have become. I am an emotional wreck.'

Saddened by the look of despair on Kate's face, Beth started to offer words of encouragement, but Kate stopped her.

'Stop it. You don't understand,' Kate repeated as she pulled her hand away from Beth's. 'It was me who arranged your kidnapping. I have hated you since my kidnapping, and I have always wanted you to suffer as much as I did.'

Beth faced Kate and quietly said two words that Kate will never forget.

'I know,' said Beth, just as the anaesthetist walked towards them.

Silence for what seemed like eternity.

Kate had run out of time to respond.

A PREVIEW OF SENSELESS REVENGE BY THE SAME AUTHOR

DUE TO BE RELEASED EARLY 2014

There is nothing unusual about adults being reported as *missing persons* in areas within and outwith Central London. When the number is highlighted as escalating for people with a similar profile and negative media attention is directed at the Metropolitan Police, the cases are transferred to the Special Crimes Division. Once again Chief Superintendent Dan Turner and Grace Fletcher, Criminal Profiler and Psychologist, are challenged by an unusual modus operandi, lack of evidence and absence of bodies. When the number of reported missing persons in this particular case reaches eleven, Dan has no choice but to make a televised plea to the community for assistance.

Lightning Source UK Ltd.
Milton Keynes UK
UKOW05n1854261113

221900UK00001B/1/P